THE GIFT THAT KILLS

by

J.K. Strange

J.K. STRANGE

The Gift That Kills

Copyright © 2026 J.K. Strange

This is a work of fiction. Names, characters, places, and incidents are the product of the author's imagination or are used fictitiously. Any resemblance to actual persons, living or dead, or actual events is purely coincidental.

Printed in the United States of America.

CHAPTER 1 — WHAT REMAINS

Jonathan didn't run far. He walked three blocks before the shaking started. Not from fear. Not from urgency. He was running from the silence.

The silence felt wrong, like a missing sound he could not name until he noticed its shape around him, pressing against his ears. The night should have been loud sirens, shouts, a neighbor's door opening on a burst of light but the world only breathed in low, indifferent hums. Each quiet second made his skin crawl.

The neighborhood absorbed what had happened without resistance. Porch lights stayed on. A television laughed somewhere behind drawn curtains. A car passed at the end of the street, tires hissing softly on warm asphalt.

Somewhere, a dog barked once and then thought better of it. Sprinklers whispered in a nearby yard, ticking their slow, patient arc over grass that had not seen what he had seen. A ceiling fan turned lazily in an open window, blades slicing the air with a soft, rhythmic whomp. A woman's shadow moved across a kitchen, arms lifted as she rinsed dishes. The world carried on.

Nothing had changed. That was what made his chest tighten.

The night air slid in and out of his lungs like it belonged to someone else. Every normal sound jabbed at him, proof that the universe was content to shrug and keep turning. Somewhere a live sports broadcast shouted about a last second play. Somewhere a laugh track rose on cue. Somewhere a neighbor chuckled at a joke that had nothing to do with the body on the floor behind him.

Jonathan stopped beneath a maple tree and bent forward, hands braced against his thighs. The rough bark at his back scraped through his shirt when he shifted. Dry leaves and stray gravel bit into the soles of his shoes, grounding him and not grounding him at the same time. His breath came too fast, then too slow, as if his body couldn't decide what it needed from him. His chest fluttered in small, shallow gulps that left his head light and his ribs aching.

His fingers trembled not wildly, not out of control but with a precision that scared him. Each small vibration felt measured, deliberate, as if some hidden part of him were taking inventory instead of panicking. The tremor didn't match the way his heart slammed against his sternum. It was too neat, too clean, like it belonged to a lab specimen instead of a young man who had just..

He cut the thought off before it finished.

He stared at his hands, half expecting to see his father's blood instead of his own. For a moment he couldn't remember when he'd scraped them on the doorframe as he shoved past it, on the floor, on the asphalt when he almost went down. The sting in his palms pulsed in time with his heartbeat. Faint reddish smears traced the creases in his skin, but nothing like the thick, slick warmth he remembered from the kitchen. That had soaked into his shirt, his sleeves, the spaces between his fingers.

He could still feel the phantom weight of his father's wrist in his grip, the way the skin had cooled too quickly. The memory slid over the back of his tongue like rust. He swallowed hard, but the taste didn't go away.

For a moment, the faces blurred together.

Henry and Suzanne laughing in the kitchen.

Tom handing him a wrapped birthday gift.

Henry crouching down to ask about school, about science fairs, about what Jonathan wanted to be when he grew up.

Another image tried to join the others like Dr Gerald's body jerking, the sound in his throat when he hit the floor, but Jonathan shoved it away, clinging to the earlier versions. In the kitchen memory, Tom's laugh had filled the whole room, booming off the cabinets while Suzanne rolled her eyes and pretended not to smile. The overhead light had glinted off the silver at his temples. There had been the warm, comforting smell of coffee and dish soap and something baking in the oven.

The birthday gift had come in crinkled blue paper with crooked tape, because Tom always forgot to buy proper wrapping until the last minute. Jonathan remembered the weight of the box, the rattle of parts inside, Tom's hopeful grin as he tore it open to find the telescope kit they'd picked out together. Tom had insisted they build it that same night, scattered lenses and screws across the table, stayed long after he was supposed to go back to the lab.

He remembered the way Tom had crouched to eye level in the yard, chilly spring air biting at their fingers as they tightened the last bolt. "You're going to see everything with this, kiddo," Tom had said, breath making clouds in the dark. "Not just what they tell you is there." He'd said it like a challenge, like a promise.

Henry crouching to ask about school hadn't just been casual small talk. He had listened, actually listened, as Jonathan rambled about a science fair project or a lecture he'd watched online. He would lean against the counter or sit forward in his chair, eyes narrowed in concentration, asking questions that made Jonathan feel like his thoughts mattered. Like he was someone worth investing time in.

Jonathan pressed the heel of his palm into his eye until sparks burst behind the lid. Hard pressure, bright starbursts. It hurt, but the pain anchored him. If he pushed hard enough maybe he could smudge out the wrong memories and leave only the harmless ones—the ones where Tom was a man in a flannel shirt with flour on his sleeves, not the man on the floor.

This wasn't how it was supposed to feel. He had imagined, in vague, guilty daydreams, that justice, if it ever came would feel clean. Sharp. Righteous. He had expected shaking, maybe, and tears. Some kind of collapse that proved he was still human. Instead, everything inside him felt suspended, like the house lights had gone down but the curtain hadn't risen yet. The grief he'd rehearsed in his head didn't fit this moment.

He slid down against the tree trunk and stayed there longer than he meant to. The bark dug between his shoulder blades, grounding him in small, uncomfortable points of contact. His jeans caught on a root and bunched around his knees. Cold crept through the seat of his pants and the backs of his legs, but he barely registered it. His lungs might as well have been on a different planet.

Time slipped its rules. The streetlights hummed, a far off car door thumped, a siren wailed in the distance and then faded again. He couldn't tell if a minute passed or ten. His phone was a heavy rectangle in his pocket, suddenly too distant to reach for. He wondered if anyone had noticed he was gone yet. He wondered if anyone ever would.

When he finally stood, his legs felt distant, like they belonged to someone else. Pins and needles stabbed up his calves as blood rushed back. His balance wobbled for a second and he grabbed at the tree, fingers scraping over the rough wood. The world tilted, then righted itself, but nothing looked exactly the same. The neat rows of houses seemed flatter,

more like painted scenery than real places people lived.

Something inside him stirred like a low, unfamiliar steadiness and for one terrifying second, it felt relieved.

It rose slowly, not like a surge of adrenaline but like a tide coming in, gentle and inevitable. His breathing evened out without his permission. His heartbeat slipped into a calmer rhythm. The edge of the panic dulled. A dense, cool focus slid into the empty spaces where the shock had been. The part of him that had been spinning finally found a center and latched on.

Relieved.

The word itself made bile burn the back of his throat. Relieved that Dr. Gerald couldn't hurt him anymore. Relieved that the waiting was over. Relieved that the worst thing he'd imagined had already happened and there was nothing left for his brain to threaten him with in the middle of the night. It wasn't the wild triumph he'd sometimes fantasized about. It was quieter, darker, a small voice whispering, It's done.

Jonathan swallowed hard. The saliva scraped down his throat like sand. He could not tell if he wanted to throw up or scream or run until his lungs burst. The new steadiness terrified him more than the shaking had, because it didn't feel like him. It felt like something that had been crouching in the dark for years, waiting for the moment it was finally allowed to stand up.

He didn't know what that meant yet.

Maybe it meant he was broken. Maybe it meant he had crossed a line he could never step back over. Maybe it meant that all the stories he'd told himself about what kind of person he was, what kind of son, had been lies, and this was the real version finally showing its face. The not knowing clawed at him, worse in its way than the blood or the memory of the gun.

He only knew he couldn't let himself feel it again.

He clung to that single decision the way a drowning man clung to debris. Whatever that cold, steady part of him was, whatever it could do, he would bury it if he had to. Chain it down. Pretend it had never surfaced. If he fed it, if he let it grow, he wasn't sure what would be left of him when it was done.

He moved on before the thought could finish forming. His feet found the sidewalk almost by habit, carrying him forward past familiar mailboxes and trash cans and cracks in the pavement he'd ridden his bike over a thousand times. Behind him, the maple tree stood as if nothing had happened there at all. Ahead, the street stretched out under the sodium glare of the lamps, ordinary and endless. He walked into it because there was nothing else he knew how to do.

CHAPTER 2 — THE BEGINNING

Fall settled over the town like a worn quilt, pretty from a distance, thin up close. Leaves drifted in slow spirals and collected in gutters. Chimneys sent frail ribbons of smoke into a gray October sky. From the street, everything looked calm.

Inside the Halden house, nothing was calm.

Jonathan lay on the couch, swallowed by blankets that couldn't keep the chill out of his bones or the heat off his skin. The cushions had molded to the shape of his body over the past few days, a hollow his weight kept returning to no matter how many times Suzanne tried to reposition him. His forehead burned beneath Suzanne's trembling hand. His lips were dry. His eyes, when they opened at all were glassy and unfocused, sliding past lamps and picture frames without recognition, like he was looking through the house instead of at it.

The television flickered silently in the corner, a news anchor's lips moving with no sound. Suzanne had hit mute hours ago when she realized she could not bear the chatter, the smiling faces, the scrolling ticker of other people's problems. Now the screen was just moving light, a ghost of normal life playing in the background of something that was anything but.

"Mom… it hurts," he whispered.

The words scraped out of him as if they had to be dragged over broken glass. Suzanne leaned closer, she had already been breathing rapidly as her heart was beating out of her chest. For a second she almost pretended she hadn't heard, as if not acknowledging it might make it less real.

Her throat tightened. "Where, baby?"

He pressed a weak hand to his chest. Even that small movement seemed to cost him. "Everywhere."

The word hung between them like another diagnosis, one the doctors hadn't written on any chart. Everywhere.

Not a knee she could ice, not a throat she could soothe with tea and honey. His whole body was a single ache she had no way to reach.

She fought to keep her voice steady. "Daddy will be home soon. Just rest, okay?"

The promise felt thin the moment it left her mouth, but it was all she had to offer. She smoothed the edge of the blanket over his shoulder as if tucking it more tightly would somehow pin him here, keep him from slipping further away.

Jonathan's eyes slid shut again. His lashes left faint shadows on flushed cheeks. His breathing stayed shallow, each breath sounding like it had to be fought for, hauled up from somewhere too deep and too dark. Between inhales there were pauses that went on just long enough to make Suzanne's heart stutter. She found herself counting silently one, two, three waiting for his chest to rise again.

Earlier in the day the hospital had given them nothing.

Machines hummed and beeped. Cold fluorescent light had bleached the color out of his skin. Blood had been drawn and spun. Charts printed, X rays pinned to lightboards. Results, numbers, graphs none of it translated into help. Nurses had moved around them with professional sympathy, voices pitched low, hands efficient and careful. It all had the shape of care, without the substance.

Dr. Lazar, a man whose confidence had once steadied Suzanne, stared at Jonathan's file with a tight jaw and unsettled eyes. He had been the one who'd patched Jonathan's broken wrist when he fell off his bike at eight, joking about "future baseball careers" while he wrapped the cast. He had been unflappable when other parents in town panicked over flu seasons and minor fractures. Seeing doubt on his face now felt like the floor tipping under her feet.

"It doesn't track," he said at last.

"What does that mean?" Suzanne asked, fingers locked together so hard they hurt. Her knuckles had gone white. The skin across them felt ready to split.

"His fever and vitals say he's in distress," Lazar replied. "But his labs…" He paused, as if even saying it out loud might make it less true. "His labs look like a healthy child's. No infection. No inflammatory markers. No organ damage."

Suzanne stared at the sheet in his hand as if the numbers might rearrange themselves if she looked hard enough—little black shapes reshuffling into a language that made sense. The monitor by Jonathan's bed ticked out a fragile rhythm behind her, indifferent.

"Then why is he…" She couldn't find the words. The air in the room seemed to congeal in her throat. "Why is he like this?"

"I don't know," Lazar said quietly. His shoulders sagged in a way she had never seen before. "This doesn't match anything I've seen."

There was a moment where Suzanne almost reached for his arm, to steady him, absurdly tempted to comfort the man who had just admitted he could not help her son. Instead she pulled her hand back to her own chest and held it there over the hollow ache growing behind her ribs.

Later, as Suzanne sat beside Jonathan's bed and stroked his hair while he stared vacantly at the ceiling, Henry lingered near the door. The hospital room smelled of antiseptic and old coffee, of plastic and too many people trying not to sweat under stress. The blinds were half-closed against a pale, washed-out afternoon light, drawing bars across the floor.

In the hallway two physicians spoke in low, urgent tones, words drifting through the crack in the door like smoke.

"…no clear etiology…"

"…metabolic readings are off like those experimental profiles downstairs…"

"…if this gets flagged, it goes above our clearance…"

Henry didn't move. Didn't breathe. The word "downstairs" slid under his skin like a razor. His mind supplied the missing noun without needing to hear it: the facility, the project, the thing at the core of the lab no one without the right badge was supposed to know about.

Downstairs.

The syllables echoed in his head, layered over the memory of new security gates being installed, of additional cameras sprouting like metal eyes in the hallways, of whispered directives about "heightened protocols." For months, the lab had hummed with a second, hidden life beneath the ordinary research. Henry had tried not to think about it beyond the boundaries of his job.

He walked away before they saw him listening, his stomach twisted into knots. As he moved down the corridor, the white walls felt closer than they had a moment ago, the fluorescent lights harsher, the air colder. His security badge bounced against his chest with each step, suddenly heavier than its plastic weight.

The clock ticked too loudly, each second a small hammer striking the inside of Suzanne's skull. The small refrigerator in the corner hummed, cycling on and off with an oblivious, mechanical rhythm. The television muttered reruns into an empty room, sound turned low but not off, the canned laughter leaking through the doorway like something obscene. Suzanne sat glued to Jonathan's side, refusing to blink too long in case he stopped breathing while her eyes were closed.

Her own body had narrowed to a single point of focus: the rise and fall of his chest under the blankets. Every time there was a slightly longer pause, her heart lurched, and she found herself leaning in, ready to shake him, to call his name.

The phone on the end table might as well have been a live grenade. Its plastic casing gleamed faintly in the lamplight, innocent and waiting.

When it rang, the sound was so loud in the quiet house that Suzanne flinched. She snatched it up. "Hello?"

"Mrs. Halden," Dr. Lazar's voice came through, oddly hollow, as if he were speaking from very far away or down a long tunnel. "We've gone over everything again. There's nothing more we can do. You should take him home. Make him comfortable."

For a moment, the words didn't make sense arranged in that order. Take him home, like this was a discharged-patient call. Make him comfortable, like she was tucking him in for bed.

Suzanne's legs nearly gave out. Her free hand groped blindly for the arm of the tall chair in the room and missed, fingers clenching only air. "You're saying.."

"I'm saying we don't have anything left to try."

There was an apology buried in his tone, but it was useless. More tests would not uncurl Jonathan's fingers. More graphs would not smooth the lines of pain from his forehead.

She hung up without answering, because if she spoke it would be a scream. The phone clacked against the table with more force than she intended, rattling a framed photo of the three of them at the county fair she placed there earlier in the day, in tending for an extended stay as per the usual. In the picture, Jonathan's cheeks were round and flushed, cotton candy smeared across his grin. Suzanne turned the frame facedown with a shaking hand.

Suzanne and Jonathan were finally at home, the house felt like it was holding its breath. Henry had gotten called in to work an hour early due to one of the morning guard's wife going into labor.

Out at the laboratory, the guard shack rattled in the growing wind.

Henry sat inside beneath buzzing fluorescent light. The shack's heater clicked on and off in a stubborn attempt to keep up with the temperature drop, filling the small space with dry, artificial warmth. Papers lay scattered on the desk—log sheets, visitor badges, tonight's schedule. None of it mattered. The lines of names and times blurred when he tried to focus on them.

His eyes kept drifting to the phone.

Each time it stayed silent, a small knot of tension coiled tighter in his chest. Each second it remained still was both a relief and an agony. No call meant nothing had gotten worse. No call meant he was still here while Suzanne was alone with a son they had been told to make "comfortable."

When it rang, his heart lurched so hard his breath caught. The sound seemed too sharp for the cramped room.

He grabbed the receiver. "Security checkpoint. Henry."

Suzanne's voice came through in fragments, skinless and raw. "Henry" she sobbed. "You have to come home. Now."

The words sliced through what little composure he had left.

He straightened so fast the chair slammed into the wall. A clipboard slid off the desk and clattered to the floor. "What happened? How's Jonathan?"

"He's… he's not waking up right. His breathing keeps… he keeps stopping and starting. Lazar said we should bring him home to die." Her words broke apart, dissolving into ragged sobs. "I can't watch him fade, Henry. I can't. You have to come home. Please."

Something in Henry cracked straight down the middle. The split felt physical, a fault line running from his throat to his stomach.

"I'm coming," he said. The words felt like the only solid things in the room. "Hold onto him. I'm coming right now."

He slammed the receiver down, grabbed his jacket, and shoved the door open.

Wind knifed into the shack, shoving ice fingers through the thin fabric of his uniform before he could pull the jacket fully on. The storm that had been threatening all evening had finally arrived. Clouds rolled low and heavy, swallowing the last traces of sunset. Rain spattered the pavement, darkening it in spreading patches that glistened under the sodium lights.

Henry ran, boots splashing through forming puddles as he sprinted toward the main entrance. The night air tasted like metal and wet leaves. He couldn't just vanish from his post; not from this place. Regulations, protocols, the chain of command years of drilled-in habit shouted at him even as his muscles drove him forward.

Someone had to know. Someone had to cover.

He barreled through the glass doors and nearly collided with two lab techs coming on shift. One cursed, clutching a clipboard to her chest. They muttered, annoyed, then went silent when they saw his face. Whatever they had been about to say died as they took in his wild eyes, the way his chest heaved, the way his fingers twitched like they couldn't decide whether to reach for a weapon or a door handle.

Henry didn't stop.

He went straight to Tom Rourke's office near the lobby security console. The hallway seemed longer than usual, each step stretching out, the polished floor reflecting his distorted shape back at him in brief, warped flashes.

Tom sat at his desk flipping through incident reports. A radio hissed behind him, low static and occasional bursts of speech from other guards checking in. He looked up, surprised. "Henry? You're supposed to be at the gate. What the...."

"It's Jonathan," Henry blurted, breath coming hard. The words tumbled out, rough and unpolished. "He's crashing. I have to get home. I'm leaving now."

Tom's posture stiffened. The supervisor mask slid into place like a visor dropping over his face. His shoulders squared. His voice tightened.

"Henry, you know better than that. You can't just abandon the checkpoint. This is a restricted site."

"My son is dying," Henry snapped.

The words hit the room like a slammed door. Even the radio seemed to hush for a heartbeat.

For a second Tom looked like he might argue again. The rules warred behind his eyes with something older and more human. Then he really saw Henry the panic in his eyes, the tremor in his hands, the raw edge to his voice that said this was not a drill, not a scare, not something that would be fine in the morning.

"Christ," Tom muttered. He scrubbed a hand over his face, fingers rasping over stubble. "All right. Go. I'll call it in as a shift adjustment and cover the gate."

Henry let out a breath he hadn't realized he'd been holding. The air left him in a shaky rush. "Thank you."

"Don't thank me," Tom said quietly. Something softer slipped through the supervisor tone, the man who had known Jonathan since he was a toddler peeking around the edges. "Just get to your boy."

The wind screamed around Henry as he ran back out into the night. By the time he reached his truck, the storm had turned vicious. Rain hammered the windshield, blurring the world into streaks of light and shadow. Thunder rolled overhead, close enough to feel in his bones, each rumble a dull drumbeat in his chest.

He started the engine with shaking hands. The key scraped once against the ignition before sliding in. The truck rumbled to life, dashboard lights blooming in a soft, familiar glow that felt alien in this moment.

"Hold on, buddy," he whispered, gripping the wheel. His knuckles went white. "Hold on for me."

He pulled out onto the road, wipers thrashing, tires hissing across slick pavement. Streetlights smeared into halos in the rain. Headlights from passing cars flared and vanished, smearing ghostlike through the downpour. Each passing vehicle felt like a threat, another unpredictable mass of metal in a world that had suddenly become more dangerous.

His mind kept flashing Suzanne alone with Jonathan. His hands hovering over their son's chest, counting breaths, begging for the rise and fall. He imagined her on the couch in in her blue and pink flowered robe, hair pulled back in a messy knot, dark circles bruised under her eyes, knuckles pressed against her mouth to keep from sobbing loud enough to scare their boy.

Don't let me be too late. Don't take him. Don't take him too.

The last word caught on old grief. A different hospital room, a different bed, a different goodbye he had never forgiven the world for requiring.

A shape exploded into his headlights.

A deer, wild-eyed, and soaked skidding as it bounded into the road. Its coat was slicked dark with rain, ribs shuddering under thin skin.

Henry reacted before thought. Training and instinct fused. He jerked the wheel.

The truck fishtailed, the back end swinging out as the tires lost grip. The world rotated in a blur of white headlights, black road, sideways rain. His heart slammed against his ribs hard enough to hurt. For a split second everything slowed, sound dropping into a muffled hum.

He remembered Suzanne's face the day Jonathan was born. Exhausted, luminous, tear-streaked and laughing at the same time as she cradled the tiny, wailing bundle against her chest.

Then flashed to Jonathan in the yard chasing leaves with an astronaut helmet too big for his head. The plastic visor fogged with his breath as he shrieked with delight, boots thudding against the grass.

The couch, the fever, the way his son's chest barely moved.

Then time snapped back.

The truck spun, skidded sideways, and shrieked to a stop inches from a ditch churning with runoff. Muddy water gushed past, carrying leaves and twigs and bits of trash, hungry and fast.

Silence surrounded him except Henry's ragged breathing and the relentless drum of rain on metal. The wipers squealed across the glass in frantic arcs.

He sat frozen, hands locked on the wheel, chest heaving. The seatbelt dug into his shoulder. For a moment there were no thoughts, only animal panic and the shock of almost dying, of almost making his son an orphan in the space of a heartbeat.

Then it all rushed in.

If I'd gone over… Suzanne would have been alone. Jonathan would have died without me there.

The image of the ditch swallowing the truck, of cold water slamming into the cab, flashed through his mind so vividly he almost tasted grit in his teeth. He saw Suzanne getting a call from some state trooper at the door, hearing that both her husband and her son were gone. The thought punched the air out of his lungs.

He swallowed hard, tasting copper and fear. "No," he hissed. "Not tonight."

The deer was gone, swallowed by the trees as if it had never existed, another ghost the storm had conjured and dismissed.

Henry forced his grip to loosen finger by finger. Pain prickled in his palms as blood returned. He straightened the truck and eased back onto the road but slower now, but with desperation tightening his throat. The speedometer needle hovered lower, but his pulse did not follow its lead.

When he turned onto their street, his heart felt like it might crack ribs. Every window in their house was lit, squares of yellow cutting through the rain. Shadows moved inside. Suzanne was pacing, hovering, breaking. The sight made his eyes sting.

He lurched into the driveway, killed the engine before it settled, and ran for the door. His boots slipped once on the wet concrete; he caught himself on the railing and kept going.

Inside, the air smelled of sweat, antiseptic wipes, and fear. It was a claustrophobic scent, clinging to the curtains and the fabric of the couch, soaked into the walls.

Jonathan lay propped on pillows. His breathing was worse, shallow and irregular, with long pauses between each inhale. Damp hair clung to his forehead in thin strands. His lips had a faint blue tint that made Suzanne's stomach flip every time she noticed it.

She knelt beside him, one hand on his chest as if touch alone could keep his heart going. Her palm rose and fell with each fragile breath, counting, begging, pleading without words.

"Henry…" she choked when he rushed in. "He stopped for a second. I swear to God he stopped breathing."

Henry dropped to his knees beside the couch so hard it hurt. Pain shot up from his kneecaps, but he barely registered it. He took Jonathan's hand, small and cold. The boy's fingers curled weakly around his.

"Jonathan," he whispered. "Buddy. It's Dad. Can you hear me?"

Jonathan's eyelids fluttered, lashes trembling. "Dad…?"

The voice was thin, but it was there.

"I'm here." Henry's voice broke on the second word. "I'm not going anywhere."

Suzanne turned away and covered her face. A sound escaped her—something between a sob and a quiet scream, strangled as she tried not to let it explode out of her. Her shoulders shook.

For a long moment they were suspended in a terrible stillness, the storm muttering outside, the house holding its breath. The ticking clock, the distant television, even the rain felt like it had pulled back, waiting to see what they would do.

Then something in Henry snapped.

"We can't just sit here," he said, standing abruptly. His voice was low, but sharp enough to cut. "We have to do something."

Suzanne whirled on him, eyes red, cheeks wet. Her hair had come loose from its tie, strands sticking to her damp face.

"What do you think we've been doing?" she shot back. "We took him to the hospital. We begged them for help. They poked him and scanned him and stared at their screens until their faces went blank. Lazar said there's nothing left, Henry. There is no more 'something' to do!"

Henry paced once, a caged animal for the length of the rug. The fibers muffled his footsteps, but the tension in his movements screamed. "There's one thing," he said. "One chance."

She stared at him. Hope and dread flared at the same time in her eyes. "What are you talking about?"

He hesitated—and the hesitation told her everything. He glanced toward the window, toward the direction of the lab as if he could see through walls and miles.

"You know something," she whispered. Anger edged the fear now, sharpening it. "You've known something since the hospital. You've been acting strange. Jumpier. What happened, Henry? What did you hear?"

He looked at Jonathan—small, slick with sweat, fighting for breath. He looked at Suzanne—exhausted, hollow-eyed, clutching their son as if she could anchor him with sheer will. He saw again the crack of the office door, heard the word downstairs like a warning and a summons.

"I overheard them," he said. Each word felt dragged out of him. "Two doctors. They were talking about Jonathan's labs. They said his numbers... match profiles they've seen in the project under the lab."

Suzanne's face went blank, all expression wiped clean by the blow.

"The project," she repeated. "Downstairs."

The word came out flat and cold.

Henry nodded.

"The place they built the extra security for," she said. "The one you told me I'm not allowed to ask about. That project?"

"Yes."

Her composure shattered. It cracked all at once, not along the neat seams she had tried to maintain. "And you're only telling me this now?"

"I didn't know what it meant," he said, but the excuse sounded weak even to him. It fell between them like something flimsy and useless. "I still don't. But they recognized something in him. That means they've seen it before. They might know what's happening."

"Or they caused it," she shot back. Her voice rose, sharp and hoarse. "Did that thought cross your mind? That whatever they're doing down there is leaking out into this town—into our son?"

Henry's jaw tightened.

He had thought it. The possibility had latched onto him in the hospital hallway and hadn't let go. He'd pictured invisible threads stretching from some machine under concrete floors straight into Jonathan's veins. He'd pictured signatures on files, decisions made in conference rooms, the faceless "they" who never had to see the people affected by their work.

He had thought nothing else since he heard those words. He just hadn't wanted to say it out loud, because saying it made it real.

"I don't trust them," he said. "I don't trust any part of that lab. But right now they might be the only people on this planet who can look at what's happening to him and recognize it."

He looked back at Jonathan, chest fluttering, fingers twitching weakly beneath the blanket. Every stutter in the boy's breathing felt like another second slipping away.

"I can't sit here and watch him die," Henry said, voice dropping. The edges of his words were raw. "Not if there's even a chance they can stop it."

Suzanne's shoulders shook. She pressed a fist to her mouth, staring between her husband and her son. Her gaze flicked toward the front door, as if she could already see the path that would take them from this living room to whatever waited below the lab.

"They'll take him away," she whispered. "They'll treat him like one of their experiments. He's a little boy, Henry. He's our boy. We don't know what they'll do to him down there."

"I know exactly what they'll do," Henry said, grim and steady. "They'll study him. They'll push him. They'll try to see how far this… whatever it is… can go."

Images flashed in his mind: sterile metal tables, restraints, needles, faceless figures in masks and lab coats leaning over his son, recording data while he cried. He tasted bile.

"And you still want to take him there?" Tears streamed down her face. "How can you even say that?"

"Because whatever this is," Henry snapped, "it's already inside him. It's already doing something to him. They started this, whether they meant to or not. They can damn well fix it."

The room went quiet except for Jonathan's thin breathing and the distant rumble of thunder. The storm outside raked its nails down the sides of the house, wind howling around the eaves.

Suzanne reached out and brushed Jonathan's hair back, fingers shaking. His skin was hot under her touch. She could feel the faint, uneven thump of his heart against her fingertips where they rested on his chest.

"If we take him there," she whispered, "we may never get him back."

The words tasted like betrayal even as she said them, betrayal of the instinct to cling, to hide him from anything that wanted to cut him open, literally or metaphorically. But there was another betrayal coiled inside: the possibility that doing nothing, keeping him here, would mean betraying his only chance to live.

"If we don't," Henry said, "we're going to lose him right here in this room."

Her knees nearly buckled. She sank down onto the edge of the couch, one hand still on Jonathan, the other braced on the cushion.

They stood in that fragile space between two impossible choices. The house seemed to lean in around them, walls listening, ceiling bowed under the weight of their decision.

Then Jonathan let out a low, broken sound—half exhale, half whimper. A sound like surrender. His fingers twitched weakly against the blanket, reaching for nothing.

Suzanne closed her eyes. The decision formed in the darkness behind her eyelids, where she could not see her own reflection.

"Okay," she whispered. "Okay. If this is the only chance… we take it."

Henry nodded once. The decision settled over him like a weight he knew he'd carry for the rest of his life. There would be no going back from this, no pretending they hadn't known what they were doing when they handed their son over to the people who had broken him.

He knelt beside Jonathan again and smoothed his son's damp hair back. His hand lingered for a moment, memorizing the shape of the boy's skull, the warmth of his skin.

"Hang on, buddy," he murmured. "Just a little longer. Dad's going to make this right."

Outside, the storm raged on. Lightning winked in the distance, hidden behind clouds, turning the sky a sickly white for split seconds at a time. Inside, a quieter storm had already begun—the kind that didn't blow over.

The kind that changed everything.

CHAPTER 3 — THE LAB

The laboratory rose out of the dark like a monument to bad decisions. The longer Henry stared at it through the wash of the storm, the more it looked less like a building and more like something that had grown there by mistake, a hard, cancerous mass no one had managed to cut out.

Henry saw it long before he reached the gate, its bulky, a jagged silhouette against a storm-tossed sky, floodlights bleaching the red brick into harsh, unnatural white. In the wet shine of the road, the building reflected back at him like a wound that wouldn't close. He had driven this stretch a hundred times on quiet nights, sipping bad coffee, thinking of overtime pay and Suzanne's tired smile, but the place had never felt like this—alive, watchful, waiting.

Jonathan lay bundled beside him, wrapped in the thick blanket Suzanne had thrown over him with shaking hands. His face was half-buried in the folds, skin pale and damp. His breath was so faint Henry had to watch for the smallest stir of fabric at the boy's mouth. Every few seconds he leaned closer, needing to see that tiny movement again, terrified of the moment it might not come.

"We're almost there, buddy," Henry whispered, though he didn't know if Jonathan could hear him. "Just a little longer." He'd said those same words on road trips and late-night drives home from the grandparents', but back then "almost there" had meant warm beds and hot chocolate, not what waited under concrete and steel.

Jonathan didn't answer. His half-lidded eyes tracked nothing, pupils dilated and glassy. A faint, confused sound leaked from his throat—more breath than voice—as if he were trying to surface through molasses and failed. Henry's fingers twitched toward him and then tightened back around the wheel. If he touched Jonathan's face again and it was colder, he wasn't sure he would keep the truck on the road.

The wipers scraped across the windshield, fighting the rain. Each pass smeared the floodlit side of the lab into bands of light and shadow. When Henry crested the last small rise, the facility opened up in front of him—the sloping roof, the blank brick walls, the distant glow of the front entryway like a single working eye. A paved approach led to the gate and the guard shack he usually occupied. Most nights, the sight meant routine: badge checks, log entries, a thermos cooling too fast. Tonight it looked like the front steps of something that ate people.

Tonight, he stayed on the gas.

The shack's interior light glowed weakly, a square of yellow in the downpour. As Henry's headlights pinned it, a figure lurched out—the night guard, raincoat half on, one hand lifted in reflex. Henry recognized the shape even through the rain-streaked glass: Davis, the kid who joked badly to cover how seriously he took the job, the one who'd asked Henry last month what it was really like "down there."

"Halden?" the man shouted, thin against the wind. "What the hell—?"

Henry didn't slow. He couldn't let himself fall back into the familiar pattern of rolling down his window, swapping a tired joke, logging his own arrival. Any delay was another breath Jonathan might not take.

The guard grabbed for the radio handset and yanked it to his mouth. Lightning flickered. Static burst across the frequency in a long, raw hiss. Whatever the man tried to say broke into fragments.

"—Rour—… come in… breach at—"

The storm swallowed the rest. Thunder rolled over the words like a closing fist.

Henry barely heard it. His entire focus had narrowed to the front entrance, to the pool of light beneath the concrete overhang. The rest of the world—the shack, the radio, Davis's alarm—blurred into background noise. He drove straight past the shack, through the open gate, tires hissing on wet pavement as he cut into the entry lane.

The guard shouted his name again, distant and useless. It sounded less like a challenge now and more like a plea: Don't do this. Turn around.

Henry slid to a stop beneath the main awning.

For a second he just sat there, heart pounding, one hand braced on the wheel, the other hovering over Jonathan. The engine ticked as it idled, wipers still dragging back and forth in frantic arcs. If he let himself think—really think about what he was doing, bringing his son here, delivering him into the belly of the place that had always felt wrong—he might lose his nerve. He pictured Suzanne on the couch with the phone pressed to her ear, Lazar's hollow voice saying there was nothing left to try.

He couldn't afford that.

Jonathan's eyes were half-open, unfocused. His lips moved soundlessly, shaping words that never made it out. A small tremor fluttered in his fingers, then stilled.

"It's okay," Henry whispered. "I've got you." The lie tasted like metal. He had never felt less like he "had" anything in his life.

He opened the driver's door and cold air knifed in with the rain. It slapped the heat from his face, stole his breath for a second. He moved around the front of the truck, wrenched open the passenger door, and lifted Jonathan into his arms. The blanket clung to them both, heavy with moisture. The boy's weight felt lighter than it should have—wrongly light, like a bundle of sticks instead of a child who had once launched himself at Henry so hard he'd nearly been knocked over.

Jonathan's head lolled against Henry's shoulder. Damp hair stuck to Henry's neck. For a heartbeat Henry smelled nothing but fever and the faint ghost of the shampoo Jonathan had used before all this started.

"Hang on," Henry breathed. "Please." The word tore out of him more like a prayer than a request.

He ran for the doors.

The entrance was brutally simple—industrial concrete, twin steel doors set beneath a narrow overhang. Years of weather had left hairline fractures in the concrete and faint rust streaks beneath the hinges. On either side of the doors, access panels glowed in the dark: a card reader lit green, a rubber-buttoned keypad, a small red status light steady and unblinking. On other nights, those lights had meant safety protocols, procedure, control. Tonight they looked like eyes and a waiting mouth.

Henry splashed through pooled water on the entry slab. It surged up around his boots, icy through damp socks. Jonathan's damp breath brushed his neck, barely there, like the faintest tickle of air. Henry angled his body to shield the boy from the worst of the wind, as if the storm were something he could fight off with his shoulders alone.

The panels hummed with a low electrical thrum that seemed to rise into his bones. It reminded him of the background buzz he felt in his teeth whenever he stood too close to the Level Three generators. The building had always had its own pulse; he heard it now like a second heartbeat, impatient and cold.

The storm made everything raw and loud. Rain hissed on the concrete. Wind tugged at his clothes, tried to peel the blanket away. Somewhere above, a loose piece of flashing rattled and banged against the roof. The building watched. He felt it in the prickle along the back of his neck, the sense that cameras were already turning toward him, that unseen eyes were narrowing.

Tonight, he wasn't here as security.

He was here as a father.

The difference felt like stepping off a ledge he'd guarded for years.

He wedged Jonathan higher in his arms, fumbled his badge free with one hand, and swiped it. His fingers were clumsy, numb from cold and adrenaline.

BEEP.

The light blinked once.

Still red.

His heart lurched. "No. Not now." The words came out more like a growl than a plea.

He wiped the badge on the blanket, streaking moisture across its worn surface, and tried again.

BEEP.

A pause stretched long enough to feel like a verdict. Henry could almost see the system weighing him, weighing this, deciding whether to obey the rules he'd enforced for so long. Rain drummed on his back. Jonathan's weight sagged heavier against his chest.

Then the red shifted to green.

Something heavy thudded inside the steel—locks disengaging, one after another. A deep mechanical heartbeat in the door. Henry let out a breath he didn't remember holding.

The keypad still waited.

Henry stared at it for only a second. The code was burned into his memory from emergency drills and from Tom's voice earlier that night, low and grim, reciting it in case "the worst ever happened." Henry had half-joked then that the worst never would.

3–1–7–5–9.

He punched it in, each digit a small act of treason. His thumb shook on the last number, but he forced it down. For a heartbeat, nothing happened. The silence roared. Then the doorway shivered.

Deep inside the mechanism, something groaned.

The twin doors dragged apart with a reluctant metallic rumble, opening just wide enough for him to slip through. Warm, sterile air rushed out, smelling faintly of disinfectant and metal, with an undertone of recycled breath and machine oil. It hit his wet skin like a slap.

Henry stepped inside.

"Henry?!"

The shout came from behind him, chased by the hiss of the closing doors. The sound reverberated off tile and glass, too loud after the muffled roar of the storm.

He turned just enough to see Tom sprinting across the lobby, jacket flapping open, shirt plastered to his chest, rainwater dripping from his hair. Tom looked furious and frightened in equal measure, the combination twisting his familiar features into something Henry barely recognized.

"What the hell are you doing?" Tom barked, voice bouncing off polished tile and a ceiling too high for any human comfort. His shoes slapped against the floor. "You can't bring him in here. This is restricted access."

Henry didn't stop. The old instinct to freeze when a superior shouted his name flared and died in the same second. He angled deeper into the building, boots thudding, Jonathan limp and hot in his arms. The warmth radiating off the boy felt wrong, feverish, as if his body were burning itself from the inside out.

"Henry! Stop!"

"I don't have time," Henry snapped over his shoulder. "He's dying." The word cracked in his throat. Saying it out loud made it more real, more final, but it also shoved everything else—regulations, clearance levels, fear—into the background.

Tom's shoes squealed on the floor as he tried to keep up. "You don't have clearance for the lower levels. You can't go down there. You know what this place is."

Henry didn't answer. What could he say—that he knew, and that knowing made this feel even more insane? The corridor ahead stretched long and bright, lined with chrome rails and fluorescent fixtures. He'd escorted enough authorized personnel down it to know the route by muscle memory alone. Every scuff on the baseboards, every camera dome in the ceiling was familiar. Tonight, each one felt like a witness.

Tonight, he didn't slow.

Tom's voice chased him, thin with panic now instead of authority. "Henry—don't go down there!" There was something in it Henry had never heard before: real fear. Not of losing his job. Of whatever waited below.

At the end of the hall, the elevator doors waited—mirror-bright, featureless except for the slim card scanner and button panel beside them. Henry's reflection flashed at him in the polished metal: wild-eyed, soaked, carrying a bundle that looked too small. He slammed his badge against the reader, breathing hard.

The reader beeped, low and reluctant, as if even the electronics were second-guessing him.

He entered the override again with clumsy, shaking fingers.

3–1–7–5–9.

For a heartbeat, the screen blinked. A small spinning icon chased itself in the corner, as if the system upstairs were arguing with the system down below.

Then a soft chime sounded.

The chrome doors slid open with a hiss and a stuttering shudder, as though the machinery resented being forced awake at this hour, for this reason. Cold air breathed out from the shaft, smelling faintly older, as if it had been sitting unused in the dark.

Henry stumbled in and turned toward the panel.

One button sat apart from the others: a single unlabeled square glowing with a faint, unauthorized light. No floor number, no name. Just that sullen glow.

Basement. The level nobody named out loud. In staff meetings it was "downstairs" or "the project." In rumors it was worse.

He hit it with his palm.

The doors began to close.

Tom's hand slapped into the narrowing gap. Metal thudded against his palm. "Henry, listen to me. They will bury you for this. They will bury all of us." His voice dropped on the last word, weighted with the knowledge of exactly how far the people above them would go to keep their secrets.

Henry met his eyes for a fraction of a second. In that flash he saw everything Tom wasn't saying—court-martials, disappeared records, closed-casket funerals with vague explanations. Tom wasn't afraid of paperwork. He was afraid of something far larger.

"I don't have a choice," Henry said. The truth of it settled heavy in his chest. If he turned back now, he would be choosing to watch his son die on their living room couch. He could live with the consequences of breaking rules. He could not live with that.

The doors shut.

The elevator lurched and began to descend. The sudden drop tugged at Henry's stomach, a hollow swoop that felt too much like the moment before impact in a car crash. For a heartbeat he imagined the cables snapping, the box plummeting them not to Level Five but straight into the earth.

The ride down felt like falling through a throat. Panel lights ticked through the upper floors and then past them, each ding and blink another swallow.

L1. L2. L3.

He had spent years riding to those levels with clipboard in hand, escorting white coats and contractors, signing off on deliveries. Those stops had always come with chatter—bored jokes, half-finished coffee, complaints about administration. Tonight, no one spoke.

B1. B2. B3.

With each level, the air turned colder. A soft vibration hummed through the walls, not quite mechanical, not quite natural, like a low animal growl buried under metal. Something in the depths of the building was awake. Henry felt it in his teeth, in the fine hairs along his arms. He had never been this far down with the doors open.

Jonathan made a faint sound in Henry's arms, a restless, pained exhale. His fingers twitched once against Henry's chest, then curled limply. Heat still rolled off him in waves, fighting the elevator's chill.

"I've got you," Henry whispered, not sure who he was trying to convince. The words came out on a ghost of breath, swallowed almost immediately by the small, humming box. He clutched Jonathan tighter, as if the strength of his grip alone could keep the boy tethered.

The elevator shuddered as it slowed. Brakes caught with a grinding sigh that reminded Henry of old hinges and shut doors.

DING.

The doors grated open with a grinding scrape.

Cold air spilled in—sterile chill threaded with the scent of electricity and something chemical and faintly organic. It was the smell of labs without windows, of things stored in sealed containers, of samples that weren't supposed to exist. Henry's skin crawled. His instinct screamed that he had no business being here with his son.

He stepped out.

The corridor beyond looked like a tunnel into another world. White light ran in a continuous band along the ceiling, painting everything in flat, colorless tones. Shadows had nowhere to hide; they were beaten back into thin, gray smears at the edges of machines. Along one side, glass-fronted rooms stretched away in a row. The glass was thick enough to mute sound, thin enough to reveal everything inside like exhibits in a museum.

Henry swallowed and walked forward. His boots thumped on the polished floor, the sound swallowed almost immediately by the insulation in the walls. Each step felt too loud, like an intrusion.

Room One: stainless-steel tables. Neat rows of instruments gleamed under overhead strips, each one aligned with unnerving precision—scalpels, clamps, syringes laid out like an alphabet of harm. A centrifuge in the corner, its orange light blinking slowly, as if thinking. He imagined those tables with restraints bolted on, imagined Jonathan's small body there, and forced the picture away before it could finish forming.

Room Two: diagnostic hardware—cuffs, leads, screens looping numbers and waveforms. Electrodes hung in bundles, the contact pads dull and waiting. On one monitor, an idle screen saver bounced a logo from corner to corner, cheerful and out of place. Some of the readouts were still active, green lines tracing phantom heartbeats from tests that were already over.

Room Three: microscopes. Dozens of them, high-powered lenses trained on slides. On one monitor, magnified cells pulsed and shifted, something foreign glimmering between them like metallic dust caught in a current. Alive or reacting—Henry couldn't tell. He only knew he didn't want it anywhere near his son. The idea that some piece of whatever that was might already be inside Jonathan made bile burn the back of his throat.

He tightened his hold on Jonathan. "Almost there," he whispered, and tried to believe it. The words echoed back off the glass with a hollow sound.

Rooms Four through Eight held things worse—surgical tools laid out with careful precision, vials labeled with strings of letters and numbers instead of names, cylinders standing upright like empty coffins, waiting. Some of the vials glowed faintly under blacklight strips, liquids too bright to be anything natural. Each label was a code that meant something to people in lab coats and nothing to a man whose only job had been to keep the wrong badges out.

Room Nine was a bank of computers, screens full of models that moved and adjusted on their own. Wireframe bodies rotated slowly, layers peeling back to reveal organs, nerves, lattices of light that mapped some invisible process. Numbers cascaded down one side of a display faster than Henry could track them. The graphs on another screen rose and fell like the outline of a city skyline.

Room Ten held tanks of translucent gel. Something dark drifted lazily in one of them, like ink in water. Henry looked away. If he stared too long he thought he saw it move with intention, not just currents—a slow, coiling twist, as if it were aware.

Room Eleven: robotic arms and surgical-assist rigs, their joints stained with discolorations that looked like blood scrubbed clean and remembered anyway. Fine tools dangled at their ends, some so slender Henry couldn't imagine what they were meant to touch. The arms were powered down now, hanging like the limbs of sleeping metal insects.

Room Twelve was colder than all the others. Frost climbed along the base of a pod sunk half into the floor, blue lights pulsing along its edges in a slow, heartbeat rhythm. Thin mist curled at its seams, drifting across the floor like low fog. Whatever was in there was kept very cold and very important.

At the end of the hall, a door rose out of the gloom.

A double-layered blast door thicker than anything Henry had seen in his years at the facility. It looked less like a door and more like the sealed plug for a missile silo. Bold red letters glared across its surface.

BIOHAZARD – RESTRICTED ACCESS

LEVEL 5 – AUTHORIZED PERSONNEL / MILITARY CLEARANCE ONLY

Beneath the words, a hazard symbol glowed faintly yellow, its stark black lines cutting through the white paint like a warning carved into bone.

Henry stepped closer anyway, heart pounding, skin clammy. Sweat crawled between his shoulder blades despite the cold. He could feel the weight of every camera in the building on his back, every line of policy he was shattering with each breath.

Jonathan let out a weak, rattling exhale. The sound dragged Henry's focus back to what mattered.

Henry pressed his forehead briefly to his son's temple. Jonathan's skin burned beneath his touch. "We're getting through that door," he whispered. "I swear it." It was a promise to his son, to Suzanne, to himself—and he had no idea how he was going to keep it.

Beside the blast door, a newer access panel waited— sleek and upgraded. Magnetic slot. Numeric pad. A white status light instead of red. The casing still had that faint matte sheen of recently installed equipment; this was one of the changes Henry had watched come in without ever being told why.

Henry lifted his badge, knowing even as he did that it wouldn't be enough. His clearance got him to the corridor. Level Five belonged to people whose names never appeared on the general staff rosters.

Before he could swipe, the panel beeped on its own. The white light flickered, as if something on the other side had reached out electronically to meet him.

The blast door hissed.

Locks began to release. He heard them thud in sequence, a deep, layered series of clanks that vibrated through the soles of his boots.

Henry froze. For a split second, some animal part of him screamed at him to turn and run, to take the open elevator back up before whoever was on the other side saw his face.

The doors parted a fraction.

On the other side stood Dr. Gerald Winston.

He was younger than most of the senior staff, sharp in the way of men who had cut their way into programs like this with nothing but intelligence and nerve. His lab coat was half-buttoned, dark hair slightly wild, eyes too bright, as if he spent more time with glowing screens than sleeping. Henry had seen him from a distance in the cafeteria, laughing too loudly with other researchers, always with a stack of files under one arm.

"What the hell are you doing down here?" Dr. Gerald demanded. His voice held authority, but something unsteady lived beneath it—shock fighting curiosity. "This level is restricted. No one—"

His gaze dropped to the bundle in Henry's arms.

Jonathan's limp body. The pallor. The fever sheen. The little jerks of his muscles when another wave of pain rolled through.

Dr. Gerald's expression shifted—not to disgust or fear, but to something more dangerous.

Calculation.

"What's his diagnosis?" Dr. Gerald asked, stepping closer. His eyes had gone very sharp, pupils pinning Jonathan like another specimen on a slide.

Henry swallowed. The words he'd already said to Lazar, to Suzanne, now had to be dragged out again. "They don't know. Lazar said they ran everything. Nothing fits. Nothing shows up. He told us to take him home and… wait." The last word scraped out of him. Wait to die. Wait for your child to stop breathing.

Dr. Gerald's jaw tightened. For a second he didn't speak. The muscles in his face worked as he looked from Jonathan to the hallway cameras and back.

"He's been like this for days," Henry pushed on. "And at the hospital, I heard them. Your people. They said his labs looked like something from down here." His voice lowered, rough with anger and fear. "They said it matched the project."

Dr. Gerald's eyes snapped to his.

"Who told you that?" he asked quietly. The tone had changed; this was not outrage at a security breach, but the cool, lethal interest of someone tracking a leak.

Henry shook his head. "Does it matter?" If he gave names, he signed someone else's death warrant, and he was already in over his head enough for everyone.

Fear flickered behind Dr. Gerald's eyes—yes—but so did something else, sharp and hungry. The look of a man who had been waiting for a problem only he could solve.

Down here, his work lived in simulations and animal trials. Models. Numbers. Projections. Good enough for reports, not enough for the kind of proof that changed careers, secured funding, rewrote the rules.

He needed a human case.

And one had just walked into his restricted level, carried in on a desperate father's arms.

"Please," Henry said, voice cracking. Pride, protocol, and self-preservation all fell away in the face of the only thing that mattered. "He's my son. If anyone knows what's happening to him… it's you. It's this place."

For a moment, the corridor held its breath with them. Even the low hum of machines seemed to recede. Somewhere behind the glass, a monitor beeped in a slow, steady rhythm that felt like a countdown.

Then Dr. Gerald stepped aside.

"Bring him in," he said.

Relief and terror hit Henry at the same time, slamming into his chest from opposite directions. Saying yes meant hope. It also meant handing his child over to the very people whose work might have caused this.

Dr. Gerald moved with sudden urgency, but his gaze never left Jonathan. His mind was already running ahead, calculating, weighing risks and outcomes, seeing graphs and models in his head instead of blankets and fever-slick skin.

The blast door boomed shut behind them.

All return paths sealed. The sound reverberated through the chamber like a final verdict.

The chamber beyond Level Five looked like it had been built for another world. It was enormous, stretching farther than Henry could process at once. Massive tanks lined the walls, each glowing with its own sickly light— deep violet fluid shot through with floating motes like distant stars in a bruise-colored sky; yellow-white reservoirs swirling in hypnotic spirals as though stirred by invisible hands.

Between the tanks, towering transparent columns rose from floor to ceiling. Inside them, diagrams moved—cell structures dividing, merging, mutating in accelerated loops. Thick cables spilled from their bases into consoles and hidden machines, veins feeding some massive artificial organism.

Puddles on the floor caught the strange lights and smeared them into rainbow sheens like oil. Each step Henry took broke those reflections apart and re-formed them around his boots.

The air was freezing. It smelled of antiseptic, ozone, and something faintly organic—like meat kept just on the edge of spoilage, never quite allowed to rot. The back of Henry's throat tasted of metal and old fear.

In the center of the room stood the cradle.

Steel and glass shaped like a pod, contoured to hold a human body. Clear tubing draped from overhead like strands of a mechanical spiderweb. In the base, a reservoir of silver fluid pulsed—thick and luminous, threaded with light that moved in a slow, synthetic rhythm, like a heartbeat that had never belonged to any living thing.

Dr. Gerald went to the console beside it and began entering commands, fingers flying. Lines of code and numbers cascaded down the screen, windows popping open and collapsing again.

"This is the only thing that might help him now," he said.

Henry stared at the cradle. At the fluid. At the waiting tubes. "What is that?" he asked, voice hoarse. The question felt almost useless; whatever the answer was, it was already too late to pretend he wouldn't use it.

"Nano-structure colony," Dr. Gerald replied. "Programmable. Adaptive. We built it to reengineer damaged tissue from the inside out—restore function at a cellular level."

The words hit Henry like blows. Reengineer. Colony. Inside. His mind snagged on each one, tearing skin.

Henry felt sick. "You've tested it, right?" Images surged up—rats in cages, monkeys under anesthesia, charts with rising and falling lines. And underneath all of that, a smaller, more horrifying image: Jonathan, eight years old, reduced to before-and-after slides in some classified presentation.

"On models. On animals." Dr. Gerald hesitated. His hands hovered over the keys. "On data."

Henry's grip on Jonathan tightened. "Not on people." He already knew the answer; he needed to hear the man say it.

"Not officially." Dr. Gerald's mouth pulled tight. "We were never given approval. Too many unknowns. Too many risks."

"So this isn't a treatment," Henry said. "It's an experiment."

"It's both," Dr. Gerald snapped. Frustration flared in his eyes, not at Henry but at the constraints he'd been operating under. "If we do nothing, he dies. If we try this, he might live."

Might.

The word hung between them like a blade.

Above them, speakers crackled. Harsh feedback squealed for a second.

"LEVEL FIVE BREACH DETECTED. ARMED RESPONSE UNIT EN ROUTE. ALL PERSONNEL STAND DOWN."

Henry's stomach dropped. The sound of the automated voice felt colder than the air. "Armed response?"

Dr. Gerald withdrew his hands from the keys and dragged a hand through his hair. The brightness in his eyes dimmed into dread. For the first time since the door opened, he looked less like a scientist on the verge of a breakthrough and more like a man standing in front of a firing squad.

"They're not coming to help," he said. "They're coming to shut this down."

He nodded toward the cradle and the vats. "They will not allow unauthorized tests. They will not allow evidence that control has been lost. And they will not let a dying child who's seen too much walk out of here."

Henry's blood went cold. His pulse hammered in his ears, but his skin felt numb.

"You're saying they'll kill us."

"I'm saying they will erase this room," Dr. Gerald replied. "You. Me. Him. Every trace." His gaze flicked to the tanks, the consoles, the cables. "If this project is compromised, they will wipe it clean and start again somewhere else."

The floor shuddered faintly beneath their feet, dust skittering across the grates.

Boots. Distant, heavy, organized. The sound filtered down through concrete like approaching thunder, in rhythm, in step.

Dr. Gerald stepped closer, lowering his voice as if the speakers could hear them. "If you want him to live, we have minutes—maybe less. Put him in the cradle. I'll start the integration."

Jonathan wheezed weakly in Henry's arms. His fingers twitched once against Henry's chest, then fell still. Gray gathered at the edges of his skin, leaching color from his lips.

Henry looked at his son. At the cradle. At the tanks. At Dr. Gerald. Each choice felt like a different kind of death.

"Tell me what to do," he said.

"Lay him inside," Dr. Gerald ordered. "I'll engage the swarm."

Henry swallowed and eased Jonathan into the cradle, adjusting him as gently as shaking hands would allow. The cold of the metal seeped through the blanket. Jonathan's head lolled to one side, his mouth falling open in a soft, rasping breath.

The glass framework closed around the boy with a soft, final hiss. It sounded too much like a lid sealing.

Dr. Gerald's hands flew over the console. Valves clicked. Tubes vibrated. The silver reservoir stirred, threads of light brightening, swirling, as if something inside had scented blood.

The alarms wailed louder. Red lights began to strobe around the chamber in time with the siren, bathing everything in pulses of crimson—boy, cradle, tanks, Henry's hands.

The building shook again, closer. Dust rained from seams in the ceiling, speckling Henry's hair and shoulders.

Henry looked toward the sealed blast doors. He heard the echo of boots now more clearly, the distant bark of commands. His body recognized the rhythms even before his mind put words to them.

"Sixty seconds," Dr. Gerald muttered, eyes fixed on the screen. "I just need sixty—"

The floor juddered. A boom overhead. Plaster dust rained down in a thicker sheet. Somewhere metal screamed in protest.

Henry's old training rose up fast and sharp. The sounds above were unmistakable.

Breaching charges. Tactical movement. He'd been on the other side of that once, years ago, kicking in a door on a drug lab that had turned out to be mostly empty. The concussion, the shouted commands, the controlled violence—it all came back in a rush.

He turned away from the cradle. "I'll buy you your minute," he said.

Dr. Gerald's head snapped up. "What are you doing?"

"Making sure they get through me before they get to him."

Henry moved back into the hall, past the pods, to the wall cabinet with red stenciling and locked glass. His boots left damp prints on the metal grating.

ARMED RESPONSE UNIT – TIER 3 ARMAMENTS

He didn't hesitate. Hesitation was for men who had more than one option left.

His elbow shattered the glass.

Shards cascaded to the floor like glittering knives, skittering across the grate with high, chiming notes. A small cut opened on his forearm where a piece caught skin; he barely felt it.

Inside: an M16 rifle, two sidearms, magazines stacked with neat indifference, a handwritten tag about command authorization dangling from one trigger guard.

Tonight, authorization was a luxury.

He grabbed the rifle, racked the charging handle, and thumbed the safety off with hands that remembered the motions after years of disuse. Muscle memory slid into place where conscious thought might have faltered. He shoved the pistols into his waistband, metal shocking cold against his skin through the damp fabric of his shirt.

For a moment he let himself look back.

Jonathan lay in the cradle beneath the web of tubes. Silver fluid trickled into the lines, slow at first, then faster, flowing like mercury toward his veins. The boy's chest rose and fell in tiny, uneven movements. Thin threads of light began to pulse faintly where the tubes met skin.

Dr. Gerald met Henry's gaze across the distance. Understanding passed between them without words: this was the point where there was nothing more a father could do with his hands, only with his body.

"Go," Dr. Gerald said.

Henry turned away.

He reached the end of the corridor as the ceiling shook with a bone-deep blast. The shockwave ran down the walls and through the floor grating into his legs. A flash through the stairwell painted the concrete in stark white for a heartbeat, followed by the muffled, stomach-turning thump of a flashbang. His ears rang, a high, needling whine pressing at the edges of sound.

White seared the edges of his vision. Instinct screamed at him to duck, to turn away from the light, but he forced himself to stand his ground.

He raised the rifle. The familiar weight settled into his hands, heavier than he remembered and yet fitting there like it had been waiting. His shoulder found the stock without thinking.

Boots thundered down the stairwell. Voices shouted over one another, bouncing off the narrow walls in jagged echoes.

"LEVEL FIVE BREACH—MOVE!"

"TARGET IS ARMED—WATCH YOUR FIRE!"

Henry braced himself and drew a breath that felt like it might tear his lungs. The air tasted of dust and metal and the sharp, bitter tang of explosives. For a split second he saw Suzanne's face, Jonathan's small hand wrapped around his thumb. Then he shoved everything except the hallway in front of him aside.

The first soldiers swung into view. Dark armor, visors down, rifles already shouldered. For a heartbeat the line of them looked less like men and more like a single organism, segmented and lethal.

The firefight was fast and brutal. Muzzle flashes strobed the hallway, turning the world into a series of frozen, red-tinged snapshots—open mouths shouting, brass casings spinning, the jagged teeth of ceiling damage above. Alarms screamed over the crack of gunfire, sirens wailing in counterpoint to the staccato bursts.

Henry fired, fell back, fired again. Years of training threaded through desperation, turning panic into practiced motion. He didn't aim to wound; there was no time for mercy and no illusion about what they had been sent to do. He moved on muscle memory—sight picture, trigger squeeze, step, cover, repeat.

One fell, armor slamming into the floor with a hollow thud. Another staggered, shoulder jerking as a round punched through his plate, spinning him sideways. Someone shouted that he was pinned, voice cracking through the comms.

Then a heavier voice cut through the chaos, cold and controlled, the sound of command accustomed to being obeyed.

"Advance line. Keep pressure. He's alone."

They pushed forward. Shields angled. Fire tightened. The corridor shrank around Henry.

Something hot tore along Henry's side—a bright, searing line that stole his breath. Another impact hit deeper, center mass, like being punched with a sledgehammer. Pain flared, then went distant and numb as his body tried to process too much at once. His legs buckled. The rifle slipped from fingers that suddenly refused to obey, clattering across the grate.

He hit the floor hard. The shock rattled his teeth. Air whooshed out of him in a raw grunt.

The ceiling swam above him, a smear of red lights and exposed wiring. The world tilted, then righted itself in sick lurches. Distantly, he heard commands—short, clipped, professional. Boots stepping over him, around him. Someone saying, "Intruder down." The words felt impersonal, as if they were talking about a problem solved, not a man bleeding out.

He tried to move—just enough to turn his head toward the blast doors. It felt like trying to lift a car with his neck. His muscles shook with the effort.

Toward his son.

Jonathan.

The name wasn't thought. It was gravity. It pulled every remaining piece of him in one direction.

Black narrowed at the edges of his vision, closing in like tunnel walls. Sound grew watery and far away.

He never heard the final confirmation.

"Command, this is Bravo Lead. Intruder neutralized. Level Five secure."

On the other side of the blast door, in the cradle, Jonathan's heart staggered—then steadied. The monitors above him flickered as his vitals crashed and then climbed again, numbers jittering into new patterns.

The silver swarm threaded through his veins, into his lungs, across the failing circuits of his body. Tiny built things woke in him and began their work—repairing, rewiring, rewriting instructions nature had never meant for him. They moved like a tide, filling capillaries, slipping between cells, changing the rules from the inside out.

The alarms still shrieked. The floor still shook. The whole structure felt like it was caught between two choices: hold or collapse.

Dr. Gerald stood between the cradle and the door, torn between the console and the boy, every inch of him strung tight. His fingers hovered over the controls, wanting to make adjustments he no longer had time to make.

"Not yet," he whispered, to the machines and the soldiers upstairs. "Just a little longer." He didn't know if he was begging the swarm to hurry or the men with guns to slow.

The first blast hit the doors.

Metal screamed. The floor shuddered. Dust puffed out from the seams like breath.

The second blast bent steel inward, warping the hazard symbol into a twisted, unreadable smear. Bolts pinged loose, ricocheting across the floor.

The third tore it open.

Smoke rolled into the chamber ahead of the soldiers, thick and bitter, tasting of burned metal and compounds Henry would never learn the names of. Rifles led the way, followed by hard, expressionless faces behind shields and visors. Their formation was neat, lethal, practiced—the kind of entry they'd drilled until it lived in their bones.

"Room clear," someone shouted, voice flat, almost bored.

Then they saw the cradle. The tanks. The monitors. The boy.

Orders snapped down the line. Weapons stayed up. A few muzzles dipped a fraction, then jerked back as training overrode human hesitation.

Dr. Gerald lifted his hands, heart pounding. His palms were slick with sweat. "He's a child," he said. "He's not your enemy. He's your only proof this works." His voice edged toward frantic.

No one answered. Silence from behind the visors said more than words.

Behind them, dragged in on a stretcher, lay Henry Halden. The white of the sheet beneath him was already blotched dark. Someone had placed a field dressing over his chest, more out of protocol than hope.

Time fractured for Jonathan as he woke.

He came back in fragments—cold air on his face, flashing red light stroking across his closed eyelids, the taste of metal at the back of his tongue as if he'd been sucking on a coin.

His lungs burned, then pulled in a breath that wasn't shallow anymore. It was deep. Strong. The inhalation shocked him; his chest expanded without the tearing struggle he'd gotten used to.

He coughed. The sound echoed against glass and metal, harsher and louder than he expected. Each cough rattled something loose inside him—a layer of weakness peeled away and left something steadier underneath.

"Easy," someone said—Dr. Gerald, close by, voice tight with contained urgency. "Don't move yet. You've been through—"

Jonathan's gaze slid past him. The doctor's face was just a blur of white coat and dark hair on the edge of his vision.

To the stretcher.

To the man lying there, motionless, surrounded by armored legs, blood pooling under the stretcher as blood spreads along the grated surface. The puddles quivered with each vibration of boots and machinery, sending tiny ripples through the red.

His father.

"Dad…?" Jonathan whispered. The word scraped out of a throat that felt raw and strange, both sore and stronger than it had in days.

The rest of the room blurred—the guns, the lights, the men. Color drained from everything but that one shape on the floor. He forced himself upright, muscles shaking but no longer failing the way they had in the living room or hospital bed. New strength surged in fits and starts, unfamiliar but there.

He swung his legs over the cradle's edge. They tried to hold him and almost did. The floor seemed too far away and then too close. He dropped to his hands, knees slamming into cold metal, the impact jolting up his bones.

"Dad," he choked. "Dad, get up. Please—Dad!"

No one stopped him at first. Maybe they were stunned by the fact that he was moving at all. Maybe they thought there was nowhere for an eight-year-old to run in a sealed Level Five chamber.

He crawled to Henry's body, leaving a slick streak behind him where his knees smeared through fluid and blood. His hands slipped when he reached his father's chest, fingers sliding on soaked fabric. He grabbed harder, bunching the shirt in his fists.

"Please," he sobbed. "You promised…" Promised you'd get me through this. Promised you'd come home. Promised you wouldn't leave Mom alone again. The promises tangled together in his head until they were one impossible plea.

Dr. Gerald took a step after him. "Jonathan—"

"DON'T TOUCH ME!" the boy screamed, voice cracking into a pitch that cut through the chamber. It wasn't just volume; there was a strange resonance under it now, a metallic edge that made even the air flinch.

Even the soldiers flinched. A few rifles jerked. Someone cursed under his breath.

At the front of the squad, Captain Braden watched with a face carved from stone. Years of carrying out orders had chiseled any softness away. When he spoke, it was flat and precise, the cadence of command that expected compliance.

"Doctor. Get the subject under control."

Dr. Gerald rounded on him. "He's eight years old. His father just died in front of him." His hands shook at his sides, either from adrenaline or rage.

Braden's expression didn't shift. If the words affected him, the impact didn't reach his eyes.

Jonathan's shoulders shook, hands pressed to Henry's unmoving chest. He felt nothing under his palms but cooling skin and the faint give of muscle slackening.

Then the lights above them flickered.

A faint metallic-silver glimmer rippled just beneath the boy's skin along his neck, across the backs of his hands. It was subtle at first, like light catching on sweat, then it repeated, undeniable.

One pulse.

Then another.

Dr. Gerald saw it. His breath caught slow at first then quick with recognition.

Braden saw it. His jaw clenched.

So did everyone else. Muted curses and whispered oaths crackled softly over comms.

"The nanotech is fully active," Dr. Gerald said softly, awe and terror tangled together. "It worked." The scientist in him vibrated with the implications; the human in him flinched.

The overhead lights strobed again, briefly synchronized with the flicker beneath Jonathan's skin, as if the building itself were reacting to what had woken inside him.

Braden's jaw tightened. "Seize the subject."

Two soldiers stepped forward and grabbed Jonathan under the arms. Their gloves bit into the thin flesh above his elbows.

"No!" Jonathan screamed, thrashing. The sound came out raw, deeper than before, edged with that same metallic resonance. "Let go of me! I have to get to him—Dad! Dad!" His heels scrabbled against the grate, finding no purchase.

Dr. Gerald lunged. "You're hurting him—stop. He's disoriented—"

Braden shoved him back with the barrel of his rifle, the gesture efficient and impersonal. "He's no longer your concern."

Jonathan's cries echoed off steel, raw and animal. He fought the armored hands dragging him away from Henry's body, heels scraping uselessly on the floor. The more he struggled, the more the silver under his skin flared and dimmed, like a storm building in his veins.

"Please," he sobbed. "Please, don't leave him. Dad, get up. Please get up…" His voice frayed with each word, thinning into ragged gasps.

They didn't let him go. Procedures and orders held tighter than his small wrists could ever hope to break.

They pulled him from the chamber. The blast doors yawned open to swallow him and then ground shut again, severing his last line of sight to Henry's body. His voice only faded later, when sedation took hold in a quiet, controlled room far from Level Five—needles sliding into veins that were no longer only his, restraints buckled around wrists and ankles, a clipboard coded with new classifications he'd never asked for. SUBJECT: HELIX-ALPHA-1.

By the time the black car turned down the familiar road toward home, Jonathan's sobs had dwindled to a hoarse whisper. His head lolled against the window glass, the outside world a smear of trees and streetlights.

"…Mom…"

He didn't see the blood they'd washed off his hands, scrubbed from under his nails until the skin went red and raw. He didn't see the forms signed over his head, the thick stack of papers that traded his future for secrecy. He only saw the door when it opened and the shape of his mother in warm light—her outline in the frame, shoulders hunched, hands shaking.

Everything that happened in the lab sank deep inside him—quiet for now, but never truly gone. The silver threads in his blood coiled and waited, carrying with them the last stand of a man who'd died buying him a few more breaths and the machine logic of a project that had never meant to save an eight-year-old boy.

CHAPTER 4 — HOME AGAIN

The knock came just after dawn.

Suzanne hadn't slept. The night had stretched into a thin, brittle thing, hour after hour of pacing and sitting and standing again, her body too wired to rest and too exhausted to do anything else. She sat upright on the couch, arms wrapped around herself, staring at the cold imprint in the cushions where Jonathan always curled during sick nights. The dent in the fabric looked like a missing person.

When the knock came again—firmer, more deliberate—her breath caught. For a heartbeat she told herself it was Henry's key, that he'd forgotten it and locked himself out, that this was some stupid, fixable mistake. But keys didn't knock.

She crossed the room too fast and opened the door.

Two men in white coats stood in the pale morning light, calm and composed as if this were an ordinary house call. Their coats were spotless, the creases sharp. One held a clipboard with a thin stack of forms clipped neatly in place. The other supported Jonathan under the arm.

Suzanne stopped as if she'd hit a wall. Cold air slid past them into the house, raising goosebumps along her bare arms.

"Jonathan?" Her voice barely worked. It scraped out thin, as if it had been left out all night with the rest of her.

Her son lifted his head. His eyes were red-rimmed and swollen from crying. When they found hers, recognition flared—along with something raw and terrified, a look she had never seen on his face before, not even in emergency rooms or bad fevers.

"Mom…"

The word cracked. It sounded older than eight.

Suzanne dropped to her knees on the porch and pulled him into her arms. Her body moved before her mind could catch up. Jonathan clung to her immediately, desperate, shaking, fingers digging into her shoulders as if he was afraid she might vanish, as if he needed to prove to himself she was solid.

"Baby—oh God—Jonathan, you're home. You're okay." She kissed his hair, breathing in the smell of hospital soap and something sterile threaded through his usual shampoo. She pulled back just enough to see his face. "Where's Henry? Where's your father?"

Jonathan went rigid. The change was instant, a full-body flinch. A wounded sound slipped out of him—half breath, half sob, as if someone had punched the air out of his lungs.

Suzanne looked up at the two men. "What happened? Why didn't my husband bring him home?" Her voice sharpened on the last word. Henry.

The man with the clipboard offered a gentle, professional smile, the kind used on distraught families in hospital hallways. Everything about him looked constructed to reassure: soft eyes, even tone, the slight sympathetic tilt of his head.

"Mrs. Halden, we're with County Medical. Your son was transported for additional evaluation after his release. He's stable now, and you were listed as the primary point of return."

Suzanne's mouth went dry. The words landed in her ears but refused to arrange themselves into anything that made sense. Transported. Evaluation. Primary point of return. "That doesn't answer my question. Where is Henry?"

A quick glance passed between them—small, practiced, almost invisible. Suzanne still caught it. Something cold slid down her spine.

The taller one spoke smoothly. "He is being held for a routine debriefing regarding last night's confusion about the facility's access protocols. It's standard procedure."

Jonathan's grip tightened like a spasm. His fingers bunched in the fabric of her shirt hard enough to hurt.

Suzanne felt it in her bones—the way children did when adults lied. She looked down at him. "Jonathan… sweetheart… what's wrong?"

He shook his head hard and buried his face in her shoulder, but not before she saw the terror in his eyes deepen, glossing over with fresh tears.

"Mom…" His voice trembled. "It was bad." The way he said bad made it sound like something too big for the word that contained it.

Suzanne brushed his hair back with shaking fingers, trying to smooth more than just the strands. "What was bad, honey? Talk to me."

Jonathan gasped for a breath that he seemed not to be able to find as the emotions were overwhelming him. His whole body cinched tight, muscles locking as if bracing for impact.

"They… they hurt Dad."

Suzanne went still. The world contracted to that one sentence, to the feel of her son's breath against her neck and the white coats on her porch.

Her heartbeat roared in her ears. "What?" she whispered. "Jonathan—what do you mean?"

His face twisted. Tears spilled. Words came out broken, catching on jagged edges inside him.

"He—he fell, Mom. He didn't get up. I saw him—he didn't—he didn't…"

Suzanne shook her head before she meant to, as if denial could physically hold the sentence back, shove it away before it hardened into truth. "No. No, sweetheart. Your father is fine. He just—he just stayed behind to fill out paperwork or something. Henry wouldn't leave you alone." The explanation sounded ridiculous even to her, thin as tissue, but she clung to it.

Jonathan shook harder. "No," he said, and the word was small but absolute. It fell like a stone into the space between them. "Mom… he wasn't breathing."

The men stepped in, quick and controlled, closing a little of the distance without seeming to move much at all. Their faces stayed open, calm, professional.

"He's disoriented," the one with the clipboard said warmly, as if explaining a child's nightmare after surgery. "Children often confuse medical events or emergency procedures. Trauma can create vivid hallucinations." His tone made the chaos Jonathan described sound like a cartoon he'd watched instead of a memory.

"No!" Jonathan screamed.

The sound tore out of him raw. It startled even Suzanne, cut right through the measured cadence of the man's voice. "I saw him! They pulled me away from him!"

Suzanne flinched as if she'd been struck. The force of his certainty rattled something loose inside her. Jonathan trembled violently, clutching her as if the porch beneath them might give way.

"Mom, he didn't get up," he sobbed. "He didn't—"

"Honey…" She cupped his cheeks, tears spilling now, her hands shaking so badly she could feel the tremor in her fingertips. His skin was warm, solid, alive under her palms. "Sometimes when we're sick or scared—"

"It was real," he whispered, and the whisper hurt more than the scream. He sounded older in that moment, like someone who'd seen too much. "Dad didn't get up."

Suzanne pressed him to her chest, trying to breathe around the pressure rising in her throat. It felt like something was wedging itself under her ribs, prying them apart.

The men watched with polite stillness, as if her grief were a symptom on a chart to be noted for later, nothing more. Their eyes moved, cataloging—time of arrival, reaction, level of resistance.

"I think that's enough for now," one of them said. "He needs rest. Memory confusion at this stage is common." The phrase sounded rehearsed, like part of a script.

Suzanne rose slowly, holding Jonathan with one arm. He clung to her like he thought they might try to pry him away. With the other she pointed at them, her finger trembling so hard it shook the air between them.

"Get off my porch."

Both men paused, as if surprised that someone would refuse them.

"We only want—"

"Leave. Now." The word came out flat and absolute, with a razor edge she hadn't known she still possessed.

A beat. Then they stepped back, nodding courteously before walking toward their car. Their shoes made soft, almost soundless thuds on the walkway, like they'd practiced leaving places without leaving an echo.

Jonathan's breathing spiked with panic. "Mom—don't let them—don't let them take me back—"

"I won't," she said instantly, fierce enough to surprise herself. The promise rose out of her like a growl. "I won't let anyone take you ever again." The words felt like a spell, like something binding.

The sedan rolled away and disappeared down the road, taillights blinking once at the stop sign before vanishing.

Suzanne shut the door behind her and locked it. Then locked it again. Her fingers fumbled the deadbolt, then checked it twice, as if mechanical security could keep out people who'd already walked off with her husband and son once.

Jonathan clung to her, shaking so hard she could feel it through her ribs. Each tremor traveled into her bones, made her own muscles want to seize. She sank onto the couch with him in her lap. His small hands fisted her shirt, knuckles whitening, and his tears soaked her collar, hot against her skin.

"Mom," he whispered, voice breaking down into air. "Dad's not coming home…"

Suzanne held him tighter than she had ever held anything in her life, as if she could anchor both of them by sheer force of will. Her arms ached; she refused to loosen them.

"Honey… you're scared," she said, because she needed it to be that. She needed this to be shock, confusion, fever dreams—anything but confirmation. "You're confused. You saw something you shouldn't have seen—"

Jonathan shook his head against her neck. His hair rasped against her skin, still carrying the faint chemical scent of the facility. "I saw him not breathing."

Suzanne's breath broke. It came out in a ragged exhale she couldn't quite disguise as anything else.

She rocked him gently, though her own world felt like it was tipping into dark water. The living room around them—the family photos, the crooked lamp, the cereal bowl still on the coffee table—tilted sideways in her mind, familiar objects in a house that suddenly felt like a set built over a trapdoor.

"It's going to be okay," she whispered, even though she didn't believe it. The words tasted like someone else's script, lines she was supposed to say because that's what mothers said. "We'll figure this out. I promise."

But deep where her fear lived, something she didn't want to name began to take root. It was small at first, a hard, cold seed lodged under her breastbone.

Something terrible had happened.

Something Jonathan had seen.

Something she wasn't prepared to face, because facing it meant admitting that the facility Henry guarded, the place that paid their mortgage and filled their fridge, might have taken more than it ever planned to give back.

Jonathan sobbed harder, burying his face in her neck. His shoulders tensed and grew firmer with each breath, the sound turning from sharp cries to exhausted, broken gasps.

And for the first time since dawn broke, Suzanne felt truly afraid.

Not just for Jonathan. Not even for Henry. Those fears were already there, raw and open.

Afraid of whatever place had sent her son back without his father. Afraid of the men in white coats and clipped explanations. Afraid of the way the word "project" had hung around Henry like a shadow since the night in the hospital.

Afraid that the lab on the hill hadn't just taken her husband. It had changed her son—and buried the truth under paperwork and polite smiles.

CHAPTER 5 — ECHOES

Jonathan slept only after exhaustion finally pulled him under. Sleep didn't feel like a choice so much as his body finally shutting down after fighting too long.

Even then, it wasn't peaceful. His body twitched. His fingers curled tight against the blanket. Sometimes he whimpered, the sound thin and choked, like he was falling even though he lay still. Every tiny sound dragged at Suzanne's nerves, proof that rest hadn't really found him, only something restless and clawing.

Suzanne didn't leave his side.

She sat on the edge of the bed with one hand resting between his shoulders, listening to the tick of the hallway clock and the distant rush of morning traffic. Every sound felt wrong—too ordinary—while her world balanced on a ledge she couldn't yet see. Tires hissed on wet pavement outside. Somewhere a neighbor's dog barked twice and stopped. The house creaked softly, settling, oblivious.

She brushed her fingers through Jonathan's hair. The strands were still damp from the shower she'd given him, trying to wash away the smell of the lab.

He didn't wake, but he flinched at the touch. His shoulders jumped under her palm, as if some part of him expected hands to hurt now, not comfort.

There were shadows beneath his eyes, already fading. The heat that had burned in him the day before was gone. His breathing was steady. Strong. Too even. It moved in a precise rhythm, like a metronome, on pace without any rough edges, nothing of the fragile weakness she'd watched with terror only hours ago.

For the first time, she really looked at him. Not just to check if he was breathing, not just to count seconds between inhales, but to take in every detail.

He wasn't just stabilized.

He was improving.

Too quickly.

Suzanne swallowed. A thought brushed the edge of her mind and she tried not to let it in. "Sweetheart… what did they do to you?"

Jonathan stirred. His eyes fluttered open, unfocused at first—then they found her, filling instantly with tears, as if waking meant being dropped back into the worst part of his memory.

"Mom," he whispered, "don't let them take me back." His fingers clamped hard on the blanket, bunching it in his fists.

She leaned down and held him. "You're safe. Nobody is taking you anywhere." The words came out fierce, more vow than reassurance.

He pressed his face into her shirt, shaking. "They took Dad," he whispered. "They took him and he didn't get up—"

Suzanne closed her eyes. The room swam for a second. "Baby… you were scared. You were sick—"

"I saw him."

The simplicity of it cut deeper than the panic.

Jonathan's voice trembled but didn't waver. "He was on the floor. He didn't move. They pulled me away. They hurt him, Mom."

Suzanne went still.

Not because she believed him.

But because she couldn't make herself dismiss it. The certainty in his tone pressed against the thin wall of denial she'd thrown up.

She smoothed his hair back, her voice barely holding. "You're home now. That's what matters. We're going to figure this out." The words felt small against the size of what he was saying.

Jonathan curled closer. His body trembled once—then stopped.

Not the gradual calming of a child.

A sudden drop. Like a switch thrown. One second his muscles shook, the next they were still, as if something inside him had decided: enough.

His breathing deepened, unnaturally fast. The rhythm shifted, locking into that same too-regular pattern.

Suzanne pulled back slightly. "Jonathan…?"

He looked up at her. His eyes were clearer than they'd been since he arrived home. Fever-glassiness had vanished. The red at the rims remained, but behind it something sharp and steady watched her.

"I'm okay," he said.

The words weren't childlike. They were measured. Practiced. They sounded like something he'd heard adults say in hallways and was now repeating from somewhere deeper than memory.

A ripple of unease slid down her spine.

"What did those men give you?" she murmured before she could stop herself. Images of needles, strange machines, cold rooms flickered through her mind, each worse than the last.

Jonathan's jaw tightened. The easy vulnerability of a moment ago snapped back behind a thin, stubborn line. "I don't want to talk about them."

She nodded. "Then we won't. Not now." She forced her voice to stay calm. Pushing him would only make whatever he was holding back burrow deeper.

He lay back against the pillow, staring at the ceiling. His fingers twitched once—sharp, reflexive, as if reacting to a signal she couldn't hear.

Suzanne caught his hand and kissed his forehead. His skin was warm but not burning, a temperature that should have comforted her and didn't. "Rest. I'll be right outside."

She stepped into the hall and closed the door partway. The click of the latch sounded too loud.

Her legs weakened. She leaned against the frame as her composure collapsed, breath shuddering out of her in a rough exhale.

Henry should have been home. The thought came like a reflex, like a missing piece her mind kept reaching for.

He should have carried Jonathan inside. He should have been here, grounding her, explaining everything with that tired, steady voice he used when things went wrong on his shift but he didn't want her to worry. He should have been the one to stand between her and men in white coats.

What if Jonathan wasn't confused?

What if he'd seen something real?

A cold knot formed in her stomach, dense and heavy. She pressed her hand against her abdomen as if she could push it out.

She forced herself into the kitchen and grabbed the phone. The familiar weight of it in her hand felt strangely foreign, an old tool suddenly untrustworthy.

The nurse was polite. Tired. Efficient. Her voice had that bleary, end-of-shift drag, the cadence of someone who had already had too many bad nights.

No record of Henry Halden.

No county medical transport.

No staff by the names Suzanne gave.

Each denial landed with the finality of a slammed door.

She hung up with shaking hands. The phone's plastic clicked against the counter, a small, hollow sound in the quiet kitchen.

They lied to me.

The thought surfaced fully formed, no longer something she tried to soften with excuses about miscommunication or paperwork errors.

She dialed the lab's number—then froze before the last digit. Her thumb hovered above the button.

If they'd lied once, they'd do it again.

Or worse. They might not bother lying. They might decide loose ends needed to be tied off. She had no evidence of anything—and they had her address, her phone, her family.

"Mom?"

Jonathan's voice came from the hallway, small and frightened, threaded with something else now—a faint edge of strain, like he was struggling with more than just fear.

She rushed back. The phone dangled from its cord for a second before swaying gently back toward the cradle.

He sat upright in bed, knees pulled tight to his chest, blanket pooled around his ankles. His bare feet looked too small on the rumpled sheet. "Everything feels… wrong," he said. "Different."

Suzanne sat beside him and wrapped an arm around his shoulders. His bones felt sharper under her hand, as if the illness had carved away softness overnight. "You're just exhausted."

"No," he whispered. "It's like something's in my head. Like I can hear things moving. Like—"

He stopped. His mouth snapped shut on the words as if he'd tasted them and found them dangerous.

Her heart pounded. "Like what?"

He shook his head hard. The motion was almost violent. "I don't want it there." His fingers clawed briefly at his temples, then dropped.

Suzanne held him tightly. "It's okay. I've got you." She said it because it was what she was supposed to say, because saying "I don't know how to fix this" would break them both.

Jonathan clung to her. His grip had strength that hadn't been there when he'd stumbled around the living room gasping for breath.

But the look in his eyes told her the truth.

This wasn't just trauma.

Something had changed inside him.

Something that started in the lab.

The place that took Henry.

The place that sent her son home without him, wrapped in a blanket and accompanied by strangers instead of his father.

Suzanne kissed the top of Jonathan's head, her lips lingering in his hair. A promise hardened into resolve like cooling metal.

She would find out what happened.

No matter what it cost her.

62

CHAPTER 6 — SLOW DISSOLVE

Jonathan slept through most of the late morning, curled on his side beneath clean blankets. His breathing was steady—but not peaceful. Every so often his body twitched, a small involuntary jerk that made Suzanne flinch each time, as if each movement confirmed that whatever had been done to him was still working its way through.

She sat on the edge of the bed, fingers combing gently through his hair, listening to the house settle into the strange hush that followed catastrophe. Pipes clicked as they cooled. A truck passed somewhere down the main road, its low rumble distant and indifferent. The ordinary sounds only made the unreality in this room feel sharper.

He should have looked sick.

But he didn't.

The fever was gone. His skin was warm—normal. Color had returned to his cheeks far faster than it should have, as if someone had simply decided to flip his body back on. The bluish tint that had terrified her the night before was entirely gone, replaced by a healthy flush that would have comforted her any other week of her life.

This isn't natural.

The thought came without her permission and refused to leave. Fevers broke; they didn't vanish like someone had pressed a reset button.

Jonathan stirred. His eyes opened, unfocused at first, then cleared when they found her. The shift from dazed to aware happened almost too quickly, like a lens snapping into focus.

"Hi, Mom," he whispered.

Her breath shook. "Hi, sweetheart." She tried to smile and felt how brittle it was.

He touched her hand but didn't cling. His fingers rested on her knuckles with a strange lightness, as if he were reassuring her instead of the other way around. His expression wasn't confused anymore. It was resigned. Wounded. Too old for eight years.

He didn't ask about Henry.

He didn't need to.

The knowledge sat in his eyes like a shadow that wouldn't lift, an understanding he shouldn't have had to carry.

"Do you feel better?" she asked. She hated herself a little for the question; better felt like the wrong metric for whatever this was.

Jonathan nodded once. "Just tired." The answer came quickly, evenly, like he'd rehearsed it.

"You rest," she said, brushing her thumb beneath his eye, chasing away a faint line of dried salt. "I'm right here."

He leaned into her warmth for a moment, then settled back, the blanket pulled tight to his chin. Suzanne stayed until his breathing softened again—not asleep, just hovering in that in-between place where his eyes drifted closed and then opened halfway, as if he didn't quite trust the dark.

When he closed his eyes for more than a few breaths, she slipped quietly into the hall.

Sunlight slanted across the wall, dust drifting through it like slow sparks. The house wore morning like nothing had happened, golden light on beige paint, the faint smell of coffee that had gone cold hours ago. Suzanne stared at the phone in the kitchen—bright yellow, ordinary, its coiled cord tangled from years of use. Every call she'd made that morning had ended the same way.

No records.

No answers.

No Henry.

They don't want me to know.

The thought sat heavy and precise. Not can't tell me. Don't want me to know.

She crossed to the window.

A dark sedan sat at the far corner of the street, engine quiet. It faced away from the house, parked just far enough that she couldn't clearly see who sat inside. Suzanne frowned, trying to remember if it had been there earlier or if it had slipped into place while she was on the phone. The windshield reflected the sky, giving nothing back but pale blue and the faint skeleton of bare branches.

A curtain twitched across the street as a neighbor moved past a window. If they saw the car, they didn't react.

The sedan rolled away slowly—too slowly—and vanished around the bend. No brake lights flashed; it simply drifted out of sight like a thought someone was trying not to acknowledge.

She stood there a moment longer than she meant to, waiting for the tightness in her chest to ease.

It didn't.

"Mom?"

She hurried back.

Jonathan sat upright, studying his hands as if they belonged to someone else. He turned them palm up, then down, flexing his fingers like he was testing new joints.

"It feels wrong inside me," he whispered.

"Where, honey?"

He touched his chest. Then his temple. "Like something keeps moving," he said. "Like it doesn't know when to stop." His brow furrowed with concentration, as if he were trying to listen to something only he could hear.

Her blood went cold. The room seemed to tilt a fraction, the walls inching closer.

"But it doesn't feel like me," he added.

Suzanne pulled him into her arms. He didn't resist— but he didn't relax either. His muscles stayed coiled, as if some part of him remained braced for impact even in her embrace. His breathing steadied too quickly, slipping into calm before it should have, as though some internal metronome had overridden his fear.

"I don't want them to come back," he whispered into her shoulder. His breath was warm against her skin, but a shiver ran through him that had nothing to do with temperature.

"They won't," she said fiercely. "I won't let anyone take you. Ever." The words came out low and sharp, a promise aimed as much at whatever watched them from outside as at his fear.

He curled closer, exhaustion reclaiming him. His eyelids sagged, but the line between his brows never fully eased.

Suzanne watched his face—the tension beneath the calm, the way control seemed to return faster than it should have, snapping into place like a program loading. Even his stillness felt deliberate.

Whatever had happened to him hadn't finished.

And she didn't know if it ever would.

CHAPTER 7 — THE CALL

The phone rang just after dusk.

Suzanne froze at the sink, water spilling over her hands until it turned from warm to lukewarm to cold. The plate she'd been washing slipped from her fingers and bumped gently against the basin, clinking against porcelain. She didn't look at it. The sound of the ring cut through the quiet house with surgical precision, sharp and insistent, like it had been waiting all day for the moment her guard dropped.

She shut off the water. Droplets clung to her skin and rolled down her wrists in thin, chilled tracks. For a heartbeat she just stood there, staring at the dark window over the sink. Her own reflection looked back—pale, hollow-eyed, someone she half-recognized.

Jonathan slept on the couch, curled inward as if bracing against something only he remembered. The blanket had twisted around his legs. One hand was fisted in the fabric as if he'd grabbed it mid-nightmare and never let go. His lashes cast faint shadows on his cheeks. Even asleep, a tiny line sat between his brows, like his body refused to fully relax.

The phone rang again. The sound bounced off the walls, louder than it should have been for such a small device.

Suzanne wiped her hands on a dish towel that did little to warm them and crossed the room. Each step felt slow and heavy, as if she were walking through water. She snatched up the receiver.

"Hello?"

"Mrs. Suzanne Halden?" The voice was male, middle-aged, carrying the weight of someone who had made a lot of calls nobody wanted.

"Yes." Her voice barely caught the syllable; it sounded thin in her own ears.

"This is Sheriff Raymond Keller, Jefferson County. I'm calling about your husband."

Her breath caught. Her free hand tightened around the phone cord until it bit into her palm. "Has he been found?" The question leapt out before she could decide if she wanted the answer.

"Yes, ma'am. A volunteer search team located him earlier today."

The pause that followed told her everything. It stretched just a fraction too long, opened up into a hollow space she could feel in her chest.

"I'm sorry," Keller said. The apology wrapped itself around the words like padding, but it couldn't soften them. "Your husband is deceased."

Suzanne slid down the wall, the phone clutched to her ear like a lifeline that had turned into a noose. Her knees hit the floor harder than she'd meant them to. The linoleum was cold through her jeans.

"How?" she whispered. The word scraped out, raw.

Another pause. Heavier. She could almost hear him picking his way through what to say, sorting phrases in his head, choosing the least brutal version of a truth that had no gentle edges.

"Mrs. Halden… your husband sustained a gunshot wound."

The word struck like a blow.

Shot.

Not an accident. Not exposure. Not a fall in the dark, or a heart attack alone in the woods. Something deliberate. Something aimed.

"There was no weapon recovered at the scene," the sheriff added carefully. His tone shifted, just slightly, from sympathy to official neutrality.

Of course there wasn't.

Her mind filled in what he didn't say—no gun near the body, no sign he'd turned it on himself. No easy box to tick on a report. Just Henry in the wrong place with a hole in him and answers nobody planned to give.

"We'll need you to come in tomorrow to make a formal identification." The words were routine, but there was a faint resistance in his voice, like he knew how obscene it was to talk about "formal identification" when a woman was still sitting on her kitchen floor holding a phone like a lifeline.

Jonathan stirred. "Mom…?"

The sound of his voice cleaved through the moment.

She hung up without answering. The click felt abrupt, almost violent. She didn't remember deciding to do it; her thumb simply moved. The dial tone hummed briefly before she set the receiver back in its cradle with shaking fingers.

He saw her face and understood immediately. Children in their town learned that look early—from neighbors, from news, from the way adults went quiet when bad things happened. Jonathan's eyes, still heavy with sleep, sharpened with sudden awareness.

She collapsed to her knees beside the couch and wrapped him in her arms. Jonathan clung to her, silent, shaking. His small frame pressed against her chest, ribs juddering under her hands. For a moment neither of them spoke. There was nothing words could do to hold the wave that had just hit them.

A car passed the house, headlights briefly washing the living room in pale light before moving on. The glow slid across family photos on the wall, over the TV screen, across the window glass, and then was gone.

The room felt different afterward. Smaller. As if something had shifted and not settled back into place. The air seemed thicker, harder to pull into her lungs.

Jonathan's fingers tightened in her shirt, knuckles going white. "It feels like before," he whispered. "Like when things don't stop."

Suzanne held him, her heart hammering, grief and anger blurring together into something she didn't yet have a name for. It burned low and hot, beneath the suffocating weight of sorrow—a spark of fury at the lab, at the faceless "they," at a world that could walk her husband out of their lives and send their son back altered.

"I know," she said softly. She didn't ask what he meant by before. She didn't need him to spell out the hospital, the lab, the gunfire echoing behind blast doors. The same feeling ran through her now—the sense of something huge and merciless grinding forward, indifferent to who it crushed.

Outside, the street stayed quiet.

Too quiet.

The quiet wasn't comforting anymore. It felt watchful, like the pause between one move and the next.

CHAPTER 8 — IDENTIFICATION

The morning felt wrong from the moment Suzanne opened her eyes. The wrongness wasn't loud or obvious; it was a thin, taut feeling under her skin, as if the day had been stretched too tight and might tear if she moved too fast.

The light through the curtains was thin and colorless, the kind that made everything feel colder than it was. It skimmed across the living room in a washed-out sheet, turning the walls a flat, tired gray. Jonathan sat awake on the couch, small beneath the blanket, staring at nothing. His eyes tracked some point beyond the television, beyond the opposite wall, as if he were looking at a place only he could still see.

He didn't ask where she was going.

He already knew. The knowledge hung between them in the space where his questions used to be.

Suzanne knelt and brushed his hair back. His hair had always been soft in the mornings, sticking up in uneven clumps; today it lay too flat, like even it was too tired to rebel. "I won't be long," she whispered. "Stay inside. Don't open the door for anyone."

Jonathan nodded without looking up. The blanket shifted with the motion, but his gaze stayed fixed ahead.

She hugged him too tightly, arms locking around his narrow shoulders until he grunted softly against her collarbone. It took effort to make herself loosen her grip and stand. The screen door clicked shut behind her— small, final, the sound of a barrier closing on something she couldn't fix.

Outside, the neighborhood looked untouched. The air held that clean, early-day chill that usually meant promise.

A jogger passed with a dog straining at its leash, the animal's breath puffing white in the air as it lunged at invisible smells. A pickup rolled by loaded with lumber, boards rattling in the bed over each crack in the road. Somewhere a lawnmower coughed to life. Ordinary life moved forward, indifferent, as if the night hadn't swallowed Henry and spat back only a phone call.

Suzanne climbed into the truck and backed out. Her hands found the motions without needing her attention; clutch, brake, mirror checks that were more habit than awareness.

As she drove, grief narrowed her vision, pulled her inward. The world outside the windshield blurred into a tunnel of asphalt and sky. She didn't check her mirrors. She barely noticed the traffic settling around her — cars stopping, starting, rearranging themselves without pattern, like pieces on a board she hadn't agreed to play.

At a red light, she caught sight of a dark sedan two lanes over. It idled there for a moment longer than necessary before turning away, its indicator blinking lazily, then vanishing down a side street.

She didn't think anything of it. Her mind filed it under background noise, another anonymous car in a world full of them.

On County Road 6, a silver car merged ahead of her, then slowed abruptly before accelerating again. Suzanne gripped the wheel, irritation flaring briefly through the fog and burning away a bit of the numbness.

She welcomed the distraction. Anger was easier to carry than the empty ache in her chest.

When she pulled into the coroner's lot, she parked and sat gripping the steering wheel until her hands steadied enough to move. Her fingers had gone stiff around the leather, joints aching. The building in front of her was squat and nondescript, red brick trying too hard to look like any other municipal office. Only the lack of windows on one side gave away what it held.

Inside, the building smelled of disinfectant and cold tile. The air had the hushed quality of places designed for bad news: low voices, soft footsteps, nothing scraping or slamming.

"Mrs. Halden?" the receptionist said softly. She wore a cardigan over her scrubs, coffee cooling by her elbow. "They're ready for you." Her eyes carried that careful compassion of someone who'd practiced it too often.

The hallway hummed with fluorescent light. The fixtures buzzed faintly overhead, adding a thin electric whine to the otherwise padded quiet. Suzanne followed as if watching herself from a distance, her feet moving while the rest of her floated a step behind. Her shadow on the linoleum didn't feel like it belonged to her.

The identification room waited at the end. The door was plain, with a simple metal handle, as unremarkable as any office, until she stepped through.

A table.

A sheet.

The attendant folded it back with practiced hands, revealing the familiar slope of a forehead, the curve of a cheek.

Henry's face emerged — still, pale, unmistakable. The stubble on his jaw was a day older than she had ever seen it. His lips were slightly parted, the color gone from them. Someone had closed his eyes; they didn't look like they were sleeping, only empty.

Suzanne's breath collapsed into a sound she didn't recognize, a low, broken noise dragged from somewhere deep in her chest. Her knees threatened to give out; she took one unsteady step forward and caught herself on the edge of the table.

She stepped closer, touching his hair with shaking fingers, smoothing down a strand that refused to lie flat. The familiar gesture only made the unfamiliar stillness worse. She rested her forehead briefly against his, the metal under the sheet cold through the fabric of her sleeves.

"I'm here," she whispered. "I'm so sorry." Sorry for not stopping him. Sorry for not knowing. Sorry for still breathing while he didn't.

The room stayed silent. The attendant looked away, giving them as much privacy as four walls and fluorescent lights could offer.

When she could finally speak, the words were thin but certain. "It's him." Saying it out loud felt like signing something she couldn't unread.

Outside, the air felt colder despite the rising sun. The light had brightened, but it only made the edges of things sharper, not warmer.

The parking lot was half-full now. A dark sedan idled near the street, engine running. Its windows were tinted just enough that she couldn't quite see the driver, only the faint outline of a head. Farther off, a silver car sat with its windows reflecting the sky, the clouds sliding across its windshield like nothing below them mattered.

Suzanne didn't know why she noticed them. They could have been anyone, going anywhere, cars like any others.

She told herself she was looking for her truck. That was the story she handed her own mind: she was just orienting herself, that was all.

She drove home with her eyes fixed ahead. Lane markers and signs passed in a blur.

At one stop sign, a car waited behind her longer than it should have before turning away. She watched its headlights in the mirror, two pale points hanging there, then peeling off down a side street only when she finally moved.

By the time she pulled into her driveway, her shoulders ached from tension she couldn't explain. Muscles between her shoulder blades burned as if she'd been bracing for impact the entire drive.

Jonathan was still on the couch when she came inside. The blanket hadn't shifted much; he might not have moved at all. His eyes flicked to the door the instant the latch turned.

She crossed the room and knelt in front of him, pulling him into her arms. His small body folded against hers in a motion that was already becoming too familiar—comforting each other around a space no one could fill.

Neither of them spoke. Words would have only scratched at the surface of what had solidified between them: absence, and the heavy knowledge that no explanation they were given would ever feel whole.

Later, when she tried to remember the drive, the details wouldn't line up cleanly. The sequence slipped in her mind like cards shuffled too many times.

Too many cars. Too many pauses.

Too many moments that felt almost deliberate—vehicles lingering in her peripheral vision, engines idling a second too long, turn signals blinking without turns.

She couldn't prove any of it. She had no plate numbers, no faces, no evidence—only the prickle at the back of her neck and the memory of dark glass.

That was what frightened her most.

CHAPTER 9 — RETURNING HOME

The drive back from her therapy felt longer than the trip there. Time stretched between mile markers, the seconds leaking out slow and uneven, as if the day itself were trying to keep her from reaching the moment when she would have to say the words out loud to her son.

Suzanne kept both hands locked on the wheel, knuckles pale, her vision blurring until she blinked it clear. Every few seconds, Henry's face rose behind her eyes— still, pale beneath the sheet—and she had to force herself to breathe past it. Each inhale felt like it caught on the image, snagging on the memory of his skin under her fingers, colder than it had ever been in their bed.

The road narrowed as she turned toward her neighborhood. Wind pushed through the early autumn leaves, scattering them across the pavement in sharp little bursts. Brown and red and gold skittered in front of her headlights, catching briefly in the beam before being crushed under tires or carried off again. Suzanne drove straight through, barely noticing.

Traffic rearranged itself around her—cars slowing, stopping, turning away. A minivan lingered in the adjacent lane for a few seconds too long, then fell back. A delivery truck turned off just ahead, its brake lights flaring and disappearing down a side street. She didn't check her mirrors. The world behind her felt irrelevant; everything that mattered was either gone or waiting at home.

Grief held her too tightly. It sat in her chest like a fist, squeezing each breath until it hurt.

She pulled into her driveway and shut off the engine. For a moment she stayed there, hands slackening, chest trembling with breaths she couldn't quite control. The truck felt too small, the air too thick, as if the cab were shrinking around her. The silence after the engine cut out roared louder than the motor ever had.

She opened the door.

A car passed the house at an unhurried pace. Another followed some distance behind. She registered neither— only the sound of tires on pavement, the sense of movement continuing when she needed it to stop, to give her a moment where the world held still long enough for her to collect herself.

Jonathan stood in the doorway, barefoot, wrapped in the blanket he'd dragged from the couch. His hair stuck up oddly on one side, and the hem of the blanket trailed on the floor, gathering dust. His eyes were swollen, his face too serious for his age. When he saw her, he started trying to be brave. His mouth pressed into a line that trembled at the corners.

Suzanne crossed the yard and dropped to her knees, pulling him into her arms. The grass was cool and slightly damp beneath her jeans, but she barely felt it.

Jonathan clung to her, trembling faintly. His fingers bunched in the fabric of her shirt with desperate strength, as if confirming she was real and here.

"I'm here," she whispered into his hair. "I'm here." It was all she could offer, a simple fact in a day where everything else had unraveled.

"I waited," he said. The words were small, but they carried hours in them.

"I know," she murmured. "I know." She smoothed a hand over his back, feeling the steady, too-even rise and fall under her palm.

Inside, the afternoon passed in a muted hush. The house seemed to understand that something irrevocable had happened and adjusted its sounds accordingly. Floorboards creaked less. Doors closed softer. Even the refrigerator hum felt subdued.

Suzanne made tea and forgot it on the counter. The mug sat there, steam curling up and fading as the liquid cooled, a small, abandoned comfort.

Jonathan sat on the couch with the television dark, staring at the blank screen as if it were showing him something she couldn't see. His reflection hovered faintly in the glass, a double image of a boy too still, too watchful.

She noticed the way he blinked less often. His eyes stayed open in long, unbroken stretches, as if he were afraid of what he might see if he let them close for more than a second.

The way his breathing stayed steady, too steady. No gasp for air when the house settled, no quickening when a car passed outside. It moved in quiet, mechanical rhythm, like something had taken over the job from his body and was performing it with clinical efficiency.

The way sudden sounds made his shoulders tense before he could stop them—a distant door slam, a truck downshifting, the clatter of the forgotten mug as she accidentally bumped it in the sink. Each noise sent a small ripple through him, a flinch he tried to smooth away.

Something inside him was shifting.

She didn't ask. Questions felt like they might crack him open, and she wasn't sure what would spill out.

Instead, she cooked him a small meal. Eggs, toast, something simple her hands knew how to assemble even while her mind drifted. He picked at it, moving the food around his plate, then pushed the plate away after a few bites.

"As the light outside softened, Suzanne tried to make the house feel normal. She folded laundry. Straightened cushions. Put away the mug she'd abandoned earlier. Every small act felt like an incantation, as if aligning objects might align something inside her.

When she lifted Henry's jacket from the back of the chair, she held it too long, breathing in the familiar scent— soap, outside air, the faint trace of the lab's sterile hallway smell—before forcing herself to lay it down. The weight of the fabric in her hands made her chest hurt.

Jonathan watched her, quiet and intent. His gaze tracked her movements with a focus that went beyond a child following a parent around the room. It was as if he were cataloging each action, anchoring himself to the way she folded, placed, smoothed, because nothing else felt stable.

Later, she sat beside him and brushed his hair back. The gesture had become a ritual, something she did as much to soothe herself as him.

"You don't have to talk," she said gently. "Just tell me if you need something."

He hesitated. She saw the moment he decided whether to speak or stay silent, the small tightening at the corners of his mouth.

"I feel strange," he whispered.

Her chest tightened. "How?"

"I feel… awake. Even when I'm tired." His brow furrowed as he searched for the right words. "Like I can't turn it off."

He pressed a hand to his chest. "And here—it feels busy. Like it doesn't rest." His fingers tapped once against his sternum, as if marking a rhythm only he could hear.

Suzanne kept her voice even. "Your body's been through a lot. Sometimes it takes time to catch up." It was the kind of thing nurses had said to her in the hospital, the sort of phrase that filled space without admitting ignorance.

Jonathan didn't argue. He just looked down at his hand, still resting over his heart.

But his fingers curled slightly, as if responding to something he couldn't quite feel, a subtle tightening in time with an internal pulse that had nothing to do with fear.

She pulled him close. He came willingly, but there was a new stiffness in the way his muscles held, as if he were trying to contain more than just emotions.

"Your teacher called," she said after a moment, choosing normal ground because the unknown was too large. "You don't have to go back until you're ready."

Jonathan stiffened. The reaction was immediate, a flinch that started in his shoulders and ran down his spine. "Do I have to go at all?"

"Not yet," she said softly. "Not until you say you are ready." She meant it; the idea of sending him into fluorescent hallways and crowded classrooms while he felt like this made her stomach twist.

He leaned into her, but when he spoke, his voice was distant, as if part of him stood a few steps away, listening.

"I don't think I'll ever feel ready."

That night, he fell asleep almost immediately. One moment he was blinking slowly at the ceiling, the next his eyes slid shut and stayed that way.

Too immediately.

His breathing settled into a deep, even rhythm that didn't match the tension in his body. His hands remained curled slightly on top of the blanket, not loose and floppy the way they used to be when he drifted off on movie nights. Suzanne stood in the doorway, watching the rise and fall of his chest, unease tightening low in her gut.

He looked peaceful.

And it frightened her. Peaceful wasn't supposed to look so deliberate, so controlled. It felt less like sleep and more like a system entering standby.

She turned off the lamp and stepped into the hallway. The darkness felt thicker than usual, pressing at her back as she pulled the door almost closed, leaving it open just enough to hear him.

Outside, the street was quiet. No distant sirens, no late-night laughter, just the low hum of a world that had decided to go on.

Later, when she tried to remember the day, the details refused to line up. Scenes slid out of order when she replayed them, like she was missing frames in a film.

Too many moments that almost made sense. A car lingering a second too long at a stop. A shadow in the corner of her eye when she glanced toward the front window. Jonathan's eyes tracking something she couldn't see.

Too many places where fear arrived before reason. Where her skin prickled, and only afterward did she notice a car idling at the corner or the faint metallic taste in the air when she touched the phone.

She didn't know what any of it meant. Only that something had followed them home.

CHAPTER 10 — BACK TO SCHOOL

Jonathan woke before dawn.

Suzanne found him sitting on the edge of his bed, shoes on, backpack zipped and resting neatly beside him. His hands were clasped in his lap, fingers wound together so tightly the knuckles had gone pale. The alarm clock beside him blinked numbers he clearly hadn't needed; he'd beaten it awake.

She stopped in the doorway. For a moment she just watched him, the small, straight line of his back, the way his shoulders were pulled in as if he were holding himself together by force.

"Sweetheart… you don't have to go today," she said softly. "There's no rush."

Jonathan didn't look up.

"I think I should."

There was no panic in his voice.

No childlike hesitation.

But it wasn't calm either.

It was controlled. Each word sounded weighed before it left his mouth, as if he were choosing them the way adults chose what to say to children.

Suzanne knelt in front of him. Up close she could see the faint shadows under his eyes, the new sharpness in his gaze. "You're allowed to take time."

He swallowed. His throat worked around something harder than sleep. "If I stay home, I'll think about it too much."

She knew what he meant. Henry. The lab. The floor of that room. The way he'd described his father not getting up. The silence between his breaths.

She brushed his hair back. "Okay. We'll try. But if anything feels wrong, you call me. Right away."

Jonathan nodded once, gaze drifting toward the window. Toward the quiet street.

Suzanne saw nothing there. Just parked cars, a trash can tipped slightly to one side, a neighbor's porch light still burning.

But Jonathan watched it as if it might move. As if he expected something to appear where she saw only asphalt and morning fog.

The parking lot buzzed with noise and motion—children laughing, backpacks thumping, teachers waving from the curb. Normal life, resuming without them. Cars lined up in crooked rows, doors opening and closing, a blur of color and motion that used to include Henry's truck on ordinary mornings.

Jonathan stiffened beside her as the noise hit him. His fingers tightened on the strap of his backpack.

"You don't have to go in," Suzanne said. "We can leave now." She meant it. One turn of the wheel and she would take him home, lock the doors, keep him where the world couldn't poke at wounds that hadn't even scabbed.

"I can do it," he whispered. "I have to." There was something in the way he said it that made it sound less like a choice and more like a test he was afraid to fail.

She squeezed his hand. "I'll be right here after school."

He stepped out of the car and walked toward the doors, posture careful, measured—like someone reentering a place that no longer fit. His backpack hung straight, no bounce in his step, no sideways glance at friends.

Suzanne waited until he disappeared inside. The automatic doors slid shut behind him, cutting off the noise for a heartbeat.

Then she exhaled.

Across the street, a dark sedan idled between parked cars. Its engine hummed quietly, headlights off, windows reflecting only sky and the vague suggestion of the driver's silhouette.

She didn't turn. She kept her eyes on the school entrance, but she felt the hairs stand up on the back of her neck.

Jonathan slid into his desk quietly. Whispers followed him like a draft.

"That's the kid who collapsed."

"He looks… different."

"Didn't he almost die?"

He kept his eyes down. The grain of the desktop became his entire world, a map of scratches and dents he could trace with his gaze instead of meeting theirs.

Mrs. Ellery stopped beside him. "Jonathan, if you need anything today, you tell me, okay?" Her voice was gentle, but there was an undercurrent of strain.

He nodded.

She hesitated, studying him. Something about his stillness unsettled her. He didn't fidget, didn't swing his feet, didn't drum his fingers on the desk like the other kids. He just sat, straight and composed, like someone waiting for a verdict.

The lessons moved on. Jonathan finished each assignment quickly—too quickly—writing with certainty that surprised even him. The numbers fell into place in his mind as if they had always been there; facts clicked together without effort.

Mrs. Ellery paused behind his desk during math. She looked at his worksheet, then looked again, brow furrowing.

"These are all correct," she said slowly. "But we haven't learned this yet."

Jonathan stared at the page. Neat columns of answers stared back. "I just… knew." The admission felt wrong in his mouth, like he was confessing to cheating when he hadn't.

She frowned, then moved on, but her hand lingered on the back of his chair a second longer than necessary.

Recess broke everything open.

Jonathan stood near the fence, hands in his pockets, watching the others play. The world felt too sharp— voices, movement, metal clatter from the chain link. Every sound came in clearer than it should have, as if someone had turned up the volume on reality. The slap of sneakers on blacktop, the creak of swings, the shriek of the whistle—all of it pressed in.

Mark and Tyler approached, moving with the loose swagger of boys who'd never been told no in a way that stuck.

"Hey, Halden," Mark said. "You back from the dead?" His grin was wide and mean.

Tyler snorted. "Guess being a freak finally caught up with you."

Jonathan stiffened. "Leave me alone." The words came out flat, more plea than threat.

Mark shoved him.

Jonathan hit the fence, breath knocked loose in a shocked huff. The chain link rattled around him, cold metal biting through his shirt.

Something inside him shifted.

His breathing slowed.

Deepened.

The roar of the playground dropped away, replaced by a low hum under his skin. His fingers loosened from the fence.

Mark frowned. "Dude… what's wrong with your eyes?"

Jonathan didn't know. He only felt the pressure building behind his ribs. A hum. A tightening coil, like something winding itself up, waiting for release.

"Stop," he whispered.

Mark shoved him again.

Jonathan moved.

Too fast.

He slapped Mark's hand aside with a sharp crack that sent the boy stumbling back, eyes wide. The contact was brief, but the force behind it shocked even Jonathan. Tyler grabbed Jonathan's shoulder, fingers digging in.

Jonathan turned and shoved him once.

Tyler flew backward, skidding across the dirt before crashing to a stop near the edge of the blacktop. Gravel tore at his palms. He stared up at Jonathan, stunned, then his face crumpled and he started to cry.

Screams cut through the yard. Children scattered back from the fence in a ragged ring.

Jonathan stood still, breathing slow, hands trembling at his sides. The humming inside him faded by inches, leaving a hollow, sick feeling in its wake.

Mark scrambled away, eyes wide with terror, one hand clutched to his chest as if it might protect him from whatever Jonathan had become.

Mrs. Ellery reached him seconds later, gripping his shoulders. Her fingers dug in harder than she meant to, needing to feel something solid.

"Jonathan—what happened?"

The world snapped back. The noise of the playground rushed in, too loud. Jonathan stared at his hands.

"I—I didn't mean to," he whispered. "I didn't—" His voice shook.

Mrs. Ellery didn't answer.

She was looking at his eyes.

Too bright.

Too sharp.

Almost fevered. The pupils were a fraction too narrow in the light, the irises catching the sun in a way that made them seem edged.

Jonathan looked up at her, panic breaking through the control.

"Please," he whispered. "I think something's wrong with me."

Mrs. Ellery swallowed.

She didn't say he was wrong.

Suzanne arrived twenty minutes later. The call from the school had been calm but urgent; the drive over blurred at the edges.

Jonathan sat in the front office, knees drawn up, eyes red. The fluorescent lights overhead made the circles under them look darker. He leaned into her the moment she touched him, forehead pressing into her shoulder like he could hide there.

Mrs. Ellery spoke carefully from behind the counter. "There was an incident. Jonathan injured two students with… unexpected force." She chose each word as if it might be used later in a meeting, or a report.

Suzanne nodded quickly. "He's been sick. He's—" She stopped herself before saying changed.

"I understand," Mrs. Ellery said. "But I've never seen a child move like that." Her voice dropped slightly, the memory of the shove still vivid.

Suzanne knelt in front of Jonathan. "Did you mean to hurt them?"

He shook his head violently. "No. Something just… happened." His hands flexed once, fingers curling and uncurling as if they remembered more than he wanted them to. Mrs. Ellery folded her hands on the desk. The knuckles were white. "Two men asked to speak with me," she said carefully.

Suzanne stiffened. "About what?" The question came out sharper than she intended.

"They said they were following up on Jonathan's medical history."

"Did you give them anything?"

Mrs. Ellery shook her head. "No. I told them they'd need to go through the district."

She hesitated. "They left cards."

She slid them across the desk.

Two names. Clean print.

Federal seals Suzanne didn't recognize.

Rowe.

Kinkaid.

"They were very polite," Mrs. Ellery said. "Almost reassuring." The word reassuring sounded wrong in her mouth.

Suzanne gathered the cards and stood. The cardstock felt too smooth under her fingers. She didn't like how steady her hands were, how quickly part of her brain began cataloging the names, the seals, the font.

She pulled him into her arms. "We're going home."

CHAPTER 11 — THE GAP

For three days, nothing happened.

No calls from the school.

No knocks at the door.

No cars that lingered too long at the curb.

The silence should have been comforting. Instead it felt like a held breath.

Suzanne kept Jonathan home. She told the office he was still recovering. The secretary's voice was sympathetic, relieved even, as if she were grateful not to deal with whatever had happened on the playground for a little while longer.

Jonathan didn't argue.

He slept.

Not restlessly — deeply. Too deeply. When Suzanne checked on him, his breathing was slow and even, his body slack in a way that felt manufactured, like something had arranged him in a textbook position for rest. She counted the rise and fall of his chest until the tightness in her own lungs eased enough to let the next breath in.

When he was awake, he was quiet. The wild, raw grief she expected never came in the way she recognized. Instead, there was a flatness under the surface, a steadiness that didn't match what he'd lived through. Children who've endured trauma can shut down emotionally, seeming detached or numb, not showing feelings even when you might expect them to.

He finished his schoolwork in minutes, then set the papers aside without comment. Problems that had taken him half a class period before now fell into place as if they were obvious. He didn't ask for television. He didn't ask for games. The toys he used to scatter across the floor stayed in their bins.

He sat by the window and watched the street, not with fear, but with attention. His eyes tracked cars as they passed, paused briefly at pedestrians, lingered on any vehicle that slowed even for a moment. Hypervigilant kids often scan their surroundings constantly, on alert for danger even in familiar places.

"Do you feel okay?" Suzanne asked him once.

Jonathan considered the question longer than necessary. His gaze stayed on the glass, following a mail truck until it turned the corner.

"I don't feel bad," he said. "I don't feel much."

That answer stayed with her. Emotional numbing after trauma can feel exactly like that: not pain, but the absence of feeling, a flatness where there should be something.

On the second day, a neighbor brought over a casserole. She stood on the porch with the foil-covered dish and the careful, condolence-soaked smile of someone who didn't know what else to do. Suzanne thanked her, accepted it, closed the door, and locked it without thinking.

Jonathan stood in the hallway, listening. His head tilted slightly, as if tracking footsteps through the door. When the neighbor's car started and pulled away, his shoulders loosened by a fraction.

On the third day, Suzanne let him step outside.

Just the yard.

Just five minutes.

Jonathan stood barefoot in the grass, eyes closed, face tilted toward the sun. The late-autumn light was thin but real, laying a pale warmth across his skin. Suzanne watched from the porch, heart hammering, ready to pull him back inside at the first sign of anything wrong—a slowing car, an unfamiliar voice, the prickle at the back of her neck she'd begun to trust more than logic.

Nothing happened.

No cars slowed.

No doors opened.

No voices called out.

Jonathan opened his eyes.

"See?" he said softly. "It's fine."

Suzanne nodded.

She almost believed him. Her body stayed half-tensed, waiting for something to crash through the calm.

That night, she slept for the first time since Henry died. The sleep wasn't peaceful, exactly, but it was deep enough that when she woke to the gray light of morning, she realized with a jolt that she hadn't heard Jonathan stir once.

CHAPTER 12 — FIRST CONTACT

On the fourth morning, the phone rang.

Suzanne let it ring twice before answering. The sound felt like a countdown, each chime marking the end of the small pocket of quiet they'd been living in.

"Mrs. Halden," a woman said, careful and professional. "This is the school. There's been… an incident."

Suzanne closed her eyes. The word incident slid neatly over panic, injury, blame.

The quiet ended without ceremony.

Suzanne carried Jonathan across the school parking lot, his backpack hooked over her arm, her hand locked around his. His fingers trembled against her skin, a fine, constant shake that didn't match his slow, measured breaths.

"Mom," he whispered, "I didn't mean to—"

"I know," she said quickly. "We're going home." She didn't ask for details; the outlines were already too familiar.

She opened the truck and helped him climb into the passenger seat. He curled inward, knees drawn tight, eyes fixed on the floor mats as if the specks of dirt there were safer to look at than anything else.

Suzanne closed the door gently. The thunk felt too loud in the heavy air of the lot.

Then she stopped.

Two men stood beside her truck.

She was certain they hadn't been there a moment ago. No footsteps. No approach. Just presence—like they had stepped out of the air itself or emerged from some blind spot she hadn't known was there.

The shorter one was broad-shouldered, his dark hair clipped close. He offered a polite nod that didn't reach his eyes. He stood with the stillness of someone who moved only when necessary, weight balanced, hands relaxed but ready.

Beside him stood a taller man, lean and pale, his expression calm to the point of vacancy. He didn't smile. Didn't blink often. His gaze carried the flat, assessing quality of someone used to looking at people as information.

"Mrs. Halden?" the shorter man said. His voice was even, practiced, the tone of someone who had said "ma'am" in a hundred uncomfortable parking lots. "May we have a moment?"

"I'm taking my son home," Suzanne replied. "Whatever this is, it can wait." Her body shifted automatically, angling herself between them and the passenger door.

The taller man's gaze slid briefly to Jonathan through the windshield.

Jonathan shrank back, clutching his backpack to his chest like a shield. His eyes went wide and flat at the same time, recognition warring with fear.

"We're here because of your son," the man said.

Suzanne stepped sideways, placing herself more squarely between them and the truck. Her pulse hammered in her throat.

"No."

The shorter man lifted a hand—not in surrender, but reassurance. The gesture was open, palms visible, textbook nonthreatening. "We're not here to cause trouble. We received notice of an incident at the school. We want to make sure Jonathan is well."

"The school didn't call you," Suzanne said. She would have heard the extra line on the voicemail, the different voice.

"No," he agreed. He reached into his coat.

She drew a startled breath.

She released a sigh when he withdrew a slim wallet and opened it just enough to reveal a badge.

Federal.

Clean.

Deliberate.

"My name is Rowe," he said. "This is Agent Kinkaid."

The names settled heavily, like weights dropped without apology.

"We've been assigned to follow up on Jonathan's medical history."

"He doesn't have one," Suzanne snapped. Not the kind you mean. Not the kind with file folders and restricted headers.

Kinkaid spoke softly, his tone almost kind. "We understand this has been a difficult transition. We're here to offer support." The word support sounded off-key in his mouth, like a borrowed line from a script.

Jonathan watched them, pale and rigid.

Something inside him recoiled—sharp and immediate, the way a body reacts before the mind can explain why. His body took a jerking breath once, then flattened again, too controlled.

Suzanne felt it in the silence he held. His fear didn't spill out; it condensed, dense and taut.

"No," she said again. "My son isn't talking to anyone. Especially not you."

The agents exchanged a brief look. Not surprise. Confirmation. As if this response had been predicted and accounted for.

Rowe adjusted his tone. "We're aware your husband worked at the facility," he said. "His death was… unfortunate. We want to ensure nothing else goes wrong."

The words landed with surgical precision. Facility. Unfortunate. Nothing else. Each one sliced close to bone.

"You stay away from my family," Suzanne said, her voice low. The edge in it surprised even her.

Kinkaid tilted his head slightly. "You won't be able to avoid us forever, Mrs. Halden. There are things you need to understand."

"Get away from my truck."

Rowe studied her for a beat, then nodded once, as if ticking a box on a list. He stepped back.

Kinkaid followed, hands sliding calmly into his pockets, posture unruffled.

"We'll be in touch," Rowe said.

It wasn't a threat.

It was a schedule.

Suzanne climbed into the truck and locked the doors. The click of the locks dropping into place was small and insufficient. Her hands shook as she started the engine.

Jonathan grabbed her sleeve. "Mom… don't let them take me." His voice cracked on the last word.

"They won't," she said fiercely. "Ever." The promise felt like a line she was drawing in concrete.

She pulled away.

In the side mirror, the two men remained on the curb, watching without urgency. They didn't write anything down. They didn't talk to each other. They just watched her go.

They didn't follow.

They didn't need to.

Jonathan stared out the window until they disappeared from view. His reflection ghosted over the glass, eyes dark, jaw clenched.

Then he whispered, "They were at the lab."

Suzanne's breath caught. "What?"

"I remember them," he said. "They were there… when Dad—"

His voice broke. The last word dissolved into air.

Suzanne tightened her grip on the wheel. The steering column creaked faintly under the pressure.

This wasn't coincidence.

Rowe and Kinkaid hadn't come to ask questions.

They had come to confirm that Jonathan Halden still existed.

CHAPTER 13 — SIGNS

Jonathan didn't want to go back to school the next day.

Suzanne offered to keep him home, but he shook his head.

"If I don't go," he whispered, "they'll talk more."

She didn't argue. They would talk either way. But she let him try.

The moment they arrived, she felt it—the way children stared too long, the way whispers followed Jonathan down the sidewalk like a wake. Yesterday's incident had already hardened into something worse than gossip.

A story.

When Jonathan entered the classroom, the noise dipped, then resumed at a lower pitch. He kept his eyes on the floor, but he could feel the attention pressing in on him, a weight between his shoulder blades.

"Did you see him yesterday?"

"He shoved Tyler like it was nothing."

"My mom said he had a seizure."

"No—my brother said he went crazy."

Jonathan slid into his seat and folded inward, shoulders rounding, trying to take up less space.

Mrs. Ellery offered a tight smile. "Welcome back, Jonathan. Let's have a calm day today."

A few kids snickered. The word calm landed like a joke.

Jonathan nodded without looking up.

During art class, he reached into the supply bin and scraped his knuckle on something sharp. The sting came first, then warmth. He pulled his hand back and saw a thin line of red bead along the skin.

He sucked in a breath.

A girl across the table gasped. "Jonathan's bleeding."

Several kids leaned closer, drawn by the smell of drama.

Jonathan pressed his fingers over the cut, heart hammering. The skin throbbed under his touch. When he lifted his hand again, the blood had smeared—but there was no new red. The skin beneath looked pale, pinched together, already settling.

Too fast.

Silence spread across the table, rippling outward.

A boy whispered, "Did you see that?"

Another leaned back in his chair. "That's not normal."

Jonathan shoved his hand beneath the table, heat flooding his face.

Someone muttered, "Freak."

Another voice, quieter but sharper: "Monster."

The words slid into him like splinters.

Mrs. Ellery hurried over. "What's going on?"

"He cut himself," a girl said. "But then it just… stopped."

Mrs. Ellery took Jonathan's hand, turning it gently. The skin was pink and unbroken, like it had been pressed too hard and released.

"It was small," Jonathan said quickly. "I barely felt it."

Mrs. Ellery nodded, but her eyes lingered a moment too long, cataloging what she'd seen and what she couldn't explain.

The room felt different after that.

Not curious.

Careful.

Recess made it worse.

Jonathan stayed near the wall, hoping to disappear.

It didn't work.

Mark and Tyler approached again, bolder with an audience. A loose ring of kids drifted closer, pretending not to watch.

"You think you're special now?" Mark said.

Jonathan didn't answer. His back pressed against the cool brick.

Tyler smirked. "He's not special. He's just wrong."

"I saw his hand," another kid said. "It healed."

Jonathan stepped back. The group followed, tightening the circle.

Mark shoved him—lightly. Testing.

"Do it again," Mark said. "Throw me like yesterday."

Something stirred beneath Jonathan's skin. Not anger. Fear.

"Stop," he whispered.

Mark shoved him harder.

"Make us."

Jonathan's breathing slowed, slipping into something steady and unfamiliar. The sounds of the playground thinned, as if they'd been pushed further away.

Mrs. Ellery's voice cut through the noise. "HEY. BACK UP. NOW."

The crowd scattered, breaking apart into guilty, darting shapes.

Jonathan pressed his palms to the brick wall, heart racing as the sensation ebbed away. His fingers dug into the mortar lines.

Mrs. Ellery crouched beside him. "Jonathan. Are you hurt?"

He shook his head.

But his hands wouldn't stop shaking.

This time, she noticed.

By the time Suzanne arrived, the atmosphere had cooled into something brittle.

Parents glanced at Jonathan, then away. A receptionist whispered behind the desk.

"That's him."

"The Halden boy."

"He hurt two kids."

"No—he healed."

"No—he threw someone."

Jonathan stayed close to Suzanne, eyes down, the words sticking to him as they walked past.

When they reached the truck, he whispered, "Mom… everyone knows."

Suzanne smoothed his hair. "Then we'll handle it. Together."

As they pulled away, traffic settled in behind them—cars stopping, turning, rearranging themselves without pattern.

Jonathan watched the road through the rear window longer than necessary.

He didn't say what he was thinking.

But Suzanne felt it anyway.

Something had shifted.

And once noticed, it would be difficult to disappear again.

CHAPTER 14 — WE'RE CONCERNED

The phone rang before Suzanne had finished making breakfast.

She froze with the spatula still in her hand, dread already curling low in her stomach. Jonathan sat at the table, cereal untouched, shoulders hunched, eyes unfocused. He wasn't watching the phone. He was watching her.

It rang again.

"Hello?" she said.

"Mrs. Halden?"

Principal Myers's voice was calm, professional—and strained in a way Suzanne recognized. Not alarm. Preparation.

"We need to discuss Jonathan's situation," Myers said. "Today, if possible."

Suzanne tightened her grip on the receiver. "Has something happened?"

A pause. Careful.

"Several parents have raised concerns," Myers said. "And some staff members have observations they'd like to review."

Observations. The word landed with weight it hadn't earned yet.

"All right," Suzanne said. "I can come this morning."

"We'd like Jonathan to come as well."

Her stomach dropped. "Why?"

"So we can understand what's happening," Myers said. "For his well-being—and for the other students'."

Jonathan looked up then, eyes wide.

"We'll be there," Suzanne said, and hung up.

Jonathan folded inward, shoulders drawing tight. "Am I in trouble?"

"No," she said immediately, kneeling beside him. "You're not in trouble. People just don't understand what you're going through."

"I don't understand it either," he whispered.

She pulled him close. "We'll face it together."

The kitchen felt smaller after that. The smell of toast lingered too long, shifting from comforting to sour. The cereal in Jonathan's bowl softened and curled at the edges, untouched. He noticed everything.

In the car, Suzanne caught his reflection in the passenger-side window. His knee bounced once, then stopped—corrected by something internal. He folded his hands in his lap and held himself rigid, as if movement alone might draw attention.

By the time they entered the school, the pressure had direction.

The front office quieted too abruptly. Conversations faltered. A secretary avoided Jonathan's eyes. The receptionist offered a stiff nod.

"Principal Myers will see you shortly."

Whispers followed them almost immediately.

"That's him."

"He hurt Tyler."

"I heard he healed right in front of kids."

"That's not normal."

Jonathan stared at the floor. Suzanne wrapped an arm around him.

This wasn't curiosity anymore.

It was fear.

They waited. Jonathan counted his breaths, careful and precise. Eye contact invited questions. Questions invited explanations he didn't have.

When they were called in, the office door closed with a soft, definitive click.

Principal Myers sat behind her desk, incident reports stacked neatly in front of her—not accusations. Records. A timeline meant to justify whatever came next. The school counselor sat nearby, hands folded too tightly.

"We want what's best for Jonathan," Myers said. "But recent incidents have raised serious concerns."

"He was being bullied," Suzanne said. "You have the reports."

"We do," Myers agreed. "But the force he used—and the speed with which his injury appeared to resolve—"

"He is not dangerous," Suzanne said.

"We're not saying he is," the counselor replied. "We're saying we may need to pause his attendance while we assess."

Jonathan stiffened. Suzanne felt it immediately—the way his muscles locked, the way his breathing shortened. She took his hand. It trembled, fine and constant, like a wire pulled too tight.

"No," Suzanne said. "He needs structure."

"Some parents are questioning whether he's safe," Myers said quietly.

"You've known my son for years," Suzanne said.

"I know," Myers replied. "That's why we're trying to proceed carefully."

Jonathan swallowed. "I didn't want to hurt anyone."

The shame arrived before blame ever could have. Jonathan absorbed responsibility instinctively, as if harm were proof of failure rather than circumstance.

"We believe you," the counselor said. "But what happened frightened people."

Jonathan's voice broke. "I don't want to be a freak."

Suzanne looked up sharply. "That word will never be used about my son."

The counselor closed her folder. "There are alternatives—home instruction, reduced hours—"

"They're exits," Suzanne said. "And we're not taking them."

Myers hesitated. "The district has requested we document everything."

Suzanne froze. "Why?"

"Because this may not be purely behavioral," Myers said carefully. "Something physical may be involved."

Jonathan trembled beside her.

A knock sounded at the door.

Myers frowned. "We're in a meeting."

The door opened partway. A secretary leaned in, pale.

"There are two men here asking about the Halden case," she said quietly. "They say it's time-sensitive."

Suzanne felt the shift immediately. The pressure changed texture.

"I wasn't informed anyone else was involved," Myers said.

"They didn't give a name," the secretary said. "Just credentials."

Authority without accountability.

Suzanne stood. "We're leaving."

Myers hesitated, then nodded. "We'll… continue this later."

Suzanne didn't wait.

She took Jonathan's hand and led him into the hallway, past staring faces, past open doors and carefully neutral expressions. Teachers paused mid-step. Conversations died unfinished.

No one intervened.

Fear had already done its work.

Jonathan stayed close—not clinging, not hiding. Just close enough that their shoulders nearly touched. His body had gone rigid, control layered over instinct. He was holding himself together.

That frightened her more than panic would have.

"They were watching," he whispered.

"I know."

"They're still watching."

Suzanne didn't answer. She didn't need to. She felt it—the weight of attention, the quiet understanding that decisions were already being made without her.

At the exit, she stopped and turned him toward her. "Look at me."

He hesitated, then lifted his eyes. They were bright with effort.

"You're not alone," she said. "Do you hear me?"

He nodded once.

"They don't get to define you. Not today. Not ever."

"They already are," he said.

The honesty of it cut deeper than accusation.

She pulled him into her arms and held him there, letting the moment stretch despite the watching eyes. Letting the building see that she would not rush or apologize.

Outside, the sunlight felt too sharp. Parents chatted near the entrance. A delivery truck backed up with an absurdly loud warning beep.

Life continued.

That, more than anything, made her angry.

In the parking lot, Jonathan's body finally surrendered. The shaking came hard and fast, adrenaline flooding a system already pushed beyond tolerance. Suzanne wrapped him tightly, one arm around his shoulders, the other cradling the back of his head.

"It's okay," she murmured. "You're safe right now."

Right now mattered.

"They weren't teachers," Jonathan whispered.

Her chest tightened. "Who?"

"The men," he said. "They were listening. Before they knocked. They knew things we didn't say out loud."

Suzanne stilled. She helped him into the car and buckled him in herself, hands steady despite the storm inside her. She scanned the lot instinctively, cataloguing faces, vehicles, exits.

She hated that she knew how to do that.

Once inside, she locked the doors. The sound was loud. Final.

They sat for a moment, engine off. Suzanne rested her forehead against the steering wheel and drew a slow breath.

You can still walk away, she told herself.

But even as the thought formed, she knew it wasn't true anymore.

Walking away implied choice.

And choice was already being constrained.

She started the car.

In the rearview mirror, the school looked the same as it always had—orderly, composed, respectable. But now she knew what lived beneath that surface.

Pressure didn't need confrontation.

It just needed time.

And people willing to look away.

Jonathan leaned back against the seat, eyes closed, exhaustion overtaking adrenaline. Suzanne glanced at him, her resolve settling into something hard and steady.

They might be documenting.

They might be watching.

But so was she.

CHAPTER 15 — CLOSE WATCH

Suzanne didn't send Jonathan to school the next day.

The meeting with the principal—the stares, the whispers, the names she hadn't wanted to hear—looped endlessly in her mind. She couldn't let him walk back into that building. Not yet. Maybe not ever.

What unsettled her most wasn't what had been said.

It was what hadn't.

The careful language. The pauses that carried more weight than answers. The way concern had shifted into documentation, into something that felt like the early stages of a file being built rather than a child being helped. Suzanne had lived long enough adjacent to institutions to recognize the pattern. This was how watchlists began—not with accusations, but with interest.

Jonathan sat at the kitchen table, knees pulled up, chin resting against them. He was quiet in a way that didn't feel like silence.

It felt like retreat.

Suzanne watched him from the sink, pretending to rinse a mug she'd already cleaned. He had folded himself inward, shoulders curved as though he were trying to occupy less space. That hurt more than anything the school had said.

"Do you want breakfast?" Suzanne asked.

He shook his head. "I'm not hungry."

She poured cereal anyway and set it in front of him. He nudged it with his spoon, never lifting it.

Time moved strangely in the kitchen. Sounds felt louder—the hum of the refrigerator, the tick of the wall clock, the scrape of the spoon against ceramic. Jonathan flinched at none of it, but Suzanne noticed how his attention flickered at each noise, cataloguing without reacting.

His knuckles—scraped raw during recess—were already fading. Barely pink now. The bruise on his forearm was gone entirely.

Suzanne looked away.

Not because she didn't love him.

Because the speed of it scared her in ways she didn't yet have language for.

He noticed.

"Please don't be scared of me," he whispered.

Suzanne dropped to her knees beside him. "I'm not scared of you," she said. "I'm scared for you."

The distinction mattered. She needed him to hear it.

His eyes shone. "I don't want this. I didn't ask for it."

"I know," she said, brushing his hair back. "None of this is your fault."

He nodded, but didn't look convinced.

Children believed adults when the world still made sense. Jonathan was already past that point.

By midmorning, the phone began to ring.

It didn't stop.

Parents. Teachers. Administrators. Voices careful with concern and edged with something sharper underneath. Suzanne recognized the tone immediately—people who wanted reassurance without responsibility.

She let most calls go unanswered. A few forced their way through.

"Has Jonathan been medically evaluated?"

"Is he safe at home?"

"Some parents are talking about pulling their children—"

She ended the call before the sentence finished.

Her hands were shaking by the third voicemail.

Outside, neighborhood kids slowed their bikes as they passed the house. One whispered. Another glanced away too quickly.

That hurt more than the calls.

Jonathan watched from behind the blinds.

"They're talking about me," he said.

"Yes," Suzanne replied quietly. "They're afraid of what they don't understand."

"I didn't mean to scare anyone," he said. "Everything just felt... too loud."

That word caught her.

Loud.

Not painful. Not angry. Not confusing.

Overwhelming.

She wrapped her arms around him from behind. "You're trying to survive something no child should ever have to."

Jonathan leaned into her, but his body remained tense, as though he were bracing for something that hadn't arrived yet.

That afternoon, a glass pitcher slipped from the counter and shattered across the tile.

The sound was sharp. Violent. Final.

Jonathan jumped back—but not fast enough.

A shard nicked his palm.

"Ow—"

Suzanne crossed the room in two strides.

But the bleeding slowed.

Stopped.

Before she reached him.

They stood there together, frozen, watching as the cut narrowed, the skin drawing together until nothing remained but a faint warmth.

The air felt wrong.

Too still. Too aware.

Jonathan's breath trembled. "Mom... what's happening to me?"

Suzanne took his hand gently. She felt no break in the skin. No heat of inflammation. Just smoothness, as if the injury had never existed at all.

"You're healing fast," she said carefully. "Faster than most people. But that doesn't make you dangerous."

She needed to believe that as much as he did.

"Why me?"

"I don't know," she admitted. "But we'll figure it out."

She didn't say what pressed at the edges of her thoughts.

Henry's work.

The promises.

The assurances that everything had been controlled.

That evening, she closed the curtains earlier than usual.

The street outside was quiet. Too quiet, maybe—but she told herself that was just the hour, the season, the weight of the day.

Jonathan didn't need to look outside to tense.

"Do you hear that?" he whispered.

Suzanne listened.

Cars passed. A door closed somewhere down the block. Normal sounds, layered wrong by fear.

"It's okay," she said. "We're inside."

She locked the door again, then checked it twice.

Later, as the house settled into night, Suzanne realized something else.

She was changing her behavior.

Curtains drawn. Doors locked. Phones silenced. Lights dimmed.

Not hiding yet.

But preparing.

That night, Jonathan lay awake, staring at the ceiling. Suzanne sat beside him, brushing his hair until his breathing finally slowed.

"Stay?" he murmured.

"I'm not going anywhere."

When he slept, she stepped into the hallway and leaned against the wall, pressing her hand over her mouth as silent tears came.

She had already lost Henry.

She would not lose Jonathan.

And even though she knew she couldn't keep him hidden forever—

she would try.

CHAPTER 16 — CARLISLE

Suzanne kept Jonathan home again the next morning.

The world beyond the windows felt tighter now, as if the air itself were holding still. Jonathan sat on the couch with a blanket wrapped around him, small and quiet, his eyes fixed on the front door the way an animal watched the edge of a clearing.

Waiting.

Suzanne tried to keep busy—dishes, laundry, anything to occupy her hands—but she checked the window every few minutes, tension coiled hard in her chest.

Late in the morning, a car she didn't recognize eased to the curb.

Not the dark sedan.

Not the silver one.

This one was newer. Cleaner. Quiet.

A man stepped out.

No uniform. No visible badge. Just a tailored suit, a long coat, and a posture that radiated control. He moved with the calm assurance of someone accustomed to being expected.

Suzanne's heart sank.

"Jonathan," she said softly. "Go to your room. Now."

He obeyed without question.

She reached the door just as the knock came.

The man smiled—polite, measured, practiced.

"Mrs. Halden," he said. "Good morning."

"Who are you?"

He produced identification with deliberate care.

C. Carlisle

Federal Oversight Division

Department of Defense

The insignia meant nothing to her—and that frightened her more than if it had.

"It's pronounced Car-lyle," he added mildly. "Most people get it wrong."

"What do you want?"

"To talk," Carlisle said. "About your son."

"No."

Carlisle didn't react. He inclined his head, patient.

"I understand your reluctance. But Jonathan's recent behavior has drawn attention."

"He was being bullied."

"Yes," Carlisle agreed smoothly. "But his recovery appears… unusual."

"You need to leave."

"Mrs. Halden," Carlisle said gently, "if I intended to take Jonathan, I wouldn't be standing on your porch in daylight."

Suzanne noticed a curtain shift down the street.

Of course he'd chosen this hour.

"We're aware of your husband's work," Carlisle continued. "And the circumstances surrounding his death."

Her breath caught.

"I'm sorry for your loss," he said. The words were precise. Correctly weighted. Empty of sentiment.

"Jonathan has experienced trauma," Carlisle went on. "Children sometimes adapt in ways that surprise even their parents."

She stepped back and began to close the door.

"You need to leave," she said. "Now."

Carlisle didn't resist.

He spoke once more before the door shut.

"Mrs. Halden," he said calmly, "there are people who will be interested in your son whether you speak to us or not."

The lock clicked.

Suzanne stood there, heart pounding, until she heard the measured retreat of footsteps.

Through the peephole, she watched Carlisle walk back to his car, adjust his coat, and drive away without urgency.

No threat.

No demand.

Just presence.

Carlisle hadn't come to frighten her.

He had come to introduce himself.

Carlisle's presence did not leave when his car disappeared down the street.

It lingered.

Suzanne remained where she was long after the engine noise faded, her back pressed against the door, her palm flat against the wood as if she could still feel the vibration of his knock. The house felt altered, subtly but unmistakably, like a room after furniture had been moved—nothing visibly wrong, yet impossible to ignore.

Only when her heartbeat slowed enough to count did she move.

Jonathan stayed in his room at first. She could hear him shifting, the soft friction of fabric, the careful way he repositioned himself to listen without revealing where he stood. Suzanne recognized the instinct immediately. It mirrored her own.

Waiting had become learned behavior.

She moved through the house, checking windows she already knew were locked. The action was ritual more than necessity. Each latch, each curtain drawn a fraction tighter, reinforced the boundary she was trying—desperately—to maintain.

Carlisle had crossed it without force.

That unsettled her more than any threat could have.

Jonathan emerged slowly, the blanket still wrapped around his shoulders. His eyes went to her face first, not the door. He had learned where danger registered before it arrived.

"Is he gone?" he asked.

"Yes."

"For good?"

She hesitated. "For now."

Jonathan absorbed the answer without comment. He returned to the couch, curling inward again, but his attention never dulled. Suzanne noticed the way his gaze flicked toward the window every few minutes, how his breathing adjusted when a car passed.

"He knew about Dad," Jonathan said quietly.

Suzanne closed her eyes for a beat. "Yes."

"Did he know him?"

"I don't know," she said. "But he knew his work."

That frightened Jonathan more than the visit itself. His father had always existed in fragments—late nights, guarded conversations, the heaviness Henry carried home even on good days. Knowing that a man like Carlisle could speak of him so easily made those fragments feel suddenly exposed.

"He said my name like he already knew me," Jonathan said.

Suzanne nodded. "That's how people like him operate."

The rest of the day passed under a different kind of pressure.

Time fractured. Minutes stretched, then collapsed. Suzanne found herself stopping mid-task, listening for sounds that never came. She replayed Carlisle's words again and again, testing them for hidden meaning.

If I intended to take Jonathan, I wouldn't be standing on your porch in daylight.

It wasn't reassurance.

It was calibration.

Carlisle had measured her—her resistance, her fear, her willingness to comply—simply by showing up.

Jonathan felt it too.

He stayed close without being asked, positioning himself where he could see her at all times. The behavior was subtle but unmistakable. Proximity had become safety.

As the afternoon wore on, Suzanne noticed how easily Jonathan tracked changes outside—the cadence of footsteps, the difference between a delivery truck and a passing car, the way certain engines lingered while others passed cleanly.

He didn't comment on it.

But she noticed.

By evening, exhaustion settled into her bones—not physical tiredness, but the fatigue of sustained alertness. She cooked dinner mechanically. Jonathan ate because she asked him to, not because he was hungry.

Carlisle had not threatened her.

He hadn't needed to.

His visit reframed everything. The school was no longer the center of concern. Curiosity had escalated into oversight. Jonathan was no longer merely unusual.

He was of interest.

After Jonathan went to bed, Suzanne sat alone at the kitchen table, hands wrapped around a mug that had gone cold. Henry's absence pressed in sharply now, his name spoken aloud by a stranger who wore authority like a second skin.

She wondered how much Henry had known.

How much he had suspected.

Whether this moment had always been coming.

Upstairs, Jonathan lay awake, staring at the ceiling. Carlisle's voice replayed in his mind—not the words, but the tone. Calm. Controlled. Certain.

The voice of someone who expected outcomes to align with intention.

That frightened him more than anger ever could have.

Carlisle had not come to frighten them.

He had come to mark them.

And both Suzanne and Jonathan understood, in their own way, that this was not an ending.

It was the beginning of being watched.

CHAPTER 17 — CONSTRAINT

The letter arrived just after noon.

Suzanne didn't open it right away. She recognized the envelope — heavy stock, unmarked except for her name printed too precisely to be casual.

Jonathan watched her from the couch.

"What is it?" he asked.

"I don't know yet," she said.

That was a lie.

She slid a finger beneath the seal and unfolded the paper.

Notice of Mandatory Evaluation.

The language was calm. Neutral. Final.

Jonathan Halden was required to report for medical assessment within forty-eight hours. Failure to comply could result in intervention under federal health and security statutes.

No names.

No signatures she recognized.

Just authority.

Jonathan read her face before she finished.

"They're not asking," he said quietly.

Suzanne folded the letter with care and set it on the counter. "No," she said. "They aren't."

Outside, a car door closed.

Suzanne moved to the window.

A dark SUV sat across the street. Engine off. Someone inside.

She didn't remember it being there earlier.

Jonathan joined her, standing close enough that she could feel the warmth of him.

Another vehicle rolled past — silver — slowing just slightly before continuing down the block.

Jonathan's hand found hers.

"They know I'm here," he said.

Suzanne swallowed. "They know where you've always been."

The phone rang.

She let it ring once. Twice.

Then answered.

"Mrs. Halden," a man said — not Rowe, not Kinkaid, not Carlisle. Someone new. Someone lower. "We're just checking to make sure you received the notice."

"Yes," she said.

"Good. Transportation can be arranged if needed."

"No," Suzanne said. "We'll handle it."

A pause.

"That would be advisable," the man said. "Please understand — this isn't punitive."

She hung up.

Jonathan was shaking.

"They're going to take me somewhere," he whispered. "Like before."

She turned him toward her. "Listen to me. No one takes you anywhere without me."

"But they can," he said. "Can't they?"

Suzanne didn't answer.

That night, Jonathan spiked a fever.

Not high. Not dangerous.

Just wrong.

His skin burned beneath her hand, then cooled too quickly. His breathing slowed until she had to count it.

When she tried to give him medicine, he vomited.

Then, an hour later, he sat up.

"I'm fine," he said.

The fever was gone.

Too gone.

Suzanne packed a bag.

Not everything.

Just enough.

At dawn, she stood in the kitchen, keys in her hand, Jonathan's backpack at her feet.

Outside, the SUV was still there.

Another idled at the corner.

They weren't hiding anymore.

Jonathan looked at her.

"Mom," he said, steady despite the fear in his eyes. "If we don't go now, they won't let us later."

Suzanne opened the door.

And stepped into motion.

Constraint did not announce itself with force.

It arrived disguised as procedure.

Suzanne read the letter again after Jonathan went to the bathroom, scanning the phrasing with the part of her mind that once believed language could be challenged, appealed, reasoned with. Every sentence was constructed to sound optional while eliminating choice entirely. Required. Failure to comply. Intervention.

The absence of a signature was deliberate. No single person to argue with. No face to confront. Authority without ownership.

Jonathan understood that instinctively.

"They wrote it like they're already done deciding," he said, not accusing. Observing.

"Yes," Suzanne replied. "That's exactly what they did."

The SUV across the street didn't move.

That bothered her more than if it had.

Movement suggested uncertainty. Idling meant patience. Someone had calculated how long they could wait without drawing attention. Someone had decided stillness was enough.

Jonathan felt it in his chest, a tightness that didn't rise or fall with his breathing. He stood close to Suzanne not because he was afraid to be alone, but because proximity felt like resistance. As long as they occupied the same space, something held.

When the phone rang, he flinched before the sound fully registered.

The voice on the line wasn't important. The tone was.

It was practiced neutrality—the kind used by people who did not need to persuade. The kind that assumed compliance as the default and framed alternatives as inconvenience rather than defiance.

When Suzanne said we'll handle it, Jonathan heard the shift. A recalibration. The pause on the other end wasn't hesitation. It was notation.

That night, when the fever came, Suzanne knew before the thermometer confirmed it.

Jonathan's body had begun doing things ahead of explanation.

The heat under her palm was uneven, concentrated and then suddenly gone, as if his skin were adjusting itself faster than her senses could track. She counted his breaths because instinct told her to, because numbers felt like anchors in a situation that refused to stay stable.

When he vomited, her heart slammed hard enough to make her dizzy.

But when he sat up an hour later, color returned to his face too quickly. Too cleanly. The fever hadn't broken. It had been erased.

Jonathan knew it too.

"I didn't try to," he said quietly.

"I know."

"I felt… wrong. And then I didn't."

Suzanne packed the bag after he fell asleep again.

She didn't turn on lights. She didn't make lists. She moved by feel, by memory, by the instinct that told her speed mattered more than completeness. Clothes. Documents. The folder Henry had insisted she keep even when she didn't want to know what was inside.

Outside, engines idled like held breaths.

At dawn, Jonathan stood beside her, backpack already on his shoulders. He hadn't been told to pack it. He had decided.

Constraint had closed in from every side—paper, presence, physiology—but the smallest space remained.

Choice narrowed until it was almost invisible.

Almost.

Suzanne opened the door not because she believed they could outrun what was coming, but because standing still would finish the work for them.

Motion was the last thing they controlled.

And they used it.

CHAPTER 18 — THE CHASE

Suzanne waited until late afternoon before deciding she had to leave the house.

The decision wasn't sudden. It had been circling her all day, tightening and loosening like a wire pulled too far and allowed to slacken just enough to avoid snapping. The refrigerator was nearly empty. Jonathan hadn't eaten more than a few careful bites since morning. Staying inside felt safer, but it was starting to feel like stagnation—like waiting for something inevitable instead of moving before it arrived.

Jonathan sat on the couch with his knees tucked up, an uneaten granola bar resting beside him. He had repositioned himself so he could see both the front door and the window without turning his head. Suzanne noticed the calculation in it. He was learning angles. Lines of sight. What mattered.

"Sweetheart," Suzanne said, kneeling in front of him, "I'm just running to the store. I'll be right back."

She made her voice light. Casual. The way she used to when errands were nothing more than errands.

His fingers tightened in the blanket.

"Can I come?"

She hesitated.

He hadn't asked to leave the house since the notice arrived. He hadn't even stood near the door unless she was already there. The request wasn't about groceries. It was about proximity. About not being alone with the waiting.

"Yes," she said. "You can come."

Relief crossed his face so quickly it hurt to see. He slid off the couch without a word and followed her to the door, staying close enough that she could feel his presence even when she wasn't looking at him.

Outside, the afternoon felt wrong—too still. The air carried sound too clearly, every distant engine sharp against the quiet. Suzanne helped Jonathan into the truck and locked the doors without thinking, the click of the locks loud in the silence.

Two houses down, a silver sedan sat parked along the curb.

It hadn't been there earlier.

At the corner, a dark SUV idled, its engine barely audible, as if even sound was being rationed.

Neither moved.

But she felt it anyway.

That sense of being aligned with something she couldn't see—threads tightening, positions being taken. Suzanne backed out of the driveway slowly, deliberately, forcing herself not to rush.

The SUV pulled out seconds later.

Then the sedan.

Jonathan leaned forward, his voice barely above a breath. "Mom…"

"I see them," she said. "Eyes forward."

She didn't speed. She didn't slow. She drove the way she always had, hands steady on the wheel, posture relaxed enough to pass for normal. If they were watching, she wouldn't give them a reason to escalate. Not yet.

At the intersection near the grocery store, another SUV eased out from a side street. It didn't block the road. It didn't cut her off.

It simply narrowed the option.

Jonathan's breathed rapidly. His hand curled into the edge of the seat. "They're doing this on purpose."

"Yes," Suzanne said. "They are."

She turned sharply onto a side road without signaling.

All three vehicles followed.

No sirens.

No lights.

Just distance tightening.

The road narrowed, pavement giving way to broken edges and patches of gravel. Fields stretched out on either side, wide and exposed, offering nowhere to disappear.

Suzanne's heart hammered, but her mind stayed unnervingly clear.

Ahead, another SUV sat partially in the lane.

Waiting.

Suzanne didn't hesitate.

She wrenched the wheel to the right.

The truck jolted violently as the tires tore through dirt and grass. Dust exploded behind them, a choking cloud that briefly swallowed the road. The engine screamed as she fought for control, steering corrections coming too fast to be graceful.

"Hold on!" she shouted.

Jonathan braced himself instinctively, body compact and controlled in a way that startled her even through the panic.

The ground dipped suddenly.

The truck spun.

Glass shattered. Metal screamed. The impact rattled through her bones, disorienting and loud and final all at once.

Then silence.

Steam hissed from the hood.

Suzanne's ears rang as she fumbled for the door handle. Her hands shook, but they worked. She forced the door open and unbuckled Jonathan in one practiced motion.

Jonathan whimpered. "Mom…?"

"We move," she said, already pulling him free. "Now."

They ran.

Branches tore at them as they crashed through brush, the sound of pursuit rising behind them—shouts, boots pounding, radios crackling. Not frantic. Not panicked.

Coordinated.

That frightened her more than anything else.

They ducked behind trees, then moved again, never staying still long enough to be cornered. Jonathan matched her pace despite the fear etched across his face, his breathing controlled, his movements precise.

Then—

A farmhouse.

Weathered but standing. A sedan sat in the yard, engine running, the driver nowhere in sight. Keys dangled from the door, swinging slightly in the breeze.

Suzanne didn't think.

She shoved Jonathan into the passenger seat, yanked the keys free, and slammed the door. The engine roared to life as she gunned it, gravel spraying behind them while the car tore down the road.

Minutes passed.

Then miles.

The road stretched empty ahead, the fields blurring into something almost peaceful if she didn't think about what they'd left behind.

Only when her hands stopped shaking did Jonathan speak.

"Did we just steal a car?"

"Yes."

After a moment, quieter: "Are we going home?"

Suzanne's grip tightened on the wheel.

"One last time," she said.

And even as she said it, she knew it was already becoming a goodbye.

CHAPTER 19 — NO GOING BACK

The stolen sedan rattled softly as Suzanne guided it through the back roads behind their neighborhood.

The sound set her teeth on edge. Every vibration felt louder than it should have been, as if the car itself were announcing their presence. She kept her speed even, hands steady on the wheel, forcing herself to breathe at the same measured pace she'd used in emergencies before. Panic wasted time. Panic made mistakes.

Jonathan stayed low in the seat, Henry's jacket wrapped tight around his shoulders like armor.

It swallowed him, the sleeves too long, the fabric stiff with the faint, familiar scent of oil and soap. He pulled it closer anyway. The weight helped. The smell helped more. It felt like proof that his father had existed, that this moment had not erased everything that came before it.

"We're not staying," Suzanne whispered. "In and out."

She didn't look at him when she said it. Saying it out loud made it real, and reality felt dangerous right now.

They parked two blocks away.

Suzanne chose the spot carefully—shadowed by trees, far enough to avoid immediate notice, close enough to move fast if they had to run. She killed the engine and sat still for a moment, listening. No doors slamming. No engines idling nearby. Just the distant hum of a normal neighborhood pretending nothing was wrong.

The house looked the same.

That was the worst part.

The familiarity hit Suzanne harder than any threat could have. Normalcy was a lie now, and seeing it intact felt like an accusation. As if the house itself didn't understand what had happened, or what was coming.

Jonathan's drawing still hung crooked on the refrigerator. Henry's coffee mug sat upside down in the drying rack, a faint ring at the base where he'd set it down for the last time. Nothing had been disturbed. Nothing warned them away.

The air inside felt stale, untouched by urgency. Suzanne's chest tightened. It was as though the house expected them to stay, to sit, to pretend this was still their life.

She didn't let herself linger.

Suzanne swallowed and grabbed the duffel.

Her movements were efficient, stripped of sentiment. She had learned long ago how to function while her heart lagged behind.

They moved quickly. Clothes. Water. Food.

Jonathan handed things to her without being asked, eyes darting toward the windows between trips. He moved with a precision that would have surprised her a week ago. He knew which drawers to avoid, which floorboards creaked. He listened while he worked.

Every sound felt amplified. The scrape of fabric. The soft click of a cabinet closing. Suzanne found herself counting each noise, measuring how far it might travel.

Then she opened the bedroom closet.

Henry's satchel sat on the shelf where he'd left it.

Suzanne froze.

She hadn't touched it since the call. Hadn't been able to. The bag felt like a boundary she wasn't ready to cross, like opening it would make his absence permanent in a way she couldn't undo.

Inside were his wallet, his badge, folded papers she didn't recognize, and a photograph bent at the corner.

Her breath caught when she saw it—Henry smiling in a way he rarely did for cameras, Jonathan younger, laughing, unguarded. A life that felt impossibly distant.

And the knife.

Jonathan stopped breathing.

Suzanne noticed immediately. The stillness in him was absolute, as if his body had shut down every unnecessary function.

"That's Dad's," he said.

126

"Yes."

The word landed heavier than she expected.

He hesitated. "Can I…?"

Suzanne didn't answer with words. She placed it in his hand.

Jonathan's fingers closed around the grip, careful at first, then firmer.

The contact seemed to steady him. His shoulders eased a fraction. The knife fit his hand with unsettling familiarity.

"It feels warm," he whispered.

Suzanne felt a chill run through her.

"It's yours now," she said. "He'd want you to have it."

She believed that. Henry had always prepared for contingencies. Always planned for what came next. If he were here, he would have pressed the knife into Jonathan's hand himself and told him to trust his instincts.

Headlights swept across the far end of the street.

Suzanne froze.

Her pulse thundered so loudly she was sure it could be heard.

"Don't talk," she whispered.

The engine noise slowed.

Paused.

The light drifted across the front of the house, lingering just long enough to mean something. Not searching. Confirming.

Suzanne didn't wait for certainty.

She grabbed Jonathan's hand.

They ran.

Adrenaline stripped the world down to motion and breath. Their feet barely touched the ground as they cut through the yard, over the fence, down the side street. Suzanne didn't look back. She didn't need to. She could feel the attention shifting, recalculating.

By the time the sedan rolled past, scanning, their house was already behind them.

Jonathan looked back once, breathing becoming normalized as the lights faded away.

He memorized it in that single glance the porch, the windows, the shape of the roof against the sky. He understood, with a clarity that hurt, that he would never see it the same way again.

"Where are we going?" he asked.

Suzanne didn't slow.

"To the farm," she said. "Somewhere they won't think to look."

Jonathan pressed the knife against his chest, feeling its weight, its certainty.

It grounded him in a way nothing else could.

Their old life was gone.

And whatever came next would not let them turn back.

CHAPTER 20 — THE FARM

The storm had thinned to a tired drizzle by the time Suzanne turned off the cracked highway and onto the narrow gravel road that split away from the world like something forgotten. Headlights tunneled through mist, the beams swallowed and reshaped by rain. Overgrowth pressed in from both sides, weeds and low branches clawing at the sedan as if the road itself were trying to close behind them.

Suzanne slowed instinctively.

The sound of gravel beneath the tires felt too loud in the open night, each crunch echoing longer than it should have. Jonathan watched raindrops race down the window, his breath fogging the glass where his forehead rested against it.

"How much farther?" he asked.

His voice was steady, but Suzanne heard the strain beneath it. The question wasn't just distance. It was endurance.

"Not far," Suzanne said. Her hands tightened on the wheel, knuckles pale against the dark interior. "The place is old. Remote."

She didn't say what echoed beneath the words.

And I never wanted to come back.

The road curved sharply, the tree line thinning just enough to reveal open land beyond it. Wind pushed across the fields unchecked, flattening tall grass in waves that looked almost intentional. Suzanne felt exposed here in a way she hadn't on the road—too open, too visible, nowhere to disappear if headlights appeared behind them.

The road widened abruptly, gravel spreading into something like a clearing. A rusted mailbox crouched in the weeds at the edge of it, its paint long gone, its metal bowed inward as if struck once and never repaired. The lettering clung stubbornly to the surface, flaking but still legible.

M. RIVERS

"My brother," Suzanne said before Jonathan could ask. Her voice sounded different when she said it. Distant. Measured. "Matthew."

Jonathan glanced at her. "Do you talk to him?"

"No."

The answer came too quickly.

Jonathan waited, then asked, "Why not?"

Suzanne swallowed. The farm appeared ahead, emerging slowly through the rain like something reluctant to be seen. "Because he stopped answering," she said finally. "And because sometimes silence is a choice."

The farm stood exactly where memory said it would—but it felt smaller than she remembered. A sagging barn leaned into the wind, its boards dark with moisture, its roof dipping unevenly. The farmhouse sat back from the road, paint peeling in wide curls, porch slumped forward as if exhausted by its own weight.

Time had tried to bury it.

It hadn't succeeded.

Fields rolled out in every direction, unbroken and empty, grass shifting under the wind like something alive. No lights. No neighboring houses. No fence lines beyond the property itself.

Jonathan leaned forward slightly. "It looks empty."

"It is," Suzanne said. "Matt signed it over before he left."

Jonathan turned that over in his head. "Is he dead?"

Suzanne hesitated, the silence stretching just long enough to matter.

"…I don't know."

She pulled the sedan to a stop near the porch. The engine ticked loudly as it cooled, the sudden quiet after it shut off almost disorienting. Rain whispered against the roof. Pain flared up her leg from the crash—a sharp reminder she'd been ignoring too long.

Jonathan noticed immediately.

"You're limping," he said, reaching for her.

"I'm okay," Suzanne said, lying without hesitation. "We just need to get inside."

A key waited beneath the mat, exactly where Matthew had insisted it always be. Suzanne bent stiffly to retrieve it, her knee protesting. The lock resisted for a moment, then turned with a sound like something old waking up.

The door creaked open.

Stale air drifted out—dust, old wood, and something spent. The smell of abandonment.

Inside, the house exhaled around them.

Furniture lay draped in yellowed sheets. Floors groaned beneath each step, not in warning, but acknowledgment. A cold fireplace sagged beneath its own ash, blackened stones stained by years of disuse.

Suzanne locked the door behind them.

The sound didn't make them safe.

It only slowed her breathing.

Jonathan wandered the living room cautiously, fingers brushing the edge of a sheet as if testing whether the furniture beneath it was real. "Did Uncle Matt live here alone?"

"For a while," Suzanne said. She set Henry's satchel on the counter, the weight of it grounding her. "After his wife left, he shut down."

"How long are we staying?"

Suzanne brushed damp hair from Jonathan's forehead, the contact lingering. "As long as it takes."

"To be safe?"

She hesitated.

"To be free."

The word hung between them, fragile and unproven.

Outside, shutters rattled as a gust pushed through the fields. Inside, the house answered with creaks and settling sounds, like an old animal shifting its weight.

They slept poorly that first night.

The house was loud in the way abandoned places always were—boards popping, pipes whispering, wind threading through cracks that daylight would later reveal. Jonathan lay awake beneath a knitted blanket, listening for tires on gravel, for the low hum of engines that never came.

Suzanne lay on the couch with her eyes open, every sense tuned outward.

Morning came gray and thin.

Suzanne moved through the house like a ghost—curtains closed, windows boarded, locks checked twice. She catalogued rooms with practiced efficiency. Kitchen. Pantry. Bedrooms. Cellar access. Barn.

Jonathan followed her quietly, absorbing routines without instruction.

Water jugs were filled. Food was sorted. Flashlights tested. Batteries counted.

They didn't talk about the crash.

Or the men.

Or what was happening inside him.

By the seventh day, Suzanne left once—back roads, cash only, eyes down. She returned with groceries and bruised knuckles from gripping the wheel too tightly.

Jonathan waited at the window until the sedan came back into view.

By the tenth, a rhythm formed.

Jonathan swept the porch each morning, the repetitive motion calming him. He walked the fence line at dusk, counting posts, memorizing breaks in the wire. Barn cats appeared and vanished like spirits; he fed them scraps without naming them.

He found an old slingshot in the barn loft and checked it every night before bed, inspecting the bands with care.

Suzanne cleaned room by room. One morning, Jonathan found her staring at a photograph tucked inside a drawer—Suzanne, Matthew, and a woman he didn't know. The edges were curled from handling. Suzanne turned it face-down without comment and walked away. Some stories were traps.

Near midnight one night, Jonathan heard it. A faint metallic hum beneath the floorboards. Irregular. Almost like a heartbeat. He pressed his palm to the wood. The hum steadied. Then faded.

Jonathan lay still for a long time afterward, listening to the silence settle back into place. He didn't tell Suzanne. She had enough to fear.

Suzanne kept a notebook hidden beneath the cutlery drawer. Not a diary. A plan. Cash totals. Back roads. Hiding places. Risk notes.

At the top of one page, written three times:

IF THEY FIND US — RUN

Jonathan saw it once.

He didn't ask.

They weren't building a life here.

They were building a pause.

And both of them knew—sooner or later—that Pause would end.

CHAPTER 21 — THE WEIGHT OF IT

The knife lay where Suzanne had set it—centered on the scarred kitchen table, catching the light like a held breath.

She had not meant to place it so deliberately. The table had been cluttered moments before—maps, a folded towel, the edge of the notebook she kept hidden beneath the cutlery drawer. But when she set the knife down, everything else had moved away from it, as if the room itself understood that this object demanded space.

Jonathan stood across from it, hands tucked beneath his arms. He didn't touch it yet. He only watched, as if the thing might move on its own.

The farm kitchen felt different with it there.

Not dangerous.

Not threatening.

Present.

"That was your dad's," Suzanne said quietly. "He carried it every day."

The words landed with more weight than she intended. Every day meant before work and after. Meant in pockets and in hands, in moments of routine and moments of emergency. Meant it had been there when she hadn't.

Jonathan nodded. His eyes didn't leave the blade.

"It feels… heavy," he said.

"It is."

Suzanne knew immediately he wasn't talking about the metal.

Not just the brass worn smooth by use. Not just the hinge that resisted slightly before giving. The weight lived somewhere deeper—behind the eyes, under the ribs. The same place grief had taken up residence. The same place responsibility nested when it arrived too early.

Suzanne recognized it.

She had been carrying it since the phone rang.

Jonathan reached out and closed his fingers around the handle.

The brass was warm.

He flinched—not in pain, but recognition. Something in him responded before thought could catch up. His shoulders eased. His breathing slowed.

Something settled, like a piece sliding into place where it didn't belong.

Suzanne watched his hand closely.

The tremor that usually lived there—the fine, constant vibration she had learned to track out of the corner of her eye—was gone.

"You okay?" she asked.

Jonathan swallowed. "It feels like… him."

The words caught her off guard. She felt them strike somewhere beneath her sternum, sharp and immediate.

Jonathan turned the knife slowly. The blade was nicked. Honest. Used. Not decorative. Henry had never trusted new things. He trusted what survived work, what showed proof of endurance.

Jonathan pressed his thumb to the hinge, careful, reverent. The blade opened with a soft click that sounded too loud in the quiet house.

Suzanne's breath caught.

The sound echoed longer than it should have, vibrating faintly in the wood beneath the table, in the hollow spaces of the house that never quite felt empty.

Jonathan studied the edge—not fascination, not fear. Focus.

The same expression he wore when he concentrated too hard, when the world narrowed and everything else faded away. Suzanne had seen it during homework, during puzzles, during moments when he withdrew so completely she worried he might disappear inside himself.

"Dad said weapons aren't bad," Jonathan murmured. "People are."

Suzanne closed her eyes.

"Yes," she said. "He did."

Henry had believed that fiercely. That objects carried intent only when guided by hands. That responsibility belonged to the person, not the thing. It had been one of the few absolutes he'd trusted.

Jonathan folded the blade again and held it flat in his palm. His breathing changed—slow, even.

Too even.

Suzanne noticed.

She always noticed.

"Jonathan," she said gently, "how do you feel?"

He didn't answer right away.

She could see him searching—turning inward, testing sensations the way he now tested pain and pressure, cataloguing responses that didn't behave the way they used to.

"Calm," he said finally.

The word frightened her more than panic ever could.

Calm meant alignment.

Calm meant certainty.

Calm meant something had stopped resisting.

Jonathan slipped the knife into the pocket of Henry's jacket and pulled the fabric tight around it, anchoring it there. The weight settled against his ribs, noticeable but reassuring.

Then he looked up at her—young again, frightened again.

"I don't want to hurt anyone," he said.

"I know."

"But if they come," he added, quieter, "I don't want to be helpless."

Suzanne crossed the room and took his face in her hands.

"You are not a weapon," she said. "You hear me? You're a boy who survived something terrible."

She made him hold her gaze.

"You don't owe the world proof of anything."

Jonathan nodded.

But his eyes flicked to the pocket where the knife rested. Where the weight lived. Where certainty waited.

Suzanne let her hands fall.

She could not take it from him—not without taking something else with it. She felt that instinctively. The knife was no longer just an object. It was a boundary. A promise. A line Jonathan needed in order to feel real again.

That night, the wind worried the eaves and the barn cats cried somewhere beyond the dark. The sounds carried differently now—less startling, more textured. Jonathan lay awake with one hand tucked inside the jacket, fingers wrapped around the handle.

The metal was cool.

Steady.

The hum came again—faint, metallic, threaded through his bones.

This time, it didn't scare him.

It steadied.

He breathed with it, unconsciously syncing his pulse to the rhythm beneath his skin. He did not think about what it meant. He did not question where it came from. It simply was—a presence he could orient himself around.

In the other room, Suzanne sat at the table with the notebook open, staring at the words she'd written days ago.

IF THEY FIND US — RUN.

She traced the letters with her finger, not reading them so much as feeling their shape. Plans were easier than fear. Lists were easier than uncertainty. Movement was easier than waiting.

Henry's knife hadn't made Jonathan dangerous.

It had made him certain.

And certainty, Suzanne knew, was the heaviest thing a child could carry. And now that he's ten he felt less like a child and more like, something else.

CHAPTER 22 — SETTLING

The town didn't announce itself.

It appeared slowly—after miles of fields and silos and roads that forgot their own names. A gas station with one pump. A diner with hand-painted hours. A post office no larger than a shed.

Jonathan noticed the quiet first.

Not the tense quiet of hiding, or the brittle silence of waiting—but the kind that came from distance. From places the world had learned to pass by.

It wasn't empty. It was simply unclaimed.

The air felt wider here. Less crowded. Sounds carried farther but meant less. A truck downshifted somewhere beyond sight. A dog barked once and then stopped. No sirens. No layered noise bleeding in from unseen roads.

Suzanne felt it too.

She hadn't realized how tightly she'd been holding herself until her shoulders dropped without permission. The road narrowed as they passed the town limits—no sign, no marker—just a change in pavement and the sense that they had slipped sideways into something smaller.

They rented a small house on the edge of town, just beyond the last line of mailboxes. One story. White siding. A porch that sagged a little in the middle. The landlord didn't ask many questions. Cash helped.

He'd barely looked at Jonathan.

That mattered more than Suzanne wanted to admit.

"This is temporary," Suzanne said, unlocking the door.

She said it the way people said things they needed to believe.

Jonathan nodded, but his eyes tracked the space the way someone measured something they might stay in longer than planned. He noted exits first. Windows second. The distance between the front door and the back.

Old habits didn't disappear just because the scenery changed.

The house smelled like old paint and sun-warmed dust. There were two bedrooms. A narrow kitchen. Windows that looked out on nothing but grass and sky.

The sky felt enormous.

Jonathan stood at the window longer than necessary, watching clouds drift without purpose. He waited for the familiar tightening in his chest.

It didn't come.

No neighbors close enough to watch.

That mattered.

The first few days passed gently.

Too gently.

Suzanne kept waiting for interruption—for a knock, a call, a car that slowed too long—but nothing broke the rhythm. Morning arrived without urgency. Afternoons stretched in a way that felt almost indulgent.

Jonathan helped unpack. Swept the porch. Learned the rhythm of the place.

He learned which floorboards complained and which stayed silent. He learned that the back door stuck unless you lifted slightly. He learned where the porch sagged enough to creak under weight.

Mornings came with birds he didn't recognize. Their calls were sharper, more deliberate, as if they knew exactly what they were saying.

Jonathan listened carefully.

Afternoons stretched without interruption. No appointments. No monitoring. No voices layered with expectation.

At night, the dark arrived honestly—no streetlights, no distant engines. When the sun went down, it meant something.

Suzanne cooked real meals again.

The act felt foreign at first, like returning to a language she hadn't spoken in years. Simple things. Eggs. Soup. Bread that came from the local bakery and tasted like it had been made by someone who knew who they were feeding.

Jonathan ate.

Not much. But enough.

Suzanne noticed he didn't flinch at sudden sounds here. A cupboard closing. A pan touching the stove. His shoulders stayed where they were.

That frightened her almost as much as it relieved her.

On the fourth day, Suzanne took him into town.

The diner was quiet except for an older couple sharing coffee and a waitress who smiled without curiosity. Jonathan sat stiffly at first, back straight, feet tucked in. He watched reflections in the window instead of faces.

No one stared.

No one whispered.

No one knew him.

The absence of attention pressed in gently, like a blanket rather than a weight.

When the waitress brought his pancakes, she asked, "You new here?"

Jonathan glanced at Suzanne.

"Just passing through," Suzanne said.

"That's how most people are," the woman replied easily. "Some stay."

She said it without implication.

Jonathan cut into the pancakes. Syrup pooled. Nothing happened.

No hum. No tightening. No shift beneath his skin.

He took another bite.

After that, routines formed.

Routines were dangerous. Suzanne knew that. They made roots before you realized they were growing.

But they also made breathing possible.

Suzanne found work cleaning cabins at a lakeside campground. The owner paid cash and didn't ask why she preferred early mornings and late afternoons. Jonathan walked the dirt road in the evenings, counting fence posts, learning where the ground dipped and where it held.

He learned the land the way he'd learned rooms before—by mapping it with his body.

The hum stayed quiet.

Not gone.

Just distant. Like something sleeping.

Sometimes Jonathan tested it without meaning to. He pressed his palm to the fence wire. He stood barefoot on the cold floor in the mornings.

Nothing surged.

Nothing answered.

At night, Jonathan lay in bed listening to crickets and wind instead of engines. The knife stayed tucked in Henry's jacket, untouched.

Suzanne checked that pocket every night without waking him.

Some evenings, she let herself imagine it.

School here. A name that didn't mean anything to anyone. A childhood that resumed—not healed, but paused long enough to breathe.

She hated herself for wanting it.

One afternoon, Jonathan came back from town with a brown paper sack.

"I met a kid," he said.

Suzanne froze.

Her body reacted before her thoughts caught up. Her hands stilled. Her breathing changed.

"Where?" she asked.

"Outside the hardware store," he said quickly. "He was fixing his bike. He didn't ask anything."

"What's his name?"

"Evan."

The name sat between them.

"And?" Suzanne asked carefully.

"He just talked about the creek," Jonathan said. "And fishing. And how the winters get bad."

Suzanne watched his face.

He looked... normal.

Not guarded. Not braced. Curious in a way she hadn't seen since before the lab.

That night, she sat on the porch alone after Jonathan went to bed. The sky stretched open above her, stars sharp and unbothered. She breathed in cold air and let the tension ease, just a fraction.

The quiet here wasn't empty.

It was patient.

Maybe this place was small enough.

Maybe the world had already moved on.

Inside, Jonathan slept deeply for the first time since the lab.

His breathing was slow. Even. Dreamless.

The hum didn't wake him. And for a little while, nothing followed them.

CHAPTER 23 — THE SLIP

The morning was ordinary.

Too ordinary.

That was what unsettled Jonathan most—the way the day unfolded without resistance, as if the world had decided to pretend nothing was wrong. A soft breeze moved through the fields, bending the tall grass in slow, rhythmic waves. Sunlight warmed the fence posts, lifting the damp chill left behind by night. Somewhere in the distance, a bird called out, sharp and brief, then went silent again.

Jonathan worked the fence line alone, hammer resting in his palm, nails lined up neatly on the rail beside him. Suzanne had wanted to come with him, but he'd insisted. The work was simple. Repetitive. Honest. It gave his hands something to do that didn't involve hiding.

He hummed under his breath as he worked—an old tune he barely remembered learning, something his father used to whistle when fixing things around the house. Sweat darkened the collar of his shirt. Dirt smudged his knuckles.

Nothing felt dangerous.

That was why it happened.

The hammer slipped.

CRACK.

The sound was sharp and final, too loud in the open air. A splinter tore loose from the board and drove deep into Jonathan's palm. Pain flared—bright and immediate, the kind that stole breath before thought could catch up. Blood welled between his fingers, warm and fast.

Jonathan gasped and clenched his hand.

For a moment, it hurt.

That moment mattered.

Pain anchored him to the present, to his body, to the ordinary rules of cause and effect. He clung to it desperately, pressing his injured hand against his chest as if that might hold the world steady.

Then the hum rose.

Low. Familiar. Wrong.

It didn't arrive suddenly. It seeped in, threading itself through his nerves, vibrating beneath his skin. The sound wasn't really sound—it was sensation, pressure, something internal aligning itself without permission.

"No," he whispered. "Not now."

The bleeding slowed.

Jonathan felt it before he saw it—the way the heat shifted, the way the pain dulled too quickly. His fingers tingled. The skin around the wound tightened, drawing inward. The splinter worked its way free, nudged out as if rejected.

The wound began to close.

Jonathan's heart slammed against his ribs.

He shoved his hand into his sleeve, breath coming too fast, pulse roaring in his ears. Panic bloomed sharp and immediate, crowding out everything else.

As long as no one saw—

"Hey there!"

Jonathan froze.

The voice came from behind him, cheerful and unguarded. Boots scuffed against dirt. A shadow stretched across the grass.

Mr. Caldwell crossed the field with a feed sack slung over one shoulder, his gait relaxed, unhurried. He waved casually, smiling in a way that carried no suspicion at all. The timing was perfect in the worst possible way.

"Morning, kid," Caldwell called. "Brought that rye mix your mama asked for."

"She's inside," Jonathan said quickly.

His voice sounded strange to his own ears—too tight, pitched just slightly wrong. He forced himself to breathe evenly, keeping his injured hand hidden inside his sleeve, pressed tight against his side.

Caldwell slowed as he drew closer. His gaze dropped, drawn by something he couldn't have named if asked.

Blood streaked Jonathan's wrist.

A thin red line, already fading.

"You hurt yourself?" Caldwell asked.

Jonathan stepped back instinctively. "It's nothing."

Caldwell frowned. Concern sharpened his expression. "Let me see."

"No."

The word came out too fast. Too loud.

Jonathan shifted his weight—and his sleeve slipped.

Just an inch.

Just enough.

Caldwell saw the wound.

Saw the torn flesh.

Saw the blood—

—and watched it disappear.

Skin pulled together in real time. The raw edges sealed smoothly, knitting themselves closed as if guided by invisible hands. Red faded, drawn backward beneath the surface until nothing remained but faint warmth and an almost imperceptible scar that vanished seconds later.

Caldwell stopped breathing.

His mouth opened, but no sound came out at first. His eyes widened, pupils blown, mind scrambling for explanations that wouldn't form.

"What…" His voice cracked. "What did I just see?"

Jonathan's stomach dropped.

Cold flooded his chest, sinking heavy and fast.

"Please," he said. The word broke in the middle. "Please don't—"

Caldwell stumbled back as if struck.

"That ain't possible," he whispered. "People don't heal like that."

Jonathan reached for him without thinking, one step forward, instinct overriding caution. "I didn't mean to—"

Caldwell recoiled violently, nearly dropping the feed sack.

"No," he said hoarsely. "No, I can't pretend I didn't see that."

His breathing came shallow and fast. He took another step back. Then another.

"Something's wrong," he muttered, shaking his head. "Something's wrong, and folks need to know."

"Please," Jonathan begged.

The word tore out of him now, raw and unfiltered. He grabbed at Caldwell's sleeve, desperation flooding his voice. "Please don't tell anyone. I didn't ask for this. I'm not—"

Caldwell yanked his arm free.

Fear overtook reason.

He turned—

and ran.

Jonathan stood alone in the field, chest heaving, sleeve clenched tight around a hand that was already whole again. The hammer lay forgotten in the grass. The fence line stretched out unfinished, innocent, uncaring.

The breeze returned.

The quiet settled back in.

But it wasn't the same.

Something had shifted. Something had slipped.

Ray Caldwell didn't tell anyone right away.

He drove home because his hands wouldn't stop shaking. Because the image wouldn't loosen its grip, no matter how many times he replayed it. Because reality, as he understood it, had cracked clean through.

He pulled into his driveway too fast and cut the engine without thinking. Sat there gripping the steering wheel until his knuckles went white.

People didn't heal like that.

They just didn't.

His wife took one look at his face when he came through the door and knew something was wrong.

"What happened?" she asked.

Ray opened his mouth to deny it. To say nothing. To laugh it off.

The words spilled anyway.

Halting. Fragmented. Precise in the way truth often was when it refused to be softened. He told her about the fence. The splinter. The blood. The way the wound had closed like it had never been there.

She tried to explain it away.

Shock. Adrenaline. Bad light. A trick of the eye.

Ray shook his head.

"I saw it," he said. "I know what I saw."

She didn't call the sheriff. She didn't laugh. She didn't argue.

She only said, very quietly, "Be careful who you tell."

Fear doesn't listen to advice.

That night, Ray stopped at the corner store. Fluorescent lights hummed overhead. A bell chimed as the door opened. Familiar faces nodded in passing.

Someone asked how things were going out by the old farm.

Ray hesitated.

Then said one sentence too many.

"Something's wrong with that boy out there."

The words felt heavier the moment they left his mouth.

By morning, two people knew.

By evening, eight.

By the end of the week, the story had teeth.

It changed shape as it traveled—smoothed in some places, sharpened in others. Details blurred. Meaning crystallized.

A boy who heals. A miracle.

Some say an abomination, something unnatural.

Something that shouldn't exist.

And somewhere far beyond the fields, beyond the town that barely appeared on maps, someone heard it—

and understood exactly what it meant.

For the first time in two years,

Jonathan and Suzanne were no longer hidden.

CHAPTER 24 — THE UNRAVELING

Suzanne sensed something was wrong before anyone said a word.

It began with looks.

Not the open curiosity she had learned to tolerate, not the passing glances that came with being new in a small place—but looks that lingered a fraction too long, eyes that slid away only after they'd taken inventory. At Turner's Market, two women paused mid-conversation as Suzanne passed, their voices thinning into silence that felt deliberate rather than polite. At the gas pump, a man she didn't recognize nodded once, then watched her reflection in the truck window instead of meeting her eyes.

Small towns always talked.

But this wasn't gossip yet.

This was calibration.

Jonathan felt it too.

Behind Turner's Market, while they loaded feed into the truck, he kept his eyes down and his shoulders drawn tight, listening in that way he did now. Suzanne recognized it instantly—the subtle stillness, the way his body arranged itself to absorb information without inviting attention. The look hollowed her stomach every time she saw it.

He wasn't nervous.

He was tracking.

Heartbeats spiked when they walked past certain people. Voices dropped or sharpened at the edge of hearing. The unconscious adjustments people made when fear entered the equation—stance widening, breath shortening, words choosing safer paths.

Jonathan felt all of it.

His senses weren't just sharper.

They were reaching.

Inside the store, the air felt thicker than it had the week before. Flour dust hung in the sunlight slanting through the windows, motes drifting slowly, suspended. Suzanne placed the bag on the counter and slid cash across without looking down, already scanning the room by instinct.

That was when she heard it.

"…that poor woman doesn't even know what's wrong with that boy…"

Mrs. Harper's voice—soft, precise, unmistakable.

Suzanne's body reacted before her mind did. Her fingers tightened around the counter edge as if bracing against a blow.

"What do you mean?" another woman murmured.

"It's just what Ray Caldwell said," Harper replied lightly, the way people spoke when they wanted to sound reasonable. "Something strange happened out on their property. Something… unnatural."

Suzanne's breath left her all at once.

The word unnatural carried weight. It didn't describe an event—it condemned it.

She grabbed Jonathan's wrist and pulled him toward the door hard enough that he stumbled.

"Mom—?"

"Get in the truck."

Her voice left no space for argument.

They tore out of the lot in a spray of gravel, tires biting too hard, engine revving louder than necessary. Jonathan watched her hands whiten around the steering wheel, the muscles in her forearms standing out sharply.

"What happened?" he asked.

"Someone talked," she said quietly.

Jonathan swallowed. He already knew the answer before he asked the next question.

"Mr. Caldwell?"

Suzanne didn't answer.

She didn't have to.

The drive home felt exposed. Fields stretched wide on either side, beautiful and merciless in their openness. Jonathan watched every passing vehicle, every dust plume on the horizon, cataloguing movement the way he once catalogued fence posts.

When they reached the farm, Suzanne parked closer to the house than usual. She locked the truck immediately after they got out, even though the keys were still warm in her hand.

Neither of them spoke.

They didn't need to.

Dusk settled heavy and slow, the sky bruising purple and gold, the fields darkening until they felt less like shelter and more like a stage. Suzanne had just finished bolting the back door when headlights appeared at the end of the drive.

Beige.

Low.

Unthreatening.

Suzanne knew the shape of it immediately.

Mrs. Lorne climbed out slowly, hands folded tight in front of her, her posture worried rather than curious. She waited by the car for a moment, as if deciding whether she should be here at all.

Jonathan hovered behind Suzanne in the doorway, silent, his presence more felt than seen.

"I thought you should know," Mrs. Lorne said gently when Suzanne opened the door. "People are stirring things up in town."

Suzanne's heart stuttered. "About what?"

The woman hesitated, glancing past Suzanne toward the interior of the house. "Ray Caldwell's been saying he saw your boy get hurt. Bad. And heal right in front of him."

Jonathan went rigid.

Suzanne felt it—the way his body locked, the way the air between them tightened.

Mrs. Lorne noticed. Her expression softened rather than hardened, which somehow made it worse.

"Stories grow when folks are scared," she added, as if that explained everything.

"What are they saying about me?" Jonathan asked.

His voice was thin but steady, stretched tight across fear.

"Oh, sweetheart," Mrs. Lorne said softly. "They don't know what they're talking about."

But fear didn't need facts.

Fear only needed repetition.

Before she left, Mrs. Lorne squeezed Suzanne's arm, her grip brief but sincere. "Be careful. When people don't understand something, they look for someone else to decide what to do with it."

Suzanne nodded once.

After the car disappeared down the drive, silence returned—but it wasn't empty anymore.

Jonathan stood beside her on the porch, the fields open and dark, the wind flattening grass in slow, sweeping motions that offered no cover at all.

"We have to leave," he said.

Suzanne didn't argue.

She nodded once. "Possibly."

The word felt like a lie even as she said it.

Then, quieter—truer—

"Very possibly."

Jonathan didn't relax.

He had already moved past possibility in his mind.

That night, the farm felt too exposed. Sounds carried farther than they should have. Every creak of the house felt amplified, every distant bark or engine note landing sharper against Jonathan's awareness.

The hum stirred beneath it all.

Low.

Uneven.

Like something waking.

Jonathan lay awake listening to it thread through his bones, no longer frightened by the sensation itself—only by what it meant. The hum wasn't reacting to injury anymore.

It was reacting to attention.

In the kitchen, Suzanne opened the notebook she'd been pretending not to keep. Her handwriting was tight, compressed, as if space itself were running out.

She added one new line beneath the others.

IF THEY START TALKING — LEAVE IMMEDIATELY

She stared at the words until they blurred.

The unraveling hadn't begun with a siren or a knock or a demand.

It had begun with a story.

And stories, once loose, never stopped moving.

CHAPTER 25 — THE LAST QUIET YEAR

Jonathan turned thirteen quietly.

It passed without ceremony, without announcement, without the kind of marking that made a day feel important. No party. No guests. No candles. Just a morning that arrived like any other, thin sunlight cutting across the kitchen floor, the sound of Suzanne moving through the house with careful efficiency. Jonathan woke with the sense that something had shifted, though nothing around him looked different. His body felt longer somehow, heavier at the joints, as if it had stretched during the night and not yet decided what shape it meant to keep.

Suzanne hugged him once before breakfast, her arms firm, her cheek pressed briefly against the top of his head. The embrace lingered a fraction longer than necessary, long enough for him to register the tension in her shoulders, the way her breath caught before she let him go. She smiled afterward, but the smile did not linger. It never did anymore.

He turned fourteen under pressure.

That birthday arrived with weight behind it, with something coiled tight beneath the surface of the day. Jonathan woke before dawn, heart already beating faster than it needed to, his body reacting to something his mind could not fully name. The air felt denser. Sounds carried farther. The house seemed to hold its breath along with him. He lay still in bed, listening to the quiet, measuring it, already aware that it was not the same quiet he had known before.

Between those birthdays stretched a year that felt both endless and fleeting—the last year the world allowed them to pretend.

Time did something strange during that year. Days blurred together, long afternoons folding into each other, while weeks vanished without warning. Jonathan learned that something could feel slow and fast at the same time, that you could live inside moments that dragged and still look back and find them gone. He did not have language for it yet, but he felt the compression, the way life seemed to be narrowing without actually moving.

Spring came, and the rumors thinned. The looks faded. The questions stopped. Life settled back into place.

Almost.

Spring brought thawed ground and the smell of damp earth. Snow receded into dark patches beneath trees, then disappeared altogether. Neighbors returned to routines, to small talk, to concerns that felt safe and ordinary. Jonathan noticed the way people looked at him less often now, how conversations no longer stalled when he entered a room. It was not relief exactly, but it resembled it closely enough to be mistaken for the real thing.

Suzanne planted a larger garden. Jonathan helped her dig the rows, taller now, broader through the shoulders, childhood receding faster than either of them wanted to admit.

The work was steady and physical, the kind that grounded him in his body. The shovel bit into soil still cold from winter, each thrust sending a dull vibration up his arms. Suzanne moved methodically beside him, her motions practiced, her breathing controlled. She spoke little while they worked. Jonathan noticed how often she paused to scan the tree line, how her gaze lingered at the fence before returning to the earth at her feet.

His hands were larger now. He saw it when he wrapped them around the handle of the shovel, the knuckles more pronounced, veins beginning to stand out beneath the skin. Suzanne noticed too. He could feel it in the way she watched him when she thought he was not looking, in the way her eyes traced the shape of him as if committing it to memory.

One afternoon he asked, "Do you think we'll ever stop running?"

They had stopped working for the day, dirt under their nails, the sun sinking lower behind the trees. Suzanne stood with her hands braced on her hips, chest rising and falling as she caught her breath. The question landed between them without force, but it stayed there, heavy and unmoving.

"I hope so," Suzanne said.

Her voice was even. Too even. Jonathan had learned to hear the spaces beneath her words, the places where truth pressed up against restraint.

"But do you believe it?"

Suzanne did not answer right away. She looked out over the rows they had planted, over the property beyond, over the trees that ringed the land like a boundary and a warning. Her jaw tightened. The silence stretched long enough for Jonathan to feel the answer forming without sound.

Her silence answered him.

Summer stretched long and heavy.

Heat settled into everything, thick and unmoving. Days expanded under the sun, cicadas buzzing until the air itself seemed to vibrate. Jonathan spent more time outside, his body restless, drawn toward open space. He moved through the property with a confidence that was new and unsettling, as if some part of him had begun mapping the land in ways he did not consciously direct.

Jonathan wandered farther across the property, sat longer by the creek, listened to sounds he never named.

The creek became a place of quiet concentration. Water slid over stones in patterns that repeated without repeating exactly. Jonathan found himself sitting still for long stretches, eyes closed, cataloging the subtle shifts in sound. Sometimes he could feel the hum before he heard it, a faint vibration that settled into his bones and lingered there. It did not frighten him. It did not comfort him either. It simply existed, and his body responded as if it always had.

He didn't tell Suzanne about the distant hums, or the way the world sometimes arranged itself into patterns he nearly understood.

There were moments when things seemed to align—light, sound, movement—into something almost recognizable. Not meaning exactly, but structure. Jonathan would sense it and then lose it, like a word on the tip of his tongue. He learned not to chase it. Chasing made it vanish faster.

Suzanne, meanwhile, grew thinner at the edges.

Jonathan noticed it in pieces at first. The way her clothes hung looser. The way she paused mid-task as if her body had briefly forgotten what came next. Headaches lingered. Fatigue clung. He watched her rub her temples in the evenings, watched her hands tremble slightly when she lifted a glass of water. She brushed off his concern every time, but her reassurances sounded rehearsed.

Jonathan noticed everything.

"You don't have to protect me all the time," he said once.

They were sitting at the kitchen table, the house quiet except for the ticking clock on the wall. Suzanne had been watching the window, eyes unfocused, attention somewhere beyond the glass.

"Yes," she replied quietly. "I do."

There was no apology in her voice. No hesitation. Just certainty, edged with something that felt like resolve.

Autumn arrived with signs they couldn't ignore.

The air cooled, leaves beginning to turn at the edges. Jonathan felt the shift in his body before he saw it in the trees. The world sharpened. Sounds carried cleaner. He became aware of absence as much as presence, of things out of place.

Tire tracks near the fence. A cut branch where no one should have walked. Evidence without explanation.

Jonathan found the tracks first, lines pressed into soft earth where no vehicle had reason to be. He crouched to examine them, fingers hovering just above the ground, his skin prickling with awareness. The cut branch came later, clean and deliberate, not the work of weather or animals. Suzanne did not ask how he noticed so quickly. She did not need to.

One night Jonathan found Suzanne hunched over a map, tracing routes with her finger.

The light was low, the house dark except for the lamp over the table. The map was worn, creased from use, its edges soft. Suzanne's finger moved slowly, deliberately, pausing at intersections, sliding along back roads. She did not startle when Jonathan entered the room.

"In case," she told him.

Her voice was steady, but her shoulders were tight, her posture guarded.

"In case of what?"

Suzanne's finger stopped. She lifted her hand from the map, folding it carefully as if the paper itself might betray them.

"In case the world remembers us."

Winter came early.

Cold arrived with sudden force, frost clinging to the ground before autumn had fully finished. Snow followed soon after, light at first, then heavier, muffling sound. Jonathan felt the quiet deepen, but it was no longer the quiet he had wished for. It was weighted now, expectant.

They celebrated Jonathan's fifteenth birthday with two candles and banana bread.

The bread was still warm when Suzanne set it on the table, the smell filling the kitchen. Two candles stood close together, their flames small but steady. Jonathan watched them flicker, aware of how easily they could be extinguished. He made a wish without words, without shape, something closer to a feeling than a thought.

He leaned into her embrace longer than he meant to, as if memorizing the shape of it.

Suzanne's arms wrapped around him tightly, her chin resting against his shoulder. Jonathan closed his eyes, focusing on the feel of her heartbeat, the familiar rhythm beneath her ribs. He knew, without knowing how, that this moment mattered. That it was something he would return to later.

He wished for the quiet to hold.

It didn't.

Strange vehicles passed too often.

Jonathan noticed them first, the way they moved through the area without purpose, slowing near the property before continuing on. He learned their sounds, the differences in engine pitch, the way tires hissed on cold pavement.

A faint drone buzzed overhead.

The sound was easy to dismiss, high and distant, but Jonathan felt it settle into his awareness like an itch he could not scratch. It lingered longer than it should have, appeared more often than coincidence allowed.

The mailbox hung open one morning, the latch bent.

Jonathan stood beside it for a long moment, cold biting at his fingers, studying the damage. Suzanne joined him without speaking. Neither of them touched it.

Neither of them spoke of it.

Silence became a language of its own, full of meaning and restraint. They moved through the house carefully, deliberately, each aware of the other without comment. Preparation happened quietly. Important things were kept close.

On the final night of the year, they stood together on the porch, snow drifting through the porch light.

The light cast a soft circle around them, flakes passing through it like slow-moving stars. Jonathan breathed in the cold air, his senses wide open, cataloging everything—the stillness, the faint creak of the porch boards, the distant sound of wind moving through trees.

"Do you think Uncle Matt would like me?" Jonathan asked.

The question rose unexpectedly, pulled from somewhere deep and unguarded. Suzanne did not answer immediately. She turned to face him fully, her eyes searching his.

"He would have loved you," Suzanne said. "No matter what."

Jonathan swallowed, the words settling heavily in his chest.

"Even if I'm not normal?"

Suzanne placed her hand over his heart.

Her palm was warm through his shirt, steady and sure.

"You are my son."

The words were simple. Final. They anchored him more firmly than anything else could have.

Jonathan leaned into her shoulder.

He felt the tension in her body, the readiness beneath the calm. He did not pull away.

Neither of them knew it was the last night of peace.

The last night the farmhouse would remain untouched.

The last night before the world came back for them.

CHAPTER 26 — A CRACK IN THE PLAN

Winter locked the farm beneath a silent, frozen shell.

It arrived without drama, without warning, the way real things always did. One night the ground was bare and dark, and the next morning it lay sealed beneath white, smooth and unbroken, as if the land itself had been erased and rewritten. Snow clung to fence posts and sagged along the barn roof. The creek slowed beneath a skin of ice, its voice reduced to a distant, patient murmur. Even the wind seemed careful, moving through the trees without urgency.

Snow softened every sound, dimmed every color, and wrapped the world in a quiet so complete it felt sacred.

The quiet pressed inward, wrapping the farmhouse like insulation. It dampened distance, blurred edges, erased footprints almost as soon as they were made. Jonathan noticed how sound traveled differently now—how even his own movements felt muted, as if the world were listening and asking him to be careful in return. He found comfort in it. In the way the snow hid things. In the way it made the land feel sealed off from whatever might be searching.

Jonathan liked it that way—hidden, protected, untouched.

He stood often at the window, watching the slow fall of snowflakes, counting the seconds between sounds. The quiet gave him space to breathe. It gave his senses something clean to rest against. In winter, nothing crept. Nothing whispered. Nothing followed.

But safety had only ever been an illusion.

The thought did not arrive with fear. It arrived as fact. Jonathan had learned the difference.

Jonathan stepped onto the porch to fetch firewood and stopped mid-step.

Cold air rushed around him, sharp and immediate, filling his lungs. His boot hovered above the snow, suspended in instinctive pause before his mind had time to understand why. His body knew first. It always did.

Footprints.

Not his.

Not Suzanne's.

Not animal.

Human.

They stood out against the snow with unnatural clarity, dark impressions pressed deep and clean. Jonathan's eyes traced them automatically, counting, spacing, measuring distance without conscious effort. His breath slowed as his awareness sharpened, everything narrowing to the marks beneath his feet.

Six—maybe seven—impressions marked the snow, each spaced wide and deliberate, as if whoever had made them had been moving carefully. Or quickly.

The prints angled toward the side of the barn, cutting across the open yard where no one had reason to walk. Jonathan felt a faint tightening beneath his ribs, the familiar low hum shifting into something sharper. He followed the line of prints with his gaze, his mind assembling possibilities it did not want to examine too closely.

They led toward the side of the barn.

And then they stopped.

The snow beyond lay smooth and unbroken, untouched by departure or hesitation. Jonathan scanned for disturbance—drag marks, scattered powder, anything that might suggest movement away from the spot. There was nothing. The absence pressed harder than any sign of struggle.

No return tracks.

No broken trail.

No sign of departure.

As if whoever had been there had simply vanished.

Jonathan's breath fogged the air. His pulse thudded in his ears.

The cold sharpened his awareness rather than dulling it. He could feel the vibration beneath the ground, faint but unmistakable, as if something had passed through the space and left residue behind. The silence felt wrong now—not sacred, but alert. Expectant.

Someone had stood here.
Watching.
Waiting.
He felt it in his bones.
In the low hum beneath his skin.
In the way the morning itself seemed to hold its breath.
"Mom," he whispered.
The word barely carried, swallowed by the cold air. He did not turn when he heard movement behind him. He knew it was her before she stepped into view, knew it by the shift in the quiet, by the way the space behind him tightened.
Suzanne stepped onto the porch behind him, rubbing at a headache that hadn't loosened all night.
Her eyes were already narrowed, already searching, already alert despite the pain she had been carrying since before dawn. Jonathan could hear the fatigue in her breathing, the way she compensated for it with control.
She followed his gaze.
Her body went rigid.
The reaction was immediate and complete. Not surprise. Not confusion. Recognition. Jonathan saw it in the way her shoulders locked, the way her weight shifted subtly as if preparing for movement.
For a long moment she didn't speak.
Then, quietly—too evenly—she said, "Don't touch them."
"I wasn't going to," Jonathan murmured.
He had not moved. Had not even finished stepping onto the porch. Some instinct had anchored him in place, held him back from crossing an invisible boundary.

Suzanne drew in a slow breath.

Let it out through tight lips.

"We're not jumping to conclusions," she said. "Could be hunters. Or kids."

The words sounded practiced, chosen for stability rather than truth. Jonathan watched her jaw tighten at the end of the sentence.

"Kids don't disappear," Jonathan said. "There's no return prints."

The statement landed between them, blunt and unavoidable. Jonathan did not raise his voice. He did not need to. The evidence lay at their feet.

She didn't answer.

Suzanne turned back inside and closed the door—not hard, not fast.

Just firmly enough to feel final.

The click of the latch echoed louder than it should have. Jonathan stood still for a moment longer, his breath steady, before following her inside. The warmth of the house closed around them, but it did nothing to ease the tension that had settled into his chest.

That afternoon, Suzanne closed every curtain in the house.

Jonathan noticed the difference immediately. The rooms darkened, the world outside reduced to thin slivers of white where fabric failed to meet. The house felt smaller, tighter, its walls pressing inward. Suzanne moved from window to window with purpose, her hands precise, her expression unreadable.

Not out of habit.

Out of fear.

Jonathan watched as she checked the locks.

Then checked them again.

Each movement was careful, deliberate. She did not rush, but she did not hesitate either. Jonathan followed her from room to room, silent, observing. He noticed the way her fingers trembled when she tested the back door, how she paused afterward as if steadying herself.

She dragged a dresser across the back door, hands shaking despite her care.

The scrape of wood against floorboards cut through the quiet, harsh and final. Suzanne adjusted the angle, pressed it firmly into place, then rested her forehead briefly against the door as if gathering herself.

"Mom?" he said.

His voice sounded too loud in the dim room.

She didn't answer right away.

Jonathan waited, his senses stretched thin, listening to the house, to her breathing, to the faint hum that had not fully receded.

"Are we leaving?"

Suzanne stilled.

Her shoulders lifted, then slowly fell.

"No. Not yet."

"But—"

"We don't run until we know who's out there."

The words carried weight. Not hesitation. Strategy. Jonathan recognized it. He nodded once, though calm already felt like something from another life, something distant and unreachable.

Jonathan nodded, though calm already felt like something from another life.

Evening settled cold and blue around the farmhouse.

The light outside faded quickly, swallowed by thick clouds and falling snow. Shadows deepened inside the house, stretching across walls and floors. Suzanne stirred a thin stew on the stove, the spoon moving in slow, steady circles. Jonathan set bowls on the table, the ordinary rhythm of the task grounding him even as his awareness remained fixed on the world beyond the walls.

Then—

CRACK.

The sound came from the woods behind the house.

It snapped through the quiet with sudden force, sharp and unmistakable. Jonathan froze, ladle suspended midair, stew dripping back into the pot without sound.

Not an animal.

Not a branch.

Something heavier.

The hum beneath his ribs sharpened, urgent, vibrating through him like a warning signal. His heart rate spiked, breath catching as his body prepared for movement.

Suzanne lifted her head.

"You heard it too."

It was not a question.

Jonathan nodded.

Another sound—closer.

The woods seemed to lean inward, the darkness beyond the windows pressing closer to the house. Jonathan's skin prickled, every sense tuned outward.

"Mom," he whispered. "Someone's out there."

Suzanne killed the stove flame with a single twist.

The click echoed loudly. The room fell into deeper shadow.

"Get your coat."

Jonathan's hands moved automatically, pulling fabric over his arms, fingers clumsy with cold and adrenaline.

"Are we running?"

"We're checking."

Jonathan swallowed.

"That's dangerous."

Suzanne tightened her scarf, hands betraying her calm.

"There are worse things than being afraid," she said softly. "Not knowing is one of them."

She cracked the back door open.

Cold rushed in.

Darkness breathed back.

Jonathan felt the shift immediately, the world outside pressing against him, testing boundaries. He stepped closer to Suzanne without thinking, his shoulder nearly brushing hers.

"Stay behind me."

They crossed the yard slowly.

Snow muffled their steps, swallowing sound, leaving only the faint crunch beneath their boots. The farm felt too wide now. Too exposed. Jonathan's awareness stretched across the open space, every shadow carrying weight, every shape suspect.

Jonathan stayed close enough to feel her sleeve brush his arm.

The trees loomed ahead, tall and listening.

Their branches creaked faintly in the wind, snow sliding from limbs in soft cascades. The darkness beneath them felt dense, layered. Jonathan's eyes scanned automatically, his senses reaching outward, mapping space.

Suzanne scanned the shadows.

"Do you see anything?"

Jonathan listened.

To the wind.

To the fields.

To Suzanne's racing heart.

He could hear it, fast and controlled, a rhythm she worked hard to keep steady.

And then—

Something else.

A breath that wasn't human.

A mechanical whisper.

Close.

It threaded through the silence, subtle and precise, raising the fine hairs along Jonathan's arms. His stomach dropped, certainty settling in his chest with cold clarity.

"Mom," Jonathan said urgently. "We need to go back."

She turned.

"What do you hear—"

CLICK.

A sharp, metallic sound snapped from the trees.

Suzanne grabbed his arm.

"Inside. Now."

They ran.

Across the snow.

Across the open yard.

Jonathan's lungs burned as cold air tore through them. His boots slipped once, then found traction. Suzanne's grip on his arm tightened, her pace unrelenting.

Suzanne slammed the door behind them, threw the lock, and braced herself against it, chest heaving.

The sound of the lock sliding home echoed through the house like a verdict.

Jonathan stood frozen beside her, heart hammering.

They didn't speak.

They didn't need to.

The house seemed to hold them, walls thick and close, the outside pressed firmly at bay for the moment. Jonathan listened hard, every nerve alive, waiting for something else—for impact, for sound, for confirmation.

Someone had been watching.

Someone who left no return prints.

Someone who had come back.

The realization settled into Jonathan slowly, not as panic but as grim understanding. Whatever had passed through their land that morning had not been curious. It had not been lost. It had been deliberate.

The quiet year was over.

And whatever came next would take everything.

CHAPTER 27 — THE FIRE HAS BEEN LIT

Blue and red lights tore through the darkness, splintering the farm into frantic color.

The snow became a mirror, reflecting chaos back at itself. Every flash fractured the night, tearing it into pieces too sharp to look at directly. Jonathan squinted against it, vision blurring, not from the light alone but from the way it made everything unreal—like a dream trying too hard to convince him it was awake.

Snow caught the strobes and hurled them back in violent flashes of crimson and cobalt.

Each pulse illuminated a different version of the farm. The barn looked whole in one instant, wounded in the next. The trees seemed to lurch closer, then retreat again, shadows sliding and reforming. Jonathan's breath came in shallow pulls, the cold biting into his lungs without registering as pain.

Engines idled.

The sound vibrated through the ground, low and constant, a mechanical heartbeat that refused to slow. It crawled up through Jonathan's boots and settled into his bones, blending with the hum already there, until he could no longer tell where one ended and the other began.

Radios crackled.

Fragments of voices spilled into the night—codes, names, clipped phrases stripped of emotion. None of it made sense. None of it mattered.

Headlights swept the barn like searching ghosts— restless, unsatisfied.

The military personnel lingered at their stations as Suzanne fired warning shots in the air form the snow covered porch.

She yelled at the group by the barn "Get off my damn property you pieces of shit before I kill all of you!"

She then saw more lights light up and red beams filled up her chest as the barn doors swung open. Just then someone cut across the snow behind her and WHACK! An agent connected hard against her head with his night stick. Suzanne fell quickly forward and hit her head on the corner of the wooden stairs.

Blood came rushing out of her temple as more agents came up.

One screamed" Get me a damn ambulance!" as if it were that easy in this small town. The nearest hospital was over 45 minutes away.

Paramedics knelt beside Suzanne's still form, their movements quick, practiced, urgent.

They worked with efficiency born of repetition, hands moving in synchronized patterns, tools appearing and disappearing. One leaned close to her chest. Another adjusted something Jonathan couldn't see. Their jackets brushed against each other as they shifted positions, blocking and revealing her in fragments.

But Jonathan already knew.

The knowing hadn't arrived with the lights or the sirens. It had settled into him the moment the noise stopped and something inside him went quiet. It was the same certainty he had felt before—when danger came close, when truth pressed in without asking permission.

He had known before they touched her.

Before they checked her pulse.

Before their eyes met over her body and flickered— just for a fraction of a second—with the truth they tried to hide.

Jonathan caught that look. He always caught things like that. The slight pause. The way one man's jaw tightened before he looked away. The way the other inhaled and did not fully exhale.

Her eyes were open.

Jonathan fixated on that detail. The way her gaze stared past the sky, unfocused, unseeing. Snow had gathered in her hair, melting slowly, dampening the strands that clung to her forehead.

But she was gone.

The certainty pressed harder now, collapsing something inside his chest. He did not scream. He did not move. His body locked in place, as if motion itself had become optional.

A gloved hand took his arm, an officer speaking softly, voice thick with rehearsed compassion.

"Son… we need some space."

The words slid past him without landing. The pressure on his arm registered only as an obstacle.

Jonathan wrenched free and staggered toward her through blood-darkened snow.

His boots slipped, nearly sending him down. He caught himself with a sharp inhale, balance returning instinctively. The snow beneath his feet was no longer white. It had turned darker near her body, stained and trampled.

"No—she was breathing—she was right here—she—"

His voice fractured, the words collapsing into a sound that scraped its way out of his throat, raw and unformed. He dropped to his knees beside her, hands hovering uselessly, afraid to touch and unable not to reach.

A paramedic pressed two fingers to Suzanne's neck.

Jonathan watched the movement with unbearable focus, counting seconds that stretched and warped. The man's expression shifted—just enough for Jonathan to see it—then disappeared behind professional calm.

"I'm sorry," he said.

Something inside Jonathan tore open.

It was not a single break. It was a ripping, violent and complete, as if something essential had been pulled apart beyond repair.

The sound that came from him wasn't a cry.

It rose from bone—from grief too heavy for fourteen years, from terror that split him clean down the middle.

It echoed off the barn, drifted into the trees, followed the path of the men who had already vanished.

Jonathan did not recognize the sound as his own. It seemed to exist independently, a force released without his consent. His chest convulsed around it, breath shuddering in uneven bursts.

Hands guided him away. Someone spoke his name. A blanket was draped over his shoulders, rough and too heavy, trapping heat he did not feel.

They wrapped him in a blanket.

Sat him in the back of a cruiser.

Spoke to him in careful, gentle tones.

Jonathan heard none of it.

The world narrowed to fragments, looping and replaying without order. His mind fractured time into shards he could not reassemble.

His mother fighting.

Her scream.

The crack of a baton.

The moment she fell.

The way she died with his name on her lips.

Each image arrived fully formed, vivid and merciless. He smelled smoke and cold metal. He felt the impact reverberate through his own body, phantom pain echoing where he had not been struck.

An officer knelt beside him, notebook balanced on his knee, breath fogging the cold air.

The man's movements were slow, deliberate. He spoke Jonathan's name again, waited for acknowledgment.

"We need to know what happened, Jonathan. Anything helps."

Jonathan stared past him, through the window, at the barn swallowed by shadow.

The barn looked smaller now, diminished beneath the weight of lights and men. It no longer felt like a place of work or shelter. It felt violated. Hollowed out.

"They weren't robbers," he whispered.

The words came easily. Certain.

The officer nodded carefully. "Okay. Who were they?"

Jonathan shook his head.

"I don't know. But they weren't here for money."

He could feel the truth of it settle deeper with each word. The men who had come that night had moved with purpose, not desperation. They had not searched. They had not taken.

A pause.

A glance exchanged nearby.

"What were they after?" the officer asked.

Jonathan looked down at his hands.

His mother's blood had dried into the creases of his skin.

The sight of it anchored him in a way nothing else could. It was real. It was undeniable.

"…They wanted my mom," he said.

It wasn't the whole truth.

But it wasn't a lie.

The words carried weight without explanation. The officer wrote something down, his pen moving slowly.

Engines still idled when another vehicle rolled up the drive with unsettling calm.

It moved differently from the others. Slower. More deliberate. It did not rush to fill space or announce itself.

A black SUV.

No plates.

Jonathan's drew a fast breath.

His body reacted before his mind could intervene. Muscles tightened. The hum beneath his skin sharpened, rising with sudden intensity, vibrating like an alarm he could not silence.

Two men stepped out—long coats, measured movements, faces carved from restraint.

They closed their doors without slamming them. They did not look around with confusion or concern. They looked like men arriving where they had always expected to be.

Not local.

Not police.

Not here to mourn.

The hum beneath Jonathan's skin sharpened, rising like an internal alarm.

Memory surged with it, uninvited and violent.

Men like this had taken him once.

Men like this had walked him into a lab.

Men like this had called it protection.

One flashed a badge too quickly to read.

The gesture was casual, practiced. It did not invite scrutiny. It dismissed it.

The sheriff stiffened.

Jonathan noticed the shift immediately—the way authority reoriented itself, the way the man's shoulders straightened, his voice lowered. Quiet words passed between them—tight, purposeful.

Then the sheriff approached the cruiser.

"No," Jonathan whispered, shrinking back. "No…"

The word tore out of him, small and desperate.

"Jonathan," the sheriff said gently, "these men are federal. They need to talk to you."

"I'm not going anywhere with them!" Jonathan shouted.

The panic broke loose fully now, crashing through the fragile control he had been clinging to.

"You've been through something terrible," the sheriff said. "They want to make sure you're safe."

Safe.

The word landed wrong.

It tasted like poison.

Safe had taken his childhood.

Safe had locked him in a lab.

Safe had taken his mother.

"This is my home," Jonathan said fiercely. "I'm not leaving."

The declaration surprised him with its force. The farm was ruined. The house was compromised. But it was still his.

One of the agents stepped closer.

"Jonathan, tonight wasn't random. You're in danger. We're here to—"

"YOU LIED BEFORE!" Jonathan screamed.

The sound ripped through the night, raw and uncontrolled.

"You took me! And now my mom—"

The words dissolved into sobs.

His chest seized, breath collapsing inward as grief surged again, overwhelming and suffocating.

The agent's jaw tightened.

"We need to secure—"

Jonathan didn't wait.

The instinct arrived whole and undeniable. He lunged for the door, yanked it open, and ran.

Shouts exploded behind him.

"STOP!"

"Kid's running!"

"Get lights on him!"

Jonathan tore across the yard, breath burning, tears freezing on his cheeks.

Snow blurred beneath his feet. The world narrowed to motion and direction, everything else stripped away. His mother's voice pounded through him with every step.

Run if they come back.

Don't let them take you.

Branches ripped at his face as he plunged into the woods.

The pain barely registered. He fell once, hard, breath knocked from his lungs. He scrambled up without thinking, hands finding purchase, legs driving him forward.

Flashlights slashed the dark behind him.

"You can't outrun us!"

But he could.

He had to.

Snow muffled his steps. Trees bent around him and something deep inside—engineered, awakened, no longer sleeping—pulled him forward, guiding him through the dark.

Not faster.

Not stronger.

Just certain.

Away from the farm and away from the sirens. .

Away from the men in long coats.

Away from the mother he would never see alive again. Jonathan Halden, fourteen years old, ran into the world alone.

And the world—

finally—noticed.

CHAPTER 28 — THE FIRST RECKONING

Jonathan Halden was no longer the boy who ran into the woods with blood freezing on his shoes.

That boy had existed once, briefly, as a thing of panic and momentum. A creature propelled by fear, guided by instinct alone. Jonathan could remember him clearly—the ragged breath, the way his legs burned as he fled, the raw terror that narrowed the world into nothing but forward motion. That boy had not known where he was going. He had only known he could not stay.

Four years had burned the child out of him.

Time had not healed him. It had refined him. Each season had taken something away—hesitation, softness, expectation—and replaced it with something colder and more precise. Hunger taught him restraint. Exposure taught him patience. Solitude taught him how to listen without needing to speak.

At eighteen, he stood taller, broader, shaped by cold seasons and colder truths.

His body carried the marks of it: lean muscle layered over bone hardened by distance and repetition. Scars mapped him in quiet places—forearms, ribs, the line of his jaw—each one a lesson remembered by the skin. He moved with economy now, every step deliberate, every gesture purposeful. Nothing was wasted.

The wilderness had stripped him down and rebuilt him—bone, instinct, discipline.

Jonathan had learned to survive before he learned to plan. Learned to plan before he learned to hunt. He had eaten what he could find, slept where he could hide, watched people without being seen. Towns were patterns. Roads were arteries. People left trails even when they thought they were careful.

His eyes no longer searched the world for safety.
They measured it.
Measured distance. Measured threat. Measured time.

Not a weapon.

Not a machine.

A purpose.

That purpose now stood beneath a flickering motel sign, watching the man who had helped murder his mother.

The sign buzzed intermittently, neon struggling against failing ballast. Letters blinked in uneven rhythm, casting red light across cracked pavement and peeling paint. Jonathan remained just beyond its glow, the light stopping inches short of his boots. He had chosen the position carefully. Light revealed. Darkness listened.

Jonathan hadn't found Daniel Rowe by accident.

He had hunted him.

Hunting was not violence. It was preparation. Jonathan had learned that difference early. Violence was loud. Hunting was quiet. It required patience, pattern recognition, an understanding of human routine. People were predictable once fear was removed from the equation.

Just as Rowe had once hunted him.

Just as Rowe had come to the farm.

Just as Rowe had stood by while Suzanne died.

Jonathan's breathing remained steady as memory passed through him. He did not relive it. He cataloged it. Rage was a liability. Purpose was not.

Three months of tracking had led here—turning whispers into maps, fragments into patterns, names into locations.

Jonathan had followed paper trails most people never noticed. Expense accounts. Vehicle logs. Temporary clearances. He learned which systems talked to each other and which did not. Learned where information leaked, where it pooled. Learned how to listen without being heard.

Rowe surfaced everywhere once Jonathan knew how to look: retrieval records, margin notes, restricted communications signed by Carlisle.

Jonathan memorized the handwriting. The phrasing. The way orders were softened into suggestions on paper and hardened into commands in practice. Carlisle's name appeared often enough to become familiar, but never often enough to attract attention.

Rowe wasn't important anymore.

Not on paper.

He drifted through small towns on quiet assignments, useful only because he knew too much to disappear completely.

That knowledge had kept him alive. It would not save him.

Jonathan watched him through a dirty motel window.

The glass distorted the image slightly, bending Rowe's outline, making his movements appear sluggish. Rowe paced the room, then stopped, then paced again. He checked the lock twice. Drew the curtain, then reopened it to peer outside before closing it again.

Rowe moved like a man who never stopped looking over his shoulder—yet never expected the past to stand up and look back.

Jonathan timed his breath with the flicker of the sign.

Jonathan slid through the cracked window without a sound.

The glass shifted just enough to accommodate him. He had chosen the window earlier, tested it, learned its limits. The room smelled of stale smoke and cheap detergent. The air inside was warm and stagnant.

"Hello, Daniel."

Rowe spun, slamming into the desk.

The reaction was pure reflex, panic breaking through habit. The lamp shattered as his elbow struck it, glass spraying across the floor. Rowe coughed, choking, blood wet on his lips where he had bitten down hard.

Jonathan grabbed his hair and yanked his head back.

Rowe cried out, the sound breaking high and thin. Jonathan felt the tremor run through him, felt the strength drain as fear took hold.

"Talk."

Rowe shook violently.

"Wh—what do you want?"

Jonathan's voice was calm.

Almost gentle.

"Everything."

He slammed Rowe into the desk again.

The impact rattled the room. Drawers jumped. The sound died quickly, swallowed by thin walls and distance.

"Start with Carlisle."

Rowe sobbed, words tumbling over each other. "He's the director—Helix oversight—I didn't report to him directly—"

Jonathan snapped his head sideways.

"Liar."

The word carried certainty. Jonathan had already mapped the chain of command. He had seen Rowe's call logs. He had listened to the rhythm of his excuses.

Rowe broke.

"I swear—I wasn't high enough—"

Jonathan leaned close, voice low and lethal.

"Then why did you call him the night you came to our farm?"

The room seemed to shrink around them. Rowe's eyes widened. His mouth opened, then closed again.

Rowe froze.

"I heard you," Jonathan whispered.

The memory was precise. He remembered the cadence of Rowe's voice, the way it shifted when he spoke to someone he feared. He remembered the pauses, the deference, the relief.

"Every word."

Rowe collapsed inward.

"He ordered it," he cried. "After your father died, Carlisle didn't want another leak—"

Jonathan went still.

The stillness was absolute. No breath. No movement. Just attention sharpened to a single point.

"My father didn't die in an accident," he said quietly.

The statement was not a question.

"Say it."

Rowe swallowed.

"It wasn't an accident."

Jonathan slammed his head into the wall.

Plaster cracked.

Rowe screamed, the sound tearing free, then dissolving into sobs as he slid down, struggling to stay upright.

"Say what happened."

Rowe gasped, pain and terror blurring his words. "You were already in the chamber. The infusion was underway. Alarms triggered. Level Five breach."

Jonathan's jaw tightened.

Each word landed with surgical precision, slotting into place alongside fragments Jonathan had carried for years without context.

"Your father held the corridor alone," Rowe whispered.

Jonathan's grip tightened.

"He fired on the team to buy time. He kept yelling your name."

Something tore and locked inside Jonathan's chest.

The sensation was sharp and contained, like a door slamming shut. The image rose unbidden—his father's voice, distorted by memory, by time, by loss. Jonathan did not let it expand.

"They ordered him neutralized," Rowe continued. "He fought until he couldn't stand."

Jonathan exhaled slowly.

"You killed him."

"No!" Rowe cried. "I wasn't there—I was in command—I heard the call. 'Target down.'"

Jonathan grabbed his throat.

Rowe's protest cut off abruptly, breath strangled into wet gasps.

"Who ordered the breach?"

Rowe clawed weakly at Jonathan's wrist.

"Carlisle!" he gasped. "Dr. Gerald wasn't authorized—lethal force on resisters—"

"Henry wasn't resisting," Jonathan said.

His voice did not rise.

"He was protecting his son."

Rowe nodded frantically.

"He bought you ninety seconds," Rowe said. "That's why you lived."

Jonathan released him.

Rowe collapsed forward, coughing violently, hands braced against the floor. Jonathan watched him without expression.

Then asked the question that mattered.

"And my mother?"

The name did not need to be spoken. The room seemed to hold its breath.

Rowe collapsed.

"She wasn't supposed to die," he said. "Sykes panicked—hit her—"

"She fired warning shots," Jonathan said.

The correction was precise. He remembered the sound. He remembered the restraint.

Rowe sobbed.

"I know. I know..."

Jonathan stepped closer.

"My mother wanted me alive," he said softly.

The words were not accusation. They were fact.

Rowe nodded, broken.

"I believe you," Jonathan said.

Relief flickered across Rowe's face.

Hope—a fatal miscalculation.

Then—

"But you helped anyway."

Jonathan drove Rowe's skull into the desk.

Bone cracked.

The sound was clean. Final.

The body fell and did not rise.

Jonathan stood still for a moment, listening. The motel remained quiet. No footsteps. No voices. No interruption.

Jonathan washed his hands in the sink.

The water ran pink, then red, then clear. He scrubbed methodically, removing blood from beneath his nails, from the creases of his skin. When he finished, his hands were steady.

He took Rowe's phone.

His keys.

His assignment folder.

Each item went into his jacket with practiced efficiency.

At the door, neon light painted his face red.

The color washed over him, briefly illuminating eyes that held no doubt.

"One down," Jonathan whispered.

Then he disappeared into the night.

CHAPTER 29 — THE LINE

Jonathan rented the room for one reason.

Not to sleep.

Not to hide.

To think.

The motel sat far enough off the highway to avoid attention but close enough to blend into the endless repetition of places people passed through without remembering. The sign outside buzzed irregularly, the same flicker he had seen the night Rowe died. Jonathan chose the room on the second floor, corner unit, sightlines clean in two directions. Habit, not paranoia. Thinking required margins.

The desk was scarred with old burns and cigarette gouges.

Jonathan traced one gouge absently with his fingertip, feeling the shallow groove where someone else's frustration had once found release. The surface carried years of careless pressure—fists slammed, drinks spilled, decisions made in rooms like this one by people who never expected them to matter later.

The lamp hummed faintly, throwing a sick yellow cone across stacks of paper he'd spread with surgical care— date, name, signature, consequence.

Each stack was aligned precisely, edges squared, weighted so nothing shifted. Jonathan had learned long ago that disorder invited mistakes. He did not allow mistakes.

NDA.

Addendum.

Addendum to the addendum.

Forty-three names.

He stared at the number longer than he wanted to.

It sat in his chest like an object with weight. Not overwhelming. Just present. Jonathan let it sit there, let the discomfort exist without rushing to resolve it. He had learned the value of that too—letting pressure reveal its shape before acting.

Forty-three people had been close enough to smell the lab that night.

Close enough to hear the alarms.

Close enough to know a child was on a table and a man was in the corridor screaming for time.

Jonathan remembered the sound of alarms differently than the transcripts did. The recordings reduced them to tones and timestamps, neutral alerts triggered by thresholds crossed. In memory, they were jagged, invasive, tearing through space with no regard for what they meant. He could still feel the vibration in his teeth when he thought about it too long.

Forty-three people had agreed—on paper—to forget.

Jonathan read each page anyway.

He didn't skim. He didn't jump ahead. He read slowly, deliberately, forcing himself to absorb the language exactly as written. Legal phrasing was designed to blur responsibility, to turn choice into inevitability. Jonathan refused to let it work on him.

Clause after clause of silence.

Non-disclosure under penalty of prosecution.

Loss of clearance.

Loss of livelihood.

In two cases, criminal liability for "operational interference."

Jonathan paused on that phrase, rolling it over mentally. Operational interference. The act of disrupting a system when it behaved exactly as designed. The system was innocent. The interference was the crime.

They hadn't just been told to keep quiet.

They'd been bound to it.

Jonathan slid on the headphones and pressed play.

The plastic cups pressed lightly against his ears, isolating him from the hum of the motel, the distant traffic, the flicker of the sign outside. The room narrowed to sound and attention.

Recording — Internal Review Board

Subject: Thomas Rourke

Timestamp: 03:14 a.m.

Tom's voice came through thin and strained.

"The alarm was tripped automatically. I followed protocol."

Jonathan leaned back in the chair, eyes half-lidded.

He pictured the room where the recording had been made. Fluorescent lights. A table too clean. A glass of water placed just out of reach. He could hear the room under Tom's words—papers shifting, someone breathing through their nose, the antiseptic calm of people who believed the story would hold if they repeated it enough.

Another voice entered.

Calm.

Educated.

Controlled.

"You manually confirmed the alert, Mr. Rourke."

Jonathan recognized the tone immediately. Not accusatory. Not sympathetic. Curious in the way people were curious when they already knew the answer.

A pause.

"…Yes."

"Why?"

Tom swallowed, loud in the mic.

Jonathan heard it clearly. The body reacting before the mind could supply cover.

"The pressure spike read as catastrophic. I didn't know—"

"Did you verify occupancy in the chamber?"

Silence.

Jonathan could almost feel the moment stretch. The mental calculus. The scramble for language that might soften what could not be softened.

"Mr. Rourke."

"No."

Jonathan rewound it.

Played it again.

No.

That was the moment.

The hinge.

The choice made without looking, because looking would have made responsibility real.

Jonathan felt the hum stir faintly under his ribs, not as agitation but as recognition. Systems broke at hinges. Lives too.

He switched files.

Another interview.

Another sterile room.

Different faces. Same posture. Same careful distance from consequence.

"Why didn't you retract the alarm once you understood Dr. Halden was inside the containment corridor?"

Tom's voice cracked.

Jonathan noticed the change immediately—the shift from defensiveness to exposure.

"Because if I pulled it back and something went wrong, it would be on me."

Jonathan exhaled slowly through his nose.

There it was.

Not terror.

Not confusion.

Self-preservation.

The most reliable motivator of all.

He let the recording run.

The questions grew sharper.

The answers grew smaller.

Breach escalation.

Corridor lockdown.

Armed response authorization.

Each phrase landed with quiet weight, stacking atop the last. Jonathan followed the sequence easily now. He had mapped it dozens of times, traced cause and effect until there were no gaps left for denial to hide in.

Henry Halden's name appeared seven times in the transcript.

Jonathan didn't flinch when he heard it.

He didn't have that kind of softness left.

The name did not reopen wounds. It confirmed them.

He stood and crossed to the window.

Outside, the highway moved like nothing in the world had ever broken.

Headlights passed.

A couple laughed in the parking lot.

Someone slammed a door.

A life continued.

Jonathan watched it all without bitterness. Continuity itself wasn't the offense. The world didn't owe him pause.

Jonathan didn't hate the lives that continued.

He hated the ones who decided his couldn't.

He returned to the desk and looked at the stack again.

Forty-three signatures.

Ink on paper. Digital confirmations. Initials placed in margins by hands that had shaken only at the possibility of consequence, not its certainty.

Only seven had authority to change what happened next.

Fewer still had chosen to act.

Jonathan separated those files first, moving them into their own pile. He handled them carefully, as if the paper itself mattered less than what it represented.

Most of the names belonged to people who'd hidden inside procedure—technicians, junior staff, guards who did what they were told and never asked why.

Some of them had even tried to slow things down.

Delay a door.

Question a channel.

Buy time in small ways that didn't look heroic on paper.

Jonathan recognized those gestures. He had survived because of seconds. Because of hesitation. Because someone somewhere had not moved as fast as they were told to.

Those names stayed on the list.

Not as targets.

As evidence.

Jonathan was not going to become an animal chewing through whoever smelled like the past.

He had lived too long in cages to mistake rage for purpose.

He reached for a marker and wrote three columns across the top of a legal pad:

PRESENT

COMPLICIT

DECISIVE

The ink bled slightly into the paper fibers. Jonathan waited for it to dry before continuing. Small discipline. Big difference.

Then he started sorting.

The guard's name was Evan Mercer.

Jonathan found him three weeks later in a hunting shack outside Scranton, filling in for a coworker who'd taken leave.

Temporary assignment.

Low clearance.

A man living the kind of life that didn't expect consequences to crawl up out of the dark.

Jonathan watched the shack from the tree line for two hours.

The cold bit through his jacket, settling into muscle and bone. He welcomed it. Cold kept the mind sharp.

Mercer laughed on the phone.

Heated soup on a camping stove.

Complained about overtime.

A heater ticked.

A radio murmured low.

A normal night, built on the assumption that the worst thing that could happen was boredom.

Jonathan pictured it easily.

A quiet entry.

A single strike.

A body cooling on old floorboards.

The hum stirred faintly under his ribs—an internal readiness he didn't invite and didn't entirely control.

It waited.

Patient.

He didn't move.

He listened again instead.

Mercer's recorded interview.

A file Jonathan had already played twice.

He played it a third time anyway.

"I received a command override. Red channel. Level Five. I didn't know who was inside."

Jonathan remembered the tone. Confused. Defensive. But not evasive.

"Did you fire?"

"…No. I held position."

"Why?"

A breath.

A longer pause than the others.

Jonathan leaned closer to the audio, as if proximity could reveal more.

"Because it didn't feel right."

Jonathan lowered the binoculars.

Mercer hadn't advanced.

Hadn't escalated.

Hadn't pressed the moment forward because it was easier than thinking.

A man could be part of a machine without being the hand that turned the key.

Jonathan stepped back into the trees and let cold air settle into his lungs until the hum quieted.

He could have killed Mercer.

The path was clear. The opportunity clean.

But killing him wouldn't correct anything.

It would only feed the part of Jonathan that wanted to stop drawing lines.

That mattered more.

Back in the motel room, Jonathan drew a single strike through Mercer's name.

Not an erasure.

A classification.

PRESENT.

He set the marker down and stared at the list until his eyes watered from not blinking.

Forty-three names.

His mother's blood had touched some of those hands directly.

His father's last ninety seconds had been spent buying time from some of those mouths. Jonathan felt the weight of that knowledge settle into him, not as rage but as gravity. It pulled everything else into alignment. Not all of them were monsters.

But monsters weren't required to build what Helix had built.

Only people willing to choose comfort over consequence.

Jonathan opened the folder at the top of the stack.

Thomas Rourke.

Photos.

Addresses.

Employment history.

A retirement plan.

A life that looked soft around the edges.

Jonathan didn't touch the knife in his pocket.

He didn't need to.

He already knew where the line was.

And Tom Rourke had crossed it with a single decision he'd spent years calling "protocol."

Jonathan zipped the folder closed and placed it carefully in his bag.

He shut off the lamp.

The room fell into darkness, the hum of electricity replaced by deeper quiet. In the dark, the hum under his ribs steadied—not hungry, not frantic.

Certain.

Forty-three names.

Only a few would die.

Not because Jonathan couldn't do more.

Because he still could choose.

And because the ones who had chosen—truly chosen—had to learn what that meant.

CHAPTER 30 — THE LONG HUNT

It took Jonathan nearly six months to find him.

Not because Tom Rourke was especially clever. Not because he disappeared into the kind of systems Carlisle favored, where contractors nested inside contractors and names dissolved into clearance codes. Jonathan had followed those trails too, had learned how quickly men like Carlisle learned to become ghosts.

Tom had chosen something simpler.

Tom Rourke hadn't vanished like Carlisle or buried himself behind contractors and clearance levels.

He had done something worse.

He went home.

A quiet suburban street in northern Pennsylvania.

Jonathan found it by accident first, then confirmed it twice more before believing it. The address surfaced in a retirement filing Jonathan had almost dismissed as irrelevant—an end-of-career form signed months after the breach. It was mundane enough to be invisible. That was the point.

White siding.

A trimmed lawn.

A rusting grill on the patio.

A swing set that creaked when the wind moved it.

Jonathan stood across the street the first night and let the image settle into him. The house did not radiate menace. It did not feel fortified or watched. It felt ordinary in a way that scraped at something deep and raw.

A life pretending the past had never happened.

Jonathan watched from a distance.

Always a distance.

Distance kept him honest. It slowed the part of him that wanted speed, wanted closure without examination. He had learned that proximity blurred judgment. Distance sharpened it.

Nights spent in tree lines, culverts, abandoned cars parked where no one bothered to look twice.

Jonathan learned the rhythm of the neighborhood. Porch lights flicked on and off at predictable hours. Dogs barked at passing cars, then settled. A man two houses down left for the night shift at the hospital at 10:15 p.m. A woman jogged every morning at 5:30, earbuds in, eyes forward, never once glancing toward the trees where Jonathan waited.

Tom lived like a man with nothing to fear.

Jonathan cataloged the routine without hurry.

He left for work at 6:40 a.m.

Returned at 5:20.

Microwaved frozen dinners and fell asleep in his recliner with the television murmuring to itself.

He had a golden retriever named Scout.

Jonathan learned the dog's name by listening. Tom said it aloud when he came home, when he filled the bowl, when he let the animal out into the yard. The tone changed every time—relieved, apologetic, affectionate. Scout responded with loyalty unearned by merit, the way dogs always did.

He talked to the dog more than he talked to anyone else.

Jonathan hated him for that.

Not because of the dog. Jonathan understood the comfort of an animal's presence, the uncomplicated acceptance. He hated Tom because he had earned that comfort after choosing otherwise when it mattered.

Henry had been a good man.

Quiet.

Careful.

Loyal.

Jonathan remembered his father in fragments now—hands steady on tools, voice calm even under pressure, the habit of thinking before speaking. Henry Halden had believed systems could be corrected, that good people inside them mattered.

Tom had been the one who pressed the alarm.

The one who had confirmed it without looking.

The one who had made the choice small enough to live with.

He hadn't killed Henry himself.

But Henry died because Tom panicked.

And Tom lived like none of it mattered.

Jonathan waited.

Waiting had become second nature. Hunger came and went. Cold arrived and receded. Jonathan adjusted without complaint. He did not rush nights that did not feel ready.

He learned Tom's habits.

Which nights he drank too much.

Which nights he cried quietly with his face buried in his hands.

Jonathan saw those nights clearly through a narrow gap in the blinds. Tom would sit forward in the recliner, elbows on knees, beer untouched on the table. His shoulders would quiver with the chill in the air; once, twice. He never sobbed. He pressed his fists to his eyes and stayed that way until the sound passed.

Guilt had hollowed him out.

But guilt never fixed anything.

Jonathan understood guilt. He lived with it too. The difference was what followed it.

The night Jonathan moved was thick with heat.

Summer pressed down heavy and unmoving, air dense enough to feel held. Cicadas screamed from the trees, their chorus relentless, a wall of sound that swallowed small noises without pause.

Tom's living room glowed behind drawn blinds.

The television flickered blue and white, casting shifting light across the room. Jonathan waited until the pattern steadied, until Tom's posture sagged into the familiar shape of exhaustion.

Jonathan crossed the yard without sound.

The grass was dry beneath his boots, brittle and forgiving. He stepped where shadows pooled, where the house itself blocked any view from neighboring windows. His breath remained slow, controlled.

The dog sensed him and whimpered.

Scout's head lifted, ears angling toward the door. The sound was small, uncertain—not alarmed.

Jonathan knelt, extended a hand.

He moved deliberately, letting the dog see him, smell him. He remembered Suzanne's voice from long ago, soft and instructive, reminding him that animals read intent before action.

The retriever sniffed, then pressed its nose against Jonathan's palm.

Warm.

Trusting.

Jonathan felt a flicker of something unfamiliar—regret, perhaps—but he let it pass without indulgence.

"Go," Jonathan whispered.

The word carried intention without force.

The dog slipped away through the fence.

Jonathan waited until he heard the faint jingle of tags fade into distance before turning to the door.

Inside, Tom sat in his recliner with a half-empty beer and a microwaved tray cooling on his lap.

The smell of processed food hung in the air. Salt and starch and something faintly metallic. Jonathan registered it without reaction.

"Tom."

The word cut through the room cleanly.

Tom stiffened.

Turned.

The color drained from his face when he saw Jonathan step into the light.

Jonathan watched recognition bloom, watched memory slam into present reality. Fear followed immediately after, raw and unfiltered.

"Jonathan," he whispered.

The name sounded like a confession.

"You pressed the alarm."

Jonathan did not raise his voice. He did not accuse. He stated fact.

Tom's shoulders collapsed.

"I had to. Protocol—"

"You chose to."

Jonathan took a single step forward. Tom retreated instinctively, his body remembering consequences his mind had worked hard to forget.

"I didn't know he had you," Tom said desperately. "I didn't know he was trying to—"

"Save me," Jonathan finished.

The interruption was precise. Tom flinched as if struck.

Tom's breath shook.

"I tried to stop it. They locked me out. I couldn't retract the alert."

Jonathan's gaze did not leave Tom's face.

"That doesn't help him."

The words landed heavier than any blow.

Tom stepped back until his legs hit the table.

"I live with it," Tom said. "Every day. I hear that alarm in my sleep."

Jonathan stepped closer.

He could hear the truth in Tom's voice. He did not doubt the nightmares. He doubted their usefulness.

"Please," Tom said. "You're not a killer."

Jonathan reached into his coat.

The pocketknife slid into his hand with familiar weight. Not comforting. Just present.

Tom broke.

"I have a daughter," he said. "She has kids. Please—"

The plea came fast, tumbling over itself, the way pleas always did when people ran out of arguments.

"My father had a son."

Jonathan's voice did not rise.

It didn't need to.

Tom turned to run.

The movement was desperate and clumsy. He made it two steps before Jonathan closed the distance and slammed him into the wall.

Frames fell.

Glass shattered.

Tom crumpled, scrambling toward the door.

Jonathan pinned him to the carpet.

The fibers pressed rough against Tom's cheek. Jonathan felt the man's panic vibrate through him, felt the useless thrashing of someone who had never learned how to fight inevitability.

"You didn't check why," Jonathan said.

His voice remained steady, each sentence measured.

"You didn't stop them."

Tom sobbed, words breaking apart.

"You didn't care enough to find out."

"I tried!" Tom cried. "I swear I tried—"

Jonathan knelt.

The movement was slow, deliberate, final.

"You're sorry now."

The statement was neither cruel nor forgiving. It was an observation.

Tom whispered, "Please don't kill me."

Jonathan paused.

The pause mattered.

It was the last place choice existed.

"I'm not killing you for who you are," he said quietly.

Jonathan looked at Tom the way he had looked at the list, the files, the signatures.

"I'm killing you for what you did."

The blade flashed once.

There was no spectacle in it.

No rage.

Just action completing decision.

Blood soaked into the carpet.

Tom stopped moving.

Jonathan stood.

He did not watch the body settle. He did not wait for anything else to happen. The house felt unchanged, as if it did not yet understand what had occurred inside it.

Jonathan wiped the knife clean. He used the edge of a dish towel from the counter, folded carefully afterward and set back where it had been. Order mattered. Disorder invited mistakes.

He stepped over the body without looking back. Outside, the cicadas screamed loud enough to swallow everything.

The sound erased the night behind him, filled the space with something ancient and indifferent.

Jonathan once again disappeared into the night.

CHAPTER 31 — THE AFTERMATH

Jonathan didn't run. Running would have meant urgency. It would have meant fear. His body refused both. He left the house at a measured pace, feet steady, posture controlled, as if nothing behind him required escape. The night accepted him without resistance. Doors stayed shut. Windows stayed dark.

He walked three blocks before the shaking started.

The distance mattered. It created separation. It allowed the act to finish echoing before consequence arrived.

Not from fear.

Not from urgency.

From the sudden, brutal quiet that followed.

The soundscape shifted almost imperceptibly at first. Cicadas dulled as he moved away from the trees. Their scream softened into background texture, then disappeared entirely. The neighborhood resumed its ordinary rhythms—porch lights glowing in patient amber, televisions murmuring through thin walls, a car passing somewhere distant with tires hissing softly over asphalt.

The world absorbed what he'd done without protest.

That was what broke him.

Jonathan slowed, then stopped beneath a maple tree, its leaves whispering softly in the heat. The trunk was thick, bark ridged and cool against his shoulder when he leaned into it. The smell of sap and dust filled his nose. Ordinary. Alive.

His hands began to tremble.

Not violently.

Not uncontrollably.

Precisely.

The tremor was narrow and contained, localized to his fingers, as if his body were isolating the response rather than letting it spill. Jonathan watched it with detached interest, cataloging the sensation the way he had learned to catalog everything else.

He stared down at them, half expecting to see his father's blood instead of Tom Rourke's.

The memory arrived without invitation, sharp and intrusive. For a moment—a terrifying moment—the faces overlapped in his mind.

Tom laughing in Suzanne's kitchen.

Tom handing him a wrapped birthday gift.

Tom crouching down to ask about school, about science fairs, about what Jonathan wanted to be when he grew up.

You're getting so tall, kiddo.

The memory wasn't fabricated. Jonathan recognized its edges, the way truth carried weight even when context shifted. He remembered the warmth of Tom's voice, the familiarity of it, the way his mother had trusted him without question.

Jonathan bent forward sharply, breath sawing out of him.

His stomach heaved, muscles contracting hard enough to hurt, but nothing came up. No bile. No relief. Just air and heat and the echo of a scream still lodged behind his eyes, vibrating without sound.

He pressed his tongue hard against the roof of his mouth until the sensation grounded him, until the present reasserted itself.

He had known Tom.

Not well.

But enough.

Enough to remember his voice.

Enough to remember the way he smelled like coffee and aftershave.

Enough to remember that Tom had once hugged his mother goodbye on their porch.

Jonathan slid down against the tree trunk, knees bending until he sat on the warm concrete of the sidewalk.

The bark pressed into his back, grounding, abrasive. He welcomed the discomfort.

He pressed the heel of his palm hard into his eye until sparks danced across his vision.

Light fractured into brief bursts, white and sharp, overriding the images trying to surface. He counted the sparks until they faded, then pressed harder, breathing through clenched teeth.

This wasn't like Rowe.

The realization carried weight, not surprise.

Rowe had been a stranger.

A function.

A cog that spoke in orders and euphemisms.

Rowe had represented machinery. Systems. Distance. Killing him had felt like severing a wire—necessary, contained, complete.

Tom had been human.

That mattered.

It mattered more than Jonathan had expected.

The understanding settled into him slowly, not as regret but as recalibration. He had crossed a line he had drawn deliberately. He had not misjudged it. But crossing it carried cost beyond calculation.

Minutes passed.

Or seconds.

Time no longer behaved properly around him.

Jonathan focused on sensation to anchor himself. The heat radiating from the pavement. The faint breeze stirring leaves overhead. The distant hum of traffic like a faraway ocean.

Eventually, he stood.

The movement felt mechanical, executed rather than chosen. He brushed dirt from his jacket, straightened the fabric, wiped his face with the sleeve until his skin felt raw.

He forced his breathing into something slow and even.

In through the nose.

Out through the mouth.

Measured.

The hum inside him—always there now—steadied.

It did not spike. It did not rage. It aligned, settling into a low, constant presence, responsive to control rather than emotion.

That frightened him more than the shaking had.

Jonathan tested it subtly, shifting his focus, tightening and loosening his grip on awareness. The hum followed. It obeyed.

Control had replaced reaction.

He moved again, this time with purpose.

Back roads.

Tree lines.

A drainage ditch that carried him away from the neighborhood and toward a strip of undeveloped land bordering the highway.

He chose paths that erased him rather than revealed him. He stepped where shadows overlapped, where infrastructure broke continuity. He crossed beneath fences at points already damaged, left no clear line of travel behind him.

By dawn, he was miles away.

The sky lightened without ceremony, pale gray giving way to washed-out blue. Jonathan watched it from the edge of a field, crouched low, his body tucked into tall grass that brushed his arms and legs.

He didn't sleep the next night.

Sleep required permission. His mind refused to grant it.

He sat beneath an overpass and replayed every second.

Not to savor it.

To audit it.

He broke the night down into fragments, examined each one for weakness.

Where he'd hesitated.

Where he'd spoken.

Where he'd allowed memory to surface.

That was the mistake.

Emotion was noise.

Noise led to error.

Jonathan understood that now with brutal clarity.

Suzanne had taught him that, even if she'd never said the words aloud.

He remembered her vigilance, the way she never allowed fear to dictate motion. He remembered her restraint more than her warmth. That was the lesson that endured.

Jonathan pressed Henry's pocketknife into his palm until the familiar weight grounded him.

The metal bit slightly into skin, a controlled pain that reestablished boundaries. He welcomed it.

This wasn't justice, he realized.

Justice required acknowledgment. It required naming what had been done and by whom.

This was something else.

It was accounting.

A ledger being balanced one decision at a time.

And he could not afford sentiment again.

Not if he wanted to survive what came next.

The news broke two days later.

Jonathan watched it from a diner television while nursing black coffee he didn't need.

The diner smelled of grease and burnt toast, the kind of place that existed everywhere and nowhere. A waitress laughed too loudly at something a cook said behind the counter. A man in a baseball cap stirred sugar into his coffee, eyes fixed on his phone.

A retired systems analyst found dead in his home.

The anchor's voice remained neutral, careful.

No sign of forced entry.

Police not ruling out a targeted act.

Neighbors described him as "quiet," "polite," "kept to himself."

Jonathan watched Tom's face flash briefly on the screen—an old photograph, softened by time and resolution. He recognized the expression immediately. It was the one Tom wore when he wanted to appear harmless.

No mention of Helix.

No mention of Henry.

No mention of the alarm.

Jonathan expected relief.

The expectation itself surprised him.

What he felt instead was a low, hollow ache.

Not grief.

Not guilt.

Absence.

Like something essential had been cauterized shut.

A place where pain once lived now felt sealed, unreachable. Jonathan tested it cautiously, like touching scar tissue. It did not respond.

He stood and left before the segment ended.

Outside, the air felt heavier, humidity pressing down. Jonathan took three steps before his phone vibrated once.

A burner he'd almost forgotten he'd set up months ago.

The vibration felt louder than it should have, buzzing against his thigh.

UNKNOWN NUMBER:

He was under observation. You weren't supposed to touch him.

Jonathan stopped walking.

The sidewalk hummed faintly beneath his feet. Cars passed behind him, unnoticed.

Another message followed.

Carlisle knows someone is moving through his old network.

You just announced yourself.

Jonathan stared at the screen without blinking.

The words carried no threat.

They didn't need to.

Jonathan deleted the messages.

Then, after a moment, powered the phone off completely.

The action was final. He did not hesitate. Tools that invited noise were liabilities.

Tom Rourke had been a door Jonathan could never close again.

The line he had drawn still held—but it now ran both ways.

The hunt was no longer quiet.

And whatever Jonathan Halden was becoming—
the world had finally started to notice.

CHAPTER 32 — HER VOICE

Jonathan heard her when he was almost asleep.

The moment hovered just before rest claimed him, the place where the body released tension but the mind remained alert enough to flinch. His breathing had slowed. Muscles softened. The concrete beneath him faded into background sensation rather than pressure. He had learned to linger there because it was efficient—because vigilance dulled without fully disappearing.

Not dreaming.

Not awake.

That narrow, dangerous space where the world loosens its grip.

Easy, baby.

The words arrived without warning, without prelude, carried on no recognizable sound. They did not echo. They did not reverberate. They landed exactly where they always had—behind his right shoulder, low and calm, as if she were leaning in to keep him from startling.

He sat up so fast his breath caught.

The movement jarred him fully awake, heart punching hard against his ribs. His hand went instinctively to the knife at his side, fingers wrapping around the handle without thought. He scanned the space beneath the overpass in sharp, efficient sweeps.

The overpass was empty.

Traffic hissed somewhere distant.

Cold concrete pressed through his jacket.

No one else was there.

"Mom?" he whispered.

The word felt fragile as it left his mouth, barely more than air. He hated the way it sounded—too small, too hopeful. He waited anyway, holding his breath, listening past the ordinary sounds of the night.

Nothing answered.

Jonathan remained still for a long count. Thirty breaths. Then sixty. He did not lower his guard until his pulse steadied and the night returned to its expected rhythm.

He pressed his fingers into his palms, grounding himself.

The pressure brought sensation back into focus, reminded him of edges and limits. He had learned to do that early, back when sleep came in fragments and nightmares threatened to bleed into waking hours.

He had learned the difference between memory and imagination.

This wasn't either.

Her voice hadn't come from inside his head.

It had come from behind him.

The distinction mattered. Jonathan replayed the moment again and again, isolating variables. Memory arrived unbidden but inward, colored by context and emotion. Imagination announced itself through distortion. This had been neither. It had possessed placement. Direction. Weight.

It happened again two nights later.

Jonathan was crouched in the woods outside a freight yard, counting rotations, listening to guards swap shifts.

The night smelled of oil and rust. Metal groaned softly as cars coupled and uncoupled. The rhythm of the yard was familiar now—predictable enough to map without looking. Jonathan counted steps between posts, timed pauses in conversation, tracked light patterns sweeping across gravel.

When the hum inside him spiked sharply—then softened.

The change was immediate and unmistakable. His body responded before his mind did, muscles tightening, breath halting mid-cycle. The spike resolved almost at once, not into threat but into something quieter.

Don't rush.

Jonathan froze.

The words slid into the space between breath and motion, stopping him without force. They weren't loud. They weren't even clear. They arrived with the same calm insistence she had used when he was younger and his impatience threatened to get him hurt.

But they were hers.

The cadence.

The patience.

The way she used to speak when fear threatened to turn into panic.

Jonathan closed his eyes.

The freight yard continued its work without noticing him. Engines idled. A laugh broke out near a loading platform. Someone spat into the dirt. Life moved forward, indifferent.

"You're not real," he murmured.

The admission was careful. Controlled. He did not want to challenge the experience. He wanted to define it.

I know, the voice said gently. But you're still listening.

The response did not argue. It acknowledged.

That scared him more than if she had been real.

If it were hallucination, grief-made-sound, he could contain it. Name it. Dismiss it when necessary. But this answered him. Not as correction. As observation.

By the end of the week, he stopped pretending it was coincidence.

The pattern emerged slowly, unmistakably. Jonathan tracked it the same way he tracked people—by absence as much as presence.

Suzanne's voice surfaced only at moments of choice.

Never during violence.

Never during planning.

Only when he stood at a threshold.

A knife in his hand.

A target in sight.

A decision that could not be undone.

Jonathan tested the pattern without consciously meaning to. He noticed the silence when his path was already set, the absence when motion required no deliberation. The voice did not intrude on inevitability. It appeared only when outcome remained malleable.

You don't have to be what they made, she said once, faint as breath on glass.

The words arrived as he stood in a darkened hallway, target breathing softly on the other side of a thin wall. His grip tightened reflexively around the knife. The voice did not tell him to stop. It did not tell him to turn away.

It reminded him there was still a choice.

Jonathan dropped the knife that night.

The sound of it striking the floor seemed impossibly loud in the quiet space. He stepped back as if burned, hands shaking now in a way he did not bother to contain. He stood there shaking, furious at himself for the weakness—

—and more furious at the relief that followed.

The relief was immediate and humiliating. It washed through him, loosening something tight and coiled. He hated it for that. Hated that part of him welcomed the reprieve.

He began talking back.

Quietly.

Carefully.

Not aloud when others might hear. Not with expectation. He treated it like negotiation rather than confession.

"I don't have another way," he said one night, staring into a dark river.

The water moved steadily, black and reflective, carrying moonlight in fractured ribbons. He watched the current for a long time before speaking again.

"They won't stop."

Her voice came slower this time.

Strained.

I know.

That was worse than disagreement.

Agreement meant acknowledgment. It meant she understood the shape of the problem and did not offer easy escape from it.

"You don't understand," he said, jaw tight. "You weren't there."

The words carried accusation despite his effort to keep them neutral. He braced for silence. For withdrawal.

A pause.

Long enough to stretch his chest tight.

Then—

I was.

Jonathan's chest tightened painfully.

The words did not claim presence where none existed. They did not rewrite history. They carried something else—recognition. Witness.

She wasn't accusing him.

She wasn't absolving him.

She was reminding him of something he had been trying to bury.

Suzanne had been there in the only way that mattered. In consequence. In aftermath. In the choices that followed.

The voice didn't guide him toward mercy.

It guided him toward restraint.

That distinction mattered more than anything else.

It didn't tell him to stop.

It told him to wait.

To watch patterns.

To count consequences.

To remember faces—not just names.

Jonathan began to notice how easily names became abstract. Lists flattened people into targets, signatures into symbols. Faces resisted that flattening. Faces demanded accounting.

If you lose yourself, she said once, so softly he almost missed it, then they win twice.

The sentence followed him for days afterward, echoing without repetition. He found himself measuring actions against it, not as rule but as weight.

Jonathan sank to his knees that night and pressed Henry's pocketknife to his chest like a child clutching a rosary.

The metal was cool through his shirt, familiar and grounding. He bowed his head without thinking, breath catching like he was trying to find it between motions.

"I don't know who I'm supposed to be anymore," he admitted.

The words felt raw, unarmored. He hated that too. He let them exist anyway.

For a long time, there was only the wind.

It moved through branches above him, stirring leaves into soft collision. The night held its distance. No answer came. Jonathan remained still, forcing himself not to fill the silence with expectation.

Then—

You're my son, Suzanne said. That's not something they can take.

The words arrived without urgency, without force. They did not counter his doubt. They reframed it.

Jonathan inhaled sharply.

The breath shuddered on the way in, broke on the way out. His shoulders shook once, then again.

For the first time since the farm, he cried without breaking.

The tears came quietly, contained, his body folding inward rather than outward. There was no scream lodged behind them. No fracture waiting to happen. Just release, measured and finite.

The voice never stayed long.

It never answered questions directly.

It never told him what to do.

Jonathan noticed that restraint too. It mirrored the woman she had been—protective without control, present without dominance.

But it anchored him.

Anchors did not pull. They held.

And Jonathan understood something then—something essential.

This wasn't madness.

It wasn't grief poisoning his thoughts.

It was memory reinforced by something deeper.

Pattern.

Imprint.

The same force inside him that healed wounds, mapped danger, and bent the world just enough to keep him alive—

had kept her.

Not her body.

Not her mind.

But her pattern.

Her imprint.

Her weight.

The understanding settled into him with surprising calm. It did not change what he was. It changed how he held it.

Jonathan rose at dawn, steadier than he had been in weeks.

The light crept across the horizon in thin bands, pale and deliberate. He watched it without hurry, breathing slow, body aligned.

The hunt was still on.

Carlisle was still out there.

But now, when Jonathan moved, he didn't move alone.

Not guided.

Anchored.

And somewhere inside the machinery of what he was becoming—

Suzanne Halden was still watching.

Still guiding.

Still refusing to let him disappear completely.

Even if the world demanded it.

CHAPTER 33 — THE ONE WHO HIT SUZANNE

Mark Sykes had once been a government field agent.

Once, that title had meant something. Authority. Purpose. Belonging. It had come with structure and uniforms and language designed to make violence sound like necessity. Sykes had worn it easily back then, slipping into the role the way some men slipped into religion— because it offered rules, and rules relieved him of the burden of thinking too hard about consequence.

Now he was what the agency left behind.

The discard pile. The remainder. The men who knew too much and mattered too little. Sykes understood that part intimately. He had watched it happen to others before it happened to him—agents quietly reassigned, careers softened into consultancy, reputations slowly blurred until they no longer posed risk. He had told himself he was different. Better. Necessary.

He wasn't.

He lived alone in a small cabin tucked into the Montana foothills, surrounded by snow and a silence so deep it felt punitive.

The land pressed in around him, not as comfort but as judgment. Snow swallowed sound, erased tracks, buried evidence. Trees stood thick and indifferent, witnesses that neither accused nor forgave. The cabin sat at the end of a narrow, unmarked road that disappeared beneath drifts half the year. When storms came, the world reduced itself to white and wind and waiting.

Retirement hadn't been a reward.

It hadn't even been voluntary.

It was exile with paperwork.

The documents had been clean. Polite. Phrases like service concluded and medical advisement had been stamped neatly across his file. A pension reduced just enough to sting. A recommendation letter vague enough to be useless. He had signed where they told him to sign. He always had.

No one had said it outright, but Sykes heard the truth in the spaces between conversations after the farm.

The pauses.

The lowered voices.

The way his calls stopped being returned.

He panicked.

The truth settled in him slowly, like rot spreading through wood. He replayed the incident endlessly, the way men did when they couldn't undo what they'd done. The justifications came first—training, threat assessment, split-second judgment. Those lasted weeks. Maybe months.

Then came the quieter understanding.

He wasn't supposed to hit her that hard.

He killed the mother.

The words had never appeared in any report. They lived only in his head, blunt and unsoftened. He had tried to phrase them differently—fatal outcome, unexpected casualty—but language refused to cooperate when he was alone.

Kincaid walked away untouched.

Carlisle climbed higher.

Rowe drank himself into paranoia.

Sykes stayed.

That had been his punishment, though no one called it that. Staying meant remembering. It meant the silence had room to stretch. It meant there were no distractions large enough to drown out the night.

Two divorces.

Each one quieter than the last. The first had come with shouting and slammed doors, accusations he could almost argue against. The second had come with resignation. A suitcase packed carefully. A kiss on the cheek that lingered out of habit rather than affection.

A bottle that never stayed empty.

Whiskey dulled the edges but sharpened the images. He drank anyway. He drank because the alternative was sleep, and sleep was worse.

Night terrors that left him clawing at the sheets, lungs burning.

He woke choking on air, heart hammering, hands clenched around nothing. Sweat soaked the mattress even in winter. The dreams never varied. They did not need to.

And Suzanne Halden.

She lived in his head now.

Not screaming.

Not accusing.

Just breathing.

That was the worst part. The calm. The steadiness. The way she had looked at him—not with fear, not even with anger, but with recognition. As if she had known exactly what kind of man he was the moment he decided force was easier than patience.

Sometimes he heard her voice when the cabin was quiet—calm, steady, impossibly present.

You didn't have to do it.

The words arrived without volume, without drama. They did not repeat. They did not vary. They simply existed, impossible to argue with.

He pressed his palms to his temples when it happened, whispering apologies into the dark.

"I know," he muttered. "I know."

The apologies were never enough. They weren't meant to be. They were habit now, like checking a lock that would never hold.

The memory never changed.

Her stance.

The rifle.

The split second where he decided force was faster than thought.

The baton striking bone.

Her body hitting the snow.

The sound Jonathan made when he realized she wasn't getting up.

That sound followed him everywhere.

It lived beneath conversation, beneath music, beneath the hiss of the heater and the wind in the trees. It surfaced when he least expected it—while washing a mug, while tying his boots, while staring at the snow piling against the door. It had no mercy and no schedule.

By the time Jonathan Halden arrived in Montana, Sykes was already half-dead.

The man Jonathan tracked bore little resemblance to the agent who had once stepped onto the farm with authority in his posture and certainty in his stride. That man had existed only briefly. The one who remained moved like something eroded.

Snow fell thick and soundless as Jonathan moved through the trees, every step deliberate, every breath measured.

The cold bit cleanly, sharpening awareness rather than dulling it. Jonathan welcomed it. The wilderness here felt honest—no walls, no corners, no places to hide mistakes. He adjusted his pace to the terrain, reading slope and drift without effort.

He had followed Sykes for months—through forgotten retirement files, medical discharges, quiet transfers designed to erase men without consequences.

The trail had been thin but consistent. Jonathan had learned how agencies buried their mistakes—not by destruction, but by dilution. Files were spread across systems, relevance minimized, attention redirected. Sykes hadn't disappeared.

He'd been hidden.

Jonathan watched him for weeks from the treeline.

Long enough to see the truth.

Sykes drank alone on the porch.

The bottle sat beside him like an accusation he refused to acknowledge. He drank slowly, deliberately, as if pacing mattered. His hands shook no matter how much he told himself it was the cold.

He cried when he thought no one could hear.

Jonathan heard everything. The muffled sounds. The sharp intake of breath. The quiet collapse inward when Sykes folded over himself, elbows on knees, face in hands.

He paced at night, whispering prayers he didn't believe would be answered.

Jonathan watched him mouth the words, the shapes familiar even from a distance. Sykes prayed like a man bargaining, not believing. He asked for forgiveness without expecting absolution. He asked anyway.

He was not a monster.

Jonathan understood that immediately.

He was worse.

He was a man who had lived.

A man who had returned to a house, poured himself a drink, and watched the seasons turn. A man who had not paid with his life for what he had done—but with time.

Jonathan felt no rush.

Only gravity.

The kind that pulled him forward without effort, without emotion. This was not vengeance. It was completion.

The night he entered the cabin, the cold cut clean and sharp.

Snow tapped softly against the windows, a steady, patient sound. Inside, the cabin glowed dimly, yellow light bleeding through thin curtains. Jonathan approached without haste, already knowing what he would find.

Inside, Sykes sat hunched near a gas heater, beard untrimmed, eyes hollow, hands shaking as he poured whiskey into a chipped mug.

The smell of alcohol hung thick in the air, layered with stale smoke and damp wool. Jonathan cataloged it without reaction.

Jonathan turned the knob.

It wasn't locked.

The door creaked.

The sound was small but decisive. It broke the cabin's rhythm cleanly.

Sykes froze.

"Hello?" he called, already knowing.

Jonathan stepped into the light.

The mug shattered on the floor.

Ceramic exploded outward, whiskey soaking into the rug like a spreading stain.

"No," Sykes breathed. "No, you're dead. They told us you died. They said—"

"People say a lot of things," Jonathan replied.

His voice carried no heat. It didn't need to. Reality was enough.

Sykes staggered backward, gripping the table.

"I didn't mean to kill her," he sobbed. "She raised the rifle—I panicked—I thought—"

"You hit her before she fired," Jonathan said.

The correction was immediate and precise.

Sykes collapsed.

The truth did not resist. It never had.

"Yes," he whispered. "I know. I see it every night. I hear you screaming. I hear her fall. I never meant—"

Suzanne's voice rose unbidden in Jonathan's mind, steady as it had always been.

Look at him.

Jonathan did.

He forced himself to see not the man from the farm, not the shape his memory preferred, but the one in front of him now.

A broken man.

A guilty one.

Still breathing.

"You came to kill me," Sykes said quietly.

There was no panic in the statement. Only acceptance.

Jonathan didn't deny it.

Denial would have cheapened what came next.

Sykes nodded. "Good. I deserve it."

He sank to his knees—not in fear, but surrender.

The posture was unmistakable. Not pleading. Offering.

"I pray for forgiveness," he said. "Every day."

Jonathan crouched in front of him.

The movement placed them at eye level. Jonathan noticed how Sykes flinched anyway, as if expecting impact.

"I believe you," Jonathan said.

The words surprised Sykes into looking up.

For a moment—just a moment—hope flickered.

"But belief doesn't undo what you did."

The hope died quickly. Jonathan watched it go without satisfaction.

Suzanne's voice again—softer now.

Finish it.

The word did not push. It did not command. It acknowledged inevitability.

Sykes swallowed. "Make it fast."

Jonathan shook his head.

"You don't deserve fast," he said. "But you deserve peace."

Tears slipped free.

Not loud.

Not dramatic.

Just release.

"Thank you," Sykes whispered.

Jonathan placed a hand on the back of his head—not gentle, not cruel.

Certain.

"This is for her."

He twisted.

The body went slack instantly.

There was no struggle. No sound beyond a brief, involuntary exhale. Jonathan supported the weight long enough to ensure finality, then let it settle to the floor.

Jonathan stood, breath even, heart steady.

He waited a full count. Ten seconds. Twenty. The room remained unchanged.

There was no triumph.

No relief.

Only arithmetic.

"Three," he whispered.

Outside, snow erased the cabin's doorstep as Jonathan disappeared into the white—

and Suzanne Halden's voice, at last, went quiet.

CHAPTER 34 — THE FRACTURE

Jonathan didn't feel relief after Mark Sykes died.

He waited for it in the way he had waited for other things—patiently, without expectation of timing, convinced that sensation would arrive eventually if he stayed still long enough. He stood outside the cabin after the snow had swallowed the doorway and let the cold bite into his face until his cheeks burned. Nothing rose up to meet it. No surge. No hollow. No recoil.

That was the problem.

He had anticipated something—release, closure, even rage—but the world remained stubbornly unchanged. Snow still fell in soft, indifferent sheets. The cold still bit through fabric and skin with the same clean insistence. His pulse stayed even. His hands didn't shake.

The absence of reaction felt louder than any scream.

He waited for Suzanne's voice to return.

He listened for it in the spaces between sounds, in the pause after breath, in the quiet moments when the night stretched thin enough to reveal what hid beneath it. He lay awake and still, eyes open, counting heartbeats, refusing sleep as if vigilance itself might summon her.

It didn't.

That silence followed him for days.

It trailed him like a shadow that refused to separate, present in every place he stopped long enough to notice it. Jonathan found himself listening for something that never came, and the longer it didn't, the more oppressive the quiet became. Silence had once been refuge. Now it pressed inward.

He moved east through Montana on foot, then by stolen rides, then by trains he boarded and abandoned without names or tickets.

Movement helped. It blurred the edges of thought. He learned which freight lines ran regular enough to trust and which ones stalled long enough to abandon. He learned the cadence of conductors' footsteps, the way their voices carried through metal cars. He rode in the spaces between destinations, never long enough to belong anywhere.

He slept in culverts, grain silos, derelict barns.

He learned the difference between shelter and safety. Shelter was a roof and walls. Safety was absence—of attention, of memory, of consequence. He chose places that offered the second.

He ate when he needed to.

Not when hunger suggested it, but when efficiency required it. His body signaled necessity clearly now. He obeyed without resentment or gratitude.

He healed when he was hurt.

Cuts closed faster than they used to. Bruises faded quickly without treatment. Pain registered, then resolved. Jonathan noted the changes without comment. They were facts. He had long since stopped pretending they were temporary.

And slowly, something inside him began to slip.

Not break.

Slip.

The distinction mattered. Breakage implied damage, dysfunction, something that could be repaired. This felt different. Like a gear shifting into a new alignment, teeth clicking into place where they hadn't before. Nothing malfunctioned. Everything worked better.

The violence no longer carried weight.

Jonathan noticed it first in the absence of aftermath. No shaking. No collapse. No delayed reaction demanding to be processed. The act completed itself and left nothing behind but a corrected outcome.

It no longer demanded justification.

He no longer replayed arguments in his head afterward, no longer weighed necessity against cost. The calculus completed itself in advance. When action occurred, it felt like confirmation rather than decision.

It simply… worked.

That terrified the part of him that still remembered being a boy.

That part existed now like a dim light behind thick glass—present, distant, unable to influence the shape of things directly. Jonathan could feel it watching, recoiling not from the acts themselves but from the ease with which they happened.

At night, memories surfaced uninvited.

They came without pattern or permission, slipping past whatever barriers he tried to erect. He did not dream them. He remembered them awake, fully conscious, as if the past had decided it no longer needed his cooperation.

Henry's voice, calm and tired, telling him to stay behind the line.

Jonathan remembered the exact tone—not stern, not fearful, but steady. The sound of a man managing both a situation and a child at the same time.

Suzanne brushing dirt from his knees, telling him pain didn't get to decide who he was.

Her hands had always been sure. The gesture was small, intimate, the kind of care that assumed injury without dramatizing it.

The farm at dawn.

Mist rising from the fields. Birds calling before the sun cleared the trees. The quiet that had once felt like permanence.

The quiet before it all shattered.

Jonathan pressed his hands to his temples when it happened, trying to force the images back down.

He counted breaths. He focused on sensation. He cataloged his surroundings. The techniques worked—until they didn't. The memories did not retreat the way they used to. They lingered, asserting themselves with a patience that mirrored his own.

They didn't obey anymore.

One night, outside a closed gas station in Nebraska, Jonathan vomited violently into the weeds for no physical reason at all.

The motion came without warning, body folding in on itself as if struck. His stomach convulsed hard enough to force tears to his eyes. He knelt on the cracked concrete, hands braced against the ground, breath tearing from his lungs in sharp, uncontrolled bursts.

Nothing came up but bile and air.

The smell of oil and old fuel hung heavy around him. The station's lights were dark, windows covered in dust and taped notices. The world offered no audience.

Something sharp and unfamiliar twisted in his chest.

Guilt.

Not for Sykes.

That realization arrived with clarity. He did not regret the act. He did not wish it undone.

For how easy it had been.

The ease frightened him more than any bloodshed. It suggested not just capability but compatibility. A system that welcomed the act rather than resisted it.

"I didn't hate you enough," he whispered into the dirt.

His voice sounded strange in his own ears—flat, analytical, stripped of self-pity.

"That's what scares me."

The admission did not lessen the sensation. It named it. That was all.

The nanotech hummed softly beneath his skin, steady and patient.

Jonathan felt it as presence rather than sound, a low consistency woven through nerve and muscle. It did not spike in response to emotion. It did not dull under stress. It remained constant, a baseline hum that suggested readiness without agitation.

It didn't care about morality.

It cared about efficiency.

Jonathan had suspected that for a long time. Now he understood it fully—not as theory but as lived experience. The system inside him did not evaluate actions by meaning or consequence. It measured inputs and outputs. Threat and resolution. Probability and outcome.

Jonathan realized then—truly realized—that whatever had been done to him wasn't just physical enhancement.

It was alignment.

The word settled into him with unexpected weight. Alignment implied intention. It implied that the changes were not accidental side effects but deliberate tuning.

His nervous system had been tuned for threat detection, response optimization, outcome certainty.

Fear registered as data. Anger registered as noise. Grief registered as inefficiency. The system smoothed those signals, reduced variance, guided action toward completion.

Killing no longer spiked his adrenaline.

It flattened it.

The realization arrived with cold precision. His body no longer reacted to lethal force as anomaly. It treated it as resolution. The surge that once accompanied danger had been replaced by calm focus.

That was the fracture.

Not the act.

Not the deaths.

The understanding.

The moment he understood he was no longer becoming something—

He was something.

Identity crystallized in that instant, sharp and undeniable. He was no longer in transition. There was no ambiguity left to hide behind. What remained was choice—not of becoming, but of use.

And if he didn't decide what that something stood for, someone else would.

That truth pressed in on him from all sides. He had seen it happen before. Systems abhorred undefined assets. They named them. Claimed them. Pointed them.

Suzanne's absence became louder than any voice.

It filled the space she had once occupied, a silence heavy with expectation. Jonathan felt it not as abandonment but as distance—deliberate, waiting. He imagined her watching him now—not approving, not condemning.

Just waiting.

Waiting to see what he would choose without her hand on the scale.

"Tell me what to do," he murmured one night, staring at his reflection in a darkened train window.

The glass showed him in fragments—eyes catching light, jaw set, expression unreadable. The image shifted as the train moved, breaking him into pieces that never quite aligned.

The reflection didn't answer.

It never would.

So Jonathan made a choice.

Not in a rush. Not in desperation. He allowed the decision to settle fully before accepting it, examining it from every angle the way he had examined targets and routes.

Not to stop.

Stopping would have been denial. It would have pretended the alignment wasn't there, that the system inside him could be ignored.

But to narrow.

The word carried structure. Constraint. Intent.

No collateral.

No chaos.

No pleasure.

Rules were not morality. They were containment. Jonathan understood that now.

Only purpose.

Only those who had touched the farm.

Only those who had given orders.

Only those who would do it again.

The criteria mattered. They created a boundary he could operate within without dissolving entirely. He would not widen the circle. He would not let efficiency dictate scope.

Violence would not be his identity.

It would be his instrument.

And instruments, he reminded himself, don't feel.

They are used.

Jonathan Halden stood, adjusted his jacket, and stepped off the train before it fully stopped—

The platform rushed past in a blur of concrete and steel. He landed cleanly, momentum carrying him forward into shadow without stumble or spectacle.

—vanishing into another city that didn't yet know his name.

Behind him, the boy he had been stayed buried in snow and blood and memory.

That boy had done his work. He had survived long enough to make choice possible. Jonathan did not dishonor him by pretending he still existed.

Ahead of him, the hunt continued.

But now—It was colder.

Not the weather.

The intention.

The narrowing of motion toward a center that would not allow mistake.

Jonathan moved into it without hesitation.

CHAPTER 35 —MAN WHO GAVE THE ORDER

Captain Ross Braden was built from the leftovers of war.

Not the clean parts that showed up in retirement photos or award citations, but the remnants that never quite reintegrated—habits calcified into reflex, instincts sharpened beyond usefulness, memories that no amount of distance could dull. Braden had been shaped by repetition: commands issued and obeyed, lives advanced and spent, outcomes measured by completion rather than consequence.

Fifty-six years old.

The number meant little to him. Years blurred together after a certain point, marked not by birthdays but by deployments, rotations, and injuries that never fully healed.

Retired with honors.

The plaque hung somewhere inside the house, Jonathan would later notice—polished brass mounted on wood, words chosen carefully to emphasize service without acknowledging cost. Honors were easy to give when the recipients lived far from the places they had broken.

Joints that cracked in the cold.

Hands that still remembered rifles.

Braden woke each morning before dawn, not out of discipline anymore but because his body refused to sleep past first light. He stretched carefully, working stiffness out of knees and shoulders, listening to the familiar pops and grinds with the detached acceptance of a man who had learned to coexist with pain rather than defeat it.

A commander whose men followed orders without question.

That had been his greatest strength—and his greatest failure. Braden had believed in hierarchy with religious certainty. Orders created clarity. Clarity saved lives. The fact that it sometimes destroyed them instead was something he had learned not to examine too closely.

He was also the man whose voice Jonathan had memorized.

The voice had carved itself into Jonathan's nervous system long before he understood why. It was the cadence as much as the words—sharp, unyielding, amplified by stress and authority. A voice that assumed obedience as natural law.

Jonathan had listened to the recording hundreds of times.

He knew every inflection. Every breath taken between commands. He knew where the boots pounded concrete in the background, where alarms layered over each other into noise so loud it drowned out thought.

The screaming.

And over it all:

"TAKE THE SHOT! MOVE! MOVE!"

That voice belonged to Braden.

Jonathan could isolate it even now, strip it clean of static and chaos. It rose above everything else because it had decided the outcome before it occurred. It had transformed a moment into a conclusion.

Henry Halden died standing in front of Braden's team, blocking the corridor, buying his son ninety seconds of life.

Jonathan carried that image with precision. He had reconstructed it piece by piece from reports, from audio, from the way men spoke afterward when they thought no one who mattered was listening. His father had not panicked. He had not begged. He had calculated. Ninety seconds was what the math allowed.

Jonathan did not come for revenge alone.

Revenge was reactive. It fed on emotion and faded once satisfied. What brought him here had weight beyond that.

He came to finish what that order started.

Braden's ranch sat alone beneath the Wyoming sky, wide and empty as a firing range.

The land stretched flat and unforgiving in all directions, broken only by fencing and low structures that existed less for comfort than function. Wind moved freely here, unimpeded, scraping sound and heat from everything it touched. It was the kind of place men chose when they wanted to believe they were alone.

Jonathan watched it for six months.

He did not rush. He did not circle recklessly. He learned the terrain the way soldiers learned kill zones—by patience, by repetition, by absence as much as presence.

Sunrise jogs.

Braden ran every morning, even when his knee protested, even when the cold cut deep enough to ache in the bone. He ran because stopping felt like surrender.

Dog feedings.

A pair of aging shepherd mixes, disciplined and alert, responded to hand signals more than voice. They were trained animals, not pets, and they mirrored their owner's temperament—watchful, obedient, easily startled by sudden change.

Lock checks.

Braden checked doors and windows out of habit rather than fear. The ritual calmed him. It imposed order on a world that had taught him how quickly order vanished.

Camera blind spots.

Jonathan found them within the first month. Old equipment, poorly updated, angles chosen years ago for threats Braden no longer imagined.

The floodlight that flickered in high wind.

The limp in Braden's left knee.

The man had retired.

His body had accepted it. His rank had accepted it. His routines had not.

The soldier in him never had.

Jonathan respected that.

Respect didn't soften his purpose. It sharpened it. Braden was not a coward hiding from consequence. He was a man who had lived exactly as he believed he should.

It made what came next harder.

And necessary.

The decision sealed itself one cold morning when Braden sat on the porch cleaning a rifle and hummed.

The sound carried farther than it should have, thin and unguarded. Jonathan froze in the treeline, breath stalled mid-cycle. The tune threaded through Jonathan's spine like a wire pulled tight, instant and unmistakable.

The same tune Braden had hummed over comms seconds before Henry Halden was gunned down.

Jonathan lowered the binoculars.

The world narrowed to clarity.

"It's time."

Wind scoured the plain as Jonathan slipped through the broken barn door Braden had never fixed.

The door creaked faintly but not enough to matter. The wind swallowed the sound whole. Jonathan moved through shadow and dust, boots finding places already worn smooth by time and neglect.

Inside, the cabin smelled of gun oil, cedar, whiskey, and old wool.

The scent was dense and layered, the smell of a man who had never fully cleaned out the past. Fire embers glowed low in the stone hearth, casting weak orange light that barely reached the corners of the room.

Jonathan waited.

Waiting here was different than it had been elsewhere. The air felt charged, expectant. Jonathan did not pace. He stood still, weight balanced, senses open.

Footsteps creaked above.

The sound traveled through the floorboards, measured and familiar. Braden moved carefully on stairs now, mindful of joints that no longer forgave impact.

A voice cut the dark.

"Whoever you are, step out slow. Hands visible."

The command was automatic, tone unchanged by retirement or age. Authority lived in it still.

Jonathan stepped into the lamplight.

Braden froze.

The recognition hit him all at once. Jonathan watched it move across the older man's face—confusion giving way to understanding, understanding to something like grim acknowledgment.

"…I'll be damned."

The words carried no humor.

"You remember me," Jonathan said.

"You look like your father," Braden replied. "Taller."

The observation was neutral, almost respectful. Braden had always assessed people quickly. He did so now out of habit.

Jonathan didn't react.

"You gave the order."

The words landed flatly. No accusation. No escalation. Statement of fact.

Braden's gaze flicked to the fire. "I gave a lot of orders. Men die in them."

"That wasn't war."

Jonathan's voice did not rise. He did not need it to.

Braden's mouth curved. "So what now?"

"I'm here to finish something."

Braden cracked his knuckles. The sound was sharp in the quiet room. "Good. I've been bored."

Violence detonated.

There was no buildup, no warning beyond posture and breath. Jonathan moved first. He had expected Braden to hesitate. He had been wrong.

Braden moved faster than expected.

Years of training collapsed into instinct. Braden closed distance with surprising speed, weight shifting cleanly despite the knee. Bone cracked as Braden's forearm collided with Jonathan's shoulder. Pain flared, bright and immediate.

Then steel sang.

Braden pulled the cavalry sabre free—old, immaculate.

The blade caught firelight as it cleared the scabbard, long and curved, a relic from a different kind of war. Braden swung like a man who had trained for this his entire life, footwork precise, grip steady.

Jonathan dodged.

Rolled.

Felt heat slice his ribs.

The cut was shallow but hot, skin opening under the blade's edge. Jonathan registered it, adjusted his stance, ignored the blood.

"You bleed just like he did," Braden said.

The words were calculated. Braden had always understood psychological leverage. He used it now without hesitation.

Something in Jonathan fractured.

Not loudly.

Not cleanly.

The break was internal, structural—a shift in alignment rather than collapse.

Braden lunged.

Jonathan blocked with a broken table leg.

The wood splintered under impact. The sabre carved air where Jonathan's spine had been a moment before, slicing cleanly through space.

"You're just his sequel," Braden sneered.

Jonathan stepped inside the blade's reach.

It was a choice made without deliberation. Distance collapsed. Risk sharpened.

Henry's pocketknife slid into Braden's abdomen.

The blade met resistance, then gave way. The sensation transmitted cleanly through Jonathan's hand, undeniable and final.

The world narrowed.

Sound dulled. Motion slowed. The moment compressed around contact.

Braden grabbed Jonathan's throat and lifted him off the floor.

Air vanished.

Vision tunneled.

The older man's grip was brutal, precise. Braden had strangled men before. He knew exactly how much pressure to apply.

"You're weaker than he was," Braden growled. "Softer."

Jonathan's thoughts scattered.

The hum inside him surged—not as panic, not as rage, but as recalibration. Systems realigned under threat.

Then something hardened.

Not rage.

Not grief.

Decision.

His hand found the knife still buried in Braden.

He dragged it downward.

The motion was brutal and efficient, tearing through tissue without hesitation. Braden screamed and dropped him.

Jonathan hit the floor, gasping—then surged up.

He drove the blade into Braden's neck.

Sideways.

Deliberate.

Blood spilled.

Steel fell.

Braden collapsed.

The sabre clattered uselessly across the floor, its era ended.

Jonathan stood shaking, staring down at the man who had ordered his father's death.

His breath came ragged at first, then steadied. Pain radiated from his ribs, sharp and insistent. He welcomed it. Pain meant the moment was real.

"Four," he whispered.

The count was not triumph. It was recordkeeping.

He cleaned the knife on Braden's shirt.

Folded it carefully.

Slid it back into place.

Outside, the cold bit his wounds.

Jonathan limped into the Wyoming night alive only because instinct had replaced mercy.

He did not look back at the cabin. He did not need to. The work was complete.

He sharpened the knife every night after that.

Not because it dulled.

Because he was.

CHAPTER 36 —MAN IN THE GLASS OFFICE

The report arrived at 4:32 a.m.

Carlisle registered the time automatically, the way some men registered heartbeats. His internal clock had been trained for years to notice moments that mattered, and this one announced itself before the screen finished illuminating. The vibration against the marble desk was soft, almost polite, but it carried weight—enough to still the faint movement of his hand as it hovered above a document he had stopped reading hours earlier.

Carlisle wasn't asleep—he hadn't slept in three nights—but when the secure phone vibrated against the marble desk, his body reacted anyway.

A sharp intake of breath.

A pause that lasted a beat too long.

PRIORITY RED.

BRADEN — STATUS CONFIRMED.

The words were sterile. Administrative. Designed to be absorbed without emotion. Carlisle felt the failure of that design immediately. He did not move for a full second, eyes fixed on the text, mind already leaping ahead of what it meant.

He opened it.

One line.

Target eliminated. Cabin compromised. Assailant unknown.

Carlisle closed his eyes.

The room around him remained unchanged—glass walls, city lights stretched thin beneath predawn haze, the hum of climate control tuned to perfection. The stillness mocked him. He let it exist for exactly three breaths before opening his eyes again.

Unknown.

There was only one person it could be.

He turned toward the photograph mounted behind his desk—Captain Ross Braden standing beside him at a classified ceremony, medals gleaming, both men composed and assured.

The photograph had been chosen carefully. It projected confidence without arrogance, partnership without intimacy. Braden had been useful that way—reliable, decisive, unquestioning when clarity was demanded. Carlisle had valued that in him.

Carlisle's hand tightened at his side.

Braden was dead.

Cooling in a Wyoming cabin.

And the wound pattern reported by forensics told Carlisle everything he needed to know.

He had not needed to read past the summary, but he had anyway, parsing the language for detail others might miss. The report had been written by professionals—precise, cautious, unwilling to speculate. Carlisle read between their restraint easily.

A precise angled strike.

Clavicle to carotid sheath.

Fast.

Quiet.

Efficient.

Carlisle pictured the motion without effort. He had seen it performed in training rooms, in demonstration footage never meant for civilian eyes. He knew exactly how much force it required, how little margin for error it allowed.

Jonathan had practiced it.

Perfected it.

The realization slid cold and smooth down Carlisle's spine, a sensation he had not felt in years. This was not the aftermath of a panicked attack or a desperate struggle. It was not improvisation.

This wasn't chaos.

This wasn't rage.

It was intention.

Jonathan wanted them to recognize the cut.

That detail mattered. The angle. The placement. The restraint. This was communication, not just outcome. Jonathan had chosen a method that would speak to men like Carlisle—men who understood what skill looked like when stripped of noise.

To see it in the photos.

To understand—without ambiguity—that Henry Halden's son had learned how to kill.

And had learned well.

Carlisle moved then, rising from the chair with controlled precision. He crossed the office slowly, the city beyond the glass still dark enough to feel distant, unreal. The reflection that followed him in the window was familiar—composed, unhurried, untroubled. It did not match the shift happening beneath the surface.

By seven a.m., Carlisle stood at the head of a sealed room beneath a federal annex.

The descent alone took long enough to allow recalibration. Security checkpoints peeled away layers of the world above, each door sealing shut with a muted finality. Carlisle passed through them without pause, credentials recognized instantly.

Eight chairs.

Fluorescent lights.

Air thick with disinfectant and fear.

The room had been designed to minimize distraction—no windows, no adornment, surfaces chosen for ease of cleaning rather than comfort. Carlisle preferred it that way. Spaces like this forced attention inward.

Two seats were empty.

Rowe's.

Braden's.

The absence registered at the edges of vision but did not disrupt the formation. Carlisle had learned long ago that visible gaps unsettled men more than bad news. He let them see it.

Carlisle ignored both.

"We have a problem," he said calmly.

The word problem carried deliberate understatement. It signaled control even as it acknowledged failure.

"And it is no longer theoretical."

A monitor flickered on.

Images of Braden's cabin filled the screen—wide shots first, then tighter frames marked with numbered forensic tags. Blood darkened wood. Furniture displaced with brutal efficiency. The scene spoke of violence without chaos.

A murmur rippled through the room.

Carlisle allowed it exactly two seconds before speaking again.

"Are we suggesting a civilian killed Captain Braden?" someone asked.

The question carried disbelief rather than challenge. Braden had been mythologized among them—too experienced, too hardened to be taken by surprise.

"Not a civilian," Carlisle replied.

He tapped the console again.

Jonathan Halden appeared on the screen.

Eight years old.

Pale.

Wired.

A child reduced to instrumentation.

Then twelve.

Older, eyes already too aware.

Then fourteen.

Hollowed.

Then nothing.

Five years of absence.

The screen lingered on the last image longer than necessary. Carlisle watched the room as much as the screen, noting the subtle shifts—straightened backs, tightened jaws, eyes narrowing in recognition.

"He survived the farm," Carlisle said.

He did not elaborate. He did not need to.

"He survived his mother's death. He disappeared. And now he has resurfaced."

"Resurfaced?" Vaughn asked.

The word carried skepticism, a reflexive resistance to uncertainty.

Carlisle met his gaze.

"He's announcing himself."

The statement landed heavily. It reframed everything. This was not an accident. Not a reemergence driven by exposure or mistake. It was declaration.

Silence settled.

"A weapon," Carlisle continued.

He did not soften the term. He had stopped pretending they were discussing anything else.

"Engineered without oversight. Adaptive. Self-correcting."

Fear finally showed on their faces.

Not panic.

Calculation.

Braden had been a soldier.

A commander.

If Braden couldn't stop him—

Carlisle did not finish the thought.

Leaving it incomplete forced each person in the room to complete it themselves. The results were visible immediately.

Instead, he outlined survival.

Security doubled.

Residences relocated.

Digital histories erased.

Families evacuated.

Safe rooms reinforced.

Movement restricted.

Monitoring widened.

Each instruction was delivered without inflection, the way surgeons spoke during procedures. Carlisle watched the room absorb it, watched men accustomed to issuing orders accept that they were now targets.

"Assume," Carlisle said, "that Jonathan Halden already knows your routines. Adjust accordingly."

The instruction carried a deeper implication: He knows you better than you know him.

Someone asked if they should strike first.

The question came from the far end of the table, quiet but insistent. Carlisle turned his head slowly, meeting the speaker's eyes.

He shook his head once.

"No."

The room stilled.

"Braden was an offensive response," Carlisle continued. "Learn from the outcome."

He did not explain further. Explanation implied debate. This was doctrine now.

The room accepted that.

Before dismissing them, Carlisle said the words he had been holding back since 4:32 a.m.

"He's coming."

A ripple of tension moved through the table.

"Just not yet."

That distinction mattered. It suggested patience. Planning. Restraint.

Jonathan Halden did not strike again for a long time.

Carlisle learned to measure time differently during that period. Days passed without incident. Weeks followed. Months stretched thin. No reports surfaced. No threats emerged. No mistakes were made.

He vanished into the seams of the country—bus stations, orchards, freight yards, roadside motels.

Carlisle read the reports that hinted at movement without confirming it—unusual data access here, a disrupted schedule there. Nothing actionable. Nothing definitive.

He worked under borrowed names.

Carlisle knew the type. Identities thin enough to slip through systems without triggering alarms. Men like

Jonathan learned those skills quickly—or were given them early.

Watched from distances that never drew attention.

Carlisle felt it in the absence of noise. The lack of error. Jonathan did not rush. He did not test boundaries. He observed.

He mapped lives.

Not just men—but systems.

Commutes.

Escorts.

Finances.

Habits.

Weaknesses.

Carlisle recognized the methodology. It mirrored his own training, refined and stripped of bureaucracy. Jonathan was not hunting targets.

He was understanding environments.

Two full years of patience.

Carlisle aged more in that time than he had in the decade before it. He slept less. He trusted fewer people. He stopped standing with his back to glass. The world narrowed around him, pressure constant and low.

Carlisle felt him everywhere—never seen, never confirmed, but always present.

A reflection in glass.

A shadow that shouldn't be there.

A pressure that never eased.

He caught himself checking angles in his own office now, noting reflections, counting exits. The behavior disgusted him even as he indulged it. He had become reactive to something he could not define.

Jonathan Halden was out there.

Not hunting wildly. Just Waiting.

And Carlisle understood, with growing certainty, that waiting was the most dangerous phase of all.

Because when Jonathan moved again, it would not be to announce himself.

It would be to end something.

CHAPTER 37 — THE NET TIGHTENS

Two years passed.

Time lost its ordinary meaning in those years. It stopped behaving like progression and began to feel like pressure—something that accumulated rather than moved. Each day added weight without release, a slow compression that bent everything beneath it.

Two years without a body.

Two years without a footprint, a fingerprint, or a camera capture that wasn't a smear of motion and doubt.

The absence itself became data. Analysts ran projections on nothing. Security firms built threat models around what did not appear. Entire departments existed to explain why there was nothing to explain.

The silence wasn't comforting.

It was suffocating.

Jonathan Halden had gone from a ghost to something far worse—a presence with intention.

Carlisle stood alone in his fortified office, surrounded by ballistic laminate and sealed panic locks.

The room had been redesigned twice since Braden's death. Walls thickened. Glass replaced with layered composites rated for blasts Carlisle prayed would never come. Locks that required multiple confirmations replaced locks that had once seemed more than adequate. Everything about the space said control.

From the outside it passed for executive polish.

From the inside, it was a bunker built from fear.

A security feed filled the wall—his new safehouse, wrapped in motion sensors, infrared lines, biometric locks, and constant armed patrols.

Carlisle could name every system by manufacturer and revision number. He had approved them personally, overridden objections about cost and redundancy. There were contingencies layered inside contingencies. Fail-safes for fail-safes.

It should have been reassuring.

Instead, Carlisle startled at his own reflection in the glass.

The man staring back at him looked thinner. Older. His shoulders held tension even at rest, as if bracing against impact that never arrived. The sharpness that had once made him formidable had dulled into something brittle.

He had aged badly.

New lines carved his face. His eyes were bruised with exhaustion. Twenty-four months of waiting had bent him inward.

Carlisle pulled up Braden's autopsy again.

The file lived on his desktop despite every security protocol advising otherwise. He had memorized it. He did not need to see it again.

He always stopped on the same frame.

The cut.

Clean.

Angled.

Beneath the collarbone, rising into the neck.

Jonathan's signature.

Carlisle stared at it until the image lost coherence, until bone and tissue blurred into abstract geometry.

"This is a message," Carlisle whispered.

The words felt inadequate even as he spoke them. Messages implied dialogue. Jonathan was not interested in conversation.

The feed switched to an exterior drone view.

Clear.

Kitchen.

Clear.

Garage.

Clear.

Bedroom.

The drone's camera swept methodically, algorithmic and blind to nuance. Carlisle watched the pattern rather than the image, tracking where it lingered and where it moved on too quickly.

Then—

A shape at the tree line.

Tall.

Still.

Watching.

Carlisle's breath caught.

For half a second, the world sharpened with terrifying clarity. The shape did not move. It did not flee. It existed, unmistakably deliberate.

Carlisle reached for the zoom.

The figure vanished.

The image resolved into empty brush and shadow.

A guard's voice crackled through the room, professional and calm. "Likely wildlife, sir. Could be a deer. Or a shadow artifact."

Another voice followed. "No thermal spike registered. Camera probably glitched."

Carlisle said nothing.

He had learned that the most dangerous thing in the room was reassurance.

He knew better.

Jonathan was testing distance.

Testing him.

Carlisle could feel it now—not as intuition, but as pattern recognition refined to instinct. Jonathan wasn't probing defenses the way an attacker would. He was measuring response time. Attention. Assumptions.

Dr. Lila Marrow's fear broke quietly.

There had been no single moment. No dramatic collapse. Just erosion—steady, incremental, relentless. Carlisle had watched it unfold through reports and intercepted messages, through requests framed as procedural concerns that all traced back to the same thing.

She lived in a reinforced condo with an armed escort.

The building had been retrofitted after Braden's death—steel-reinforced doors, laminated glass, controlled access points. Her schedule was randomized. Her routes were altered daily. Every precaution taken.

But paranoia eroded her in inches.

Curtains slightly off.

A pen moved.

A sound beneath the floor she couldn't place.

She logged each anomaly. Filed each concern. Security teams responded promptly, professionally. They found nothing every time.

Then the alarms screamed.

The sound tore through the building at 2:11 a.m., shrill and absolute. Security teams flooded corridors. Weapons came up. Protocols snapped into place with well-practiced precision.

Her front door stood open.

No forced entry.

No prints.

No alarms tripped.

The escort found nothing.

They swept the condo room by room, checked vents, ceilings, service access points. Every system reported green.

Marrow found a maple leaf on the kitchen counter.

Wet.

Fresh.

From a tree half a mile away.

Carlisle read the report twice.

Jonathan hadn't entered to harm her.

He had entered to be remembered.

Marrow resigned the next morning.

Filed for relocation.

It didn't matter.

Fear had already rooted itself too deeply.

Carlisle watched her departure through administrative notes and asset transfers. She left behind equipment, files, pieces of her life she could no longer stand to see. She did not ask for reassignment. She asked to disappear.

Director Vaughn unraveled faster.

Where Marrow's fear turned inward, Vaughn's exploded outward. He tried to fight the pressure with aggression, with displays of control that only exposed his instability.

Car alarms at 3:17 a.m. for a week straight.

Each time, Vaughn bolted upright in bed, heart racing, weapon in hand. Each time, security found nothing but tripped sensors and untouched vehicles.

Tires deflated.

A fake tracker taped beneath his bumper.

Small things.

Intimate things.

A note under the wiper:

YOU'RE NEXT.

Jonathan hadn't written it.

He didn't need to.

Vaughn barricaded himself behind guards and drones, then disappeared overseas within a year.

The official explanation cited health concerns and strategic reassignment. Carlisle approved the paperwork without comment.

One less weakness.

Jonathan didn't kill.

Not yet.

Carlisle understood the restraint now. It was no longer mercy. It was leverage.

Jonathan became pattern without rhythm—a shadow where none should exist, a flicker in peripheral vision, a presence guards felt but couldn't confirm.

Dogs growled at nothing.

Handlers adjusted routines. Veterinarians were consulted. Nothing explained the behavior.

Sensors blinked once, then never again.

Carlisle stopped trusting the green lights. He trusted only the gaps—the moments when systems failed too cleanly to be accidental.

Jonathan didn't tighten the net with violence.

He tightened it with absence.

Two years after Braden's death, Carlisle convened what remained of the original group.

The invitation was narrow. The list shorter than it had ever been.

Three people.

A table too large.

Empty chairs that felt accusatory.

Carlisle let the silence settle before speaking. He had learned its value.

A satellite infrared scan glowed on the screen—guards marked in red, terrain in blue.

One faint heat signature hovered just outside the perimeter.

Barely there.

But real.

Carlisle felt the familiar cold spread through him.

"He's closer," Carlisle said. "And he's patient."

The statement wasn't speculative. It was acknowledgment.

"What does he want?" Marrow asked.

Her voice sounded thinner than Carlisle remembered. Fear had altered her cadence, made her cautious even with words.

Carlisle didn't hesitate.

"He wants us to know he's here."

The truth landed heavily.

Jonathan stood on a ridge above the fortress as autumn frost whispered through the grass.

The air was clean and sharp. The kind of cold that clarified rather than numbed. Jonathan breathed it in slowly, letting it settle through him.

Below, the complex glowed with artificial light—layers of security radiating outward like a diagram. Guards moved in predictable loops. Drones traced lazy arcs overhead.

Jonathan saw all of it.

He took out Henry's pocketknife and let the moonlight catch the blade.

The steel reflected pale and steady, unchanged by time or blood.

"Soon," he said.

The word carried no urgency.

Not tonight.

Tonight, the net only tightened.

Jonathan remained still as the frost deepened, patience absolute.

And far below, Carlisle felt—without knowing why—that the space around him had grown smaller.

CHAPTER 38 —MAKING OF A WEAPON

Jonathan Halden did not become lethal overnight.

The idea itself offended precision. Lethality was not a switch that flipped or a moment that arrived. It was accumulated—earned through repetition, failure, correction. Jonathan understood that instinctively. Whatever had been done to him in laboratories had accelerated certain processes, sharpened certain perceptions, but it had not replaced the need for work.

He built himself slowly—bone by bone, scar by scar— over two silent years.

The years blended together without notice. There were no markers to separate one from the next, no holidays or anniversaries to punctuate time. Jonathan measured progress instead by endurance gained, errors reduced, reaction times shortened. His body kept its own calendar.

No mentors.

No instructors.

Only repetition.

That absence mattered. Jonathan trusted no external authority. Guidance created dependency. Dependency created vulnerability. Every lesson he learned, he learned through failure and consequence—painful, honest, impossible to forget.

He lived light.

Anonymous.

Temporary.

He did not accumulate possessions beyond what fit in a pack he could abandon without regret. Clothing chosen for durability and disposability. Tools selected for reliability rather than sentiment, with one exception he allowed himself without apology.

Cash only.

Cheap motels.

Towns that forgot him as soon as he left.

Jonathan learned which places asked questions and which didn't. He favored the latter. Front desks staffed by people too tired or underpaid to care. Buildings that smelled like bleach and old carpet, where anonymity was a feature rather than an oversight.

Every morning before dawn, he ran.

The hour mattered. Darkness hid inefficiency. Cold clarified breath. Jonathan moved before the world fully woke, when streets belonged to utility workers and delivery trucks, when no one noticed a lone figure pacing through industrial zones or empty neighborhoods.

Not for speed.

Speed was fragile. Speed faded.

For endurance.

For the ability to keep moving after others failed.

Jonathan ran until his lungs burned.

Not the shallow burn of exertion, but the deep, clawing ache that demanded surrender. He ignored the demand. He learned to breathe through it, to let oxygen arrive when it arrived rather than chase it.

Until his legs collapsed.

Sometimes it happened suddenly, muscles seizing without warning. Sometimes it crept up gradually, weakness pooling until motion simply stopped. Jonathan accepted both outcomes as data.

Until he woke unsure how long he'd been unconscious on cold concrete.

The first time it happened, panic flared briefly—body down, exposed, vulnerable. The second time, he adjusted his route. By the third, he accepted it as part of the process. He chose places where collapse carried minimal risk, where discovery was unlikely.

He didn't care.

Caring would have required alternatives. Jonathan did not believe in alternatives anymore.

His body existed for one purpose: to carry him to his targets—and away from anyone who tried to cage him again.

The framing mattered. Escape was as important as approach. Jonathan trained for withdrawal as deliberately as he trained for engagement. He ran weighted, then unweighted. He practiced sudden changes in direction, abrupt stops, controlled falls that dissipated impact rather than absorbed it.

He learned how to disappear while exhausted.

At night, he practiced with Henry's pocketknife.

The knife never left his person. Not out of sentimentality, but because consistency mattered. Grip familiarity mattered. Jonathan trained with what he would use, not approximations.

Meat scraps.

Carcasses.

Discarded mannequins.

Bundles wrapped to mimic bone resistance.

He scavenged materials with care, choosing textures and densities that approximated human anatomy. He learned how much force it took to penetrate cartilage, how angles changed resistance, how grip altered precision.

He drilled upward thrusts beneath the collarbone.

Arterial angles.

Grip reversals.

Silent sequences.

Each movement repeated until thought was no longer required. Jonathan drilled in darkness, in cramped spaces, in weather that numbed fingers and blurred vision. He practiced until error became rare, then practiced until it vanished.

Calluses split his palms.

Small scars tracked his mistakes.

Jonathan cataloged them without resentment. Each mark represented correction. Pain was instruction, not punishment.

Pain instructed him.

Every night ended the same way—Jonathan kneeling, sharpening the blade in slow, deliberate strokes.

The ritual mattered. Not because the knife dulled quickly—it didn't—but because the act imposed stillness. It forced reflection without indulgence. Steel whispered against stone, the sound steady and controlled.

Prayer, spoken in metal.

Jonathan did not frame it that way consciously, but the discipline carried the same weight. Focus. Repetition. Acceptance of imperfection without surrender to it.

He trained his mind harder than his body.

The body adapted quickly. The mind resisted longer.

Breath control.

Heart-rate suppression.

Blind-spot movement.

Emotional shutdown.

Jonathan practiced slowing his pulse deliberately, forcing calm under exertion until his heart obeyed command rather than circumstance. He learned to breathe shallow when necessary, to move without the rise and fall of chest that betrayed presence.

He practiced moving through spaces without being registered—learning how eyes slid past him, how attention skipped over shapes that did not announce themselves.

He learned how emotion interfered.

Fear accelerated heart rate.

Anger narrowed vision.

Grief slowed reaction.

Jonathan did not eliminate these responses.

He muted them.

He slept in abandoned houses where animals scraped the walls.

Raccoons in attics.

Rats in basements.

Insects in the dark.

Jonathan learned the difference between human noise and animal movement, between threat and nuisance. He slept lightly, alert even in rest, body conditioned to wake without panic.

Sat motionless in culverts through storms.

Water rushed inches from his boots. Cold seeped through fabric. Jonathan remained still, counting seconds, breath controlled, until the storm passed. Stillness became a skill as valuable as motion.

Remained still as coyotes circled him.

Their curiosity was cautious. Jonathan did not challenge it. He let them pass, let them lose interest. He learned patience until it replaced fear.

Jonathan didn't just sharpen a knife.

He sharpened himself.

The distinction mattered. Tools were extensions of will. The body was the primary instrument.

The world changed shape around him.

Jonathan noticed it gradually, then all at once.

Homes became choke points.

He saw entrances and exits without effort, measured room dimensions by glance, assessed cover and concealment instinctively. Familiar spaces felt smaller, constrained by possibility.

Mirrors became exits.

Reflection revealed angles, blind spots, alternate paths. Jonathan learned to use glass as information rather than vanity.

Streetlights became timers.

He counted intervals, learned the rhythms of illumination and shadow. Light dictated movement. Darkness offered opportunity.

People became variables.

Not threats.

Not targets.

Variables.

Jonathan assessed behavior patterns, not morality. He watched how people moved, how they reacted to disruption, how quickly they noticed absence. Empathy did not vanish—it became data.

He didn't grow cold.

He grew exact.

Exactness allowed restraint. Precision limited collateral. Jonathan valued both.

The boy who cried beside his mother's body remained buried in snow and blood.

Jonathan did not try to exhume him. That boy had served his purpose. He had survived long enough to allow choice. Carrying him forward would have been cruelty.

What walked now was purpose.

Cameras caught him sometimes—but never fully.

Jonathan allowed it.

A silhouette on a roof.

A shadow in a garage.

A figure watching from a ridge at 3 a.m.

Enough to be felt.

Never enough to be caught.

Presence without confirmation unsettled systems more than absence. Jonathan understood that now. He let himself be sensed just beyond certainty, a pressure without shape.

One winter night in an abandoned lumberyard, Jonathan stood before five wooden posts carved into human shapes.

He had chosen the place carefully—isolated, forgotten, layered with old industrial noise that swallowed sound. Snow drifted through skeletal beams. The air smelled of sap and rust.

The posts were rough approximations, but Jonathan did not need detail. He needed spacing. Height. Angle.

Snow drifted.

Breath fogged.

Jonathan centered himself.

He moved.

Five strikes.

Five identical cuts.

Five perfect angles beneath imaginary collarbones.

The sequence flowed without hesitation. Motion connected seamlessly, transitions smooth and economical. There was no flourish. No excess.

Wood split.

Snow dusted into the wounds like powdered bone.

Jonathan stepped back.

Calm.

Ready.

He assessed the results with professional detachment. Depth consistent. Angle correct. Recovery time minimal.

Not to kill.

Not yet.

But to tighten the noose until the men who destroyed his family felt it with every breath.

Jonathan understood the difference now. Killing was outcome. Pressure was process. He had mastered the first. He was refining the second.

He folded Henry's pocketknife.

The familiar click echoed softly in the empty yard.

Slipped it into his pocket.

And walked into the cold.

The night closed around him without resistance.

The net was almost tight enough.

Almost.

Jonathan moved on, carrying with him the stillness he had earned—patient, exact, and no longer in doubt about what he was.

CHAPTER 39 — FEELING HUMAN

Jonathan Halden had spent years carving himself into something precise and efficient.

He had done it deliberately, with intention sharp enough to cut clean through doubt. Silence had been his scaffold. Discipline his mortar. Scars his measurements. He had taken what the world had given him—loss, fear, enhancement without consent—and shaped it into something narrow enough to survive.

A weapon built from silence, discipline, and scars.

That framing had once steadied him. It had allowed distance from regret, from yearning, from the soft parts of memory that threatened efficiency. Jonathan had believed that if he could make himself exact enough, nothing unnecessary would slip through.

But every so often, something did.

Not violently.

Not dramatically.

Something small. Unimportant. A gesture. A sound. A smell that did not belong to the hunt.

And those moments frightened him more than any man he had ever hunted.

Because they did not announce themselves as threats.

They arrived quietly.

The bunkhouse smelled of fermented apples and damp soil.

The scent clung to everything—clothes, hair, wood— an earthy sweetness already tipping toward rot. Fruit crates leaned crookedly against the walls, sticky with residue that attracted flies too sluggish to be chased away. They hovered and landed and lifted again without urgency, as if even insects were tired.

A single bulb flickered above the door, its light weak and uneven, casting tired shadows over the orchard crew as they unwound after a fourteen-hour shift.

Jonathan noted the way bodies loosened when work ended. Shoulders slumped. Voices dropped. The men moved with the unselfconscious familiarity of people who had shared discomfort long enough to trust it wouldn't turn on them.

Jonathan sat just outside their loose circle.

Close enough to blend.

Far enough to retreat.

He sharpened Henry's pocketknife on a smooth river stone he'd carried for months. He didn't need to sharpen it. The blade already held an edge keen enough for purpose. But the ritual mattered. Each draw of steel against stone anchored him.

Each stroke produced a faint whisper—metal against memory.

The sound slid beneath conversation without intruding, steady and controlled. Jonathan kept his eyes down, body angled slightly away, posture signaling disinterest without hostility. He had learned how to be present without inviting attention.

Laughter drifted around him.

It came in waves, cresting and breaking as jokes landed and missed. Bottles clinked. Someone cursed amiably at a sore shoulder. Men talked the way exhausted men do— unguarded, unfiltered, trusting the dark.

Trust was always what unsettled him most.

Hector dropped onto a crate beside him, brushing dust from his jeans.

The crate creaked under his weight. Jonathan registered the sound, the proximity, the shift in air.

"You ever talk," Hector asked with a grin, "or do you let that knife do all the speaking?"

Jonathan didn't look up.

"It's quieter than I am."

The answer came without effort. He did not plan it. He did not soften it.

Hector laughed—warm, easy.

The sound moved through the orchard like something alive.

It carried no edge. No calculation. Just release.

For a brief, dangerous second, Jonathan felt the corner of his mouth twitch.

The sensation startled him more than gunfire ever had. Muscles that had long forgotten how to respond that way threatened to remember.

Then Hector wiped sweat from his brow with the back of his hand.

The gesture was nothing.

Thoughtless.

Human.

It cut deeper than any blade.

Henry used to do that.

The memory arrived fully formed, unfiltered by distance. Every evening. Same motion. Same tired grace. Sun on his shoulders. Dirt embedded under his nails. The way he would pause, hand dragging across his forehead, exhale slow and content after honest work.

Jonathan saw it with brutal clarity.

The orchard vanished.

The smell shifted from apples to motor oil and dust. Cicadas replaced flies. The weight of memory pressed inward until the present thinned dangerously.

Jonathan snapped the knife shut.

The click was sharp enough to fracture the moment.

"I need to sleep."

Hector's smile faded.

The transition was subtle but immediate. Concern replaced humor.

"You alright, man?"

Jonathan didn't answer.

He stood and walked into the orchard, boots sinking into damp earth. Apples hung heavy above him, pale and swollen, glowing faintly in the dark. Wind threaded through the branches, carrying ghosts he couldn't outrun.

He did not stop walking until the sounds of laughter fell behind him.

Two days later, he was gone.

Jonathan did not leave notes. He did not say goodbye. He departed the way he always did—quietly, efficiently, without a rise. By the time the crew noticed his absence, it would already be old news.

The motel leaned toward collapse, neon buzzing pink across cracked asphalt.

Jonathan stood on the second-floor railing, hands resting lightly on rusted metal as he watched headlights smear into white streaks along the highway below. Cars passed with indifference, each carrying lives he would never touch.

Two pipeline workers waved him over, beers in hand.

"One drink won't kill you," one called.

The invitation was casual, uninvested. Jonathan evaluated it quickly. Visibility here required participation. Declining too often attracted curiosity. Accepting once diffused it.

Jonathan joined them because invisibility required cooperation.

The beer was warm and bitter. He drank only enough to satisfy the moment, careful not to alter his edge.

"Where's home?" the taller one asked.

The word tightened something in his chest until breathing hurt.

Home.

The concept had no stable definition anymore. The farm existed only as ruin. Everywhere else was transit.

Jonathan said nothing.

The shorter man laughed. "Just like my little brother. Won't talk unless you poke him."

Suzanne's voice surfaced instantly.

You're quiet, Jon. But I see you. I always see you.

The memory carried warmth. Not command. Not restraint. Just recognition.

Jonathan's fingers trembled around the bottle.

He noticed it immediately.

Too much.

Too visible.

"You okay?" someone asked.

Concern again.

Connection.

Jonathan set the beer down with careful precision.

Too careful.

"I should rest."

Inside his room, neon bleeding through thin curtains, he opened Henry's pocketknife.

Not to sharpen it.

Just to hold something that had survived her.

The metal felt cool and familiar in his palm. Weight without expectation. He sat on the edge of the bed and breathed until his hands steadied, until the hum beneath his skin quieted.

He left before sunrise.

The construction camp cafeteria rattled with noise—metal trays clanging, shouted jokes bouncing off sheet walls, wind hammering the structure until it shuddered. Jonathan ate fast, eyes down, movements economical.

The foreman sat across from him.

The man had the posture of someone who had spent his life assessing bodies for utility. Jonathan felt the scrutiny immediately.

"You move like you've had training," the foreman said. "Saw you fall today. Rolled clean. Military—or someone taught you young."

Jonathan's fork froze.

The moment telescoped inward.

Fluorescent lights.

Dr. Gerald's voice.

Pain is information.

Again.

"I learned young," Jonathan said.

The words tasted metallic.

"Parents?" the foreman asked.

The word slammed into him.

Not curiosity.

Not malice.

Just assumption.

Jonathan stood so abruptly the chair shrieked across concrete.

"No."

The response was sharper than intended. Heads turned. Conversation faltered. Jonathan registered the attention too late.

He didn't sleep that night.

Sleep gave the past too much room.

Memories slipped through defenses when his mind relaxed. He lay awake, cataloging exits, listening to wind worry at the camp walls, counting breaths until dawn diluted the pressure.

By dawn, he was packed.

By noon, gone.

By dusk, forgotten.

Jonathan never fled danger.

Danger sharpened him.

It gave him boundaries, objectives, clarity. Threat simplified the world into solvable equations.

He fled people.

Hector felt like Henry.

The motel laughter felt like Suzanne.

The foreman's attention felt like the lab reaching for him again—hands poised to measure, to categorize, to claim.

Every connection woke a ghost.

Every ghost reopened a wound.

Every wound reminded him what he had lost—and what he had become.

He could stalk a man for months without sound.

He could kill with a single, upward strike beneath the collarbone.

He could move through America like smoke, leaving no trace heavy enough to follow.

But he could not sit beside laughing men without wanting to disappear.

He could not see a familiar gesture without drowning in memory.

Jonathan Halden was a weapon learning—slowly, painfully—how to feel human again.

And that humanity terrified him far more than violence ever had.

CHAPTER 40 — THE FIRST WARNING

Dr. Lila Marrow stirred her tea in slow, trembling circles.

The porcelain cup chimed softly against its saucer with each rotation, a sound so delicate it bordered on fragile. Steam curled upward, carrying the faint bitterness of bergamot and citrus oil. The smell usually calmed her. Tonight it turned her stomach.

Her hands had never trembled before.

Not during Helix's darkest experiments.

Not when she signed off on procedures that made junior researchers avert their eyes. Not when she stood behind observation glass watching bodies react in ways biology textbooks insisted were impossible. Her hands had been steady through things other people couldn't even look at.

Not during congressional hearings.

She had answered questions with measured precision, voice level, posture immaculate. She had spoken about oversight and containment and unintended outcomes without once betraying the fact that she knew exactly what those words concealed.

Not even during Braden's autopsy, when she realized exactly what Jonathan Halden had become.

She had recognized the cut immediately. Not because it was brutal, but because it was correct. She had seen enough controlled violence to know the difference between savagery and intention. That wound had been a thesis statement.

But the last two years had eroded her.

Not all at once. Not dramatically. Fear had arrived in increments, the way corrosion did—quiet, patient, irreversible.

The anonymous leaf on her doorstep.

The first time, she had dismissed it as coincidence. A gust of wind. A prank. The second time, she had logged it. The third, she had begun photographing it before removal, documenting moisture, species, placement.

The faint tapping beneath her floorboards.

Once. Twice. Always stopping before she could triangulate the source. Inspectors found nothing. Cameras caught nothing. Her sleep thinned.

The widening gap between what she knew and what she feared.

Knowledge had once insulated her. Now it sharpened every imagined threat into something plausible.

Tonight the tremor was constant, a small earthquake beneath her skin.

She felt it in her wrists, her jaw, the shallow pause in her breathing she could not correct. She moved through the house slowly, deliberately, completing routines she no longer trusted to protect her.

She had just finished locking the final window when the porch motion detector chirped—one soft, mechanical beep, barely louder than a breath.

Marrow froze mid-step.

The pause stretched. Her mind raced through possibilities faster than her body could follow. Animal. Glitch. Guard error. Jonathan.

Outside, the guard muttered into his radio, bored and dismissive.

"Unit Six responding. Probably a raccoon."

Her pulse thudded once, hard.

A raccoon didn't make the air feel colder.

A raccoon didn't raise the hairs on her arms.

A raccoon didn't—

She stopped the thought before it could finish. Panic was sloppy. Panic obscured detail. She forced her breathing shallow and controlled, the way she had taught trainees to do when fear threatened performance.

She moved to the window, breath shallow.

The porch lay still under the humming light. Silent boards. A lonely chair. Nothing out of place.

Except the guard's flashlight stopped.

Not drifted.

Stopped.

That distinction mattered. Marrow leaned closer, forehead nearly touching the glass.

The beam illuminated the railing—

—and the teacup slipped from her fingers.

It shattered across the hardwood, spraying shards and brown liquid like blood. The sound was violent in the quiet house, sharp enough to tear a scream from her throat that never quite made it out.

Carved into the wood, clean as if sliced by surgical steel, was a mark.

A perfect upward strike beneath an imagined collarbone.

Jonathan's cut.

His signature.

The same wound pattern found on Captain Braden's corpse.

Marrow felt her knees weaken. Her vision tunneled. The room tilted as if the house itself had lost balance.

Her voice barely escaped her throat.

"Oh God… he was here."

The guard stumbled back, rifling for his radio, hands suddenly clumsy.

"Control—we've got a… possible breach—"

But there was no breach.

Jonathan didn't break in.

He didn't test locks.

He didn't trip alarms.

He simply walked close enough to touch her house.

Close enough to reach her.

And left a mark to tell her:

I could have killed you.

I didn't.

Not yet.

The understanding slammed into her with nauseating clarity. This wasn't escalation. It was calibration.

He wasn't hunting tonight.

He was circling.

And Marrow knew why.

She had made the list.

After the breach—after Henry Halden's death and Jonathan's disappearance—Carlisle had ordered containment. Silence. Legal closure. Systems were to be protected. Liability minimized.

It was Marrow who had compiled the post-incident matrix.

Forty-three names.

Ranked by proximity.

Exposure.

Liability.

She had built the list the way she built everything—methodically, defensibly, without emotion. She had convinced herself she was preventing chaos, protecting the institution from collapse.

She had overseen the NDAs.

Signed off on the severance agreements.

Catalogued the recorded interviews—who panicked, who hesitated, who followed orders too quickly.

She remembered her own notes in the margins. Phrases like procedural adherence and acceptable deviation. The language of insulation.

She had told herself it was damage control.

Jonathan had called it something else.

She had seen the reports later—access logs tripped, archived files opened, interview recordings pulled and re-pulled. Someone had listened to everything.

Including hers.

Her calm voice on tape.

Her measured language.

Her recommendation at the end of the summary:

Subject poses long-term risk. Monitoring advised. No further action required.

The words replayed in her head now, venomous and precise. She had signed Jonathan's future away with a sentence written in passive voice.

Marrow bolted for her phone, nearly slipping on the tea pooling around her bare feet. Her fingers shook so violently she almost dialed the wrong code.

Carlisle answered on the second ring, voice composed, as if he'd been expecting the call.

"Dr. Marrow."

"He was here," she gasped. "Jonathan Halden—he carved the mark. Right on my porch. My guards didn't see him. They didn't hear him. He walked up like—like a ghost."

Silence stretched across the line, cold and analytical.

Carlisle let her words settle, dissected them for utility, not comfort.

"Are you certain it was him?" Carlisle asked.

"Of course it was him!" she snapped.

Her voice cracked, emotion bleeding through the polished veneer she'd spent thirty years cultivating.

"The carving—it's identical to Braden's wound. He's targeting me next. Carlisle, he's—"

A long inhale.

A longer exhale.

"Lila," he said slowly, "I believe you're reacting to stress. Halden is precise. If he intended to kill you, he would have."

Her knees nearly buckled.

The implication crushed her more thoroughly than panic.

"So what am I supposed to do?" Marrow whispered. "He's stalking us. He's in my yard."

"I understand," Carlisle replied quietly.

There was no warmth in the understanding.

"I need more agents," she demanded. "Relocation. Reinforcements. Anything."

More silence.

Carlisle reviewed resource maps in his head. Threat probability. Asset value. Replacement difficulty.

When he finally spoke, his voice had thinned to something small and razor-sharp.

"Resources are limited."

Marrow blinked.

"I beg your pardon?"

"We cannot protect everyone equally," Carlisle said. "Operational necessity requires prioritization."

Everyone.

Meaning: not you.

Her voice collapsed.

"Carlisle... please."

"You're on your own for now," he said.

The line went dead.

She called back.

No answer.

Again.

Straight to encrypted voicemail.

Her chest tightened until breathing hurt. She pressed both hands to her temples, rocking as if she could hold fear inside her skull through force alone.

"He left me," she whispered. "He left me to die."

Wind rattled the windows and she screamed, dropping to the floor.

Her guards swept the yard, shouting into radios, flashlights slicing through the dark.

It didn't matter.

They weren't guarding her from a man.

They were guarding her from something that could walk into her life whenever it chose—

—and vanish just as easily.

Jonathan didn't need to kill her.

Fear was already doing the work.

She slid into the corner of the living room, arms wrapped around her knees, rocking gently—the instinctive sway of someone trying not to shatter.

"He's not hunting yet," she whispered.

"He's circling."

And then the truth landed with perfect, icy clarity.

He wasn't circling the weakest.

He was circling the ones she had ranked as acceptable losses.

Miles away, inside a fortified office lined with panic locks and bullet-resistant glass, Carlisle locked his phone and rubbed his temples.

The room reflected him back in fragments—angles of glass, layered reflections that made him look multiplied, distorted. For a fleeting second—an almost human flicker—he wondered if leaving Marrow undefended had been cruel.

He dismissed it.

Cruelty implied intent. This was logistics.

Braden was dead.

Vaughn had fled.

Two others were missing or compromised.

Jonathan Halden would kill again.

And Carlisle had no intention of being next.

If sacrificing Marrow bought him a month, a week, a single breath—

She was acceptable collateral.

The thought did not trouble him as much as it should have. He noted that too, filed it away as another necessary adaptation.

He checked the satellite feed of his safehouse.

Clear.

For now.

But something gnawed at him, a pressure behind the ribs he hadn't felt since the night Henry Halden breached the lower levels of the lab.

A pressure not of fear—but recognition.

Jonathan wasn't warning Marrow.

He was warning him. And Carlisle finally understood: Jonathan Halden was done circling. He was closing in.

CHAPTER 41 — THE SECOND WARNING

Jonathan didn't need blood to cause wounds.

That understanding had come slowly, hard-earned through observation rather than instinct. Blood was loud. Blood attracted response. Blood narrowed the field into something simple and final. Fear, by contrast, widened it. Fear lingered. It metastasized. It rewrote behavior long after the source vanished.

He didn't need violence to break a man.

Not yet.

Fear was still the sharper blade.

He stood on a ridgeline half a mile from Carlisle's fortified estate, motionless beneath the black lattice of winter pines. Snow gathered on his hood and shoulders until he looked less like a man than something carved and abandoned there, a shape the storm had decided to keep. The wind hissed through the branches and cut across his face, but he barely registered it.

Cold had become background noise. Sensation existed only when it mattered.

Below him, the estate pulsed with anxiety.

Jonathan felt it even from this distance, the way one could feel machinery straining under load. Armed guards marched in rehearsed loops, their boots crunching too loudly against the frozen ground. Too much sound. Too much effort to prove presence. Dogs worked the perimeter in tight, nervous arcs, handlers tugging at leashes already pulled taut. Floodlights swept the property in wide, frantic passes, beams overlapping and correcting, never fully satisfied.

It was not a fortress.

It was a performance.

Jonathan watched everything.

The rhythm of footsteps.

The lag between patrols.

The micro-pauses where a guard hesitated, unsure whether to trust training or instinct.

The way fear introduced hesitation where discipline should have lived.

He noted the small errors—the half-second delays, the unnecessary glances over shoulders, the subtle tightening of grips on rifle stocks. Fear lived in those details. Fear degraded efficiency before it ever reached panic.

He waited four hours before taking a single step.

Waiting was not passive. It was active measurement. He let patterns repeat until they were predictable, then waited for deviation. He let the guards tire themselves out, let adrenaline bleed into exhaustion.

When he moved, it was not toward the estate.

He didn't breach the fence.

He didn't silence a guard or touch a camera.

Instead, he moved around the estate's outer shell, staying just beyond thermal detection, passing beneath branches that fractured the floodlights into broken shards of light. He followed the terrain, not the perimeter, letting the land itself swallow him.

The earth knew how to hide things.

Carlisle's people did not.

The southeast edge sloped into a narrow drainage ditch, muddy and neglected, a forgotten seam where attention thinned. Jonathan had marked it days ago, watched how patrols skirted it without truly seeing it. He knelt at its edge. Cold seeped through his boots, but his breathing remained slow, even.

He reached into his jacket and withdrew a small cloth bundle.

Not a weapon.

A memory.

Inside lay a single wooden match.

Jonathan knew its weight without looking.

He knew the faint rasp of the grain beneath his thumb, the slight resistance just before ignition. He remembered the sound it made when struck—sharp, intimate. A sound meant for quiet rooms.

Henry had used matches like these every morning, lighting the fireplace while the house was still dark. Jonathan remembered sitting at the table, legs swinging, watching the brief flare of flame against his father's tired smile. The smell of woodsmoke curling through the kitchen. The peace of a life small enough to feel real.

A life Carlisle had helped erase.

Jonathan pressed the match into the mud until it stood upright, thin and deliberate, impossible to mistake.

He did not strike it.

Fire would have been spectacle.

He didn't linger.

Lingering invited chance.

When he rose, the treeline accepted him without a sound, the darkness closing behind him as if he had never been there at all.

At 4:11 a.m., a perimeter guard froze mid-step.

"What the hell…?"

His voice was low, uncertain. The guard crouched slowly, eyes locked on the match planted in the mud. There were no footprints. No disturbed earth. No sign of intrusion, no explanation his training could reach for.

Just the match.

Waiting.

"Control, this is Unit Twelve," he said into his radio, voice tight. "You need to see this."

Eight minutes later, Carlisle arrived.

A robe hung crookedly over body armor, thrown on without thought. His hair was still damp, his expression sharpened by the kind of fear that followed him out of sleep and refused to let go. He stared at the match as if it might move on its own.

"Explain," he said.

The word carried no volume. It didn't need to.

"Sir, cameras show nothing," the guard said, words tumbling over each other. "No motion alerts. No heat signatures. No—"

"Then how," Carlisle interrupted quietly, "did it get here?"

No one answered.

Silence stretched, thick and accusing.

Someone near the back spoke barely above a whisper. "Someone knows how to move where we aren't watching."

Carlisle crouched, studying the match between two gloved fingers.

It was insignificant.

Harmless.

And it shook something deep in his chest that armor couldn't reach.

He understood the message immediately, and hated himself for how long it took to exhale afterward.

Jonathan could have breached the fence.

He could have killed a guard, shattered the illusion of control in a way that cameras would replay for weeks. He could have stood beneath Carlisle's bedroom window and let him feel a presence he couldn't explain.

Instead, he had left a memory.

A promise.

Carlisle straightened slowly.

By sunrise, orders were already cascading outward.

Infrared trip lines expanded.

Dog rotations doubled.

Floodlights were repositioned, their angles recalculated, overlapping until shadows vanished entirely.

Thermal drones lifted into the sky.

Blind spots were mapped, sealed, reinforced.

Fencing was upgraded.

Drills reinstated around the clock.

Millions were spent.

Hundreds were mobilized.

All because of a single match.

And still, Carlisle couldn't escape the truth pressing against his ribs.

Jonathan had stood close enough to touch the fence.

He had been there.

He had chosen not to act.

That restraint terrified him more than any overt attack ever could.

From the ridgeline, Jonathan watched the response unfold.

Guards moved faster now, radios hissing constantly, beams of light lurching over the snow in overlapping patterns that solved nothing. The system was reacting to itself, feeding panic back into procedure.

He didn't smile.

Fear wasn't a trophy.

It was information.

Every frantic adjustment revealed something new. Every overreaction carved fresh weaknesses into the perimeter. Jonathan cataloged them without hurry.

He turned Henry's pocketknife over in his palm, the cold steel grounding him, reminding him where this began and why it couldn't stop yet.

Not tonight.

Soon.

The incident report reached Lila Marrow before sunrise.

She sat in her locked condo, knees drawn tight to her chest, reading the details again and again. A match planted at Carlisle's home. A symbol pulled straight from Jonathan's childhood. Precision without spectacle.

Her voice trembled when she spoke aloud. "He's not going for Carlisle first."

The words echoed back at her, heavy and undeniable.

Understanding followed immediately, unwelcome and absolute.

Jonathan wasn't choosing targets at random.

He wasn't striking the strongest or sparing the weakest.

He was shaping the terrain itself.

Closing exits.

Forcing movement.

Guiding them all toward a narrowing point they refused to see.

He wasn't killing yet.

He was positioning.

He was preparing the world for what came next.

And the worst part—the part that hollowed her chest with dread—was that he was doing it with patience.

With restraint.

With memory.

The second warning had been delivered.

The third would not be symbolic.

CHAPTER 42 — THE LAST SANCTUARY

The snow had swallowed the road by the time Dr. Lila Marrow reached the safehouse.

The tires lost traction twice on the final ascent, the SUV fishtailing before the driver corrected with practiced precision. Pines crowded close on either side, their branches bowed beneath the weight of snow, muffling sound until the engine felt like an intrusion rather than reassurance. Marrow watched the forest slide past through the fogged window and felt the unmistakable sensation of being funneled.

The cabin crouched at the edge of the frozen Montana forest, its heavy log walls hunched beneath a roof crusted with ice. Steel reinforcement hid beneath the wood— bones meant to withstand a siege. It should have felt secure.

Tonight, it felt like a trap.

She stumbled out of the SUV, boots crunching through ice and powder. The cold was immediate and punishing, a living thing that clawed through her coat and into her chest. Wind cut across the clearing with a sharpness that stole her breath and brought tears to her eyes. Her fingers slipped twice on the keypad before the lock accepted the code.

The delay felt catastrophic.

The door shut behind her with a low, final sound.

The kind of sound that sealed things.

Inside, heat rolled out from the stone fireplace, thick with the scent of burning pine. The contrast made her dizzy. Her body had not caught up with the reality that she was no longer exposed, and adrenaline had nowhere to go.

Six men in tactical gear waited.

They were positioned deliberately—two near the windows, one by the hallway, one near the kitchen, one standing guard by the reinforced back door, one centered in the room like a fulcrum. Hard faces. Scarred hands. Bodies built for violence and trained to deliver it efficiently.

Men who had done this before.

The team leader stepped forward. His voice was calm, controlled, designed to transmit confidence.

"Dr. Marrow. Are you ok?"

She shook her head, breath still unsteady. Words arrived before thought could restrain them.

"He's coming."

One of the men frowned. "Who?"

She swallowed. The dryness in her throat made the word scrape.

"You know who."

The name didn't need to be spoken.

It pressed into the room anyway.

Jonathan Halden.

The men shifted—not fear, exactly, but recognition. The kind that tightened grips and narrowed eyes. The kind that acknowledged the difference between theory and encounter.

"We lock it down," the leader said. "You stay inside. Nobody gets through this perimeter without going through us first."

He believed it.

Marrow tried to.

She wrapped her arms around herself, feeling the tremor in her muscles refuse to subside. She told herself this was different from the condo. Different from the warnings. This was a place designed for exactly this scenario.

A place meant to hold.

Outside, the darkness pressed close, the forest leaning in as if it were listening.

Snow muted everything, the world reduced to shapes and breath and the soft, traitorous sound of movement. The clearing around the cabin glowed faintly under floodlights, their beams fixed and measured, less frantic than Carlisle's estate had been. The perimeter was tighter here. More thoughtful.

Jonathan noted the difference.

Two guards moved along the east wall. Boots crunching softly. Breath fogging in controlled bursts. Their spacing was disciplined, their movements were intentional, precise. These were not men who expected boredom.

They reached the generator.

Jonathan had already been there.

The shadow detached itself from the dark.

It was not sudden. Not dramatic. It was simply there, where absence had been a moment before.

Jonathan's arm locked around the first guard's face. The motion was precise, practiced until it lived beneath thought. A hand sealed his mouth before sound could form. Henry's pocketknife slid into the soft hollow above the collarbone and punched upward.

The man's legs buckled.

Jonathan guided him down.

Quietly, carefully.

The second guard heard only a muffled sound.

"Davis?" he murmured. "You good?"

Snow shifted behind him.

Jonathan surged up from the drift where he'd been buried. He slammed the man into the cabin wall. The impact rattled bone and breath. The rifle discharged once—wild, useless—its report swallowed by the forest.

Jonathan drove the blade under the ribs, angling up.

Two.

Steam rose as blood soaked into the snow.

Jonathan flexed his fingers once.

Pain registered—then flattened.

The hum steadied, damping shock, sealing torn vessels faster than nature allowed. His breath evened without conscious effort. He did not pause to assess the bodies. He did not need to.

He moved on.

Inside, the gunshot hit Marrow like a physical blow.

The sound punched through the walls, reverberating through the cabin and into her bones. Her mind rejected it for half a second, clinging to the belief that this place was insulated from consequence.

"What was that?" she whispered.

The interior guard raised his radio. His posture changed—alert, purposeful.

"East team, report."

Static.

"Davis? Carter?"

Silence.

The guard turned to Marrow. "Stay behind the couch."

His tone was firm now, stripped of reassurance. He moved toward the back door, weapon raised, steps measured.

It opened.

Closed.

The sound was soft. Final.

Marrow was alone.

Outside, the guard stepped onto the stoop.

His boot brushed something hard.

He looked down.

A gloved hand stared back.

Recognition hit too late.

Jonathan erupted from beneath the stoop, twisted the man down, crushed him against the frozen ground. The impact knocked breath loose in a sharp, wet sound. A blow split Jonathan's cheekbone—pain flared white—

—then dulled.

The knife went in at the base of the neck.

Three.

Jonathan wiped blood from his face with the back of his glove. His ribs throbbed beneath the cut fabric of his jacket, each breath sending a reminder through his chest.

He welcomed it.

Pain meant contact. Contact meant the moment still belonged to him.

Around the front of the cabin, the remaining two guards hugged the walls now. Closer. Tighter. They had adjusted quickly.

"Footprints," one said. "Too small for—"

Jonathan dropped from the eaves.

The impact jarred his already aching ribs. He drove one guard into the wall, felt bone crack beneath his forearm. The second charged.

Bodies collided.

A boot cracked into Jonathan's ribs, driving breath from his lungs in a harsh, involuntary exhale. Stars flared behind his eyes. The hum surged, clamped down, stabilized.

He shoved backward, smashed both men into the wall. Frost rained down from the eaves, scattering like powdered glass.

The knife flashed once.

Then again.

Four.

Five.

Silence returned.

Jonathan stood still for a moment longer than necessary, letting his breathing settle, cataloging damage. Blood dripped from his sleeve onto the snow. His vision swam slightly, then corrected.

He turned toward the cabin.

Inside, the final guard pulled Marrow toward the hallway.

His grip was tight enough to bruise, his breath hot against her ear.

"Move," he said. "Now."

The back door rattled.

Once.

Twice.

Each impact echoed through the small space, reverberating in Marrow's chest like a countdown.

The guard told her to run.

She couldn't.

Her legs refused the command, locked by something deeper than fear.

The door opened just enough.

Jonathan's hand shot through and dragged the guard forward. The movement was violent, abrupt. Bone crunched as they crashed into the kitchen, bodies colliding with cabinets and counters.

The blade buried itself in the man's chest.

Six.

The sound he made was brief.

The cabin went quiet.

Marrow stood in the hallway, gun hanging uselessly at her side. She had raised it without remembering how. Her hands shook so badly she doubted she could pull the trigger if she tried.

Jonathan turned toward her.

Blood streaked his face. One eye swollen shut. Breath ragged now, no longer perfectly controlled. He looked real in a way she hadn't expected.

Not monstrous.

Wounded.

Human.

He stopped several feet away.

"Don't," he said.

Not to her.

To himself.

She raised the gun, shaking. "Please."

The word tore itself loose without permission. It tasted like betrayal.

"I'm not here to torture you."

His voice was rough, strained by exertion and something else she could not name.

"Then why?"

"To finish what you started."

Her sigh was a sort of acknowledgement of what was to come.. She looked past him. Towards the fire place roaring with a flames, the walls, the lie of safety she had carried here like a talisman.

She understood then that nothing she said would matter. That justification had no currency left between them.

She put the gun in her mouth.

Jonathan didn't move.

The shot was deafening.

The sound ricocheted through the cabin, through the trees, through Marrow's body as it collapsed. Jonathan flinched despite himself, a reflex he could not suppress.

He knelt beside her body only long enough to confirm it was over. The clinical part of him noted the angle, the absence of hesitation in the final act. He did not judge it.

He searched her pockets, found the keys, guided her hand to the safe in the study.

It opened.

Inside: binders, photos, drives. One marked with his name.

Jonathan sat on the floor and read until his hands shook.

Read about containment protocols.

Read about projected outcomes.

Read about risk modeling that quantified is life in percentages and margins. When he finished, he closed the binder.

"Now I know," he said softly.

The words were not a threat. They were acknowledgment. He stepped back into the storm. Snow erased his tracks almost immediately. The fire crackled behind him. The storm went on and so did he.

CHAPTER 43 —WARNING NO ONE HEEDED

The news reached Carlisle before sunrise.

He had been awake for hours, staring at a wall of live feeds that offered nothing except proof of his own futility. Every camera showed stillness. Every sensor reported nominal. Every alert queue sat empty. The absence felt like mockery.

A secure line buzzed once on his desk.

The sound snapped through him.

He answered with fingers that didn't feel steady.

"Report."

"Dr. Lila Marrow is deceased."

Carlisle shut his eyes.

For a moment, he allowed himself to imagine a different sentence forming at the other end of the line. Relocated. Evacuated. Under protection. Something that suggested continuity.

"How?" he asked.

"Inconclusive."

A lie.

Carlisle recognized the cadence immediately—the careful vagueness, the bureaucratic pause meant to dull impact. Inconclusive meant no external breach. Inconclusive meant clean. Inconclusive meant Jonathan.

"All security personnel neutralized," the voice added.

Carlisle exhaled slowly.

Not relief.

Calculation.

Jonathan had escalated again—not in noise, not in spectacle, but in certainty. Each step forward was narrower, cleaner, less negotiable than the last.

He stared at his reflection in the office glass.

The man looking back at him barely resembled the one who had once spoken with ease about acceptable risk and strategic loss. The face was hollow-eyed, cheeks drawn, skin grayed by fluorescent light and weeks of sleeplessness. He looked like someone who had mistaken control for permanence.

He needed help.

Not men with guns.

Not committees.

Someone who believed systems always won.

Someone like Elias Kincaid.

New York City woke too fast to notice fear.

It never had time for it.

The city surged into motion before dawn fully loosened its grip, subway doors clattering open, delivery trucks grinding through intersections, steam lifting from grates like breath from something vast and indifferent. Millions of lives collided and passed through each other without acknowledgment.

Fear drowned here.

On the forty-second floor of a mirrored tower, Elias Kincaid sat behind reinforced glass, broad shoulders squared, posture still military despite the years. His suit was expensive, tailored to a body that had once been armor. His confidence was older than money. It had been forged in rooms where outcomes were decided before words finished forming.

Carlisle's name flashed on the encrypted line.

Kincaid didn't look surprised.

"Kincaid."

"He's killed her," Carlisle said.

There was no preamble. No attempt to soften the statement.

"Marrow?" Kincaid asked.

"Yes."

A pause.

Calculating.

"Knew the day would come."

The dismissal landed harder than denial would have. Carlisle's jaw tightened.

"You're underestimating him."

"I'm contextualizing him," Kincaid replied. "He beats men. Systems don't bleed."

"You're wrong."

Carlisle leaned forward now, palms pressed flat against the desk, voice low with something close to urgency. "He learns. He adapts. He isn't reacting anymore."

Kincaid stood, walking to the window.

Below him, the city unfolded in rigid grids and flowing arteries. Glass reflected glass. Traffic flowed and stalled and flowed again. People moved in patterns too dense to isolate.

"This city runs on layers," Kincaid said. "Cameras. Redundancy. People everywhere. If he comes for me, he drowns."

"You forget what ghosts fear," Kincaid added.

Carlisle stiffened. "And what is that?"

"Being seen."

He ended the call.

Carlisle stared at the dead screen long after the connection severed. He wanted to call back. To press. To force understanding.

He didn't.

He already knew it wouldn't work.

Across the street, beneath scaffolding dusted with snow, Jonathan Halden stood motionless.

He blended into the city without effort. Dark coat. Neutral posture. No fixed stare. Just another figure waiting for a light to change, another body occupying space without announcement.

He watched the tower.

The building's skin mirrored the world back at itself, an architectural insistence on separation. Inside, Kincaid believed he was insulated by layers thick enough to suffocate threat.

Jonathan understood something Kincaid did not.

Cities didn't protect men like Kincaid.

They buried them.

Fifteen months earlier, New York had swallowed Jonathan whole.

The first day had been disorienting.

Port Authority at dawn—noise layered on noise, bodies moving in overlapping currents that never stopped colliding. The smell of grease and metal and damp concrete pressed into him from every side. Digital signs flashed departures and delays in relentless sequence.

Jonathan didn't fight it.

He let it take him.

He moved when others moved. Stopped when they stopped. Allowed the city's momentum to carry him until his own presence dissolved into it. The crowd became concealment.

He slept where no one noticed absence.

Public libraries between floors. Overnight trains. Stairwells that smelled like disinfectant and neglect. He learned which spaces reset at morning and which were ignored indefinitely.

He worked jobs that didn't ask questions.

Loading docks. Night cleanup. Construction sites that changed faces weekly and never tracked names beyond first. He kept his head down and his pace steady. Reliable. Forgettable.

He dressed like the background.

Neutral colors. Nothing new. Nothing distinctive. Shoes worn just enough to avoid attention. Jackets that matched the season without signaling intention.

He learned which badges beeped twice before turning green.

Which scanners hesitated when someone moved with confidence rather than hesitation. Which security guards noticed faces and which noticed only behavior.

He never stole access.

He copied it.

Library terminals gave him paper skeletons.

Public records. Zoning maps. Corporate filings that traced ownership through layers of shell entities until patterns emerged. Observation gave him flesh.

Habits.

Routes.

Blind corners.

The hour when the service elevator lagged before resetting. The stretch of sidewalk where cameras overlapped imperfectly. The security desk guard who drank too much coffee and missed small inconsistencies.

He mapped Kincaid the way surgeons mapped arteries.

Where information flowed.

Where pressure built.

Where intervention would cause collapse.

Jonathan didn't rush.

The city rewarded patience.

He learned Kincaid's rhythms without ever entering his orbit. Board meetings. Private dinners. The routes between offices and residences that never changed because consistency was mistaken for control.

By the time the city forgot him, Jonathan knew every way into Kincaid's world.

Now, he stepped back into the crowd.

Kincaid believed systems beat individuals.

Jonathan was a system.

Not because he commanded others.

Because he integrated.

He adapted.

He learned from every surface he touched.

The warning had been written already—in Braden's body, in Marrow's cabin, in the match planted in mud.

No one heeded it.

They would.

Jonathan shifted his weight as the light changed.

The crowd moved.

He moved with it.

The city accepted him without resistance.

Above him, glass reflected nothing of consequence.

Below him, tunnels carried lives in endless circulation.

Somewhere inside the tower, Elias Kincaid believed himself untouchable.

Jonathan didn't hurry.

Time was already working for him.

CHAPTER 44 —MAN IN THE BLIND SPOT

The city breathed around him.

It was not a metaphor Jonathan indulged often, but here it fit with uncomfortable precision. New York inhaled and exhaled in cycles of traffic and footfall, noise and lull, light and shadow. The breath carried grit and heat and the constant abrasion of motion, and it never paused long enough to notice any single particle within it.

Wind funneled between high-rises in long, metallic groans that rattled loose signage and sent paper cups tumbling along the sidewalk. A bus belched exhaust into the cold morning air, sour diesel washing over the curb. A taxi screeched as it swerved around a delivery truck double-parked in a bike lane. A street vendor's grill hissed—meat and onions charring—mixing with the chemical sting of winter sidewalk cleaner and the coppery undertone of rusted scaffolding.

Jonathan moved through it all like a man made of fog.

Present, but unnoticed.

He didn't fight the flow of pedestrians. Fighting created friction, and friction invited attention. He drifted with it—an eddy of silence inside a storm of noise— matching pace without mirroring posture, aligning trajectory without sharing intent. The city rewarded this kind of humility. It mistook absence of assertion for absence of threat.

New York didn't hide him.

It consumed him.

By now, Kincaid's building felt less like a target and more like terrain, a place Jonathan knew with the same instinctive clarity as forests and fields and back roads. Only here, the trees were steel and the predators wore suits.

Terrain was honest. It followed rules.

Buildings did too.

He knew the morning guard rotation down to the minute. The first guard arrived just before seven, always yawning, always rubbing frost from the corner of the security booth window as if the cold were personal. Jonathan had watched him enough times to recognize the exact moment fatigue overtook vigilance. Lobby doors unlocked on schedule, obedient to a timer and nothing else. No human judgment, no deviation.

The second guard took the east post with a thermos that always carried the faint smell of cinnamon. Jonathan had once followed the scent to confirm the man's path without ever seeing him. Kincaid's sedan pulled up at the same time each day, tinted windows reflecting the rising light, a private world insulated from the street.

Predictability was comfort mistaken for strength.

At 6:59, Jonathan slipped through the loading dock pushing a borrowed janitorial cart he'd used before. The cart itself was unremarkable—scratched plastic, squeaking wheels, a mop head stained beyond redemption. The mop handle rattled against the bucket with each step—just enough noise to sell reality, not enough to invite attention.

Noise mattered. Too little felt deliberate. Too much felt sloppy.

The guard barely glanced up.

"Cold one today," Jonathan said, pitching his voice scratchy and low, the opposite of his natural cadence. He had practiced this register until it felt as easy as breathing, a voice that suggested fatigue rather than confidence.

The guard shrugged. "Could be worse."

Jonathan moved on without lingering.

Lingering was a form of confession.

He didn't look toward the lobby. He didn't search for cameras with his eyes. Searching telegraphed uncertainty. Instead, he let his body behave like it belonged and relied on the building's own arrogance to keep him invisible.

Over the last two months he had mapped it floor by floor until it lived behind his eyes.

Not diagrams. Not drawings.

Pressure sensors beneath the marble that triggered half a second later than expected. Swipe-access limitations that funneled staff through predictable arteries. The freight elevator's timing, its momentary lag before doors sealed. The stairwell door that complained if opened too quickly, metal protesting impatience.

He knew which guards dragged their feet, which paid attention, and which were bored enough to miss anything that didn't announce itself. Boredom was the city's greatest vulnerability. It dulled edges faster than fear.

Today, he pushed deeper—into a section he had never entered but had studied until he could feel its geometry in his bones.

Two levels underground, Kincaid kept a private training floor.

Not a public gym.

Not a corporate perk.

A controlled space for former operatives, high-value clients, and men who needed to sweat where their ghosts couldn't follow. The floor existed in blueprints and rumors, in maintenance logs and power draw anomalies. Jonathan had never been inside.

Which meant he would be today.

He rolled the cart into a maintenance corridor and stopped beside a gray door marked with an authorization warning. The badge reader glowed red, patient and indifferent.

He didn't use the clone.

Too risky.

Too traceable.

Cloned access left echoes—timestamps that could be reconciled later, patterns that begged for explanation. Jonathan preferred solutions that left no questions at all.

Instead, he pulled a thin strip of metal from his pocket, improvised from scrap found behind a construction dumpster—flexible, sharpened at one end. He slid it between door and frame, felt the tension, coaxed it with small movements.

Wiggle.

Lift.

Twist.

The lock clicked, less picked than persuaded.

The door opened.

Warm, filtered air washed over him, thick with rubber mats, eucalyptus spray, and the faint chlorine edge of a recovery pool. The lighting was soft but clinical, designed to flatter strength and conceal weakness. Polished steel machines reflected bodies back at themselves, optimized for men who treated pain like a budget line item.

Jonathan didn't touch anything.

Touch left traces.

He stood still and listened.

The hum of HVAC. The distant rhythm of feet. A low mechanical whir that suggested motion elsewhere.

Footsteps approached—heavy, steady, measured.

Jonathan eased behind a corner and flattened himself to the wall until he became another hard edge in a corridor full of hard edges. He controlled his breath until even the rise of his chest disappeared into geometry.

Kincaid entered in a gray workout shirt and black compression pants, sweat already gathering along his neck as if he'd warmed up somewhere else. Two guards followed, not dressed to exercise—dressed to react.

They carried themselves differently than lobby guards. Less carefree. More readiness.

"Same interval training as last week?" one asked.

"No," Kincaid said. "Increase incline. Decrease rest."

"Sir, your knee—"

"My knee is my business," Kincaid snapped.

Jonathan watched through the reflection in a weight rack, taking in details Kincaid wouldn't know he was giving away.

He moved like a disciplined man, powerful and practiced, but he still favored the left leg more than he realized. The compensation showed up not in stride, but in recovery—how long it took him to settle after exertion.

When he stepped onto the treadmill, he tapped a PIN into a custom control panel—four quick digits, rehearsed, casual.

Jonathan tracked the rhythm.

The finger placement.

The pattern of certainty.

Two.

Two.

Seven.

Two.

Sloppy.

Overconfident.

Reused.

Jonathan stored it without judgment.

He slipped back into the corridor before anyone's head turned, leaving the air as undisturbed as he'd found it. He didn't need to stay. He'd already taken something vital.

Kincaid's condo was a separate fortress.

Polished marble.

Gold-warm lighting calibrated to soothe.

A doorman with perfect posture and white gloves that never showed dirt.

Jonathan approached it as different men on different days: a courier with a clipboard and tired eyes, a confused tenant pretending not to understand the buzzer, a survey contractor checking foundation pressure lines. Each role required only minimal performance, enough to be believed and quickly forgotten.

Each time, he collected the same truths.

Camera angles.

Guard placement.

Door timing.

Which residents held doors for strangers and which ignored everyone as a rule.

Human behavior was more consistent than architecture.

On the fourth attempt, he didn't enter.

He watched from across the street, hood up, hands wrapped around a steaming coffee cup that kept him looking ordinary. The cup burned his palms slightly. He welcomed it.

One resident dropped her keycard with predictable clumsiness. Another let strangers slip in without looking. The doorman stepped away from his station at exactly the same time each afternoon for a phone call that lasted fourteen seconds.

Fourteen seconds was enough.

Jonathan stored it all where it couldn't be searched or seized.

Patterns.

Flaws.

Rhythms.

No fortress was perfect.

Kincaid's was no exception.

He secured a vantage point from above—a rooftop with a broken lock he repaired just enough to reenter, not enough to draw attention. He lay flat on cold concrete, breath fogging into the night. The cold pressed into him, steady and impartial.

From there, he watched Kincaid's life as rectangles of light.

A high-floor living room.

A silhouette pacing during late-night calls.

Occasional guests, their arrivals and departures telling their own stories.

Curtains snapping shut when paranoia surged.

Once, lightning carved the sky and for a fraction of a second the city became a skeleton of light. Kincaid stood framed in the flash, staring out with a face carved from exhaustion and pride.

Jonathan didn't blink.

He knew that posture.

A man pretending he wasn't afraid.

Good.

Fear made men predictable.

Kincaid Solutions also maintained a secondary monitoring hub on the twelfth floor, where junior staff handled internal CCTV. Jonathan needed inside.

He didn't force entry.

He waited.

Watched the watchers.

Learned what boredom did to vigilance.

One guard fell asleep after midnight, chin sinking to chest in a slow surrender. Another took long bathroom breaks. Another flirted with the receptionist until his attention became a joke shared by everyone but him. Another microwaved fish at one in the morning and carried its stink like a warning label.

He went in once more with a stolen janitor badge, a mop, and the quiet confidence of a man who belonged wherever he decided to belong.

In the dim glow of monitors, he memorized blind angles near Kincaid's office, elevator refresh delays, exterior alley cameras that glitched for seconds during reboot cycles, stairwell corners that dissolved into grainy static.

Then he saw it.

A true blind spot.

A three-second window where a camera rebooted and recorded nothing at all.

Three seconds was an eternity in the right hands.

Jonathan didn't test it.

Testing invited scrutiny.

He left as silently as he arrived, a ghost under fluorescent light, the kind people never remembered even if they tried.

Late one night, he passed Kincaid on the sidewalk.

Kincaid stood outside his building with his collar high, phone at his ear, a black SUV idling too close to the curb. His voice carried irritation, not fear.

Jonathan walked by like any other man headed somewhere else, neither slowing nor turning, letting proximity do nothing more than confirm what he already knew.

"…I don't care what Carlisle says," Kincaid growled into the call. "Marrow was weak. But I'm not dying because that boy has a grudge."

Jonathan's breath fogged in the cold.

"I'll handle it my way."

Jonathan didn't look back.

He didn't let his pace change.

But he took every syllable and put it where it belonged, cataloged alongside everything else arrogance offered.

A few steps later, the SUV engine rumbled louder.

Jonathan didn't break stride.

He smiled—faint, almost invisible—there and gone.

Kincaid had no idea that the hooded man walking past him was the one he feared.

Not yet.

But the city knew.

Every alley.

Every rooftop.

Every broken lock Jonathan fixed just enough to return.

Every camera that flickered at the wrong moment.

Every gust of wind that carried his shadow across a busy sidewalk.

Jonathan Halden moved through New York like a rumor sharpening into truth.

Kincaid's doom wasn't approaching.

It was already here.

He just couldn't see it—because Jonathan lived in the one place even strong men never learned to check.

Their blind spot.

CHAPTER 45 — THE NARROW LINE OF FEAR

Kincaid hadn't slept in two days—not real sleep.

What he'd had were brief outages. Blackouts that ended before rest could do its work. Each time his eyes closed, the same images surged forward with predatory insistence: a cabin soaked in blood, walls breathing with heat, the metallic tang of iron in the air. A boy standing in the corner of his office, silent and unmoving, watching. A boy who didn't die.

The images didn't arrive as dreams. They arrived as interruptions—memories that didn't belong to him but insisted on residency anyway. He had tried medication. He had tried alcohol. He had tried exercise, pacing his private gym until his knee flared and forced him to stop. Nothing quieted the reel.

Coffee cups littered his desk—half-drained, gone cold—fingerprints smeared into the cardboard like evidence of time he couldn't get back. He noticed the pattern without meaning to. He always drank the first half fast, then forgot the rest. The habit annoyed him. It felt like another small failure.

Three security briefings lay open, pages wrinkled from being flipped too hard, too often. His tie was gone. His collar hung open. His sleeves were rolled to the elbows as if he'd been fighting something invisible and losing.

He stared at the bank of monitors in his private surveillance room on the forty-first floor.

The room had been built to project control. Black glass. Matte steel. Screens arranged to imply omniscience. Tonight it felt smaller every minute, the walls tightening, the air thinning, the screens too bright. The hum of electronics pressed into his skull until he wondered if it was new—or if he'd only just started hearing it.

"Zoom in," he snapped.

A guard obeyed, hands steady enough to function but not steady enough to escape Kincaid's notice. Kincaid's attention fixed on the alley camera behind Kincaid Solutions. It flickered during its scheduled reboot. It always flickered.

That had never mattered until it did.

"Why is that still happening?" Kincaid demanded, voice cracking despite his effort to keep it level.

"System refresh protocol, sir," the guard said, swallowing. "Engineering scheduled—"

"I don't care who scheduled it."

Kincaid slammed his fist into the console. Equipment rattled. His knuckles split; a thin bead of blood welled up and slid down his skin. He didn't look at it. Pain felt secondary now, like something happening to someone else.

"Fix it. Now."

"Yes, sir."

Kincaid dragged both hands down his face, pulling skin until his eyes felt hollow and bruised. Fear had cracked him open, and once it did that, it didn't let a man close again. It didn't scream. It whispered. It suggested. It pointed.

Below him, Jonathan stepped out of a maintenance stairwell onto the twelfth floor with a mop bucket rolling ahead of him, its wheels humming softly against polished flooring.

He felt it immediately.

Not danger yet.

Pressure.

The building's rhythm had shifted, tightened by intent rather than schedule. Jonathan had learned to recognize that sensation the way others recognized weather changes—subtle, pervasive, undeniable. He cataloged it without panic.

As he passed a darkened conference room, he caught the reflection of two guards at the far end of the corridor.

They weren't usually there.

The deviation registered, slotted into place beside a dozen others. Increased staffing. Repositioned coverage. Kincaid had reacted to something—perhaps the blind spot, perhaps the accumulated absence that had begun to scream louder than presence.

Jonathan didn't slow.

He didn't react.

He didn't let his face change.

He turned a corner as if he'd taken it a hundred times, the cart's rattle steady and unremarkable. Inside him, something clicked into sharper alignment. Kincaid had altered the pattern.

That made everything riskier.

Jonathan welcomed it.

Men under pressure became predictable. Predictable men made mistakes.

He moved into another corridor—clean, sterile, lined with abstract art that suggested taste without substance. Colors chosen to soothe. Lines chosen to imply motion without direction. His boots whispered along carpet engineered to swallow sound.

Footsteps began behind him.

Too fast.

Too focused.

Too intentional.

He didn't turn. He walked until the hallway split into a Y, three branches angling away from each other. He chose left without hesitation, not because it was correct, but because commitment itself reduced scrutiny.

"Hey! You!"

Jonathan pushed the cart left, rounded it smoothly, and slipped through a service door he'd memorized weeks earlier. The latch closed without a sound. He pressed himself flat against the metal wall, breath held, muscles loose, body making itself smaller than it should have been able to.

The trick was not tension.

Tension drew attention.

Through the wired glass, a guard burst into view. "Service corridors are restricted!"

A radio crackled, urgent. "Possible intruder on twelve."

Intruder.

Not janitor.

Not staff.

Progress.

Jonathan's fingers curled around the worn leather sheath beneath his jacket. Henry's pocketknife sat there, familiar weight and familiar promise. He didn't plan to use it today. Not here.

Plans were ideals. Survival was arithmetic.

The guard reached for the service door.

Jonathan stayed perfectly still—no shift of shoulders, no change in breathing, nothing for the eye to catch. He counted heartbeats until his pulse aligned with the ambient hum of the building.

Then the radio barked again, louder. "Kincaid wants all teams to Sub-Level Two. Now. Possible breach."

The guard cursed, spun, and sprinted away toward the elevators.

Jonathan let his breath out in a slow thread and moved deeper into the service tunnels.

He'd tripped something early.

The building was tightening around him.

Time to vanish.

He burst through a fire exit into the parking garage.

The air hit him thick and stale—oil, rubber, concrete dust—fluorescent lights buzzing overhead, flickering just enough to irritate the eye and fray the nerves. The garage amplified sound without clarifying it, a bowl of echoes and blind corners.

"There! On me!"

Jonathan ran.

Boots pounded concrete. His breathing stayed controlled. His heart climbed but didn't spike. The hum beneath his ribs flattened the surge, redistributed energy where it was needed most.

Guards poured into the garage, black uniforms and hard shouts, weapons raised. Jonathan vaulted a curb, cut between two sedans, sprinted toward the ramp.

"Cut him off!"

"Two on upper level!"

His mind mapped the space instantly—dead-end row, upper ramp, exit gate, staff parking—and he chose the back row, the one with tighter angles and more cover. He ran where vehicles were parked unevenly, where shadows broke lines of sight.

A shot cracked.

A side mirror exploded inches from his shoulder. Glass sprayed the air, glittering briefly before skittering across concrete. A car alarm screamed into life and wouldn't stop, its pitch shrill enough to distort direction.

Jonathan dropped, rolled under a pickup, and came up running, legs burning but steady.

"He's headed for staff parking!"

He reached an old gray sedan.

Locked.

Next car—unlocked.

He slid inside. The interior stank of cigarettes and sweat, upholstery worn thin by other people's impatience. His hands moved without thought, the kind of mechanical fluency earned from farm equipment and old engines and junkyard lessons. The ignition coughed, then caught.

"He's in a vehicle!"

Jonathan floored it.

The sedan fishtailed, tires scrabbling for traction on dusty concrete. He corrected without slowing, steering into instability rather than away from it.

A security SUV lunged to block the lane.

Jonathan jerked the wheel.

The impact was brutal.

Metal slammed metal.

The world snapped sideways.

Airbags detonated with a violent punch. His skull rang. Blood flooded his mouth, copper and heat. Pain flared through his ribs where the belt had bitten hard, compressing breath into something thin and sharp.

He tore himself free, shoved the door open, and staggered out into the buzz of alarms and shouting.

He didn't stop to orient.

Orientation wasted seconds.

He ran.

Another SUV barreled down the ramp toward him, engine screaming, tires squealing as it fought physics.

Jonathan bolted for the lower exit, lungs searing, vision bright at the edges. The garage fell away behind him in a howl of engines and radios and frantic footsteps.

He burst outside.

Cold air slapped him hard enough to feel like punishment. Snow spiraled. Horns screamed. The street surged with life that refused to organize itself around pursuit.

Jonathan ran straight into traffic.

He cut between hoods and bumpers, forcing drivers to brake too late. Tires screeched. A hand slammed on a horn, long and furious.

A delivery truck clipped him.

Pain detonated across his side—sharp, electric—and his feet left the ground. He hit pavement and rolled, elbows scraping, shoulder slamming, then came up again before his body could fully register what it had endured.

Collisions cascaded behind him.

Metal screamed.

Glass burst.

Drivers shouted and spilled out of cars, furious and terrified and confused. Guards followed, then stalled, trapped by civilians and traffic and the city's sudden refusal to become a clean battlefield.

Jonathan cut down a sidewalk and dove into a subway entrance.

Warm, stale air rushed up to meet him. The smell of brake dust and electricity swallowed everything else. The city took him back without pause, without judgment, without memory.

Gone.

Above, Kincaid watched the monitors as everything unraveled below—smoke, wreckage, a smear of blood on concrete that the camera couldn't decide to focus on. Voices overlapped in his earpiece. Status updates turned into excuses. Commands turned into noise.

The blind spot flickered again.

That three-second lapse suddenly felt like a gaping wound in the building's skin.

Kincaid backed away from the screens, breath shallow, his mind trying to deny what his body already knew. His reflection fractured across black glass, multiplied and distorted.

"He's here," he whispered.

Not a file. Not a rumor.

A presence. And by the time a man understood what lived in his blind spot, it was already too late.

CHAPTER 46 —SPACE BETWEEN BREATHS

Jonathan hid for three days.

Not because he was wounded.

Because the world had come too close.

That distinction mattered to him. Wounds were measurable. They obeyed rules. Damage announced itself through pain, limitation, friction. What had pressed too near in the garage and the street afterward had not been damage—it had been proximity. Exposure. The sense that the city had brushed against him and left fingerprints where there should have been none.

He took shelter beneath an abandoned theater scheduled for renovation, a maintenance crawlspace no one bothered to lock anymore.

The building had been closed long enough that the city had forgotten it, but not long enough to erase it entirely. Posters still clung to the brick façade outside, their colors bleached, corners peeling like old skin. Inside, dust lay in a fine, undisturbed layer across everything. Old show flyers curled against the concrete walls, names and dates fading into nothing. Pipes ticked softly as they cooled. Footsteps passed overhead.

Somewhere deeper underground, a train moved through the city like a distant mechanical pulse.

Jonathan lay still and let the sound pass through him without attaching to it. He had learned the difference between noise and threat. The train was neither. It was simply evidence that the world continued whether he acknowledged it or not.

He lay on his back with his hands folded over his chest and listened.

Listened not for pursuit, not for footsteps or radios or the subtle hum of surveillance, but for himself. The space inside him that no longer spoke unless he made room for it.

His body repaired. There was no effort involved. No concentration required. He did not direct the process. It simply happened, quietly and efficiently, the way systems functioned when nothing interfered with them.

The cut along his ribs sealed within minutes of stillness. Internal microfractures smoothed out without leaving tenderness behind. Inflammation never had time to bloom.

By the end of the first hour there was no pain left to catalog, only memory.

That was what lingered.

Memory did not close. It did not scar over. It did not obey biological timelines. It waited, patient and exact, for moments when his guard dropped.

Jonathan focused on his breathing anyway.

In for four.

Hold for two.

Out for six.

The rhythm wasn't for healing.

It was for grounding.

He had learned long ago that breath could anchor the mind when nothing else would. Not as meditation, not as calm—but as structure. Something repeatable. Something that could be returned to when thought began to drift too far in any direction.

He counted until numbers lost meaning and only timing remained.

When he sat up slowly, he half-expected stiffness or soreness, some proof that the chase had been real.

There was nothing.

His muscles responded immediately, clean and responsive. His joints moved without hesitation. His balance settled where it always did, precise and centered.

His body felt normal.

Fully functional.

Perfect.

That unsettled him more than pain ever could have.

Pain would have confirmed consequence. Pain would have reminded him that something had been paid for the distance he covered, the speed he maintained, the impacts he absorbed.

Perfection suggested something else entirely.

He pulled out his notebook.

It was small, unmarked, carried in an inner pocket where it stayed close to his body. He did not open it right away. He rested his thumb against the edge of the paper, feeling its texture, grounding himself in something that did not optimize or correct or anticipate.

He didn't write about Kincaid.

Not yet.

That part of him needed distance, space to cool back into precision. Emotion too close to intent produced error. He knew that as surely as he knew the layout of any building he had ever mapped.

Instead, he wrote things that didn't belong to a weapon.

The way steam rose from subway grates like breath in cold air.

The smell of roasted nuts near a street vendor who never looked up.

The sound the city made late at night when traffic thinned and everything felt briefly exposed, as if New York itself were holding still, waiting to see if anyone noticed.

He wrote slowly, carefully, as if the act itself required restraint. His handwriting surprised him. It was smaller than he remembered. Tighter. Controlled. Each word placed deliberately, with no excess.

When he finished, he stared at the words, confused by his own handwriting.

He hadn't written like this in years.

Not since before the farm. Before silence had become a tool instead of a refuge.

That night, hunger arrived—not sharp or urgent, but insistent.

It made itself known not through pain but through a gradual thinning of focus, a subtle hollowing that suggested something missing rather than something wrong.

After midnight he slipped out and bought soup from a bodega that never closed.

The bell above the door rang once. The man behind the counter barely looked up. Jonathan paid in cash and received a plastic container that radiated warmth through his gloves.

He ate sitting on the curb, plastic spoon scraping softly against the container.

Rainwater pooled near his boots, reflecting streetlight halos that wavered with each passing car. He ate slowly, aware of texture, temperature, the way steam fogged his glasses before dissipating.

A woman passed with a child bundled too tightly for the weather.

The child laughed—sudden, bright, unprompted.

Jonathan froze.

Not from fear.

From memory.

For a fraction of a second the city peeled away and he saw snow-lit fields, a porch light glowing warm against the dark, his mother's voice calling him inside before the cold settled too deep.

There was no pain in the memory.

Just absence.

The absence pressed harder than grief ever had. Grief burned. Absence hollowed.

He stood abruptly and left the empty container behind.

Back beneath the theater, he lay awake until morning, staring at the low ceiling.

The concrete above him held the day's warmth faintly, a dull echo of heat that faded as hours passed. He watched shadows shift imperceptibly as the city moved overhead.

He didn't sharpen the knife.

He didn't replay security footage in his head.

He didn't run contingencies.

That alone felt dangerous.

He existed in the narrow space between breaths.

The place where thought did not immediately turn into planning. Where awareness did not demand action. Where the world could be observed without being solved.

On the third day he folded the notebook closed and added one final line, written smaller than the rest.

Don't confuse silence with emptiness.

He read it twice.

Then once more.

The sentence did not feel like instruction. It felt like warning.

He slid Henry's pocketknife into his pocket and rested his hand there longer than usual.

The weight of it was familiar, grounding, unchanged by everything else that had altered around it. Steel did not adapt. It did not learn. It waited.

His body was ready.

It always was.

The danger wasn't damage.

It was how easily the world could still reach him when he wasn't looking.

That realization settled deeper than any threat assessment. It did not demand immediate response. It demanded acknowledgment.

Jonathan Halden stepped back into the city.

The hunt would continue.

But now he understood something new—something Carlisle never accounted for.

You don't need to be broken to feel fragile.

And fragility, when acknowledged, can be controlled.

CHAPTER 47 —FIRST CLOSE ENCOUNTER

Kincaid liked control.

Polished wood tables. Controlled lighting. Controlled conversations with people who believed they were powerful until they understood how much they depended on him. Control was his currency—his oxygen—the invisible force he wrapped around every room he entered.

Tonight was no different.

The steakhouse was closed to the public, its windows shuttered, its host stand abandoned. Warm, honeyed light filled the dining room, turning cutlery and glassware into museum pieces. Outside, rain tapped softly against the glass, steady and patient.

Inside, a political campaign was buying reassurance.

"…we're expecting full national exposure by the primaries," the chief of staff said, swirling a glass of scotch with a hand that didn't quite belong to the gesture. "Our donors want assurances. No surprises."

Kincaid cut into his steak with small, controlled movements. "You're not paying me to prevent embarrassment," he said calmly. "You're paying me to anticipate threats you don't know exist."

The candidate studied him over the rim of a wine glass. "And you really think your firm can do that?"

"I know we can."

He did not mention Jonathan Halden. He never did. The ghost that had slipped his grasp wasn't leverage.

It was a wound.

Rain hit him the moment he stepped outside—cold, sharp, insistent. Neon bled into puddles. Taxi headlights carved through wet dark.

Then Madison Square Garden emptied all at once.

Thousands of bodies spilled into the street, laughing and shouting, phones lighting the rain like drifting sparks. Traffic snarled. Sirens wailed. Umbrellas collided.

Chaos took shape.

"Stay tight," Kincaid snapped, and his security moved instinctively.

Across the street, Jonathan stepped out from the recessed doorway of a closed electronics store. Rain soaked his hood. Cold water slid down his neck. He had planned to observe and leave.

Then the concert let out.

A citywide blind spot formed in real time.

Jonathan watched Kincaid step into the flood of bodies, watched the guards tighten, watched patterns dissolve. This was opportunity. He stepped off the curb, and the crowd swallowed him.

He let motion dictate him. Matched pace. Matched sway. He became a correct answer inside the chaos.

He spotted Kincaid instantly.

Men like Kincaid never blended.

Twenty feet.

Ten.

Eight.

No adrenaline spike. No acceleration. Just alignment.

Kincaid's skin prickled. He turned, scanning faces and umbrellas and noise. Nothing. The instinct didn't fade.

"He's here," Kincaid whispered.

Jonathan closed to five feet. Three.

A body slammed into him from behind, driving his shoulder into Kincaid's.

Pressure registered. Angle assessed. Force mapped.

Then the sensation vanished—corrected as quietly as static clearing from a signal.

Kincaid turned sharply.

Jonathan's hood slipped back for less than a second.

Their eyes met.

Recognition passed between them—not complete, not rational, but primal.

Kincaid's breath caught. "Hal—"

Jonathan moved.

Sideways.

Gone.

"STOP HIM!"

The crowd reacted perfectly wrong.

Jonathan slipped behind a group taking selfies. Flash exploded. Bodies surged. A taxi fishtailed. Jonathan crossed without breaking rhythm. Rain erased edges.

He dissolved.

Kincaid stood in the street, soaked and panting, while the city ignored him. His guards closed in, shouting questions he didn't answer. Lightning lit the glass beside him and for a split second he saw a boy's reflection staring back.

Then rain took it.

Two blocks away, Jonathan stood beneath the awning of a closed shop. His pulse had never spiked. His breathing had never broken rhythm. Whatever force the collision might have imparted had already been normalized—cellular corrections completing themselves without sensation or ceremony.

He felt nothing.

That was the point.

He allowed himself the smallest smile—not triumph, but confirmation.

"Now you know I'm real," he whispered into the rain.

The city swallowed the words.

Kincaid fled with fear gnawing at him.

Jonathan remained—unseen, unhurried, already adjusting the next variable.

The hunt had crossed a line.

And Kincaid had stepped over it first.

CHAPTER 48 —CALM BEFORE THE COLLAPSE

Rain continued through the night, a steady metallic patter against glass and concrete that made the entire city feel like it was breathing through clenched teeth.

The sound was constant enough to become structure. Not soothing—never soothing—but predictable. Each drop struck with the same dull insistence, turning time into something measurable again after the rupture of the street. Rain imposed order where chaos had briefly ruled, stitching the city back together one wet surface at a time.

Subways exhaled steam through glowing grates.

The vapor rose in ghostly plumes, caught the light, then dissolved—appearing and disappearing without warning, as if the ground itself were struggling to breathe. The platforms below stayed crowded. People moved shoulder to shoulder, unaware that above them fear had begun to reorganize power.

Neon smeared across rain-slick pavement like bruises in motion.

Colors bled into one another, reds dissolving into blues, blues into sickly greens, every reflection warped by water and speed. The city looked injured when it rained— alive, but struck.

Buses rumbled down glossy streets and released long, shuddering breaths at every red light.

Inside Kincaid's penthouse, nothing breathed cleanly. Not even him.

He paced the length of the windows, a restless silhouette against the city's bruised glow.

The glass reflected him back in fragments—shoulder here, face there, a smear of motion where he moved too fast for the light to keep up. He did not like seeing himself like this: broken into pieces, unresolved. He preferred clean lines. Defined edges.

His tie lay discarded somewhere on the floor.

It had been loosened first. Then removed entirely. A symbolic surrender he hadn't registered until later.

His shirt clung damply to his back where rain had soaked through during the street encounter.

The fabric stuck cold against his skin, an unwelcome reminder that the city had touched him. That something had slipped through layers he paid to keep intact.

His security presence had tripled since then.

Contractors lined the hallways in black, boots planted wide, eyes alert but uneasy. They spoke in low voices, radios murmuring constantly, hands never straying far from weapons. They had been briefed. Not fully—but enough to understand this was not a drill.

Two remained inside the penthouse, rigid and silent— and even they weren't calm.

They had seen the moment Kincaid cracked.

They had watched fear take him.

That frightened them more than any briefing ever could.

Kincaid spun and jabbed a finger at the nearest guard, the tremor in his hand impossible to hide.

"I want every camera within six blocks reviewed. Every traffic cam. Every private feed. I don't care who owns it—get access."

He heard the edge in his voice and hated it. Authority should glide. This scraped.

"Yes, sir."

"And I want a composite of every male wearing a dark hoodie during that window."

The words piled up too fast. He knew it. He couldn't slow them.

"That'll be hundreds—"

"Then start narrowing."

The interruption was sharp enough to cut.

The words didn't carry authority anymore.

They carried strain.

The guard swallowed. "Yes, sir."

Kincaid stalked to the liquor cabinet.

He did not savor the ritual. No appreciation for crystal or age or burn. His hands shook as he poured whiskey into a glass that had cost more than most people's rent and drank half of it in one swallow.

The burn barely registered.

Behind his eyelids the moment replayed on a loop: the collision, the hood slipping back, Jonathan's eyes.

No expression.

No hesitation.

A ghost wasn't supposed to have a face.

But now it did.

Jonathan Halden was alive, grown, sharpened—and hunting.

Kincaid slammed the glass onto the counter.

It shattered across the marble, splintering into bright fragments that skittered across the surface like startled insects. Whiskey spread in a dark stain. One of the guards flinched.

"Sir—"

"Get out," Kincaid said.

"Sir?"

"I said get out."

This time he didn't shout.

The lack of volume was worse.

The guards exchanged glances and withdrew, the door sealing behind them with a muted finality. Silence rushed in, thick and oppressive, broken only by rain and Kincaid's uneven breathing.

Kincaid gripped the counter until his knuckles blanched.

He leaned forward, shoulders tense, head bowed—not in defeat, but containment. He had spent a lifetime learning how to cage emotions until they obeyed. Tonight, the bars bent.

"You think you can scare me?" he whispered.

His voice echoed too much in the empty space.

"You think you can break me?"

His voice wavered, but beneath the fear something else stirred—a warped resolve trying to harden into shape.

Anger. Not clean, not focused. Desperation masquerading as determination.

"I'll root you out," he said softly. "Even if I have to burn this city down to do it."

The words surprised him with their intensity. He meant them—and that realization unsettled him more than fear ever had.

Hours later, the penthouse lights were still blazing.

Kincaid paced with a phone pressed to his ear.

These weren't business calls.

They were political ones—the kind made after midnight when men decided rules were optional and consequences belonged to someone else.

"I need access to your data team," Kincaid snapped. "And your private intelligence arm."

"That's not—"

"It's part of the contract. You want protection. I'm telling you what the threat is."

"And what threat is that, exactly?"

The hesitation was real.

Saying Jonathan's name felt like feeding it.

Like acknowledging it made it stronger.

"A rogue element," Kincaid said finally. "A violent one."

"Is this related to the incident earlier?"

Kincaid's pulse jumped.

"There was no incident," he lied. "Just a sighting."

A pause stretched long enough to become judgment.

He could hear it in the man's breathing on the other end. Calculations being made. Risk being reassessed.

"We'll need full details before committing resources."

They sensed weakness.

Kincaid heard it in the careful tone, the way the man didn't say it outright but didn't need to.

"I'll be in touch," the chief of staff said.

The line went dead.

Kincaid hurled the phone across the room.

It struck the glass wall, bounced, and skidded to a stop.

He stared out at the city with his chest tight, and for the first time in his life the ground beneath him felt unstable.

Two blocks from the river, Jonathan sat alone in a narrow basement apartment that smelled faintly of dust, old brick, and radiator heat.

The space was barely livable. One room. Low ceiling. Paint blistered where moisture had crept in and never left. It was temporary. That was the point.

Rain tapped patiently against the barred window.

The sound filtered down through concrete and steel, muted but persistent.

The radiator hissed.

The bulb overhead flickered.

Jonathan sat at a metal table salvaged from a dumpster and scrubbed until rust no longer flaked.

He did not rush. Pressure remained consistent. Each pass removed another layer of decay. When he finished, the surface bore scars—but it was stable. Functional.

Spread before him lay the pieces of the next movement, arranged with surgical care: a folded Midtown map marked in red pencil, security rotations written in tight shorthand, a calendar grid filled with patterns, a small notebook with worn pages, and his father's knife.

He had learned that preparation was not about volume.

It was about clarity.

He picked up the pocketknife and turned it slowly.

The blade caught the light and fractured his reflection into pieces.

He watched his face break apart—eye here, cheek there, mouth distorted—and felt nothing.

There was no residual pain from the night before.

No soreness.

No stiffness.

The collision had registered as pressure only—a brief input—and the nanos had corrected alignment before sensation had time to bloom.

He hadn't even slowed.

He wasn't nervous.

Not excited.

Not afraid.

The encounter hadn't rattled him.

It had clarified.

The variables had resolved cleanly. Kincaid's reaction time. His instinctive retreat. The way fear overtook calculation.

Kincaid was unraveling.

Fear had cracked him open.

And fear forced men into patterns.

Jonathan rose and moved to the window.

Through the rain, the city blurred into streaks of color.

Somewhere nearby, Kincaid paced polished floors and drowned in panic.

Jonathan pressed the flat of the blade gently to the glass.

The cold traveled through steel, through skin, into bone.

"Soon," he murmured.

This wasn't revenge anymore.

It was correction.

A system adjusting itself after detecting a flaw.

He returned to the table and circled a location on the map with deliberate pressure.

Kincaid Solutions — Executive Garage, Sub-Level Three.

A funnel.

A choke point.

A place where movement collapsed into inevitability.

He had been there once.

He would be there again.

Tomorrow night, the variables would align.

The storm would break.

By sunrise, Kincaid finally stopped pacing—barely.
He made one final call.
"Get the armored car ready," he said. "Double the men. We're moving to the Jersey safehouse."
His head of security hesitated.
"That's not advised. The city gives us more coverage—"
"I don't want coverage," Kincaid snapped. "I want distance."
A pause.
The hesitation on the line carried weight.
"It'll be ready in an hour."
Kincaid hung up, chest heaving.
He had never run before.
The decision tasted wrong, like metal on the tongue.
Outside, the rain thinned to mist.
The city looked deceptively calm.
Kincaid didn't understand what Jonathan already knew.
When frightened men flee, they choose speed over thought.
And speed leads straight into traps.
Tomorrow night, the path would narrow.
The exits would choke.
And at the end of it—
Jonathan Halden would be waiting.

CHAPTER 49 — THE CITY WATCHES

It was the kind of night New York never truly slept through—wet, humming, restless in a way that felt deliberate.

The rain didn't fall hard enough to cleanse. It lingered instead, persistent and needling, turning every surface slick and reflective, multiplying light until the city looked bruised and overexposed. This was the weather that made people uneasy without knowing why. Not storm. Not calm. Something in between.

Rain fell in thin, slanting curtains, needling the streets and beading along neon signs until color bled and smeared into motion.

The effect flattened distance. Everything felt closer than it should have been. Sounds overlapped. Edges dissolved. The city became a single organism breathing unevenly, arteries lit by headlights and signals.

The tower that carried Kincaid's name rose from the sidewalk like a dark tooth, its windows glowing in staggered rows that disappeared into low clouds.

It dominated the block not by size alone but by certainty. A building that assumed permanence. A structure designed to look down rather than out. Jonathan had learned long ago that places like this advertised confidence the way animals advertised size.

Jonathan stood across the street with his hood up, coat zipped, hands buried deep in his pockets.

He had chosen the spot because it allowed waiting without waiting. A recessed bus shelter. A darkened storefront. Enough foot traffic to dissolve him, enough distance to see without being seen.

Rain soaked the fabric and crept cold into his wrists, but he barely noticed.

Cold sharpened awareness. It narrowed sensation to what mattered. Everything else fell away.

From here, the building was a vertical mirror filled with moving shadows—people reduced to silhouettes and light.

Most people saw glass and money and height.

Jonathan saw patterns.

He watched the front entrance without moving, letting time pass until it felt like another layer of the city.

He did not rush observation. Rushing distorted data. He waited until rhythm replaced curiosity, until the lobby traffic stopped drawing attention and started repeating itself.

The lobby team rotated with mechanical precision: two at the desk, two at the turnstiles, one at the inner elevator bank, one patrolling the rear door.

The spacing was intentional. Coverage without redundancy. Confidence without excess.

Six on the ground floor alone.

He could feel the rest above—more bodies, more radios, more weapons humming quietly beneath tailored jackets.

The building had adjusted since the encounter in the street. That much was obvious. The posture of the guards had changed. Less boredom. More tension in the forearms. The kind of alertness that came from fear rather than routine.

Lightning flickered behind the clouds, briefly turning the glass façade into an opaque slab, the city erased and replaced by its own skeleton.

For a fraction of a second, everything reduced to structure.

Jonathan checked the cheap watch on his wrist.

Kincaid would be back soon.

Tonight was a late night, and late nights always carried looser seams—tiny gaps a man could slip through if he knew where to press.

Pressure created errors. Fatigue widened margins. Jonathan had learned that on farms and in labs and on streets that didn't forgive hesitation.

He stepped off the curb with the crowd when the light turned green.

Taxi tires hissed past.

A bus roared by, lights smearing across wet asphalt like dragged paint.

Rain soaked into his cuffs and climbed higher up his legs, and he welcomed it.

Cold made him quieter.

Cold made him careful.

He kept his head down and moved with the current.

Four people entered the revolving door together, shoulder to shoulder, and the lobby swallowed them in warm, filtered air tinged with polished stone and expensive coffee.

The temperature change registered immediately. Moisture beaded on his skin, then cooled. The smell of money—cleaning agents, fresh fabric, controlled climate—replaced the street.

Inside, the space opened upward like a cathedral built to worship confidence.

Tall ceilings.

Brushed steel columns.

Black marble polished until it reflected faces back at themselves.

The architecture forced awareness upward and inward at the same time. A subtle reminder of hierarchy. Of who belonged and who didn't.

The security desk sat like an island, terminals glowing softly, guards wearing boredom the way men wore armor when they didn't want to show vigilance.

Jonathan could see how awake they really were in the tension of their forearms, the way their eyes never stopped scanning even as their expressions stayed neutral.

He didn't head for the turnstiles.

He veered right.

A woman rushed in from the rain, shaking her umbrella and swearing under her breath.

Her irritation was genuine. Her focus inward. She was already late somewhere and annoyed at the world for noticing.

Jonathan timed his step behind her.

When she dropped her access badge fumbling for her bag, he was already bending.

"I've got it," he said, offering it back with a neutral half-smile.

His voice carried just enough warmth to disarm without inviting conversation.

"Oh my God, thank you," she laughed. "I'd lose my head if—"

"Long day," Jonathan said. "It happens."

She swiped and passed through.

The sensor flashed green, and before it clicked back to red Jonathan followed in her slipstream, bumping the turnstile lightly as if he misjudged his step.

Quick enough that the system registered only one pass.

The desk guard glanced up, saw two people, saw the badge in her hand, and let his eyes slide away.

People saw what they expected to see.

Jonathan moved with a cluster toward the elevators and stepped into the first car that opened.

He turned to face out like everyone else.

He didn't press a button.

Others did—thirty-four, eighteen, forty-nine—without ever noticing him.

The doors closed with a soft pneumatic sigh.

As the car rose, Jonathan slid his thumb under the rubber lip of the emergency hatch and tested it gently.

Loose.

Maintenance schedules cut corners when confidence replaced fear.

He listened to the elevator's hum, the slight sway at twenty, the change in tone as it climbed higher.

Every building had its own voice. This one spoke in precision and arrogance.

At thirty-four, three people stepped out.

At forty-five, the last man left without looking back.

The doors shut.

Jonathan's expression flattened.

He pushed the hatch aside quietly and pulled himself into the narrow crawlspace above the car.

Effort dragged heat up through his shoulder and down into his ribs—old damage waking under strain.

Not enough to stop him.

Enough to remind him he wasn't made of steel.

He lay flat, breathing shallowly, listening through a thin skin of metal and cable.

The car continued upward, empty, obedient.

When it reached the low sixties, he used a thin strip of flexible metal and pressure instead of finesse.

The release popped.

The doors parted a fraction.

He widened them and slipped out like a draft of cold air.

The executive floor was warmer, lit lower, carpet engineered to swallow sound.

Minimalist artwork hung in careful intervals, chosen to suggest taste without revealing anything personal.

No photographs.

No sentiment.

Only signals.

Cameras watched the junctions—small black eyes built to catch the intruder who hurried, who panicked, who made obvious decisions.

Jonathan did none of those things.

At the far end stood a heavier door—wood, frosted glass panel, gold letters:

R. KINCAID — EXECUTIVE SUITE.

In front of it, a broad guard lounged in a leather chair, pistol holstered, attention split between his phone and the corridor.

Jonathan didn't walk straight at him.

He slipped into a darkened glass conference room and let the tint swallow him.

The glass reflected just enough to watch without being seen.

He studied the guard's rhythm: an up-glance every thirty seconds, a head tilt during radio checks, the subtle shift of weight when boredom edged toward vigilance.

He waited for the smallest human flaw.

A voice floated down the hall.

"Hey, Rico, you want anything from the machine?"

Rico turned his head.

"Yeah. Salt chips. Not the cracked pepper crap."

Laughter.

Footsteps.

Attention drifting.

Jonathan moved.

He kept to the blind side of a camera dome, glided along the wall, and when Rico's eyes swung back Jonathan was already behind him.

A hand clamped over Rico's mouth.

Jonathan's forearm slid under his chin and braced cleanly against the side of his neck.

Rico thrashed hard—strong, desperate—but there wasn't space to stand.

Jonathan tipped the chair backward and used its momentum to lever Rico into his own weight.

The choke was efficient, not cruel.

Rico's boots scraped once against carpet and then went heavy.

Jonathan lowered him gently, dragged him into the conference room, propped him behind the door, and took the radio and keycard.

The radio crackled.

"Rico, you good?"

Jonathan pressed transmit and kept his voice low, indistinct.

"Yeah. Just tired."

"Same."

The channel clicked off.

Jonathan stepped back into the hallway.

There were more.

Twelve on duty tonight.

Rico had only been the first point of friction, the smallest resistance.

The real weight waited deeper in.

He didn't move toward Kincaid's door yet.

He moved away from it.

Angled down the corridor that curved toward the service core.

Cameras watched this stretch in overlapping cones, their coverage tidy and confident.

Jonathan slid through the gaps he'd memorized over months of watching—two steps hugging the wall, a pause beneath a vent shadow, then forward again as the camera completed its lazy sweep.

Two guards stood near a break area, posture loose but eyes sharp.

One leaned against a humming refrigerator, arms crossed, the faint smell of reheated food lingering around him.

The other stood by a narrow window, watching rain streak sideways across the glass.

"You think he's really going to Jersey?" the one at the window muttered.

The other snorted.

"He's too addicted to this view. Paranoid bastard loves watching people from up high."

Jonathan stepped into the doorway.

"Hey," he said quietly.

Both men turned.

The first barely had time to inhale before Jonathan's open palm drove into his throat.

The sound that came out wasn't a shout—it was a ruined attempt at air, a wet, broken gasp.

The guard collapsed, hands clawing uselessly at his neck, eyes already widening in shock.

The second went for his gun.

Jonathan kicked his knee backward.

The joint gave with a sharp, sick pop that echoed too loudly in the confined space.

The man screamed—too loud, too sharp—and Jonathan smashed his head into the wall hard enough to turn the sound into a choking grunt.

An arm wrapped around the neck.

A twist.

A dull crack.

Silence returned to the hallway like a lid set back on a pot.

Jonathan dragged both bodies into the break room, killed the light, and shut the door.

He stood still for three breaths, listening.

Nothing yet.

Three down.

The floor began to tighten.

Guards shifted closer to the core, drawn by instinct and procedure.

Jonathan could feel the structure changing, the way prey moved when it sensed pressure but hadn't yet located the source.

Two stood at a corner junction, heads bent over a tablet, camera thumbnails flickering blue-white across their faces.

Jonathan approached from behind while their attention was trapped in the glow.

He didn't speak.

He drove the closest guard into the wall.

Bone struck plaster.

The man went slack immediately.

Jonathan pivoted and drove a knee into the second guard's stomach, folding him.

An elbow came down across the back of the neck, stunning but not killing.

The guard hit the floor gasping.

Jonathan crouched and forced the man to look up.

"What do you know about Jonathan Halden?"

"I—I don't—"

The man's voice broke, tears cutting clean tracks down his face.

Jonathan tightened his grip just enough.

"You work for Kincaid. That means you've heard the story."

The guard swallowed hard.

"He said—you were unstable. A threat. That you killed Rowe. That you—"

"Then he knows I'm coming."

"Yes," the guard sobbed. "Please. I'm just—"

Jonathan snapped his neck without ceremony.

He dragged both bodies into an empty office and shut the door.

Five.

The structure tightened further.

The remaining guards held closer now—two at the elevator bank, one near the emergency stairs, one outside Kincaid's door, and two inside a glass-walled monitoring hub that overlooked the floor like a perched nest.

Jonathan couldn't take the hub cleanly without triggering a cascade.

So he changed the shape of the problem.

He approached the stairwell from the far side and let the heavy fire door swing inward with deliberate slowness.

The guard turned, expecting a colleague.

Jonathan's boot came up fast.

The door slammed into the man's face with a crunch that sounded wrong in carpeted quiet.

Blood sprayed the metal frame.

The guard stumbled back, hands flying to his nose, swearing through red.

Jonathan slipped into the stairwell, grabbed him by the vest, and dragged him down three steps.

The man's spine met the metal railing with a hollow clang.

Breath left him in a hard grunt.

Jonathan twisted and finished it.

Six.

He didn't bother hiding the body.

Speed mattered now more than cleanliness.

The elevator guards were alert—hands hovering near holsters, eyes scanning hard angles.

Jonathan slid along the wall until he owned the geometry.

He needed one heartbeat where attention leaned the wrong way.

An elevator chimed.

The doors opened.

Empty.

Both men glanced into the car for a fraction too long.

Jonathan tore a fire extinguisher from its case and swung it in a brutal arc.

It smashed into the back of the nearer guard's head and dropped him instantly.

The second spun, gun halfway out.

Jonathan jammed the extinguisher between them, pinning the man's forearm and trapping the draw.

The guard headbutted Jonathan across the bridge of the nose.

Stars exploded.

Blood flooded Jonathan's mouth.

Pain sharpened the world into clean edges.

Jonathan twisted anyway.

He forced the wrist until the pistol came loose and clattered across marble.

The guard threw a desperate punch.

Jonathan ducked and returned it with an uppercut that displaced the man's jaw with a dry, unmistakable click.

Seven.

Eight.

A gunshot cracked from farther down the floor—someone in the hub reacting too fast, too blind—ripping through the quiet like a siren.

Radios flared to life.

Footsteps shifted.

The air changed from complacent to awake.

Jonathan looked up at the glass-walled hub.

Two men inside were already moving, radios lifting.

One shouted, "Executive floor under attack—"

Jonathan yanked the pin and dumped a choking white cloud toward the opening.

Powder swallowed the space.

Coughing.

Swearing.

Blind movement.

One guard stumbled out, hands groping.

Jonathan met him with the extinguisher—ribs, then chin—and the man crumpled, blocking the threshold at a useless angle.

Inside the haze, the second guard fired blind.

The shots found his partner, loud and final.

Jonathan shoved the collapsing body inward, slipped low beneath the powder, and moved like a shadow under fog.

The remaining guard turned a fraction too late.

Jonathan took him from behind, arm locking around the throat, squeezing until the kicking slowed, the clawing weakened, the body went slack.

Nine.

Ten.

Radios still screamed, but Jonathan turned their meaning into background noise and moved forward.

Two left.

Kincaid's personal detail.

He wiped blood from his face with the back of his wrist.

His nose throbbed.

His shoulder burned from the earlier climb.

The accumulated strain made his limbs feel slightly delayed, as if the night itself had thickened the air.

He ignored it.

The man outside Kincaid's door was older than the rest, bigger too.

Scars cut pale lines beneath one eye.

His shoulders didn't sag.

He held a radio in one hand and a pistol in the other, muzzle low but ready.

The radio hissed.

"Evans, report. We've got shots fired on sixty-one."

Evans didn't answer.

He stared down the corridor at bodies, powder, blood, and the wrong kind of silence—

—and then he stared at Jonathan.

Jonathan didn't rush.

He walked.

Evans raised the pistol.

"Drop to your knees. Hands on your head."

Jonathan stopped five yards away.

"Don't," he said quietly.

Evans repeated the order, voice steady.

He stepped forward, gun trained center mass.

Sweat shone at his temples despite discipline.

"You really don't want to do this," Jonathan said.

"I really do."

Evans shifted his weight—left foot forward.

A tiny mistake.

Jonathan went up and in, not away from the gun but inside its line.

His hand slammed Evans' wrist.

The shot tore into the ceiling.

Heat kissed Jonathan's side as the muzzle scraped past.

They hit the door together.

The frame rattled.

Evans recovered fast and wrapped Jonathan in a crushing bear grip, arms cinching around ribs and wounded side.

Jonathan's breath stuttered.

Pain flared bright enough to bleach the edges of his vision.

Jonathan hooked a leg behind Evans' knee and twisted.

They went down hard.

The gun skidded out of reach.

Evans fought like a man who understood exactly what dying felt like.

Jonathan did too.

He got his forearm under Evans' jaw, set the pressure, and turned.

Resistance held for a moment, then gave.

Eleven.

Jonathan lay there for a second, breath ragged, chest burning.

Blood ran hot at his side.

The graze wasn't fatal—but it was real.

He pushed himself up.

The twelfth waited inside.

Jonathan stood and turned the brass knob.

The door opened on silent hinges.

The office felt like another climate—warmer, quieter, insulated from consequence.

Amber light softened the edges of polished wood and glass.

Bourbon lingered beneath faint cigar smoke.

Commendations lined the walls in frames and shadowboxes: medals, plaques, old unit insignia arranged like proof that history could be curated.

Manhattan glowed beyond the windows, rain streaking the glass into silver veins.

Richard Kincaid stood near the sideboard, half-turned as if he'd been reaching for a drink.

He froze when he saw Jonathan.

His eyes dropped first—to the blood darkening Jonathan's shirt, to the arm hanging wrong, to the knife at his belt—

—then lifted slowly, calculation snapping into place.

"…You," Kincaid breathed.

Jonathan stepped inside and let the door close behind him with a soft click.

The sound landed heavier than it should have.

"You've been looking for me," Jonathan said.

Kincaid gave a short, disbelieving laugh.

"For years."

"And you still didn't see me."

Kincaid's jaw tightened.

"Do you have any idea how many people have died because of you?"

"Because of you," Jonathan corrected.

The air compressed.

Rain traced thin lines down the glass like counting marks.

Kincaid moved first—

—and the city held its breath.

CHAPTER 50 — KINKAID COLLAPSE

Kincaid moved quickly—not for the desk, not for a weapon, but straight at Jonathan. He slammed his shoulder into Jonathan's chest with trained aggression, driving him backward. Jonathan slid across polished wood and hit a wall of framed commendations. Glass exploded. Metal rattled. Kincaid's forearm crushed into Jonathan's throat.

"You think you're some avenging angel?" Kincaid snarled. "You're a mistake that lived too long."

Jonathan's fingers dug into the arm, nails scraping skin. "Henry was a father," he rasped. "You called him a breach."

Kincaid slammed him again. A shadowbox shattered at their feet.

"He was a liability," Kincaid said. "Just like you."

Jonathan shifted his weight, slipped a leg inside Kincaid's stance, and heaved sideways. Pressure broke for half a second—long enough. Jonathan drove his shoulder into Kincaid's ribs and sent them crashing into the sideboard. A decanter bounced and shattered. Bourbon splashed across the floor, sharp and sweet.

Kincaid grabbed the back of Jonathan's head and smashed his face into the desk. Wood met bone with a dull, hollow sound. Jonathan's vision burst into white flecks. Blood filled his mouth.

Again.

And again.

Jonathan's hands scrabbled and closed around a heavy nameplate. On the next downswing he twisted and drove it into Kincaid's cheekbone. Skin split. Kincaid recoiled with a curse.

Jonathan surged, driving him into shelves. Binders rattled loose. Papers spilled like pale snow. Kincaid punched Jonathan across the nose. Cartilage shifted. Pain lanced behind Jonathan's eyes and the room tilted.

Jonathan stepped into it anyway and headbutted Kincaid. The collision was ugly. Both men staggered. Kincaid recovered faster, rage and training keeping him upright. He kicked Jonathan's leg and sent him down to one knee. Jonathan's hand went to his side by instinct. The graze burned. Blood slicked his palm.

Kincaid moved in to finish it with weight.

Jonathan twisted, used momentum, and drove Kincaid into the desk corner. The edge slammed into Kincaid's lower back. His breath left him in a sharp gasp. Jonathan dragged him along the desk, knocking pens, files, and a photograph face-down to the floor.

Kincaid tore free and shifted, putting the desk between them.

Jonathan saw the flicker.

The drawer.

They hit it from opposite sides. Jonathan grabbed for Kincaid's wrist, but Kincaid had the angle. His hand plunged into the drawer and closed around cold metal.

Too late.

The first shot punched into Jonathan's left shoulder. It didn't feel cinematic. It felt like a hammer—heat and impact stealing the arm from him. His fingers went numb. The second shot hit low on the right side, below the ribs. Pain tore through him so hard his breath collapsed.

Jonathan hit the floor.

Warm light turned blood into a dark shine as it spread beneath him. Kincaid stood over him, gun trained down, chest heaving. Jonathan tried to pull air. Failed. Tried again.

Kincaid didn't kneel. He didn't check vitals.

"Should've stayed a ghost," he panted. "You came back into my world."

He backed away, lowered the gun, and set it on the desk like punctuation. He pressed a hand to his face where blood leaked from split skin and turned toward the windows, needing the city to tell him this was over.

On the floor, Jonathan didn't rise.

He didn't reset.

He didn't bounce back.

Inside him, the system did what it always did—not resurrection, not miracle.

Triage.

Clotting where loss threatened collapse. Tightening around ruptures. Buying minutes the way Henry once bought him seconds.

The pain stayed.

The weakness stayed.

Jonathan stayed still because moving too soon would end him.

Kincaid spoke to the glass, voice shaking. "Carlisle will deal with the fallout. He wanted to keep you hypothetical. I deal in realities."

He laughed once, brittle. "You're not real anymore, Halden. You're dead."

Jonathan's fingers curled against the slick floor.

A decision.

He slid his good hand toward his belt until it found the worn handle of Henry's pocketknife. His shoulder screamed when he tried to push. He stopped. Breathed. Waited for the spin to ease. Then moved in increments— an elbow, a knee, a slow drag behind the desk where Kincaid's sightline couldn't reach.

Blood ran down his hip.

Breath came shallow and ugly.

He waited until Kincaid's breathing settled, until attention sank into the illusion of safety—the fatal moment when a man believes the worst is finished.

Then Jonathan rose.

Not smoothly.

Quietly enough.

"Kincaid."

The name came out hoarse, scraped thin by pain.

Kincaid turned. His face emptied.

Jonathan stood with blood soaking his shirt, one arm hanging useless, the other braced on the desk. His eyes were clear. His body was paying for every inch.

"You…" Kincaid whispered. "How—"

His gaze snapped to the gun on the desk.

Too far.

Jonathan watched the calculation flicker and fail.

"You should've finished it in the corridor," Jonathan said.

"You're a monster," Kincaid spat.

Jonathan took a step. Pain sliced white through his side. He took another, slower.

"My father didn't ask to die for your orders," Jonathan said. "My mother didn't ask to run. I didn't ask to become your project."

Kincaid backed toward the windows, hands searching. He grabbed a crystal paperweight and hurled it. Jonathan ducked. It shattered against the wall. Kincaid lunged for the desk.

Jonathan cut him off.

He grabbed Kincaid by the collar and drove his face into the desk edge. Blood splattered dark across wood. Jonathan spun him and slammed him into the window. The glass flexed and thrummed but held.

Kincaid's nose was crooked. One eye swelled shut. Fear finally stripped away the polish.

"What are you?" Kincaid breathed.

Jonathan stepped close. "Something you built," he said. "Something you lost."

The pocketknife opened with a soft click.

"You kill me and there are others," Kincaid rasped. "Systems. Layers."

Jonathan nodded once. "I know."

He tilted Kincaid's head back and drove the blade beneath the jaw—clean, sure, practiced. Breath turned wet. Blood fanned across glass and slid downward with the rain.

Kincaid sagged.

Jonathan lowered him until he sat slumped against the window, legs sprawled. The city reflected in his eyes as they fluttered.

"How… are you alive…?" Kincaid whispered.

Jonathan knelt despite the protest in his side. "My father bought me time," he said. "My mother bought me distance."

Kincaid exhaled once.

Then nothing.

Jonathan closed the knife, wiped it on Kincaid's shirt, and slid it back into his pocket. He stood slowly. Upright didn't mean fine. Pain radiated. Blood soaked. The system held—barely.

He cleared the pistol and set it on the desk where it would be found.

This wasn't disappearance.

It was an answer.

Jonathan braced against the doorframe until the room stopped tilting, then slipped out into the hallway, leaving Elias Kincaid cooling beneath the indifferent glow of the city he believed he owned.

Outside the glass, New York kept breathing. And now, it knew.

CHAPTER 51 — THE MAN ABOVE IT ALL

Jonathan didn't find Victor Langford's name on a hit list.

He found it on a donor wall.

The plaque gleamed beneath soft museum lighting—brushed steel, clean font, arranged to suggest benevolence rather than power. Names carved there weren't meant to feel dangerous. They were meant to feel generous. Civic. Necessary.

Jonathan stared at it longer than he should have.

After Dr. Marrow was dead and her private files lay scattered across cabin floorboards, Jonathan took everything that looked like it might matter—hard drives, notebooks, encrypted sticks labeled in neat shorthand that meant nothing until you understood what you were looking at. Some of it cracked in hours. Some took weeks. A few pieces resisted until he stopped forcing them and let patterns emerge on their own.

The cabin—cold, empty, unmoving—became a sorting room. Paper stacks. Data dumps. Tangled cords that looked like nerves when firelight caught them at the wrong angle. Jonathan slept in the same chair three nights in a row because the mattress smelled like smoke and someone else's life. He woke with a stiff neck and a shallow ache in his side that still hadn't fully faded since New York, and he forced himself upright anyway.

Sleep didn't restore him.

Stillness did.

He made coffee in a pot that didn't match its lid. Drank it black and bitter. Read until words blurred and numbers began to feel like faces. He learned the shape of Marrow's thinking by how she organized her fear—what she archived carefully, what she buried in subfolders, what she mislabeled in hopes no one would look twice.

The deeper he went, the less the files looked like medicine and the more they looked like finance. Grant approvals. Defense-contract language buried inside "research partnerships." Black-budget funding streams labeled with phrases designed to sound harmless—strategic viability study, adaptive survivability review, continuity trials.

Helix wasn't just a program.

It was an investment.

A machine fed by money, not ethics.

Jonathan saw how the language shifted whenever outcomes worsened. How the words softened as the human cost increased. Mortality became "attrition." Children became "viability cohorts." Pain became "stress response indicators."

He found Langford three layers deep in a spreadsheet so bloated the laptop fan screamed, the cheap plastic casing vibrating like a trapped insect. Five million here. Twelve million there. Performance bonuses tied not to survival rates, but to adaptability metrics under live-fire conditions.

That phrase sat on the screen like something diseased.

Jonathan leaned back in a motel chair—because he wasn't in the cabin anymore. Not after the power flickered and the cold crawled in through the seams. He'd moved on, carrying the files like contraband. The motel room smelled like bleach, stale cigarettes, and damp carpet that hadn't been replaced in decades. The air conditioner rattled even when it wasn't on, like it had forgotten how to be quiet.

He clicked a link.

A photograph appeared—one of those heroic corporate portraits where glass and sky did half the work.

Victor Langford.

Early sixties. White hair arranged to look effortless. Skin tanned without labor. A smile shaped carefully enough to resemble warmth. Hands clasped as if posing for history itself.

Founder, Langford Dynamics.

Beneath it, awards stacked like armor. Defense innovation. Humanitarian leadership. Children's health benefactor.

Jonathan read that last one twice.

A man praised for helping children, whose money had funded technology built out of a dying child.

His hand tightened on the mouse until the plastic creaked.

He scrolled.

Langford had spoken at panels. Given polished talks with soft lighting and applause placed exactly where it belonged. His favorite phrase surfaced again and again, a mantra for men who needed permission to sleep.

Progress demands hard choices. History does not remember the cost. Only the breakthroughs.

Jonathan shut the laptop.

The room fell into darkness except for the neon sign outside. It flickered red, then blue, then red again, painting the peeling wallpaper in pulses like a slow-forming bruise. Jonathan sat for a long time and listened to pipes knock behind the walls. A truck groaned past on the highway. Somewhere down the hall, a television laughed at something that wasn't funny.

Langford had never held a gun on Henry.

He'd never chased Suzanne's car through the rain.

He'd never stood in the lab when Jonathan died on the table and came back wrong.

But it was Langford's money that pushed everything forward. Langford's signature that turned Helix from theory into weapon. Langford's impatience that demanded faster results, more aggressive trials—and then walked away clean.

The others had gotten blood on their hands.

Langford made sure they had something to wash it off with.

Jonathan reached into his jacket pocket and felt the familiar outline of Henry's pocketknife. Not because he needed it—because the contact grounded him. The handle was worn smooth where his father's thumb used to rest. That small softness in the wood, evidence of hands that built instead of destroyed, was the closest thing Jonathan had to a prayer.

He didn't speak.

He decided.

Helix funding didn't have a single obvious path from Langford's accounts. It had dozens. Shell corporations. Offshore entities. "Nonprofit collaborations" whose boards were empty titles and names that dissolved under scrutiny. Langford Dynamics never touched Helix on paper.

It just touched everything that touched it.

Jonathan learned quickly there was no point untangling every strand. That was how investigators disappeared into complexity. That was how the system protected itself.

So he looked for weight.

Where did the largest transfers land? Which names repeated? Which accounts behaved like reservoirs instead of conduits? Which funds lingered instead of passing through?

A company called Gulf Strategic Holdings kept surfacing. On paper it was logistics. In reality it moved defense hardware, experimental tech, and personnel under labels designed to make you stop reading before you asked questions.

One entry in Dr. Marrow's logs snagged Jonathan's attention like a hook: a private demonstration request for a nanite survival prototype, a briefing aboard a GLS vessel, a note that V. Langford would be present.

No date attached.

But the vessel name was.

GLS Halcyon.

Jonathan spent the next week living in the cold glow of public terminals—libraries, truck stops, anywhere no one cared how long you stayed. Coffee. Vending-machine food. He tracked the Halcyon the way he used to track storms on the farm: watching where the air shifted, where birds vanished, where patterns broke.

It wasn't small.

It was a private megayacht.

Registered to an empty shell. Flagged overseas. Docking along coastlines where the water was warm and the money warmer. Its port history read like indulgence—Miami. Nassau. Key West.

And one name that didn't belong on tourist maps.

Lanely Point.

Jonathan circled it on a stolen paper map. The ink bled where he pressed too hard.

Lanely Point didn't have a bus stop. It barely had a road.

He got off in the nearest real town—a faded strip of gas stations and seafood shacks that smelled like diesel, old fry oil, and brine—and walked the remaining miles with a duffel over his shoulder. Sweat dampened his back. Salt wind dried it into a crust that tugged at his skin.

The farther he went, the quieter it became. No music. No laughter.

Just wind across marsh grass, reeds hissing, gulls crying like something hungry.

Lanely Point emerged from haze like a place built to be forgotten. Chain-link fencing. A peeling security booth. Low warehouses hunched under corrugated roofs. A fuel tank marked with warnings bleached pale by sun.

Beyond it—the docks.

Metal, not wood. Wide enough for trucks. Stained with oil and tide marks like the water kept trying to reclaim them.

At the end of the longest dock, bobbing in murky green, sat a ship that didn't belong.

The Halcyon.

Sleek. White. Polished like bone scraped clean. Even from a distance, Jonathan could see the helipad.

He didn't approach that day.

He watched.

He read angles. Counted cameras. Noted where shadows pooled beneath overhangs. Studied the guards—two at the gate, one on the dock, one in the booth—with the rigid posture of ex-military men convincing themselves they were still necessary.

By sundown, Jonathan knew three things.

The Halcyon didn't stay long.

Victor Langford wasn't always aboard, but when he was, security doubled.

And Lanely Point was only a door.

There was somewhere else the ship went when passengers mattered.

He just had to find it.

The easiest way to watch a place was to become part of it.

Jonathan got a job moving crates. Cash pay. Minimal questions. The man who hired him had a sun-ruined face and the permanent squint of someone who'd stopped trusting people a long time ago.

"You work, you sweat, you don't steal," the man said. "You don't ask about the fancy ship and you don't get close to it."

"Got it," Jonathan said.

He got closer than anyone—just not the way they measured closeness.

He learned rhythms. Truck schedules. Cargo transfers. Crew habits. Smoke breaks. Which guard hid cigarettes. Which dozed after midnight. Which talked too much when boredom loosened their mouths.

"Langford's ship's in early," one guard said.

"He's bringing suits."

By night, Jonathan knew what mattered.

Langford didn't trust land.

He trusted water.

And water only slowed consequences—it didn't stop them.

By the time storm season rolled in, Jonathan already knew how he'd get there.

He waited for noise.

For wind.

For rain.

For a storm loud enough to hide a man clinging to steel beneath a barge.

When the engines fired and the dock fell away, Jonathan lowered himself into warm, fouled water and held on.

Ahead lay an island built on money, fear, and silence.

Jonathan closed his eyes and let the storm carry him toward Victor Langford.

Toward the man above it all.

CHAPTER 52 —FORTRESS ON THE EDGE OF THE WORLD

The Maine coastline looked like the bones of something ancient that refused to stay buried—jagged granite ribs, black cliffs rising like broken teeth, and the Atlantic hurling itself against stone with a violence that never learned fatigue. Out here, the ocean didn't soothe. It attacked. Waves detonated against the rock with cannon-boom force, flinging white spray high into the air. Fog rolled in heavy sheets, swallowing the tree line and spitting it back in brief, ghostly flashes. The wind came sharp and salted, clawing at exposed skin, the air tasting of iron and rust.

Jonathan had learned long ago that landscapes like this were honest. They didn't pretend to be safe. They didn't offer comfort they couldn't keep. The coast gave nothing freely, and it took everything eventually. That made it easier to trust.

Perched on the cliff's edge—clinging to the violence like an apex predator—stood Director Ethan Carlisle's mansion. A fortress pretending to be a home. Three stories of quarried stone wrapped around a reinforced steel skeleton. Hurricane-rated glass glowed warm against the gray. Floodlights swept in steady arcs like lighthouse blades, carving tunnels through fog that never stayed cut. A security fence traced the cliff line, humming faintly when the wind shifted. Sensors winked along railings and corners, pinpricks of technology embedded into the architecture like parasites. It didn't look built to survive storms. It looked built to dare them.

Jonathan crouched at the forest's edge where the pines pressed tight and dark, branches bending and groaning under the ocean wind. Fog slid between trunks like a living thing. He stayed still long enough for cold to settle into his clothes, long enough for his breath to feel like part of the weather.

Stillness was not waiting. It was preparation.

His right side burned where the bullet had bitten him in New York. The wound wasn't fresh, but it wasn't finished—every deep breath tugged at it like a loose thread. His shoulder ached with a dull, constant throb that made his left arm feel heavier than it should. The nanites kept him upright. They didn't make him comfortable.

Pain was a variable now, not a warning. Something to be measured and compensated for, not avoided.

He didn't need comfort. He needed timing.

He watched the property the way he'd watched buildings and men—quietly, clinically, patiently. He tracked the sweep of the floodlights. Counted seconds between arcs. Watched guard silhouettes dissolve into fog and reappear on the same routes, as if the ground itself had drawn their paths. He wasn't waiting for an opening. He was studying a battlefield.

Carlisle had designed this place the way he designed everything else: layered, redundant, overconfident. The architecture assumed threats would come from the road, from the air, from places that could be anticipated and countered with money. It did not account for someone who treated terrain as an accomplice.

Jonathan marked the gaps where floodlights overlapped too much, blinding their own cameras. He noted how fog confused infrared just enough to soften edges. He listened to the wind distort sound, to the ocean swallow anything that fell too far or screamed too late.

Inside the mansion, warmth and wood and money pretended fear didn't live there. But fear always leaked. It pooled in habits. It clung to voices, to fingertips, to the way a man checked a locked door twice.

Carlisle stood in his cedar-paneled study while fire snapped in the hearth. A wall of security monitors filled his vision—multiple angles, multiple assurances. Redundancies stacked like prayers. He stared at them the way a drowning man stared at the edge of a boat he couldn't reach.

The house had been designed to make him feel untouchable. Tonight, it felt like a coffin lined with screens.

The secure line rang before sunrise.

He answered with hands that no longer obeyed him. "Report."

The voice on the other end was thin with panic. "D-Director... Kincaid is dead."

Carlisle's face slackened, as if his skin had forgotten how to hold itself up. "How?"

"Sir—his office. His team. It's... it's a bloodbath. Cameras caught... someone. Tall. Hooded. We think—"

"You think what?" Carlisle snapped, and felt his own voice split.

A pause. Then the words no one wanted to carry. "We think it was him."

Carlisle stared at fog and cliff and moving light on the monitors. Below the windows, the ocean hammered the rocks like it was trying to climb. He swallowed and tasted salt even in the warmth of the room.

For a moment—one traitorous moment—he pictured Henry Halden in the corridor again. Bleeding. Blocking the path. Buying time with his body. Carlisle had convinced himself for years that memory was contained, filed away with the rest.

It wasn't.

"No," he whispered. "Kincaid had redundancies. Fail-safes. He was supposed to—"

"He didn't stop him, sir."

"That's impossible."

Silence. Then, smaller now, almost ashamed: "He tore through a high-security tower. Alone."

Carlisle's knees softened. He caught himself on the desk, fingertips whitening against polished wood. "Where was he last seen?"

"Leaving the building. After that... nothing."

Carlisle lifted his eyes to the monitors as if they might answer him. Fog thickened along the cliffside, swallowing floodlight beams and turning them into pale, useless spears.

"We assume he's coming here," he said—and hated how inevitable it sounded.

The words felt less like a prediction than an admission.

Within minutes, the fortress woke fully. Boots thudded across wet stone. Radios crackled, voices layered and tight. A recon team pushed into the treeline. Drones rose into the fog, rotors whining like insects. A K9 unit strained at its leash, dog coiled with nervous energy, handler's jaw clenched until it hurt to look at. A sniper took position on a balcony, scope glinting once before vanishing behind sweeping light. The service road sealed. The gate detail doubled. Floodlights crossed and recrossed the same ground, as if light alone could pin a man down.

Jonathan watched it all from the trees, fog sliding over his shoulders like a cloak. He smelled the place before he moved—diesel from generators, wet bark, ocean iron, the sharp bite of gun oil carried on the wind. Beneath it all was the human scent no system could hide: sweat, adrenaline, fear.

Fear made people loud. Fear made them predictable.

His side twinged when he shifted. He held still until the pain dulled back into something workable. He waited for the lights to pass, for the drone to pivot away, for two guards to turn their heads in the same direction at the same time.

Then he moved.

Not fast. Not frantic. Exact.

Fog covered him. Wind stole his sound. The fortress's own systems masked his approach—every sweep and sensor convincing the people inside they were seeing everything.

The ground under his boots was slick with pine needles and wet stone. He placed each step where sound would die instead of travel. His breathing stayed shallow, synced to the gusts that rattled branches and howled through fencing.

The first team died in the trees without knowing they'd been found. A choke. A blade. A body eased into mud so gently it could have been sleep. The second man turned toward a sound that wasn't there, and Jonathan was already behind him—hand at the jaw, twist, silence. The third lifted his rifle and fired into fog. Muzzle flashes bloomed uselessly white. Jonathan stepped inside the line of fire, closed the distance, and ended it with one efficient movement.

There was no satisfaction in it. Only subtraction.

A radio hissed. Someone called for a status check. No one answered.

A drone pivoted, caught a sliver of heat, and washed the ground in sterile white. Jonathan broke into a run, pain flaring sharp in his side. He kept his breathing controlled. He moved through trees and rock like he'd been built for it—which, in a way, he had.

The K9 hit first, bursting from the fog with a savage snarl.

Jonathan caught it midair with his good arm, redirected the bite away from his throat, and dropped to one knee under the impact. His injured side screamed as it struck the ground. For a half-second, his expression tightened.

"I'm sorry," he whispered.

He ended the animal quickly. Not cruelly. Just decisively.

The handler screamed. Jonathan closed the distance before the man could raise his weapon and silenced him with the same finality.

Somewhere above, a recon voice crackled: "Director, possible movement near—"

The sentence never finished.

A man went over the cliff, the scream swallowed by surf before it could become warning. Two more followed in brutal, efficient quiet. Fog accepted them the way the ocean accepted everything else.

Inside the mansion, the monitors flickered—then died.

Carlisle lurched toward the wall of screens. "All units, respond!" he shouted. "Respond!"

Static answered him. Only static.

His chief of security stood rigid behind him, face pale. "Sir… we believe he's neutralized them."

Carlisle turned slowly, something old showing in his eyes. "How many?"

"Sixteen, minimum. Possibly more."

Carlisle's mouth moved, searching for words that didn't exist.

Sixteen meant layers. It meant protocols. It meant men who were supposed to buy time.

"He's not human," the chief whispered.

Carlisle's fingers dug into the desk. His voice came out thin and raw. "He's something we made."

Outside, the main gate detail held position, weapons raised, fog curling around their boots.

Then the fog parted.

Jonathan stepped out of it like consequence.

One guard tried to speak—an order, a warning. Jonathan didn't let the words finish. He moved through them in three clean beats. Three bodies collapsed into wet stone and fog.

He passed through the gate, and the fortress swallowed him.

Warmth hit him like a lie—cedar, leather, whiskey in crystal. Military plaques and curated confidence lined the halls. Spaces designed to insist power lived here, that safety could be purchased and displayed.

Fear rotted it anyway.

The air inside was too still. Too controlled. Jonathan felt the change immediately—how sound carried farther, how pain echoed louder in enclosed space. His shoulder protested as he adjusted his grip. He didn't slow.

A guard lunged from a side hall. Jonathan slammed him into the wall, weapon clattering away. Another came from behind—Jonathan turned, used momentum, and sent him through a glass table that exploded into shards. Radios screamed. Jonathan crushed one under his boot and kept moving.

He climbed the main staircase slowly. There was no point rushing now. The house was already collapsing. Every shouted order arrived too late.

"Secure the hall!"

"Protect the Director!"

"He's inside—he's inside!"

Bullets tore the air. Jonathan ducked and rolled, shoulder protesting, side flaring hot. He used the pain the way he'd learned to use everything else—as information. As fuel. He disarmed one man and broke him against marble. Drove another into a wall hard enough to crack plaster beneath a painting worth more than most houses. He didn't pause. He didn't savor. He walked.

At the end of the upper corridor, the study door waited—solid wood, expensive hardware, the quiet center of all the fear in the house.

Behind it, fire crackled. The ocean pounded. Carlisle breathed fast and shallow, trying to outrun something already in the room with him.

Jonathan set his hand on the door.

Pain pulsed with his heartbeat.

He pushed anyway and the door opened.

Carlisle spun with a pistol raised, both hands shaking. The Atlantic wind battered the glass behind him like an animal trying to break in.

For a heartbeat, they stared at each other—creator and consequence.

Carlisle's voice fell to a whisper that sounded like prayer. "…God help me."

Jonathan shook his head once.

"No," he said softly as he stepped over the threshold. "You only ever needed to fear me."

CHAPTER 53 — THE SUNSHINE TURNS BLACK

The storm was still hammering Carlisle's cliff house when Jonathan found the photo.

Rain drove through the shattered window in sharp, slanting sheets, soaking the ruined study. Papers skittered, caught, and stuck to puddles, sliding through smeared blood like they were trying to escape the room. The fire had burned down to a restless glow, throwing heat that couldn't compete with the ocean-cold wind pouring in through the glassless wall.

Jonathan sat on the edge of Carlisle's broken desk, boots planted amid debris. His body had begun to register what the night had cost him. Not collapse—never collapse—but a deep, accumulating weight. His shoulder throbbed with a slow, rhythmic insistence. His side burned where the bullet had torn through him in New York, the wound sealed but not forgiven. Every movement pulled at it, reminding him that even systems built to endure still paid in increments.

He ignored it.

Pain was background noise now. Information, not warning.

His hands were still slick when he peeled open a leather folder and slid the glossy print free.

A retirement party.

Soft-focus decorations. Paper hats on thinning hair. A drooping banner sagging over a sheet cake:

CONGRATULATIONS, ALAN — ENJOY RETIREMENT.

For a moment Jonathan didn't breathe.

The image didn't belong here—didn't belong anywhere near blood and storm and the wreckage of a man who had thought himself untouchable. It was too bright. Too normal. The kind of photograph meant to be framed, to live on a shelf, to be pointed at during quiet conversations about how time passed faster than anyone expected.

In the center stood a man in a cheap tropical shirt and an almost-convincing smile. Thicker glasses.

Deeper lines at the mouth.

Hair thinner, cut shorter.

A plastic lei hung crooked around his neck like a joke that didn't know it was a joke.

From across a room, Jonathan might have missed it.

Up close—framed by lightning in broken glass—he didn't miss anything.

He saw the eyes.

Behind wrinkles.

Behind the forced smile.

Behind the pretense of an ordinary man at the end of an ordinary career.

Dr. Gerald.

Jonathan's chest tightened, and for a moment the study wasn't cedar and blood and storm.

It was white light.

Cold light.

It was restraints biting into his wrists and ankles.

It was the smell of antiseptic layered over old fear.

It was Gerald leaning over him with coffee-and-antiseptic breath, glasses slipping down his nose, hands shaking just enough to notice.

We're losing him, Gerald had said once, voice thin, almost pleading.

We're losing him, as if that were a natural disaster and not a choice being made in real time.

Jonathan drove his thumb into the corner of the photo until it creased.

Under the printed banner, in neat blue pen, someone had added a note:

20 years of service — Gulf Shore BioResearch.

There.

The first real thread.

Jonathan exhaled slowly through his nose, forcing his body back into the present. The storm howled through the open wall. Somewhere below, something heavy struck stone and rolled, the sound swallowed by surf. The house groaned as if it were reconsidering its place on the cliff.

He turned the photo over.

Carlisle's stiff handwriting stared back at him like a final spiteful gift.

Ridge / Winston — Florida relocation.

Ridge.

Alan Ridge.

Jonathan said it out loud, testing it in the ruined room.

"Alan Ridge."

It felt wrong in his mouth—too smooth, too practiced. A lie worn down into comfort. A name sanded until it no longer caught on anything sharp.

The wind howled through the broken wall. Somewhere downstairs, a loose door banged in a rhythm that sounded almost like a heartbeat trying to restart.

Jonathan slid the photo inside his coat. The glossy edge stuck for a second to drying blood on his fingers, then gave.

He walked away from Carlisle's body without looking back.

He started with paper, because paper didn't lie.

It just hid.

Motel rooms.

Bus stations.

Public libraries that smelled like dust, old plastic, and disinfectant.

Jonathan moved the way he always did when he needed to disappear into process—quiet, methodical, unremarkable. He spread Carlisle's stolen documents across chipped tables and held the retirement photo down with whatever he had at hand: salt shakers, coffee cups, the heel of his hand.

He studied background details like they were evidence at a crime scene.

A faded logo on someone's shirt.

Gulf Shore BioResearch.

A partial view of a wall plaque—Excellence in Clinical Innovation—with the year cut off by a shoulder.

A plastic cup with a catering company's name printed on it, the kind of detail no one thought to hide because no one believed it mattered.

Jonathan tracked the catering company first.

Their records were guarded by nothing more than lazy passwords and an overworked clerk who had never imagined anyone would care who ordered coleslaw and rolls for a retirement party three years ago.

One night, Jonathan sat in a weedy motel parking lot with the glow of a stolen laptop lighting his hands. Trucks hissed past on the highway, headlights slicing through the dark. Somewhere nearby, a neon sign buzzed like an insect trapped in glass.

The air was still northern-cold—Florida heat days away—and the search finally coughed up a single invoice entry that made his pulse go quiet and flat.

Client: Gulf Shore BioResearch

Event: Retirement Celebration

Honoree: Dr. Alan Ridge

Location: Private residence, Gulf Shore, FL

The street address was half-redacted with marker.

Jonathan stared at the screen for a long time, then closed the laptop and sat there until the cold worked its way through his clothes.

Later, he printed the record and held the paper to a lamp. The ink wasn't thick enough. With patience—angles, light, time—the ghost of letters seeped through.

He didn't need every number.

He had a town.

He had a fake name.

He had a face that wasn't fake at all.

He bought a one-way ticket south.

Florida hit him like walking into a wet towel straight out of a scalding shower.

The air in Gulf Shore was heavy and bright, smelling of hot asphalt, salt, and fryer oil from a seafood shack near the main intersection. Palm trees rattled in a warm breeze that never cooled anything. Sunlight overexposed everything—too cheerful, too clean—like the town was trying to convince itself nothing bad ever happened here.

Jonathan stepped off the bus in the same dark coat that had followed him through rain, forest, and snow.

Here, it made him stand out.

Eyes slid over him, curious, then away.

He shrugged the coat off, slung it over his arm, and kept moving.

Gulf Shore wasn't big.

Two main roads.

Churches with banners that faded faster than belief.

A community college with sun-bleached signs.

A hospital that smelled like bleach and old linoleum.

Pastel rental houses along the beach pretended hurricanes were a myth.

Jonathan went to the company name first.

The building that used to say Gulf Shore BioResearch now had a sun-faded FOR LEASE sign out front. Cracked asphalt. Weeds pushing through tar. The outline of the old logo bleached into stucco—a pale helix-shaped ghost.

Jonathan stood at the rusting gate and stared at it.

He pictured Dr. Gerald walking out those doors on his final day.

Cake frosting on his fingers.

Applause fading.

A joke about finally getting some rest.

Smiling because he thought the worst chapters were behind him.

Jonathan's jaw tightened.

He looped the building and found a side door with a rotten frame and a broken latch. It took almost no effort to slip inside.

The air was stale, layered with old chemical ghosts—alcohol, latex, disinfectant, metal. Stripped-out labs stretched in both directions. Empty shelving. Tape shadows on floors where equipment used to stand.

Every step echoed too loud.

The admin office still had filing cabinets.

Jonathan pried them open one by one.

Most were empty except for dust and a single paperclip.

Some held shredded confetti that used to be contracts.

But in the last drawer, misfiled behind outdated maintenance forms, he found a thin personnel folder.

RIDGE, ALAN J. — CLINICAL RESEARCH DIRECTOR.

A headshot stared back at him.

The same face from the party, younger—tie instead of a Hawaiian shirt.

Same eyes.

Performance reviews followed: dedicated, meticulous, exceptional intellect.

Jonathan almost laughed at that one.

A change-of-address notice sat clipped at the back.

The forwarding address was blacked out with thick marker.

Jonathan held it up to the light slanting through a grimy window and angled the page until the ink block glowed at the edges.

Pieces came through.

Gulf Shore Estates (Phase III).

A retirement neighborhood.

Of course.

He slid the folder into his bag and left.

He didn't go there that day.

Or the next.

He learned the town's skeleton first.

Street names.

Quiet patrol loops.

Which neighborhoods had HOA "security" that was really just bored men with flashlights.

Which houses had cameras that worked and which ones were plastic shells meant to scare kids.

Which dogs barked at everything.

Which barked only when someone unfamiliar passed too close.

He rented a small, mildewed room above a boat repair shop that backed onto a canal. The owner took cash, no questions, and always smelled like gasoline and beer.

At night, Jonathan pinned the retirement photo to the water-stained wall and stared at it until sleep dragged him under.

Dr. Gerald's smile didn't change.

He found "Alan Ridge" by accidentally finding someone else.

At a café on Main—burnt coffee, sugar, local flyers taped to the wall—Jonathan took a stool near the window and listened. Two women behind him talked about HOA meetings, grandkids, a neighbor's dog.

Then one of them said, laughing, "Did you see Alan's yard this week? He's going to get one of those little orange violation tickets. Again."

Jonathan's hand stopped halfway to his cup.

"Which Alan?" the other asked.

"Alan Ridge. The doctor. The one who always forgets his garbage day."

They laughed like it was harmless.

Jonathan didn't.

Later that afternoon, he walked the direction they'd gestured—north, inland, toward streets he hadn't mapped yet. The heat sat on his shoulders like weight. Bugs buzzed in the shrubs like static.

A white sign greeted him at the entrance in cheerful script:

Gulf Shore Estates — Phase III.

55+ Community.

He walked in like he belonged.

Golf carts hummed past. Identical mailboxes lined the street like teeth, every lawn trimmed to the same obedient height.

Except one.

A pale blue single-story house with a struggling hibiscus out front and grass just overgrown enough to irritate the kind of people who enjoyed rules.

The mailbox read:

A. Ridge.

Jonathan stopped on the sidewalk across the street.

Through gauzy curtains, something moved—a shape crossing the living room. Older. Slower. The figure turned just enough for the light to hit his face.

Profile.

Nose.

Mouth.

Jawline softened by years.

The blueprint was older.

The structure was the same.

Dr. Gerald Winston.

Alive.

Comfortable.

Nowhere near steel and concrete.

Living in a place where the worst consequence was a paper slip about trash cans and grass height.

Jonathan's fist tightened at his side until the knuckles went white.

He didn't cross the street.

He kept walking—slow, calm—eyes flicking over everything.

Streetlights.

Camera angles.

Motion sensors.

Which houses had dogs.

Which neighbors watched.

Where shadows pooled at night.

From that day forward, Gulf Shore Estates had a new resident.

A shadow that never quite stepped into the light.

Dr. Gerald changed in slow degrees.

At first, he was just another retiree who waved at neighbors and left his front door unlocked when he was "just going to the mailbox."

Then came the first envelope.

Jonathan watched from a bench beneath an oak as Dr. Gerald opened the mailbox and froze. Mixed among catalogs and a utility bill was a plain envelope with no return address.

His name was written carefully on the front:

Dr. Gerald Winston.

Not Alan.

Not Ridge.

Gerald.

The envelope shook slightly as he tore it open.

From across the street, Jonathan watched color drain from his face. Dr. Gerald swayed and caught himself on the mailbox door like it was the only solid thing left in his world.

He turned slowly, scanning the street.

Cars.

Houses.

Trees.

Bodies.

His gaze passed right over Jonathan.

To him, Jonathan was background.

Inside the envelope was only the retirement photo.

No note.

Just the past, returned to sender.

Dr. Gerald went inside and didn't come back out.

A week later, another envelope appeared—slid under the front door at night.

Jonathan didn't need to see Dr. Gerald's face to know when he found it. Hours later, the man's silhouette stood in the front window long after midnight, unmoving, staring into dark that stared back.

This time it was a single photocopied sheet.

A page from an old lab log.

Dr. Gerald's handwriting.

One line circled in red:

SUBJECT–01: Nanite integration successful. Prognosis: unknown.

The next day, a new deadbolt appeared.

A cheap camera went up above the entry, crooked by a few degrees.

Fear didn't hit Dr. Gerald like a punch.

It seeped in.

His world shrank.

Long walks became short ones.

Short ones became none.

Trips to the café turned rare.

He hovered in the yard only long enough to grab mail, then retreated inside like the air itself had teeth.

A neighbor knocked once, offering help with the pile of envelopes.

Dr. Gerald smiled too wide and said he'd been "under the weather."

That was true enough.

Sleep deserted him.

He started talking to himself in the kitchen, hands shaking around tea gone cold.

"You saved him," he whispered. "You had to try."

Other nights, different words slipped out.

"You stayed. You stayed."

And out on the street, every few days, his instincts flared at nothing he could prove.

A figure at the end of the block.

A shape rounding a corner.

A man in a cap sitting alone in the café.

Always too far to be certain.

Always gone when he looked twice.

Dr. Gerald stopped going out after dark.

By the twelfth month, Gulf Shore knew Dr. Alan Ridge as the strange old man who rarely left his blue house.

Jonathan knew better.

He knew the exact timing of lights at dusk.

The squeak in the third porch step.

The pattern of Dr. Gerald's cough on humid days and how it rattled deeper than it should.

He knew there was a lockbox on the coffee table.

He knew there were journals stacked near the TV, spines lined like vertebrae.

He wondered what was in them.

He wondered if his name appeared.

The night he decided to take him came after a day of dead heat that wouldn't break.

The sky went yellow-gray, storm-colored but undecided.

The air felt wrong—still, heavy—like the whole town was holding its breath.

Jonathan sat on his usual bench beneath the oak, shirt clinging to his back, watching the living-room light glow in sticky dusk.

He thought of Henry on a sterile floor.

He thought of Suzanne bleeding out where no one came in time.

He thought of Carlisle and Marrow and Kincaid— each one breaking in their own way as the chain tightened around them.

Everything had led here.

A blue house in a Florida retirement community.

A man in a soft chair.

A monster in a name that wasn't his.

The sun went down, but the heat stayed.

A lawn sprinkler ticked somewhere.

A dog barked once, then quit.

The distant ocean was only a faint salt taste in the air.

Dr. Gerald's living-room light burned steady.

Jonathan stood.

The sunshine that had bathed Gulf Shore all year felt thin now.

Hollow.

Already dark at the edges.

He stepped off the curb.

And walked toward the house.

CHAPTER 54 — THE END IS NEAR

Jonathan had known this moment would feel quieter than the others.

Not weaker.

Not smaller.

Just quieter.

There were no alarms screaming here. No sirens. No men with weapons and radios and rules to break. No glass towers or fortified cliffs or steel corridors built to pretend accountability lived inside them. There was only a street designed to soothe—curves instead of corners, identical mailboxes, lawns clipped to submission, light posts spaced at comforting intervals.

A place where consequences went to retire.

Jonathan stood across from the blue house longer than necessary, letting the heat settle into his muscles, letting the neighborhood teach him its rhythms one last time. Porch lights clicked on in sequence as dusk deepened. Somewhere down the block, a garage door whined shut. A television laugh track erupted and died. A golf cart hummed past and disappeared.

Everything ordinary.

Everything complicit.

He felt the weight of Henry's pocketknife in his jacket—not because he planned to use it, but because it reminded him how far violence could travel before anyone noticed it was happening. How it could start with paperwork. With funding approvals. With men who convinced themselves that saving one child justified breaking another.

He crossed the street when the sprinkler cycle clicked over, mist drifting low and harmless across the asphalt.

Jonathan stepped off the curb and walked toward the house.

The lawn was damp from evening irrigation, grass cool against his shoes. Sprinklers ticked somewhere down the block—a metronome for a neighborhood that believed routine was protection. Cicadas screamed and then fell quiet as he crossed into the shadow of the hibiscus. The living-room light burned steady, a square of yellow comfort framed by gauze curtains.

He did not hurry.

He didn't need to.

Every detail was already mapped. Every sound cataloged. Every variable collapsed to certainty. He could feel the house breathing—air cycling through vents, heat rising toward the ceiling, the faint electrical pulse that said someone was home and unaware.

The third porch step squeaked, exactly as he knew it would. He shifted his weight and it stopped. The cheap camera above the door blinked once, searching for meaning in the dark. It found none.

Jonathan waited three seconds longer than necessary.

Inside, Dr. Gerald stood at the sink with a mug he had reheated twice and forgotten again. The ceiling fan clicked and turned. Click. Whirr. Click. He rubbed his temples, swallowed, and tried to steady his breathing as if breath alone could hold the past outside.

He had been doing that a lot lately.

Trying to out-breathe memory. Trying to convince himself that the envelopes had been coincidence. That the photo had been a prank. That the photocopied lab page had been a mistake.

He had scrubbed the kitchen counters until the laminate dulled. He had moved the journals twice and then put them back exactly where they had been, as if order could disguise guilt. He had stopped sleeping more than an hour at a time.

Tonight, he had told himself, he would go to bed early.

When the knock came, it was soft—polite enough to be mistaken for a neighbor.

Dr. Gerald froze.

The mug slipped from his fingers and struck the sink with a dull crack that didn't quite break it. His heart hammered so hard he felt it in his teeth.

Another knock followed, firmer now. Patient.

"Who is it?" His voice came out thin.

The answer was silence.

He edged toward the door and peered through the peephole. The porch light threw a clean circle onto empty boards. No face. No body. Just the suggestion of movement at the edge of vision, a wrongness the eye couldn't pin down.

A memory surfaced without permission.

A lab corridor.

A gurney.

A child's chest rising and falling too fast.

He wiped his palm on his pants and told himself this was nothing. A kid. A prank. A wrong house.

His hand shook as he reached for the chain.

The door opened inward.

The chain snapped taut—then failed with a dry, tired sound. The door came the rest of the way open under a single, controlled shove. Dr. Gerald stumbled back, his heel catching the rug.

The figure filled the doorway.

Black from head to toe. A smooth, featureless mask that swallowed the porch light and gave nothing back. No eyes. No mouth. No expression to bargain with.

Dr. Gerald screamed.

The sound tore out of him raw and animal, a sound he hadn't made since the night the monitors flatlined and then—impossibly—spiked again.

He lunged for the counter, for anything that might matter. A gloved hand caught his wrist and turned it just enough to steal the strength from it. Pain bloomed and vanished as quickly as it came—precise and impersonal. He tried to twist away, to run, but the room was suddenly very small.

Jonathan felt the man's pulse under his fingers.

Fast.

Irregular.

Fragile.

"Please," Dr. Gerald sobbed. "I don't—"

The words ended when the needle kissed his neck.

Cold spread with surgical speed, a clean flood that loosened his knees and softened the edges of the room. The mug shattered somewhere behind him. The fan kept turning.

Click.

Whirrrrr.

Click.

Dr. Gerald's thoughts fragmented—images slipping out of order, sentences losing their ends. He tried to say a name and couldn't remember which one mattered. His hands clawed weakly at fabric that didn't yield.

The masked man lifted him before he could fall. Dr. Gerald's feet dragged once, then left the floor. He gasped on large gasp, then his breathing slowed, then found a dull, obedient rhythm that was not his own.

Jonathan adjusted his grip to protect the man's airway automatically, a reflex learned in rooms where life was reduced to protocols and margins. The irony did not escape him.

They moved through the house without sound.

Past the lockbox on the coffee table.

Past the journals stacked like bones.

Past the framed retirement photo sitting facedown on a side table, as if the house itself couldn't bear to look at it anymore.

Jonathan paused long enough to glance at the spines of the journals. He didn't open them. He didn't need to. He already knew what they contained—justifications written to survive reflection. Notes meant to soften memory. Language that turned a child into a subject and suffering into data.

Past the window where the living-room light still burned, unwavering—convincing anyone who glanced that all was well inside.

At the door, the figure paused long enough to reach up and straighten the crooked camera with two fingers. It blinked, satisfied.

Jonathan did that not for the machine—but for the people who would review the footage later and see nothing worth noting. A house undisturbed. A routine uninterrupted.

Outside, the night accepted them.

The humidity wrapped around Jonathan as he stepped off the porch, thick and clinging. Crickets resumed their song as if nothing had happened. Somewhere nearby, a sprinkler head clicked and sprayed a lazy arc of water across a sidewalk.

A car door opened and closed softly. An engine turned over, low and steady. The headlights stayed dark as the vehicle rolled away from the curb and merged with the neighborhood's quiet loops, leaving the porch light on, the fan clicking, and the house breathing as if nothing had happened at all.

As the car disappeared, Jonathan glanced once in the rearview mirror.

The blue house sat exactly as it always had.

All was well.

For now.

CHAPTER 55 — THE FINAL RECKONING

Dr. Gerald's scream shattered against the concrete walls and came back wrong.

"HELLO?! SOMEBODY HELP ME! ANYONE!"

The echo stripped the words of meaning, flattening them into noise. It did not behave like sound was supposed to behave. It didn't fade so much as collapse, as if the room itself absorbed desperation and returned only its shape. Gerald's chest convulsed as he fought the restraints, breath tearing in and out while the rope burned into his wrists. His shoulders screamed in protest as he twisted, tried to rock the chair, tried to lift it enough to matter.

It didn't move.

The chair was bolted to the floor.

The concrete around its base had cracked and settled long ago, spiderweb fractures filled with grime and time, as if the room itself had accepted the chair as permanent. A metal grate shrieked beneath his shoes when he strained, then went still again, the sound cutting off too abruptly, like a throat closing.

Water dripped somewhere beyond the reach of the light.

Slow.

Patient.

Unconcerned.

The sound dragged memory with it—coolant lines beneath research wings, sublevels never shown on floor plans, rooms designed to contain problems rather than solve them. Rooms that existed only so failure could be hidden somewhere quiet.

Gerald began to start hyperventilating as recognition crawled through him. He had not been in this room before, but he had been in rooms like it. Rooms where the walls were thick, where nothing accidental ever happened.

"PLEASE!" he sobbed. "WHY ARE YOU DOING THIS? WHAT DO YOU WANT?!"

His voice cracked and failed. The ropes creaked. The bulb overhead swayed faintly, its weak yellow light trembling as if it wanted to look away. The motion made the shadows stretch and compress, pulling the corners of the room in and out of focus.

Then the air shifted.

Not dramatically. Not loudly. Just enough.

A redistribution of weight where there should have been none.

Dr. Gerald froze.

His breath stalled halfway in, lungs burning as instinct screamed at him to stay quiet, to listen. Every experiment he had ever overseen had taught him this much: when the environment changed without explanation, something had entered the system.

"Hello?" he whispered.

Silence.

And then the darkness began to take shape.

It didn't rush him. It didn't speak. It simply resolved, as if the shadows themselves had decided to stand upright. Gerald's body locked, a low, broken sound leaking from his throat before he could stop it. His pulse thundered in his ears, drowning out the drip, the sway of the bulb, even his own thoughts.

"Please," he whispered, shaking hard enough to rattle the chair. "I don't know who you are. I don't—please don't hurt me."

A footstep answered him.

Slow.

Deliberate.

Certain.

The sound was wrong in a way Gerald couldn't articulate. Not heavy. Not light. It carried no hesitation. The figure stepped into the edge of the light.

Boots scraped softly over concrete. Old stains darkened the leather—oil, mud, something rust-colored that might have been blood. The bulb caught fragments—worn denim, a black jacket zipped to the throat, the faint silver glint of a knife at the hip.

The man stopped three feet from the chair.

The bulb swung wider, revealing hands that were steady.

Too steady.

Not the hands of a killer in frenzy. Not the hands of a man discovering violence for the first time. These were hands that had learned exactly how much pressure was necessary and never used more.

Gerald swallowed hard. "Why?" he rasped. "What did I do? I'm just a retired doctor. I'm nobody."

The figure tilted his head slightly.

That small, measured motion erased the last of Gerald's hope.

It meant attention. Recognition. Memory.

The man raised both hands to his face.

"No," Gerald whispered. "Please—don't—"

Gloved fingers found the edge of the mask and lifted it free.

Not fast.

Not theatrical.

Slowly.

Purposefully.

Jonathan stood where the mask had been.

Older. Harder. Built out of years Gerald had refused to look at.

The boy Gerald remembered—pale, shaking, burning with fever beneath lab lights—was gone. What stood in front of him was structure. Weight. A body shaped by consequence rather than intent.

"…Henry's boy," Gerald breathed.

Jonathan's jaw tightened once.

"Not a boy anymore," he said. "But yes. His son."

The name hung between them like an accusation, heavy enough to bend the air.

Jonathan stepped fully into the light. His posture was controlled, but not relaxed—like someone holding himself together by force. The old scar in his shoulder burned, the way it always did when he carried too much tension for too long. His side throbbed faintly, a reminder that survival had a cost even now.

"You shouldn't be here," Gerald stammered. "They told me you were gone. There were reports—fire—accidents—"

"You didn't look," Jonathan said quietly. "You didn't ask where I went. You didn't want to know."

Gerald flinched as if struck. "Jonathan… I saved your life."

There it was.

Jonathan let the words sit between them. He had rehearsed this moment in silence for years, not with speeches, not with rage, but with a careful accounting of truth.

"You saved my body," Jonathan said. "And doomed everything else."

He began to circle the chair.

Slow.

Measured.

The way someone moves when time is no longer a concern.

"I learned to read fear," Jonathan said, "long before I learned to read books. I learned what panic smells like. What lies sound like when people tell them to themselves."

Gerald shuddered, tears leaking down the deep lines of his face.

"You made a mistake," Jonathan continued. "And instead of stopping, you built a machine out of it. You fed it data. You fed it money. You fed it me."

The knife slid free with a soft metallic whisper.

Gerald sobbed once. The sound broke, turning into something animal and small.

The blade moved.

The sound was wet.

Intimate.

Wrong.

Dr. Gerald's body jerked against the restraints. Blood spread through his shirt, steaming faintly in the cold air. His eyes went wide—not only with pain, but with shock. Not disbelief. Understanding.

Jonathan didn't look away.

For a moment—just one—something crossed his face.

Not rage.

Not mercy.

Recognition.

The awareness of a closed loop.

Then it was gone.

Dr. Gerald's breaths thinned, each one shallower than the last.

"I tried," he whispered. "You were… supposed… to be… proof…"

His chest rose.

Fell.

Stopped.

Jonathan waited.

He counted without numbers, the way he always did. The way he had learned to wait for systems to settle.

Then he wiped the blade clean and slid it back into its sheath. The motion was practiced. Familiar. It cost him nothing.

There was no satisfaction.

Only quiet.

Jonathan turned toward the stairs and climbed. Each step pulled at his wounds, but he welcomed the sensation. Pain meant presence. Pain meant he was still here.

At the top, he paused, listening.

Nothing followed him.

The basement returned to stillness.

Blood dripped beneath the chair, patient as a clock.

The bulb kept swinging.

The basement smelled of damp stone, rusted metal, and blood.

And beneath it all—so faint it could almost be imagined—the air hummed.

Not machinery.

Not electricity.

Something deeper.

Something that had learned how to wait.

Then Dr. Gerald's right hand twitched.

Just once.

The rope creaked.

Seconds passed.

His eyelids fluttered.

Once.

Twice.

Then opened.